THE
CRETAN
CIRCLE

Goldshaw Books

£15

THE
CRETAN
CIRCLE

A story of ancient Minoans and modern Cretans

Bill Mayor

Published by Goldshaw Books
31 Newchurch-in-Pendle, Burnley BB12 9JR
www.goldshawbooks.co.uk

First published 2006
Copyright © Bill Mayor 2006

ISBN 0 9552606 0 4

Edited and typeset by Freelance Publishing Services, Brinscall, Lancs
Printed in Great Britain by Biddles Ltd, King's Lynn

Preface

Siga siga, as the Greeks say, slowly, slowly. And slow has been the history of this book.

The original idea came to me on a green bus from Hania to Paleochora, winding down the long curves to the coast, grey hills rising on either side, brief glimpses of blue sea, the smudge of Gavdos on the horizon. I promptly forgot all about it. Only later, watching the many greys of night creep along the dramatic coast, did it come again into my mind. It has been there ever since, a story of that coast and those mountains, and the splendid people who dwell there.

And not only the people of today, but those who have lived and worked and fought and loved on this land for five thousand years and more.

Maybe the modern Sfakians are the descendants of the Minoans, And maybe there are, yet to be found, other disks of hard clay incised with spirals of hieroglyphs like the enigma of Phaistos.

And, maybe, the problems of tourism and exploitation which confront the south-west coast of Crete today are similar to those faced by the Minoans after the destruction of their magnificent palace in the 16th century BC.

Why not?

It makes a good story.

Bill Mayor

Bill Mayor is retired from the drudgery of commerce and lives with his wife, Sue, in the shadow of Pendle Hill in Lancashire, England.

He has travelled extensively and returns every year to his first love, the beautiful island of Crete.

Acknowledgements

Among the many friends who have encouraged me and helped with the preparation and writing of this book are

My wife, Sue
Alistair Mayor
Rachel Saynor
Jason Saynor
John and Jackie Davies
Peter and Aileen Baldwin
Frances Hackeson
Sean O'Brien
Irini Kilaiditi Corrigan
Tony Fennymore
and Alison Androulakakis

My sincere and grateful thanks are due to all of them.

Crete
16th century BC

Chapter one

Noon in late summer

Hot wind howled against the palace stones, seeking every crevice, every crack, every chink in the ancient walls. Dust spiralled angrily in the corners of the courtyards, urged madly on by the unending gale then lying still for brief moments before resuming its dizzy dance. Heat lay heavily on the land. There was no relief from the streaming air and the ancient stones groaned under its onslaught. Dry, burdened with dust, the wind poured down the slopes of the mountain and swirled over low grey foothills before hurling itself unremittingly at the steep white sides of the chalk ridge on which the palace cowered. The wind tore through the line of plane trees guarding the old buildings on top of the hill to tear the remaining few leaves from tired branches and twist them on its unseen wings over the ridge. Relentless it raged down the southern slope to ravage the buildings of wood and stone in the town under the ridge, to tear branches from walls, dried leaves from roofs.

To the north of the palace the sacred mountain towered high, the small scar of a cave below its bare summit showing dark against grey rock burnished to a dull lead by the gale. At the foot of the mountain, forests of cypress dotted with the darker green of olive bowed in the stream of air, leaves changing from dark green to light grey and back again as the waves of the hot torrent passed. For days there had been no respite from the twin torments of burning sun and scalding wind and the land was exhausted, desperate for relief that did not come. The only comfort was the vulture which, soaring on the thermal built by the palace ridge throughout that long hot summer, was a constant, unfailing companion to the people of Phaistos.

The rituals of the palace went on, but in a half-hearted, routine fashion. In the town beneath the hill the people were lethargic, numbed by the gale and the heat. The yearly cycle of planting, tending, harvesting was broken at this season, and listless men and women sat in the shade waiting for the wind to drop and the heat to make way for the refreshing autumn rains. The flocks of sheep and goats were high in the hills and those who were left behind on the hot plain were jealous of the solitude of the shepherds. They had energy only for their own needs and resented the constant demands of the palace for food and water which had to be carried daily up the steep slopes by the young people of the village.

This labour had to be carried out many times each day but, despite its hardship, it was tolerated by the youngsters because it offered the chance for girls and boys to be together and free from adult eyes. Today it was the task of Sirute and Jasumatu and, despite the howl of the torrent of dusty air and the unrelenting heat, it was a pleasure to them both. Sirute was a slim, strong girl of fifteen, the eldest of five daughters of Witejame, the village headman, who had lost his wife in childbirth several summers ago. Witejame ruled the village and his family with a ruthless and remote fairness. He had not taken another partner after the death of his wife, preferring to devote his time and energy to his service of the palace and the priest-king. A strong, thickset and undemonstrative man, his relationship with his beautiful eldest daughter was one of mutual tolerance and respect rather than affection but he cared for her well. He was aware of the attraction between Sirute and Jasumatu and had a high regard for the solid and respectful young man who had been chosen to be acolyte to the old priest. He watched the pair start the dusty climb to the palace before turning his attention back to the bronze axe-head that he was polishing.

Sirute followed the donkey to the sluggish river where Jasumatu was pouring the brackish water which he had raised in a bucket into the large jar.

"Don't make it too heavy," she smiled, "I'm not very strong today and it's too hot.

Jasumatu gave her his slow grin, "You may not be very strong, but you are very beautiful. Come on, let's go."

The young man and the girl were similar in height and wore identical tunics of rough brown wool which were belted at the waist. They lifted the heavy pithoi into the yoke on the donkey's back and urged the reluctant animal up the well worn, stony path which wound up the steep south side of the palace hill. The wind was cheated here by the mass of the hillside and swirled angrily about them as they climbed, and the vulture watched their progress from high above.

Asumunde, Priest-King of Phaistos, grumbled to himself as he crossed the palace courtyard. The heat was intense between the high buildings and the wind did nothing to alleviate it. Dust and sand, caught in a vortex, stung bare legs and arms and irritated old eyes; like the people in the town at the foot of the hill, the priest was exhausted by its constant, erratic intrusion. He fought his way across the burning stones to the high doorway at the north of the courtyard and into the dark passage beyond. Here, out of the sun but shielded from the wind, the heat was even greater and he sweated under his purple murex-stained robes as he turned the corner into the passage to the storerooms in the north-east corner of the palace. The storerooms faced north and into the wind, and the stones themselves were cooler here and Asumunde shivered as he entered the Room of the Jars. He stooped as he entered; a tall man with an angular frame about which his ceremonial robes hung like dustsheets over a forgotten statue. His dark and lined face, creased by years of sun, taut from the wind, relaxed in the gloom as his old eyes adjusted slowly to the darkness, and the sanctuary calmed him. Here in the presence of his predecessors, Asumunde felt at peace as he moved slowly along the tiers of funerary jars which lined three of the walls of the dark room. In these ponderous pithoi were the mortal remains of an unbroken line of priests which stretched back into a dim past, away from Crete, to Alashiya, to Anatolia and Syria and beyond. A continuous line of succession of which he would one day – and soon, he sometimes hoped – be part. In this room there was a comforting sense of being a member of a community and one could share the burden of power with others who had experienced, and overcome, and survived. And died in the service of Phaistos.

The dark pithoi moved past him with a step matching his own as he progressed further into the store. As he passed each earthenware jar, he dusted it lightly with a familiar touch, greeting its heavy roundness with affection; his feather brush raised small puffs of fine dust, which hovered in the still air. Who would dust his own jar, Asumunde wondered as he turned to come back out of the darkness towards the glare of the doorway; who would care as he had done? He knew that his choice of Jasumatu had been a popular one with the people but wondered, as all old men wonder, whether his successor would have the same stamina, the same dedication.

Asumunde paused as he came to the door; here on his right was his own pithos, awaiting his own remains. The baked clay roundel which would one day seal his jar had not yet been imprinted with the pictographic script which would record his achievements. The carved seal-stones that would impress into damp clay the story of his life were still hidden in the secret place where he himself had put them.

He remembered his anxiety when the last priest, who had guided him so well and been such a dear friend and support, had told him that he would die soon, and shown him where the seal-stones were hidden. He remembered the care with which they had mixed the clay and wrapped it in cloth to keep it moist while the seal-stones printed the old man's story, first on one side and then on the other, in the inward spiral which was the tradition. He remembered the sadness with which he had later placed the roundel in the neck of the funerary jar and cemented it into place. He remembered the isolation that he had felt as the pithos was stored in the Room of Jars and he had turned to face his people. And soon it would be another's grief, another's responsibility.

On such a day as this, when the earth groaned under the sun and the wind, Asumunde thought that might be welcome. He turned in the darkness and moved down the second line of jars dusting as he went, the heavy bronze sword which hung from his belt occasionally tapping a jar as if to bring its sleeping occupant awake. The sword was another part of the tradition of the palace. It had been cast long ago with a dark bronze blade and a hilt of gold. Along the length of the broad blade and inlaid with gold and silver were a series of pictographs similar to those of the jar seals. Great copper and bronze ceremonial double axes which stood between the horns of consecration in the dining hall of the palace carried the same symbols, symbols of power and continuity which could be read only by the priests and their acolytes. He had never used the sword in anger but there were dark stains of blood to show that it had not always been merely a symbol. His predecessor had hinted of its use in sacrifice in times of crisis, and palace lore suggested that such sacrifice had not always been of animals. Asumunde dreaded the possibility that he might one day have to raise the weapon in the bright sunlight and bring a human life to an end. He did not doubt that he would do it but he prayed that he would never have to; such an act of violence was abhorrent to him and in the safe world of the new palace he believed that it would never be necessary.

Asumunde turned in the dark at the end of the long line of jars and made his way slowly back towards the dazzle of light at the doorway, the gold of his sword hilt catching the light and throwing splinters of brightness across the dark bulk of the old jars.

As he shuffled along flicking his feather duster at the grey dust, he remembered his early days as Priest King of Phaistos. He recalled the pride he had felt at his succession and the weight of responsibility which had followed it; he recalled the early days during which he had completed the rebuilding of the old palace which had been destroyed by an earthquake many years before. This had been a time of great enterprise and the whole community had come together in a concerted effort to build a new palace of such beauty that it outshone the functional structure over the hill at Knossos. The elegant building which now graced the ridge above the Messara plain was his own creation and would be his memorial, and he was content. The work of construction had united the tribes and the community was stronger for his efforts and the land was enriched by the structure which he had created. What better memorial could there be?

Yet, despite the tranquillity which the Room of Jars always brought him, Asumunde was uneasy. Coming out of the passage into his private inner court he looked up at the sky, seeking the vulture, which had been a constant sentinel during these hot windy days. It was not in sight and he felt forsaken. The wind tore at him with hot gritty fingers and in the heat the earth seemed to groan. It was not just the groaning of his old bones but the very rock of the court seemed to stir and turn under the sun and the howling wind.

The sun and the wind Asumunde knew; uncomfortable, oppressive, but familiar. The swaying of the trees and the rattle of their dried leaves he knew and accepted. But today, in the heat of the afternoon, something was different. The earth moved, and the vulture was gone.

Asumunde walked into the darkness of a short passage which led out into the main courtyard, deeply black to his eyes save for a small triangle of searing white stone formed by the sunlight slanting through the massive doors. The bright harsh glare outside was suddenly frightening, as was the gloom of the passage. He hesitated, caught between dark and light, deeply unsure; the day had become threatening and his familiar palace alien. As he hesitated he remembered the old tales of the destruction. Nothing was written, and the telling exaggerated, but the people's tales told of a great shaking of the earth which caused the collapse of the old palace. Of a shaking of the land which lasted for days and which was so strong that all the buildings fell in storms of dust, killing many under the falling stones. This was the lore, passed down through many generations by the bards. Indeed, he had seen the fallen stones himself, and had built his new palace with them and on them, and many were still strewn down the western slope of the hill. But the old palace was not built as strongly as his new Phaistos where skilled stonemasons using modern techniques had fashioned a much more robust structure. Asumunde could remember the occasional tremor when the land had stirred itself, but his building had not suffered. A pillar might move, a lintel fall, but the stone was good and the structure sound.

But the stories told of destruction which was so complete that the entire palace had become uninhabitable for many years; surely that could not happen again? Asumunde reached out an unsteady hand to touch the stone wall of the passage as if to reassure himself of its substance. He felt the rough surface of the stone and the chisel-marks of his stonemasons and was comforted. Wiping his sweating forehead with a corner of his robe, he strode out into the wind-whirled court.

Sirute and Jasumatu had driven the donkey with its heavy load of water up the track from the town so happy in each other's company that the task had seemed easy. Their work completed, they climbed the steps and followed a corridor which led through into the main court and, turning left again on entering the court, went to sit in the shade of the vestibule.

"One day," Jasumatu waved his arm across the court, "One day, I will stand here in my purple robe, with the sword at my side, and you will come and worship me."

Sirute looked at the brown face of the young man beside her and giggled. "One day," she said "I will lie in that room over there, with-out my robe, and you will come and worship me, and you will stay for longer."

"How can you say that to your priest elect? Have you no re-spect?" He grinned at her.

Jasumatu was half-serious but his dignity was lost when the girl came to stand in front of him as he sat on the stone bench, and taking his head between her hands, pressed his face into her breasts. Sirute bent and kissed him.

"It will not be long now."

Jasumatu wrapped his arms around her waist and looked up into the pale face above him, painted with shadow and framed with long jet-black hair.

"Soon I will go to the cave for the two months of peace before our marriage – I can hardly wait."

"Hardly wait for the peace, you mean, not the marriage."

Sirute pulled his hair sharply and, escaping his arms, ran out into the sunlit court, the wind swirling her brown skirt. Jasumatu ran after her in the hot afternoon but she evaded him easily and, with her hair streaming behind her, was quickly at the far end of the court. She stood, hands on hips, looking down at the town beneath the hill, and then turned into his arms as he came to her. They kissed and stood for a moment before turning and walking back, arms around each other's waists, across the burning glare of the pavement towards the priest's rooms at the northern end of the court. The upper slopes of the sacred mountain showed faintly through afternoon haze above the high buildings. The wind continued its restless, burning torment.

As Sirute and Jasumatu turned from the southern parapet, Asumunde emerged tall and stern from the doors of his rooms at the far end of the court, and the wind howled around him as he made his way across the burning stones towards them, robes bright purple in the strong light and striding in a pool of his own shadow. Others moved in the courtyard; a small man carrying a jug of wine crossed from left to right; two women, shielding their eyes from the flying dust with their robes, came out of the storerooms and crossed the court towards the Room of Pillars in the south-west corner. But the vulture was absent, no longer gliding on the high, hot wave of air over the hill.

Asumunde felt more confident now that he was out in the open, and he and the young couple walked towards each other across the hot pavement. The unease which he had felt in the dark passage from the inner court ebbed as he came into the strong light and into the view of his people. Now in public, he walked straight and tall, confident in the respect of his subjects. The golden hilt of his sword sent signals of his authority about the court, and his stature gave reassurance. The vulture may have gone, but Asumunde was going about his normal tasks, so all was right in the palace, and none should fear.

But all was not right. The courtyard moved sideways as he walked across it and then it rose and fell and moved sideways again. The two large pithoi framing the door to his apartments did a little dance, raising dust. In the Room of Pillars there was a crash as one fell, leaving a lintel sagging at an unreal angle. The pavement rippled like the disturbed surface of a still pond. A large block of stone in a storeroom edged its way over lower blocks to rest, rocking, before falling ponderously to crush several small pots. Heavy stone walls fluttered like curtains in a breeze. Doors opened and people rushed out into the courtyard, turning as they ran to watch the buildings sway behind them. The man carrying the jug of wine lay on the hot stones and the dark red wine spread around him like blood on the white pavement. The two women lay tangled together in horror, holding each other as they watched the buildings around them totter and sway.

9

Asumunde had stumbled at the first shock, falling to his knees in the heat and the wind, and then, unable to rise, watched the comic dance of the young couple coming towards him. Sirute and Jasumatu grabbed at each other in fright before falling to the pavement in an untidy heap. The wind blew dust in unkind eddies into their faces as they lay.

Then, save for the rush of the wind, there was silence. No more movement. An unbelievable stillness. A pause. A holding of breath. A slow acceptance. A slow understanding. A tentative lifting of heads. A kneeling. A careful standing. An exchange of glances. A rising of prostrate companions. Then a chatter, a fearful look around the court. Then a babble of voices raised in fear and question and a rush back into the buildings in search of loved ones and workmates. It was all over in a moment and the afternoon heat struck again and the incessant wind renewed its onslaught. All that was left was fear. The ground moved again in a shuddering aftershock as the security of the last three centuries passed and the reign of the second palace of Phaistos approached its end.

And the vulture returned and soared again on its wide wings above the unquiet palace.

Chapter two

The court of Phaistos was filled by a babble of people hastening in fear from the palace, looking back in fright at the buildings and gathering in concerned groups in the late afternoon sun. The wind hustled between them in dusty swirls, still irritating but now ignored. Asumunde rose slowly to his feet and brushed the white dust from his robe, restoring its leprous complexion to one of more regal purple and looked around the familiar courtyard with alienated eyes. The tall buildings around the court stood intact and over them to the north the peak of the sacred mountain rose, darker blue in the lowering afternoon light. To the south the brown hills of late summer shimmered in the heat. These sights were commonplace. But the agitated gathering in the slanting sun was not, and Asumunde saw that the crowds were looking towards him, seeking his reassurance.

The old priest rose to his full height and straightened his robe, adjusting the hang of his sword so that it again swung freely at his hip and reflected the sunlight. He sought out Jasumatu in the frightened mob and beckoned him to his side. With a show of confidence, he walked towards the centre of the court and, with Jasumatu beside him, stood tall, gaunt and regal, casting a long dark shadow in the hot sunshine. He slowly raised his arms into the air, turning, as he did so, to hold the attention of the multitude. The crowd fell silent, only the wind spoke its quiet litany, and the vulture held steady overhead.

"Have no fear, my people."

His high clear voice cut through the toils of the wind.

"Have no fear. These tremblings are only the stirring of our mother earth as she turns in her sleep. They cannot harm us. We have a safe home, built by our own hands and strong; it will not fall. We have felt the gods breathe before but our vulture watches over us and we have not been harmed."

Asumunde took the glinting sword from its scabbard and pointed it at the soaring bird above, scattering golden reflections over the crowd.

"Have no fear. I, and Jasumatu, my chosen successor, will guard you."

He felt their need for reassurance like an urgent tug on his robe and despite his earlier misgivings he knew what he had to do now to satisfy his people. "Bring me a goat", he said and raised the sword high over his head. "Bring a goat, and we will make sacrifice to the gods and our tribute will pacify them."

A small and frightened goat was dragged through the crowd to the sacrificial stone altar which stood in the centre of the courtyard, and presented to Asumunde. He bowed and gestured that the animal should be given to Jasumatu who came forward to stand beside him.

"Let it be known …" Asumunde spoke in his high, clear voice. "Let it be known that I have chosen Jasumatu to be my successor and your priest, and that he has my full authority and my confidence and trust. Give him your faith as you have given it to me and he will not fail you."

Watched in silence by the surrounding crowd, Asumunde held out the gleaming sword and offered it to Jasumatu. The dark gold of the afternoon sun exploded on its blade as he brought it down on the trembling beast on the altar. A single neat stroke cut the goat's throat and its blood gathered in the altar trough before pouring in a crimson arc into a golden cup held at the stone spout. Jasumatu held the cup high and showed it to the people before raising it to the sacred mountain. Lowering it he took a sip, the blood warm and sticky to his lips. His voice was strong. "I drink this to the gods of the mountain; may their sleep be deep and silent. We have made this sacrifice in hope of their favour and tomorrow I will go to the sacred cave and make supplication to them."

He looked around the throng. "I will go to take the prayers of Asumunde, and your prayers, to the gods."

The crowd was silent during the sacrifice, intent on the two imposing figures at their centre. Sirute watched the young man who had been chosen for her in his first public role, and was proud. She heard of his intention to go up into the mountain with secret delight for it was the custom for young men to retreat to the sacred cave for several weeks prior to taking a wife, and she knew that she was to be his bride. Now, as the crowd chanted his name, she stood apart, savouring the moment. The crowd's clamour increased as their relief at being spared by the earthquake grew, and they shouted their approval of the sacrifice. Sirute joined them in shouting, "Asumunde, Jasumatu!" into the hot afternoon air. On wide wings, a lighter grey now in the failing light, the vulture sailed high above then stooped steeply over the palace.

Asumunde raised his arms for quiet and the throng fell silent.

"My people," he said. "The sacrifice has been successful and the gods are content. Tonight we will feast and celebrate the last full moon of the summer. Return when the moon rises behind the mountain and we will eat together. Go now and finish your work and do not be afraid."

Asumunde, tall and purple-clad with white hair and beard framing his dark face, made his way slowly towards his rooms at the north end of the court. Jasumatu waited for Sirute to join him before following the old priest through the double doorway into the dark, cool passage beyond. The crowd watched them go before leaving in chattering groups. The courtyard was clear again, white in the sun except for the dark patch on the altar in which the goat lay with its blood stiffening on its coat, and the red stain on the pavement where the wine had been spilled. The dying wind, erasing the memories of the earthquake and the sacrifice, gently covered blood and wine with pale dust. The vulture made one last pass over the palace on the quietening air and flew on strong wings to its lair in the crags of the purple mountain.

Night had fallen over Phaistos. A dull pewter in the sky behind the black bulk of the sacred mountain foretold where the moon would rise. Cooking fires blazed orange and red in the town, making the rough houses into cubes and pyramids of darkness. Burning hand-held lanterns wound a meandering trail through the buildings and up the track to the palace. The wind had dropped and the night was warm and still and cicadas shrilled from unseen shrubs. A large fire burned brightly at the southern end of the palace court casting a red glow on the building; the open windows in the massive walls seemed like the mouths of deep and gloomy caves in the face of a cliff. Flames cast a glow down the hill causing parts of the path to be lost in deep pools of darkness in which the procession stumbled as it climbed. The twisting track made some climbing figures red like ghouls entering Hades and others black shades outlined against the fire. The people of Phaistos climbed hoping that the sacrifice had been successful, but also in fear that the earthquake would return. Some believed in the power of the priests, others were not so sure and made the climb for the expected feast rather than in faith that the sacrifice would satisfy the angry gods.

Sirute and her father Witejame had been early at the palace helping to build the fire and to set tables with bread and wine. They watched from a window in the west court as the townspeople, faces bright with firelight and anticipation, swirled in a slow arc around the fire under the flicker of smoking lanterns held in brackets along the walls. As they watched, a sliver of yellow moon appeared from behind the sacred mountain and grew quickly into a disk and killed the stars. Its cruel light made Witejame's face older and colder, cruelly emphasizing the wrinkles of his forty years; the same light turned Sirute into a beautiful wraith with perfect pale skin and large dark eyes in an oval of jet-black hair.

Father and daughter were silent as jugs of wine circulated and the crowd below them grew restive and noisy. The goat, together with others that had been sacrificed during the afternoon, turned slowly on a spit above the sparking fires. As the full moon dimmed the brightness of the flames, a winding black river opened in the sea of pale faces as Asumunde moved slowly through carrying the gleaming double axe whose blades sent flashes of moonlight like icy arrows about the crowd. Behind him came Jasumatu holding the ceremonial sword with both hands, its bright blade pointing to the sky. The crowd grew quiet as the solemn procession passed through but the moon was unimpressed and regarded the ritual with a cold cynicism, depressing the mood. Its pall reduced the proceedings from meaningful ritual to gaudy pageantry and what should have been a consecration became an orgy. Asumunde and Jasumatu reached the fire and, outlined against the flames, turned to face the crowd. Asumunde felt the change of mood; attempting to regain control he raised his axe and the people slowly fell still silent again.

"Feast, my friends," Asumunde's powerful voice sought to recover the solemnity of the autumnal ritual. "Feast, and thank the gods for our deliverance from the quaking of the earth and for the success of our sacrifice. Tonight we should celebrate because the hot winds of summer are gone and the rains of autumn will soon arrive and the season of planting and harvest will begin. A double celebration! Let us pray for a quiet earth and a plentiful harvest! Be strong and brave and of good hope now that the land is still again! Enjoy the bread and wine which the earth has produced and the harvest that is to come. Eat the meat and drink the wine and be merry!"

The old man pointed the axe at the dark scar of the cave on the moonlit flank of the mountain.

"Give thanks to the gods of the mountain."

In the great courtyard of the palace, bathed by the pale light of the moon, the people of Phaistos raised their arms in the night and pointed to the silver mountain.

"We fear you, care for us."

The old prayer circled the court in the still night air. And in the dark distance there was a flash of lightning and the first thunder of autumn rumbled quietly in response.

The goats were eaten, their charred flesh pulled greasily from the spits, dribbling fat into the spitting fires. Wine flowed in purple rivers and, from ritual sacrifice, the night turned into pagan riot. Dancing began to the beat of drums, and the crowd, restless and melancholy, joined in with desperate abandon.

Asumunde's authority was lost in debauchery. The purpose of the sacrifice was forgotten and the yellow moon watched a wild night of drunkenness sink into a sickly dawn. Witejame and other palace elders urged Asumunde to restore the dignity of the evening but his efforts were worthless. His people, wearied by the heat of the summer and the relentless wind and now frightened by the earthquake, sought escape in wine and dance.

Chapter three

Autumn arrived with the first gentle rains and the hot northern wind faded away to be replaced by softer winds from the sea. The dry brown landscape bore a hint of green as grass spread along the walls and beside the paths of the village. Now the rivers started to flow again and the sacred mountain was softened by cloud, and the air smelt sweet. Grapes were harvested and trodden and the first fermentation bubbled in massive pithoi. Children plucked bursting, sticky figs from the trees and ate them greedily, delighting in their sweetness. The people of Phaistos were happy again and the summer fears had been forgotten. The rituals of the palace resumed their monotonous and tranquil rounds and the vulture returned to hunt along the crags of the palace ridge and over the endless emerald carpet of the forest.

Shepherds brought their flocks down from the hills and came back into the village, desperate for company and wine and loving. Their arrival was greeted with joy by young girls and kindly mothers but resented by young men who had spent a hot summer on the plains and were jealous of their vigour and energy. The shepherds, smelling of sheep and smoke, spread through the town and enlivened it. Girls became restless in their presence and men hostile. Fights broke out in public and embraces were exchanged in private as the nights lengthened and the cool of late autumn crept into the misty mornings. This was the busiest time of the year for a community that lived on its efforts in the fields and woods and the energy of the young men and women was directed to ploughing and hoeing and winemaking. Witejame and the older men, remembering the excesses of their own youth, hoped that a rigid routine of hard work would produce chastity and peace. It had failed then, and it failed now, and the quarrels and love-making continued and the old men grumbled and the young men lusted and fought, and the girls were happy and the town was content.

High in the sacred cave on the mountain Jasumatu watched the turning of the year in solitary peace, awaiting the call to descend to his marriage to Sirute. The first three weeks had been enjoyable and he had passed his time in carving. His gift to his bride-to-be was a wooden vulture hacked rather than carved from a twisted piece of olive wood and the work had taken all his time and skill, but as it neared completion his impatience dulled his ambition and he spent more of his time in thought than work. The uncertainty of his future as the acolyte of Asumunde weighed on him and he began to fear the responsibility which would be thrust upon him in the service of the palace and to question whether he was suited to the life of a priest. These were normal worries for a young man in his position but accentuated by his solitary state and meagre diet, and intensified by the increasing cold. Dream-filled restless nights of lust in the imaginary embrace of his young bride did not help and Jasumatu began to count the hours to his release and recall despite his fears for the future.

Jasumatu climbed the mountain from the cave to its rocky peak every day to tire himself and to increase his strength and endurance. He carried rocks for extra load and soon a sizeable cairn accumulated as he added his daily burden to the pile, and for further exercise he built a primitive shelter. This hard work passed the day tolerably well but did little to calm the feverish imaginings of the nights. His haggard face and wildly growing beard would have made him, if any had been there to see him, a figure of madness. He knew that his actions were becoming erratic but did not have the need to control them and his wild runs down the mountain from his lonely shelter on the peak to his cave refuge below became increasingly irrational as he leapt across the rough limestone, falling frequently and further damaging his already scarred limbs. He came to take pleasure in his pain in the hope that it would obscure his twin torments of hunger and lust. It was time to go; Jasumatu searched desperately for the sign that would beckon him back to Phaistos.

One cold clear night when the mist covered the palace and town beneath him and the nearly full moon took the life from the stars, Jasumatu started the precipitous descent from the peak to his cave and his supper of dry bread and water. Accustomed to the track he took little care and was not surprised when he found himself lying on the cold rough stones while the moon rocked in the sky. The stones harsh under his side were familiar but the movement of the moon was not, nor was the fall of boulders as the whole hillside seemed to slide away under his feet. Jasumatu held hard to the cold rock as the mountain moved, trembled, shook itself like a wet dog: a long shake, nose to tail, and as suddenly, lay still again. Around and below him scree and larger boulders chattered and slipped to new resting places; a final quiet crack and all was silent again. He lay rigid in fear until, urged by the sharp stones and the cold, he got to his feet and stumbled down the mountain and back to the sacred cave where fear now haunted the shadows. In the newly alien dark of the once familiar retreat Jasumatu pulled his cloak tightly round his body and burrowed into the crushed dry bracken which formed his bed; curled in a tight ball. With wild eyes staring out into the night, the future high Priest-King of Phaistos trembled through the long night and waited for the dawn.

The town below the palace lay shrouded under a thin mist through which the moon shone fleetingly. Dying campfires were glowing dully, deep red in the dark between the shallow pools of light cast by the occasional torch from which black smoke rose vertically to join the softer mists above. The village was silent and most of its people slept in their huts on rushes or bracken, the children seeking the warmth and comfort of their parents and older siblings. Some dogs lay amongst them, others prowled the sleeping town seeking scraps of meat and bread; cats watched disdainfully from concealment, ignored the noisy dogs, and leapt with deadly precision to take rats or mice. Only the guards were awake, circling the village slowly, carrying torches to deter the wild goats and pigs who were the only living enemies of the peaceful community.

The earthquake struck silently and without warning, breaking a thousand dreams with a frightening reality. A hundred fragile huts collapsed onto their sleeping occupants covering them with dust and rocks and heavy beams which broke bones and killed children. Women screamed, men shouted in fear, babies cried and dogs barked, torches fell firing dry straw, fire spread quicker than understanding. The awful shaking continued for ever then stopped without warning then came again and again; the horror continued unabated throughout the long night as men and women heaved desperately at fallen buildings in the darkness, aided only by the fleeting moon and the dying fires.

Witejame's hut stood at the foot of the palace hill slightly apart from the main part of the town, larger and more heavily constructed than others. The old man slept on the hard soil floor of an inner room; his daughters preferred beds of fern and the comfort of blankets. Sirute slept high in the palace above, kept in the isolation and privilege which are the bane and blessing of the intended bride of the priest-king elect.

The sudden earthshock dislodged the flat stones which pinned the rush roof of Witejame's hut. They slid to the ground with a rattle which was masked by the rumble of the stone wall of the room as it collapsed slowly inward, shaken into a low pile by the continuous tremble of the earth. The collapse of the wall caused the heavy roof beam which ran the length of the hut to pivot about its wooden central support. It swung wildly, allowing branches and rush coverings to fall on the girls to add to their fear and confusion. They scrambled out through the open door into the brighter dusty light of the night, screaming and holding each other tightly in panic. Blankets around them, hair wild in the moonlight, they turned together to see the roof beam fall heavily across the low mound of stones which now formed their father's grave. With hands torn and frantic, Witejame's daughters pulled stone from stone, log from log, to reveal their father's face, white in the moonlight, while the screams and the silence of the devastated village spread around them in the now still night.

The second palace of Phaistos had withstood many shocks and survived. It survived this earthquake, physically. A few pillars were dislodged, a few lintels collapsed, and some of its heavy building blocks moved a little. Ornaments shattered to the floor, and plaster was cracked; lamps moved to the edge of shelves, teetered and plunged to the hard flagstones below. Flames ran across rivers of oil but flickered and died. Structurally the palace survived and all its inhabitants escaped unharmed. But its composure was lost, its security destroyed. Since the destruction of the first palace so long ago, there had been few earthquakes and its people had become complacent and unsuspecting. This earthquake did not destroy the building, but it destroyed the lives of its inhabitants. The world would never be the same again for the people of Phaistos.

Chapter four

When the earthquake struck, Sirute and her two friends were standing by the southern boundary wall of the courtyard. The ground moved beneath their feet and they clutched at each other in sudden panic. The movement went on endlessly, a progression of shocks big and small, of imperceptible tremors followed by hammerblows growing to a crescendo as Africa struck Europe and turned Crete on its axis. The movement threw buildings to the ground and cracked the pavement, pillars fell and frescoes collapsed into dust, hillsides slumped in streams of rubble. Oil from broken pithoi spread through shattered storerooms and caught fire from falling lanterns. People screamed under tumbling masonry or were silent in shock; animals escaped and ran in fright, adding to the chaos. A calm and peaceful night in the ordered palace was transformed in a moment to a scene from hell, a scene of fear and horror and death.

The tremors seemed to go on forever until, suddenly, everything was still again, and silent but for the crackle of the fires and the screams of the injured. Sirute and her friends had been thrown to the ground by the tremors but were unharmed by the falling buildings and the spreading fires. In the stillness they lay tense, fearful of the next shock, reluctant to move. Sirute was the first to realise what had happened and struggled to her knees to see that Turusa was also moving. They looked at each other with wide fearful eyes in the orange glow from the fires, mirroring each other's horror. Between them Janati lay still. Sirute lifted her head onto her lap and wiped the dust from Janati's face with the corner of her robe. Holding her friend in her arms her tears fell wetly on to the other girl's face as she held her.

"What are you doing to me?" Janati opened her eyes and gave Sirute a slight smile. "Why are you crying, why are we on the ground? What's happened?"

From behind her came a groan as Turusa got stiffly to her feet and stretched and spat dust from her mouth. "I'll tell you what's happened, you silly girl. We've had a little earthquake, that's all. Just a little one. Now get up and let's get to work. There's going to be a lot to do. But take care; it may not be over yet."

The big girl led the way towards the piled stones of the fallen buildings and together they worked through the night, digging in the rubble, binding cut limbs and faces, covering the dead and consoling the living.

Halfway through the tragic night the three found themselves together and for a moment's respite sat on the broken wall and looked down onto the burning town below.

"I wonder how things are down there." Sirute thought of her father and sisters. "I ought to go to see if they're all right."

"They must look after themselves; we've enough to do up here," Turusa was firm.

"Come on, wash your face and let's get back to work and help who we can. Time for thought later. Time to decide why this has happened again. So much for Asumunde's sacrificed goat, that didn't do much good, did it?"

"You mustn't say things like that, Turusa, Asumunde always does what he thinks best, doesn't he?"

"Like sending your precious Jasumatu up to the mountain just when he's needed? Is that for the best?"

"Come on, Turusa, that's not fair", Janati pleaded with her angry friend. "How was he to know that this would happen?"

"Because that's his job." Turusa turned to look down on the burning town below.

"That's what he is supposed to do, to know about these things, and stop them. And he's failed. I hate to think what desperation he plans next; I wonder if we should send for Jasumatu? He would be a bit more sensible."

"No," Sirute surprised them all by her sharpness. "No. We will not send for Jasumatu; that's Asumunde's choice and his only. I will not spoil our betrothal. And, besides, he's safer there, up in the mountain."

The three girls looked involuntarily up to where the sacred mountain towered over of the smoke of the fires of the burning palace, and wearily went back to the horrors of the night.

No one dared to sleep in the palace that night other than Asumunde, lost in tortured dreams in his own room. Those who had laboured so long that their weariness had overcome their hopes brought mattresses and straw and slept out under the intermittent blaze of the moon as it broke through the blanket of smoke above the palace. A short sleep and a broken one. With the dawn came news from the town and of Witejame's death; Sirute was exhausted by the trauma of the night and heard of her father's demise and swift burial through a pall of weariness. She had suffered a surfeit of tragedy through the last few hours and was too tired to comprehend this personal loss. The news only roused her to join again the gruesome work of the search for the dead and the rescue of the injured in the palace.

Asumunde lay restless in his cot, isolated from the action, his mind offering yet more unrealistic solutions to what should have been practical problems. His people needed leadership and he was lost in nightmares. The management of the palace, based as it was on the omnipotence of the Priest-King, had failed its people in its greatest test and brought to an end three centuries of security.

By mid-morning, all the fires in the palace and in the village had been put out and all the injured had been taken from the wreckage. Broken bones had been bound to splints and cuts cauterised with wine and bandaged tightly; faces had been rinsed of the dry dust and thirsts quenched. People wandered aimlessly through the destruction of palace and town seeking friends, delighting in discovering those alive and despairing for the dead. As the morning wore on there was a general movement up to the palace and to the great court and soon crowds were gathered there, talking quietly, brought together by a common need for friendship and comfort, and most importantly, for guidance.

Some called for Asumunde but no one dared disturb him; some criticised him and blamed him; some tried to organise further recovery and repair work but their efforts were ignored. The power of the palace had lain for so long in the hands of the priest that without him there could be no organisation. But Asumunde lay alone, lost in his nightmare and in the horror of what he had chosen to do.

At length it was decided that Sirute and Turusa should go to Asumunde and ask for his help. They took with them a flask of wine and a little water and dry bread, not knowing how well he was, or indeed, if he was injured. They had been chosen because they were young and female and would not suggest a challenge or criticism, but it was with fear that they approached his room. Neither had been there before and they needed great courage to knock on the solid wood door, let alone enter. Even Turusa found her hands trembling and her first tentative knock was feeble. Summoning all her courage she knocked again, more firmly this time, and heard the old man's curt call to enter. The priest lay in his purple robe with his back to the girls as they came into the darkness of the stifling room. The drapes which obscured the windows had not been opened and narrow gaps between the strips of thick cloth allowed arrows of sunlight to strike golden targets on the floor making the surrounding gloom more intense.

Turusa coughed quietly. "Asumunde," she said softly, "Are you well? We have brought you some water and some wine. Please take them and refresh yourself. Your people need you."

The robe shook and an arm extended from it, moving through a sunbeam in an unexpected flash. "Give me the water."

Taking the beaker from Sirute the priest drank noisily. "Now go," he said, turning back to the wall, "I do not want you here."

"But, Asumunde, we need you." Sirute knelt beside his cot with Turusa standing beside her forcing her to go on. "Everyone is in the courtyard and no one knows what to do. We need you to tell us what we must do now. Please, help us, help everybody."

The old man was silent, covered by his royal robe, sprinkled with sunspots. The girls were uncertain, faces pale in the reflected light, frightened to stay but reluctant to go. The silence stretched; dust drifted through the sunbeams with only its gentle fall marking the passage of time.

The angular form under the rich robe stirred. Asumunde turned over; he raised his head from the cot and a ray of sunshine shattered on the untidy halo of his grey hair; he lifted his left arm and pointed. "We need a sacrifice."

The dreadful words slid slowly through the dust motes in the sunbeams.

"Phaistos must make a greater sacrifice to its gods. The gods of the mountain are displeased and have tried to destroy us. They demand more."

The words hung in the fragmented sunlight; they were not the words of the priest. They had a life and a death of their own. The gaunt arm moved palely in the gloom and pointed a bent finger at Sirute; a fingertip hit a sunbeam.

"The gods must be appeased or Phaistos will perish. You, Sirute, will be the sacrifice. You are their choice."

The gaunt finger pointed at Sirute, "You will be the sacrifice."

Nothing stirred but the golden specks of dust, given brief life in a sunbeam. Sirute sank to her knees on the rough matting which covered the floor of Asumunde's cell. She threw her arms around Turusa's legs and buried her face in her friend's robe; Turusa remained standing, strong and determined.

"You swore you'd never do it," she whispered, her voice slicing through the silence. "You can't sacrifice Sirute. What good will that do? Even you cannot stop the earthquake. You did not stop it before, when you killed the goat; killing Sirute will not stop it now. You can't take her from us. She's my friend and I love her, everyone loves her."

Her anger and horror overcame her fear and she moved toward the purple-clad figure on the bed, towering over him in her white dust-stained gown, ignoring the clinging Sirute who still clasped her knees and was dragged across the floor by the strength of her friend's desperation.

"You're mad." Turusa screamed at him, "It's evil and stupid and pointless. You can't kill her. I won't let it happen; the people of Phaistos won't allow it. Jasumatu will not allow it, Witejame will not …"

There was a violent movement from the bed; Asumunde pulled himself upright with a jerk, his bright cold eyes staring into hers. "Witejame is dead," he said in a flat hard voice. "He will not interfere. Jasumatu is in the mountain and will not return in time."

The tall priest got slowly and menacingly to his feet, the dappled sunlight bringing spots of brilliance to the royal purple of his robe. He loomed over the girls, his anger flaring, and Turusa retreated before him, leaving Sirute prostrate on the floor between them.

"And you, do you dare to thwart the will of your priest and king? I speak for Phaistos and for the gods of my ancestors. They demand sacrifice. How can you defy them? You are nothing. Do not dare to question me." Asumunde raised his arm and pointed to the door and the dark corridor beyond. "Go before I destroy you too,"

Sirute stirred on the rough floor matting, lying at the priest's feet. "Go, Turusa," she said quietly. "Go now, and leave me to my fate; it is what I was born to. It is my destiny, and I accept it, and now that my father is dead, and Jasumatu is away, I must do what I can for our people and the palace."

"No, you must not," Turusa still dared to challenge Asumunde. "I will not let this happen to you. You must not agree to it, Sirute. It will not help anyone; losing your life won't save the palace, your death will not bring your father back to life. All you can do is give this old man a chance to regain his power and his authority and that's not worth dying for."

Sirute got slowly to her feet and stood in front of the priest and faced her loyal friend. Her pale robe outlined her slim frailty against the dominating bulk of the man. A golden spot of sun multiplied in her black hair and made her face dark except for where the gleam of tears lit her eyes.

"I love you, Turusa," she said softly, "But I must accept what Asumunde says. And it is also my wish. Please go now and leave me to my fate." She crossed the room through the streaks of sunlight to take her friend in her arms and hold her tightly, and to cry desperate tears into Turusa's hair. "But don't forget me, Turusa. Promise that you will tell Jasumatu how it was, and how much I love him."

Turusa hugged her quickly and turned away. With dry eyes, upright and implacable, she walked through the spattered light to the door where she turned again.

"Asumunde, you are an old fool. Any sacrifice is wrong and futile, and Phaistos will not forget, nor will the people forgive you for what you intend to do."

Taking a stride back into the room she stood outlined in light against the gloom of the open doorway and hissed her hatred at him. "And I swear by the gods of the mountains: I will not forgive you. Watch for me, old man, wait for me. Do not forget. Count your hours carefully and treasure them, for they will be few. Watch for me. I will be there when you die in agony and I will rejoice at your death."

The altar threw a black shadow across the debris-strewn pavement in the late afternoon sun and the ruins of the courtyard buildings made a fitting background to its sombre bulk. Beyond the altar a massive pair of horns of consecration loomed darkly against the pale landscape adding an air of ritual to the barbaric scene. The crowd, still and silent, were gathered in groups amongst the piles of rubble; some had climbed onto fallen blocks to get a better view; some of the injured had been carried out into the hot sunshine and were shaded from its glare by their companions. The smoke from the smouldering town and palace hung like a like a shroud in the still air and hushed the cries of the unseen vulture soaring above.

There was movement at the north end of the court and the crowd froze further into its stillness as if all present simultaneously had caught their breath. A small procession emerged from the priest's rooms and picked its way through the fallen masonry. Asumunde, in a long black robe with a dust-stained hem, wearing the sacrificial sword in a leather scabbard at his waist, wound through the rubble heading inevitably toward the waiting altar. Behind him came four men carrying a litter of wood and canvas covered by a brightly patterned rug on which the tightly bound figure of Sirute lay, clad from head to toe in pure white silk. Her black hair framed her pale face and she stared blindly at the sky as if seeking Jasumatu in the sacred mountain. A tall man in a red robe carrying an immense axe with a double head of gold bearing symbols like those on the disks in the Room of Jars followed the litter. Through the jumble of fallen stones and the silence of the waiting crowd the small procession reached the altar and stood, motionless, as the axe was placed upright in its notch between the horns of consecration. The symbol of the power of the palace of Phaistos, pagan, unfeeling, dominant, rose over the courtyard, black against the pale haze of the sky.

Sirute lay gracefully in her white dress on the draped rug, seeming already dead under the influence of the opium. Asumunde drew the bronze sword from its scabbard and with its point indicated that she should be placed on the altar. Gentle hands lifted the girl's unconscious body and placed it on the hot stained black stone. Her black hair fell over her face and Asumunde brushed it back to reveal her pale neck. At his touch, Sirute stirred slightly and a whisper of a smile touched her lips.

The crowd held its collective breath and even the wind was still.

The vulture soared, silently, high, high above.

In the stillness, Asumunde's clear voice could be heard through the palace and over the ruined town; his words travelled to Kommos on the edge of the blue sea and to the summer palace of Triada. They spread over the wooded foothills and climbed the sacred mountain; they were heard wherever the power of Phaistos reigned.

"The priests of Phaistos have laboured through the ages to please the gods of the mountain. This palace was consecrated to them. But we have angered the gods. They have withdrawn their blessing and destroyed the palace and now they demand further sacrifice.

I, Asumunde, your priest and king, hear their anger and accept their command.

"I offer this maiden in sacrifice to them in the name of my people and of my ancestors and of the Palace of Phaistos.

"I do this in the certainty that the gods will be satisfied and that the palace and the people of Phaistos will be spared further destruction."

The crowd were silent and watchful, unconvinced but held in thrall by their history and their ingrained respect for the Priest-King and the awful drama unfolding before them.

Taking the sword in both hands, Asumunde brought it down across Sirute's throat and cut her jugular vein. The virginity of the white neck and dress was defiled by the scarlet blood as it pulsed, staining the world and taking her life. Her body slowly settled into sleep and a gentle sigh escaped from her open lips as her blood spread over the altar and ran in crimson curtains down its sides.

The vulture called harshly overhead and the mountains grumbled quietly and ominously in the distance.

The dreadful deed was done.

Asumunde stood with bowed head, still holding the sword whose bronze blade was now tarnished by the dark stain of the sacrifice. He knew he should now convince his people of the value of the sacrifice, tell them how the gods would be glad, tell them that there would be no more earthquakes and that the palace and town would be rebuilt. He knew that this was the time when he should show his authority and reassert his power. But he was an old man and tired and had lost his self-belief. The euphoria he had experienced before the sacrifice had been replaced by doubt and by revulsion at what he had done. Sadly, finally, he turned away from his people and abdicated his dominium for ever.

The people of Phaistos, traumatised by the terrible events of the hours since the earthquake, were strangely unimpressed by the ceremony. There had been no reaction to the sacrifice, they had seen so much death; if there was any surprise it was in Asumunde's abrupt withdrawal afterwards. In silence they slowly left the court. Sirute lay still, her crimson bed contrasting with the silk white of her gown and the alabaster white of her face.

Asumunde walked with bowed head through the departing crowds with the sword dangling from his right hand and dripping viscous drops of blood to dry quickly on the hot pavement. He felt sick and despondent. His fanatical belief in the worth of the sacrifice had evaporated to leave an emptiness which contained a bursting doubt. He had imagined the drama of his role, he had seen himself raising the bloodied sword to the approval and acclaim of his subjects, reassuring them with calming words, promising security and the rebuilding of the palace. And now he was lost in the dwindling crowd, dejected and rejected. In a moment of clarity he realised that his people had accepted the sacrifice but did not believe in it; they recognised it as part of an old ritual which they were as yet unready to question. But they were in no doubt as to its irrelevance. They no longer believed that the death of a beautiful young girl would stop the earthquakes. The power of the priests of Phaistos, which endured for five hundred years, was ebbing away forever.

Soon the court was empty but for the dead Sirute, and Turusa and Janati, and the departing remnants of the crowd. Palace servants came to remove the double axe from between the stone horns and to remove Sirute's body but were stilled by a quiet voice.

"Wait." Turusa's command was unexpected and firm. "You must not move her yet."

Janati and Turusa came to the altar and gently closed the eyes of their friend and wiped the drying blood from her neck, arranging the still lustrous black hair to conceal the awful wound. They turned her body and crossed her arms over her chest and covered her with a cloak of dark blue; with two white roses on top. Janati's tears flowed but Turusa was cold.

"You may take her now," she told the carriers. "Bear my friend with care."

Turusa stood before the altar in the lengthening shadows of the afternoon and called after Asumunde. At the far end of the devastated courtyard the old priest stopped and turned to face her.

"You will die for this murder, Asumunde; I will revenge the death of my friend. Count the last hours of your life, and start to count now." She was implacable and unwavering, shooting arrows of cold hatred across the court. She held her hands up high, the fingers stained with Sirute's blood and her voice carried clearly across the court. Count the hours, and enjoy them if you can; they are numbered on the bloody fingers of my hands." Taking the weeping Janati's arm, she turned her back on the priest and led the way through the courtyard back to the propylon, and to the earthquake victims who lay within it.

Asumunde watched the women depart then returned to his rooms. Weary, defeated, he sat on his cot with his head in his hands. Through the haze of his exhaustion he remembered the previous afternoon and his pleasure in making the embossed disk. Taking it now in his hands he tried to recall the pleasure he had felt in its creation. He turned it over and read again the story which the disk told of his life and his achievements, and was satisfied. Jasumatu should be recalled, he decided, and the disk should be entrusted to him to ensure that it was used for his funerary jar. He placed it carefully on the wide window ledge of his room. Then with a damp cloth he carefully cleaned the blood from the incised sword and hung it on a hook in the wall above his bed. He lay down on his cot and memories of the day crowded his mind; the earthquake, the injuries and deaths, his waking to see Sirute and Turusa in his room, the preparation of the opium to sedate Sirute, the blood cascading from her neck to the white dress, and finally the strong implacable Turusa and her curse. With part of his mind Asumunde rejected the girl's condemnation, knowing it to be unjust, recognising his great contribution to Phaistos. But another part of him accepted his inability to protect the palace which he had built and his disappointment of the people who had trusted him, and his despair deepened. With heavy heart he sought solace in the Room of Jars and, lighting an oil lamp, he walked slowly past the stored bones of his ancestors, finding some comfort in their company. He reached the far end of the double line and turned back towards the light from the open door.

As he turned, the floor rocked and rose again, dropped under his feet and groaned in pain. One of the jars of the remains of his ancestors fell heavily to the floor, shattering into a thousand pieces and filling the glow from his oil lamp with bright dust. Terrified, Asumunde ran for the sanctuary of the doorway, his old bones complaining and slow. A second shock struck and the floor moved again under his running feet and he fell painfully to his knees. The Room of Jars rocked and turned again and he dropped his lamp and the flame went out. The clay lamp-bowl shattered to allow its oil to spread over the shuddering floor. Now drenched in the oil, Asumunde crawled across the floor between the falling jars and tumbling masonry toward the dust-filled light until a powerful shock caused a large wooden beam to fall onto his legs. He was trapped in the darkness and debris, and rubble poured around him. His screams filled the room of his ancestors and reached out into the passage beyond and met Turusa as she ran down the staircase from the propylon. She heard the priest's cries and turned and took a lamp from a wall niche. She fought her way over the shaking floor and through falling masonry back towards the priest's rooms against rising clouds of dust Following the sound of the screams she came to the broken doorway of the Room of Jars and, bending down under the fallen lintel, she held her lamp to reveal Asumunde's face drawn in pain and outlined in the dark oil.

She smiled at him.

"Please, get me out," Asumunde whispered through the dust and darkness. "My legs are trapped and I can't escape. Please, please help me."

The earthquake grumbled again beneath them, bringing more rubble down from the roof.

Turusa looked at the old priest with the unfeeling eyes of a cat regarding a captive mouse. "You killed my friend and I swore to kill you. Now the earthquake which you sought to appease by that

29

pointless sacrifice will be your death, and I will be glad. Your gods have failed you. Die in agony and fear."

Her eyes glinted cold in the light of her lamp. "And as you die, remember Sirute, who, unlike you, did not deserve her death."

Turusa held the glowing wick of her lamp to the river of oil which covered Asumunde. Blue flames shot along the river and ignited the priest's hair and beard in a sparkle of gold. His face turned dark red and his screams grew as the flames spread down his robe searing his trapped limbs. Crouched in the darkness, Turusa watched until the terrible cries died away and the flailing frantic arms were stilled and the upturned face turned black. Only when she knew that he was finally dead and had died in agony and terror did she release his eyes from her terrible gaze.

The earth moved again and she left him to his death in the company of his ancestors. Her revenge had been swift and sweet and awful and brought to an end the reign of the second great palace of Phaistos.

Chapter five

Through the long day Jasumatu watched from the cave on the sacred mountain as the smoke from burning Phaistos drifted slowly to the east on the wings of a soft wind from the sea. He had been isolated from his people for six weeks and the poor diet of figs, olives and cheese and dried bread had weakened his grasp on reality; at times he felt godlike in his remoteness, high above the world and its petty tragedies; at others he became frantic in his need to know what had happened to Sirute and the palace and desperate to descend and find out.

Torn between a desire to descend and a belief that he could not do so unless Asumunde ordained it, Jasumatu spent a restless day before climbing to the ruined sanctuary on the peak late in the afternoon. He watched the sun sink slowly until as it touched the distant hills then, cold and hungry, he got to his feet and turned from the still bright sky and ran down the path, spirits lifting with every downward leap. In his urgency he was soon down the limestone track to the cave where he collected his cloak and a small oil lamp. He put all his remaining food and water into a leather satchel and with a last look around his hermitage, started down the long slopes of the mountain. Phaistos, Sirute and his family lay below in the night and Jasumatu raced down the mountain towards them through the darkness.

The trail was difficult to find, steep and covered in the debris of the earthquake, but his determination leant certainty to his footsteps and, light-headed with hunger, he saw himself flying across the mountain. The vulture, circling on silent wings high in the night, came to follow him as he crossed the lower slopes to the woods on the plain.

There was no track through the thick forest which covered the dry chalk downs between the foothills of the sacred mountain and the ridges which guard Phaistos and Jasumatu found the going hard and his legs growing weary. The moon had not yet risen; it was dark

31

in the forest and he had to feel his way forward through the trees and over the rough land. At the river he stopped to drink and sat on the bank looking up at the black mass of Phaistos on the ridge, ominous against the growing light of the moonlit sky. As he looked up at the palace his earlier certainty ebbed away to be replaced by a fear of what lay ahead. He hesitated, irresolute, fearful of what lay ahead.

The earthquake that brought the death of Phaistos struck suddenly, shockingly, in the darkness. The land shook with such abrupt force that Jasumatu was thrown into the jumble of boulders in the river bed and struck his head heavily. He lay unconscious as the earth groaned and twisted, turned, shook and trembled beneath him. Small avalanches of stones rushed into the valley, larger boulders cut a path through the bushes before coming to a juddering halt against trees or larger stones. Small animals cowered, bigger ones ran in terror, a fine white dust rose from the shattered chalk to reflect the silver moonlight. Bleeding into the river, Jasumatu recovered his senses to find the whole dark world in terrifying motion. Terrified, he hugged the moving ground as it lurched endlessly under him.

Then suddenly all was still again. The world was silent, held its breath and waited. Small stones clattered, animals stirred, lifted heads, listened. A fragile peace returned. Nature soon forgot but the palace on the ridge was changed for ever.

Exhausted, frightened and bleeding from the cut on his head, Jasumatu crawled up the steep chalk escarpment through the night, his way impeded by fallen trees and unstable rock falls. Boulders moved at his touch; fine dust filled his lungs and his eyes and made his face a red scarred mask of white like that of a damaged, tragic clown.

After a long struggle he came to the northern gate of the palace which led into the granaries and the storerooms. The doorway had collapsed and he had to climb over its fallen lintel to get into the narrow passage beyond, where a roof fall impeded his progress. The passage had low walls and a brush roof and did not appear much damaged and it was only when Jasumatu came to the corridor leading to the priest's room that he realised the full extent of the damage. Enormous blocks had fallen from the walls and filled the courtyards. Fractured columns leant across them; there was the smell of burnt wood and straw mingling with the sweetness of rivers of spilt wine and oil. Here were bodies crushed and broken; here were men and women alive and screaming; here were others tugging ineffectively at people trapped by fallen stones and beams. Fires raged furiously, casting wild illumination over the scene of devastation.

By instinct alone the young man crawled through his fallen kingdom until the light from a small fire led him into one of the inner courts filled with terrible screams which chilled his blood. There was a room across the courtyard which seemed full of flames and, black against the fire, was the figure of a woman. Carrying a lighted lamp in her right hand, she moved backwards towards him haloed by the brightness beyond. As Jasumatu crossed the flame-lit court towards the room of the jars, Turusa turned to face him.

"Oh. It's you. At last," she said, dully, without surprise. "I've killed him." She gestured toward the dying flames behind her. "And Sirute is dead, too. He sacrificed her to try to save the palace, and so I killed him. She was my friend. Where were you when she needed you?"

Early next morning they took Sirute to the shaft graves outside the desolate town, a procession of silence weaving a torturous route through the rubble. A small procession, for many had been killed or injured, and others were still attempting to recover lost friends and family from the ruins, but a procession nevertheless. Led by Jasumatu and Turusa and in the stillness of early autumn with a sorrow of mists hanging from the branches of the trees, the people of Phaistos laid their princess and sacrifice to rest in the cold rock grave. Sirute was dressed in a fine white gown and wore the golden necklace and earrings that Witejame had given to her at her betrothal. Jasumatu fastened round her neck a necklace of golden bees which he himself had brought for her from the northern palace at Malia. Her hair, freshly washed and shining black against the white dress, was bound in an amber clasp. A green glass bracelet adorned the ivory white of her wrist and the gentle half-smile was frozen forever on her lips.

They carried her slowly through the still morning and laid her in a cool grave on a bed of rushes. Some placed libation cups beside her; others cups of wine and oil. Dates and figs were put at her side with corn to sustain her on the journey into death. In a final gesture of farewell Jasumatu put a small bronze dog which she had loved as a child beside her hand and Turusa laid a single red rose on her chest.

Sirute's white lips were cold to their last kisses; their tears ran glistening from her icy cheeks into the depths of her hair. Heavy stones covered the grave and Sirute's faint smile faded forever into the darkness. The procession returned in silence, winding slowly through the mounds of rubble which had once been the town of Phaistos.

Unseen, above the thin autumn mist, the vulture circled.

33

Chapter six

On the third day after the earthquake Jasumatu called a meeting of the survivors on the slope outside the west gate of the destroyed palace. He and Turusa had been tireless in organising the recovery of the dead and injured from the ruins, leading rescue parties into the debris and risking further hurt in releasing those who remained trapped in the rubble. Many bodies had been found and buried and the badly injured had been made comfortable and left to die in peace. Some with lesser wounds had been saved and now lay awaiting recovery with broken limbs bound to splints and cuts poulticed and tied with healing leaves. Some with bad burns from the oil-fed fires had been given opium to ease the pain and now lay vacant in the sunshine awaiting a slow death. The population of the palace of Phaistos had been halved by the tragedy and all of the people in the town had lost children or parents in the terrible fires which had devastated the timber buildings. Many animals survived and had been rounded up and corralled, and dogs and cats wandered uneasily through the desolation. Stores of grain and olives and oil which had survived intact were located and kept safe and a number of the treasures of the palace had been found; there would be no famine that winter and some of the history of Phaistos would be preserved for the future.

Jasumatu called a meeting of the survivors to take place at noon. He had earned respect for his efforts in the hard and dangerous work of recovery but the gulf between him and the people he was to have ruled as priest-king remained deep. He did not have the easy familiarity that Turusa was able to exert through the power of her personality. He had been isolated too long from the ordinary people and despite all his efforts he remained distant and cold, and communication did not come easily to him. When able to lead through example he could be effective, lacking neither strength nor courage, but he could not bridge the gap between him and his people by words alone. He earned the respect of the people, but not their love.

In the full hot glare of noon in late autumn he and Turusa stood on the wide, shallow stone steps which led up into the fallen palace. He had chosen the place with care, outside the palace but above the town, indicating a new, easier, relationship between priest and people, but the shallow slope succeeded only in making him either too distant or too low to command attention. Turusa realised this at once and arranged for a large broken stone block to be brought and placed on the steps; precariously balanced on this Jasumatu announced his plans for the abandonment of Phaistos. Turusa stood a little way behind him, supporting but not undermining his authority; the crowd listened quietly in the still air, some standing, some of the injured supported by friends, some carried on couches, all intent on the young priest's words. The vulture, previously circling high above, came closer as if to hear his plans.

"My friends. We have suffered much together and I shall ever regret that I was not here to share the final tragedy with you. You have worked hard to recover and without your efforts our future would be desolate. The palace of Phaistos is destroyed and many of your houses with it, but we are here and we are strong and fit and determined. We will survive and the spirit of Phaistos will live with us."

The vulture swooped overhead.

"We will survive. But we will leave Phaistos."

The crowd stirred, people shuffled their feet and looked at each other, seeking agreement and reassurance, afraid to voice their fears and surprise in public.

The vulture circled lower.

"When I was young," Jasumatu continued, "I sailed west along the coast, past the white mountains to a green land with wide forests where the sea is always blue and full of fish. A land with fresh water and good soil, where olives and corn grow, and the wild goat lives in the mountains. A land which is free from other men and where the winds are soft. A land which does not shake itself to destroy us. A land in which we can raise our children in safety. This will be our new home."

The crowd was silent in the slanting light of the afternoon, undecided and unconvinced.

Turusa moved down the staircase to stand in front of Jasumatu. Her clear voice spoke personally to everyone in the crowd. "Jasumatu is right. It is sad to leave Phaistos where we have worked and lived and where many of our loved ones lie buried. Where we know every flower, every tree. But we must think of our future. Our children must be safe from danger and from hunger. Could you feel safe here,

35

again? We will go with Jasumatu to a new land, a land of safety and plenty where we can build a new Phaistos together. Let us forget the terrible past and go together to make a new and happy home in the west."

The people looked up now, believing her, wanting to trust her; the vulture waited.

Turusa moved back to stand beside Jasumatu in the golden light of the late afternoon. "Trust us," she said quietly. "We will lead you well."

"In the springtime," Jasumatu continued, in the silence following Turusa's plea, attempting to regain some of the authority which had slipped away to her, "We will sail from Kommos to make a new life and take the spirit of Phaistos with us. It will not be easy. There will be hard work for everyone but, if we are together, we can build a new home where we can be secure and content, and where we can put these terrible times behind us. I am confident that this is the right thing to do."

The people were sceptical of the confidence of priests: where had Asumunde's certainty led them? But Turusa was one of their own, and they trusted her. Life was hard, why not suffer it elsewhere? Restless for change, maybe sensing the end of the priestly authority, they voted to leave Phaistos and the security of five hundred years.

The vulture circled lazily high above and, apparently content with the resolution, flew westwards into the setting sun.

* * * * *

Four months later, at the third new moon of the year, the people of Phaistos left forever the fallen palace and ravaged town beneath the sacred mountain. A fleet of ships, big and small, lay heavily loaded at Kommos, awaiting a fair wind to assist their journey to the west. The ships were loaded with all that could be usefully saved from Phaistos; cereals and salt, oil and olives, glass and grapes, cups and copper, beads and bowls, tools, ropes, swords. Ducks were in cages and cats also; dogs stood proudly on deck, excited by the activity and ready for the journey. Sheep and goats had already left in the care of their shepherds to go to the high pastures for the summer from where they would descend, in autumn, to the new homelands in the west.

The fallen palace had kept many of its treasures. Heavy blocks of stone which had fallen from the walls and roofs prevented access to a great number of the rooms and the people lacked the will to move them unless they could be sure of recovering something worthwhile or valuable. The sacred bronze axes had been found intact and the sacrificial sword had been discovered on the floor of Asumunde's room, beneath his bed. Turusa did not want to take the sword to the new place, stained as it was with Sirute's blood, but Jasumatu insisted. To him it was the single most important symbol of tradition and authority and he believed it should be kept despite its awful association. He decided that he would not wear it as Asumunde had always done but saw that it was carefully stowed on one of the larger ships.

Jasumatu wanted to preserve as much of the history and tradition of Phaistos as possible and would have liked to have taken the funerary jars of his predecessors to their new home. He had earlier found a way into the Room of Jars to remove the blackened corpse of Asumunde to give it a solemn burial and now crawled again in fear between the blocks of the fallen walls. Many of the jars were shattered and he had to force his way in the darkness over the crushed dry bones of his ancestors. Despite the cloth that he held over his face, his eyes and throat filled with the detritus and he retched in the fine dust which his slow passage threw up into the flickering flame from his oil lamp. Resolute in his horror and discomfort he persisted and eventually forced a way through into the depths of the chamber only to find that virtually all the jars had been broken in the earthquake. Disappointed in his attempt to recover the jars complete, he collected as many of the intact inscribed clay sealing disks as he could find and soon a considerable pile grew outside in the courtyard. If he could not recover the jars and their grisly contents, at least he was able to preserve the written record of his predecessor's lives. It was with some satisfaction that he was able to store over fifty disks carefully packed in straw in a great pithos deep in the hold of the ship.

The engraved seal stones, which had been used to inscribe the clay discs over the years, could not be found and he did not discover the disk which Asumunde had made on the day before his death. During the earthquake this had fallen from the window ledge where the old priest had placed it to dry, directly into a store room under his quarters and had been buried under tons of rubble. It would not be found again for thirty-four centuries.

On the last morning Jasumatu and Turusa climbed the ridge to the palace and walked up the wide stone steps. The way into the main courtyard had been partially cleared and they crossed the rubble-strewn flagstones to stand by the altar on which Sirute had died, and

37

turned to look at the ruins of the palace. In the clear air of spring the twin peaks of the sacred mountain dominated the scene, climbing high and pure over the destruction.

"This could have been yours," Turusa said quietly, "A beautiful palace, a beautiful bride, and power. And now they've all gone. Do you regret it?"

Jasumatu looked around the silent ruin. "I miss the palace. It was such a magnificent building. And it carried so much history. It can never be replaced. But it was only a building. Sirute I will not see again and her loss will stay with me forever, but she is still alive to me in my heart."

"You have never blamed Asumunde for her death and that pointless sacrifice."

"How can I blame him? I would have done the same if I believed that it would save the palace. It was his duty."

Turusa looked into his eyes and saw his confusion. In a moment of tenderness she sympathised with him and understood how the responsibilities to the palace and to the cult of priesthood still conflicted with his love for Sirute. But she also saw his weakness. And she realised that this weakness brought the plans for the future of Phaistos into jeopardy; the intention to move the entire tribe into new and unknown territory would bring many difficulties and dangers, and strong and resolute leadership would be necessary. She herself would have made a capable leader but she knew that the people would only be led by a man. She needed Jasumatu as a public face for her determination. Phaistos needed a leader whom the people could acknowledge.

Turusa hardened her heart and stilled her sympathies. "It may have been his duty, but it was wrong. He took the life of my friend and your bride, and you still cannot condemn him. What are you? How can you stay uncommitted? There is a time for understanding and calm and there is a time for anger and determination; that time is now. You cannot, you must not, side with those who took Sirute's life in such a pointless and futile gesture. The future of Phaistos lies in leadership and example, not in vain ritual. Ritual brings fear; leadership brings security and contentment. You have to lead; whether you are priest or king does not count for anything now; you have to lead as a man."

Jasumatu walked to the edge of the damaged courtyard and looked down on the deserted town under the ridge. He shook his head and turned back to Turusa. "I was to have been the Priest-King of Phaistos," he said quietly. "You may not understand, but this was my honour and my duty and is still so. My duty, my responsibility to Phaistos and to my ancestors is greater than anything else, even my love for Sirute. Even the love of my people. If I fail in that duty, I shall not live."

Turusa and Jasumatu stood side by side, but apart, on the courtyard of the fallen palace and each wept in the spring sunshine for the long history which was ended, and in fear of an uncertain future.

"I promise you one thing, Turusa." With tears running down his face Jasumatu looked up at the mountain behind the palace. "I will never use the sword in sacrifice, no matter what happens to us. I do not believe that such things can influence the gods and I will never do it."

Turusa wiped her eyes roughly with the sleeve of her red gown. "I believe you, now. But I also heard Asumunde say the same. And I tell you this; if you ever break your word, I will kill you, too. As I killed Asumunde."

Turusa looked unflinchingly at Jasumatu, her face damp with her tears but resolute and cold in the morning sunshine.

"Remember that, I mean it."

Jasumatu did not doubt her.

They stood in silence, reluctant to leave.

A soft, cool spring wind crept down from the mountain and they both shivered to its touch.

"Come, it's time to go."

They crossed the court for the last time and did not look back as they descended the staircase and followed the familiar track down the hill to the waiting people and the road to Kommos and the laden ships.

As they left the palace the vulture flew high above and led them towards the sea.

Chapter seven

The fleet set out from Kommos early next day on a favourable wind from the east and straggled along the coast, hugging the land as closely as possible. The bigger ships were heavily loaded and unwieldy and their captains were reluctant to take them far out to sea knowing that the oarsmen would have great difficulty against the prevailing westerly current should the wind fail. They crept along the shore beneath the high cliffs and prayed that the light easterly breeze would hold throughout the day. The bigger ships had a single mast with a large rectangular sail and were directed by steering oars at either side of the stern. These craft were very seaworthy but were vulnerable to sudden changes in the direction of the wind. Their captains had to be constantly alert to any variation which, catching the ponderous sail, might lead to a capsize. These boats were not capable of sailing into the wind as they lacked a keel, and at the first sign of a contrary breeze the sail had to be taken down and the oarsmen brought into action. When they carried loads as heavy as now the boats sat low in the water and the action of the oars was inefficient and very tiring to the crew and they were slow through the water. The journey they now undertook was hazardous and fraught with difficulties and required the best of conditions.

Ramati was the most experienced captain and in consultation with Jasumatu had planned a route which might be accomplished in four days but which was more likely to take ten if the weather was less than perfect and the fleet had to hug the land for safety.

The small boats went ahead to find moorings for the night and to search for fresh water. Heavily loaded as it was, the fleet had no capacity to carry supplies for longer than a day and Ramati hoped that water could be found each night and stocks replenished. At this time of the year the rivers which entered the sea on the early part of their journey would be running and further along the coast he knew of springs which could be used.

The first day passed easily and without incident. In the evening the leading boats found a sandy beach, sheltered from the east wind, and set up camp where a river brought fresh water down from a great gorge carved through the mountains. The tribe spent a light-hearted night around its campfires and under the stars, glad that the journey had at last started and that the sad work of clearing Phaistos had been completed. There was a new spirit of excitement and anticipation and a relaxed and happy people made an early start next morning as the gentle east wind returned and guided them on.

The wind strengthened as the day passed but the sky remained clear and the voyage became an enjoyable and pleasant cruise. Small boats showed off their skills and circled the larger ones; foolhardy swimmers dived from the big ships and tried to impress the women on board, children fell in by design and had to be rescued with much fuss and concern and then rubbed with large cloths until their skin glowed. A carnival atmosphere prevailed and the tribe had not been happier since before the first earthquake. The fleet made a dramatic picture; dark hulls under deep red sails suspended on the white-edged blue of the sea, under the grey limestone of the sea cliffs and the pale blue of the sky. The world had never seen a finer sight.

Afternoon lengthened into evening and the grey bulk of Cape Lissos loomed ahead, lying on the sea like a long finger with a knuckle slightly bent and under a cuff of cliff which rose steeply from it.

The cape formed two harbours, one to the east and one to the west, both providing safe havens for shipping but both vulnerable to coastal winds. The easterly bay has a fresh water spring which emerges from under its steep cliffs; the westerly cove has a better anchorage and flat ground for a camp. It is a further day's sail to the next fresh water beyond Lissos and the intervening shore is steep and inhospitable. Ramati, on the wings of a freshening easterly, had no choice. He signalled to his fleet that they should make for the western bay and the smaller boats dashed off enthusiastically along a rocky limestone coast to make the turn into the sheltered cove and to set up camp on the headland. As the breeze increased with the evening and a hard, storm-threatening brightness crept across the sky from the west, the bigger boats followed more hesitantly, constantly aware of the sharp teeth of the land on their right.

The sea turned dark and steep waves were capped with laces of white as the wooden ships with sails reefed crept along the coast under a following wind. As each came to the westerly point of the headland, the sail was dropped completely and all hands were put to the oars. In the lee of the land it was just possible for oarsmen to propel the awkward craft against the wind to their intended moorings

41

and it was with great relief that the anchors were dropped and the boats made safe in the lee of the cape. The euphoria of the day had been quickly lost under the challenge of the hard steel sky and the needles of rock and the increasingly erratic wind which now gusted down from the mountains.

Ramati and Jasumatu were on the largest ship which carried the greater part of the palace treasures. They were the last to come to make the turn around the headland into the more sheltered waters of the west bay. By now the land was dark and made more so by the brittle brilliance of the sunset. The heavy ship made the turn slowly, with choppy waves lapping over the low gunwales. Ramati ordered the sail to be dropped as the crew took to the oars and in the growing darkness the craft edged around the point and followed the shore of jagged rock towards its intended anchorage in the bay. Now the land was dark as they sailed into the east and into the night sky; the oarsmen strained at heavy oars made difficult to manage by the steep waves. Progress was painfully slow with Ramati and Jasumatu at the prow attempting to navigate, peering into the black sea and passing instructions back to the men on the steering oars. The craft crept along, silent passengers and crew straining eyes and ears, confused by the crash of the waves on the broken shore and the lights of the campfires of their tribe on the headland.

On the high scarp cliff above the headland the east wind turned on steep rock and hurled down the bare hillside, turning the leaves of the olive trees silver as it passed. It leapt down the slopes and rushed across the west bay of Lissos to hit the ship carrying Ramati and Jasumatu on its left side, and turned the heavy craft into the shore. A pinnacle of sharp rock lay just under the surface, urchin covered and sculpted to a knife edge, hidden by the dark sea. Its point made a clean cut in the wooden hull of the ship and the momentum of the laden vessel slowly tore it through successive planks as Jasumatu's flagship, carrying most that had been saved from the palace of Phaistos, impaled itself on the fatal point. The shock threw the oarsmen and Ramati to the deck. Dark water poured into the torn hull and the ship came to a shuddering halt and rested, tilting slightly to its left, unnaturally immobile amidst the turbulence of the sea. The sea rose quickly in the craft and men scrambled through the chaos of rope and oars and floating stores desperate to grasp something solid in the turmoil. To add to the danger the mast broke its stern stays and leant forward at a perilous angle threatening to turn the craft over into the steep waves. Jasumatu clung to the great arc of the prow and watched his crew and their passengers scrambling for the inhospitable rocks where they found a difficult landing on the sharp teeth of the limestone. Some were dragged ashore, cut and shocked, by the occupants of the earlier ships who had watched in horror the wrecking of the flagship. Others held fast to the stricken ship shouting for help, shivering in the shock of the cold water. Dogs swam to the rocks and pulled themselves out and shook, scattering tiny specks of rainbow in the sunset.

The ship filled with water leaving only the curves of the prow and stern and the oddly-angled mast above the waves. In black despair Jasumatu slipped into the sea which slapped him cruelly in the face as if to reprimand him, and swam to the shore to join the silent, horrified crowd on the alien headland. The sun set and the world was a cold and desolate place.

It was too late to attempt to salvage anything from the flagship that evening and the people spent an uncomfortable night on the headland exposed to the increasing gale. By morning a full storm raged over the tribe huddled miserably in the driving rain, watching impotently as the steep waves pounded the wreck.

Apart from the others, in the lee of a large limestone outcrop from which the wind blew cold raindrops into his face, Jasumatu crouched, young and lonely. Turusa watched for some time from a distance and then made her way through the scrub and the rough rock to him. Resentful of her intrusion into his grief, Jasumatu pretended not to see her approach but watched covertly and envied her strength. She had a grey blanket wrapped around her and her long fair hair streamed in the wind; she seemed indestructible as she came to stand beside him and looked out across the bay. They stayed silent for some time, she tall and resolute, he crouched defeated and shivering under the rock.

"It wasn't your fault, you know. You have to believe that."

"First I lose my palace, then Sirute, and now I lose the treasures and the ship."

Awash with self-pity Jasumatu buried his face in his hands and wept salt tears into the fresh rain. Turusa watched him in silence for a while, partly sympathetic but wholly contemptuous. But the tribe needed leadership and he was all they had; she sighed and put her hand on his shoulder. She would support and encourage him again, for herself and for Phaistos. She patted his shoulder as one would with a small child, to console him.

"Be strong, Jasumatu," she said, "You are the priest and the king of Phaistos, you cannot blame yourself for these things. The people need your leadership and your guidance. You must not disappoint them."

"But what can I do now? There is nothing left."

Turusa looked down at the young man sitting in the rain and pitied his weakness. She knew that he was a good man and knew that his people acknowledged his kingship rather than respected it. He was a man out of his time, considerate and imaginative, tender even, but not a leader. Torn between sympathy and contempt she watched him weep for a future, which was lost forever. "Come," she said roughly, suddenly irritated. "Stop this. We need you and we need you strong. Only you can hold us together. Don't forget that it was your idea to leave Phaistos. You cannot just give up."

"But what are we going to do?"

Turusa was angry now. "This is what you are going to do. You are going to get up and rejoin your people. There are things to be done with the wreck, and stores and cargo to be salvaged and you must organise it. We should save what we can and put it in the other boats and then, when the storm drops, we will go on to our new home. We can't stay here and we cannot afford to lose what is on that ship."

Turusa had never resented the lowly status of women as much as now. She felt clear-sighted and determined and hated to have to manipulate Jasumatu to do things which were so obvious to her. But that was the way of Phaistos and she was useless without him. She shrugged to herself. If she had to use Jasumatu for the good of the tribe, then she would. She consoled herself with the thought that he would only be the puppet of her will and, swallowing her pride, took him in her arms. She hugged him and took his head between her hands. She held his wet face, streaked by tears and rain and looked into his eyes, willing him to respond.

"You are our leader and our king. We all need you and your strength. Lead us in what we must do, before it is too late."

"It is too late." Jasumatu turned away from her, "I cannot do it."

Turusa urged him yet again, "You can do it, and you must. It is not too late. We must start now."

But it was too late. Under the beating of the waves the hull of the ship was being torn to shreds on the needle rocks and, as Jasumatu and Turusa watched from the shelter, the mast dipped down toward the sea. The broken craft freed itself from the restraint of the limestone, turned slowly onto its side and disappeared under the waves. The coast was steep and the wreck fell down an underwater cliff face to its final resting place in shingle and weed deep beneath the surface.

The remaining deck-stored cargo broke free in the fall and was scattered down the slope and the shattered hull came to rest on its side on the pale sand with the treasures of the palace of Phaistos within it.

Wet, cold and miserable, the tribe huddled on the exposed headland not wishing to leave their moored vessels and reluctant to abandon the site where the flagship had been lost. The storm persisted throughout the day and made any attempt to salvage cargo from the wreck impossible. A diver volunteered to go down to ascertain how the wreck lay but the sea was cold and the storm had raised a silt which obscured all but the most general picture. He reported that the ship lay on its left side and with the gunwales smashed where it had struck the sea floor. The mast lay beside the hull like a broken limb, he reported, sticking out at an angle. The submarine cliff and the scree at its foot were littered with debris from the ship, which was already being covered by the fine silt raised by the storm. In the conditions it was not possible to salvage anything and the diver showed little enthusiasm for further investigation. Surrounded by an inquisitive and solicitous crowd he was taken away to a warm fire and dry clothes, a hero for the day.

Although the tribe as a whole had agreed to the emigration from Phaistos some had had reservations and these now raised their voices in criticism, encouraged by the cold and driving rain. A murmur of mutiny grew as the day lengthened and Jasumatu's role in bringing them to this desolate place and in the loss of the flagship was debated and criticised. The arguments for a return to Phaistos grew stronger and more heated and resulted in angry and deep divisions in what until then had been a united people. The feeling of depression spread and even those most resolute and determined and supportive of Jasumatu began to waver.

Turusa and Ramati attempted to raise the spirits of the people by organising parties to build huts and encouraging others to cross the flat headland to climb down the steep cliff into the easterly bay to the well to replenish the fresh water supplies. The wind died down a little towards evening and fires were lit to heat food and to warm wet and cold limbs and Turusa and Ramati urged Jasumatu to speak to the people and quell the unrest. Reluctant and unsure of himself, Jasumatu wandered off to the point of the headland alone and sat looking out over the calming sea towards the dying light of the west.

After some time deep in thought and with more resolution in his manner than his mind he came back to the camp and beckoned the people to gather together in the circle of fires. Coated in the gold light from the glowing fires and outlined against the western sky

45

Jasumatu stood alone before his tribe. For the first time since the destruction of the palace Turusa did not come to stand beside him as he spoke and his voice was quiet against the slap of the waves on the shore.

"My friends," he said, "tomorrow you will continue your journey to your new home. I will not be with you. Ramati and I and two or three others will stay here to attempt to salvage all we can from the flagship. We will keep one of the ships and follow when our work here is done. The rest of you must go on."

Ramati looked at him in surprise and was about to object when a glare from Turusa stilled him. His innate respect for the priesthood kept him quiet as Jasumatu continued.

"My friends, my people. You will sail as soon as the wind becomes favourable. Turusa will lead you to the safe havens in the west of which I have told you and where you will find the land of plenty which I have promised you. You will be happy there. You must forget about the palace and about the loss of the ship; these things will only strengthen us and help us to meet the challenges of the future. The people of Phaistos are strong; believe in yourselves and you will be strong."

The people looked at one another, the promise of his firm words enhanced by the prospect of an early departure from this inhospitable place. Ramati said nothing but Turusa grasped the opportunity to exert her authority. "Your priest has spoken," she said, moving to stand in the centre of the circle of fires. "We will leave tomorrow as he directs, and I will lead you to our new home; his power is now in me and I will not fail him, nor will I fail you. Now sleep, for there is much to be done tomorrow."

Had Jasumatu suggested a course of action less acceptable to the people of Phaistos he would have encountered opposition to his proposal. His statement had been made in an uncompromising fashion, allowing for no question or argument, and would not have been accepted if his plan had not coincided with the wishes of his tribe. But the people wanted to leave this inhospitable headland; they were fearful of a return to the old palace and had accepted the somewhat unsubstantiated appeal of the new lands to the west. They were prepared to accede to any suggestion, however dogmatically made, which assured escape. Jasumatu did not win any hearts by his statement but made no further enemies and the people retired to their makeshift quarters with no open dissension. The wind died, the sea stilled and the cold turmoil of the last few days faded under the warm promise of early spring as the tribe enjoyed a mild moonlit night under a clear sky. In the cool blue hour between the setting of the moon and the dawn the gentle easterly wind returned, to promise an easy sail along the high cliffs to the west.

In the early morning, enthusiasm regained, optimism in their hearts, and with their dogs safely aboard and their cats and ducks in baskets on deck, the tribe of Phaistos set sail on their interrupted pilgrimage into the slowly brightening west; behind them the sun rose to light their way and the vulture came leisurely down from the hills to follow.

Chapter eight

The optimism of those members of the tribe who set sail in the departing fleet was not matched by those who were left behind on the sharp rocks of the headland; Ramati and the two men who had been chosen to stay behind stood some way apart from Jasumatu and sadly watched their friends and families sail away in the dawn on the wings of the breeze, the dark red sails of the ships made crimson by the low sun. With heavy hearts the four men waited until the last ship had disappeared behind the white marble of the next cape then turned reluctantly to the task of collecting the storm-thrown debris of the wreck.

Some of the lighter stores had broken free from the deck and had risen to the surface, some had come into the shore to be snared by the jagged rocks and others still bobbed about on the sea. Jasumatu and his men worked through all that first day to gather what they could and to decide what was worth salvaging. Two piles were collected on the headland, one to be kept and the other discarded. Jasumatu wanted to keep almost everything but the others, more practically, considered the utility of the recovered items and the ability of the remaining heavily laden ship to carry them.

Stronger arguments arose when Jasumatu insisted on diving to attempt to recover some of the palace treasures from the damaged hull. The wreck was deep and the divers could only stay down on it for less than a minute; the water was cold and dark, and the men grew quickly exhausted over what they regarded as a pointless task. Little was recovered but Jasumatu's stubborn insistence forced them down time and time again. He did not spare himself in the enterprise but achieved only his own exhaustion, and his consequent irritability strained his relations with his men to breaking point. Jasumatu's priestly training had not extended to leading men in practical and dangerous circumstances and his lack of understanding and his abrupt and dogmatic orders brought resentment. By the end of the second day there was a wide rift between the young priest and the others.

Ramati, a previously loyal man, sided with his men against Jasumatu's increasingly unrealistic and erratic demands and defended them against the young priest's criticisms. He had some hopes of leadership himself and was jealous of the tribe starting to build their new home without him; he understood more than most the problems which the people would encounter in the new land, and how they would have to decide quickly on the site and make it secure. Jasumatu should have recognised that this practical and capable man should have been with his family and his tribe at such a critical time.

If the recovery from the wreck had been more successful the differences between the young priest and his conscripted helpers might have been overcome, but by nightfall the continuing failure to bring anything worthwhile to the surface led to an open declaration of war. With deference, but with defiance, Jasumatu was banished from the men's camp. A stronger man might have dominated his crew and remained within the fold, but Jasumatu could only slink away and spend a cold night bedded as best he could on the unrelenting limestone, restlessly watching the slow westerly march of the stars and haunted by flitting dreams of Sirute and Phaistos. Later in the night he fell into a deep sleep and when he awoke in the early dawn the remaining ship and the stores had gone and the bay was empty. Ramati and his men had loaded their ship in the darkness; aided by the growing easterly wind, they had made a silent departure before dawn. The last remnants of the tribe of Phaistos had abandoned both their priest and the forlorn pile of treasures from the palace and had sailed to join their families and friends in the west.

Alone on the desolate cape in the slanting morning light, Jasumatu contemplated the bay and the rugged grey landscape which lay beyond it. Its awful emptiness accentuated his loss and isolation. Head back, arms raised, hands clenched in anguish, he stood on the white headland and screamed into the gale as he mourned the loss of his palace, his love and the fellowship of his people. Giving himself up to despair and self-pity, he raged at the gods who had destroyed his life. The day passed in cold, lonely misery.

Much later hunger and thirst drove him from the cape to cross the bluff to the easterly bay to find the spring where he had a drink with fresh water and refilled his flask. He found some olives on the immense trees growing under the cliff and in painstaking hours in the afternoon was able to catch a few small fish by enticing them into a reed basket. In the evening he ate some raw fish and olives and dates then slept in a cave shielded from the wind, huddled in his blanket.

Jasumatu woke stiff and cold in the warmth of the morning and as the daylight grew he climbed back up onto ridge between the two bays, wondering what to do. He could not stay where he was, that was certain. He knew that he had none of the skills necessary to survive by living off the land and it was clear that there were only two other possible options. He could go east, back to Phaistos; the route lay along the curve of the dark blue bay beneath the towering cliffs, and beckoning in the far distance he could make out the shape of the sacred mountain against the brightening sky. It would not take more than two or three days, and he knew the land. But Phaistos was empty of its people and torn and destroyed and he could not face its silence or its memories.

He looked west, where the land was brighter in the morning light, and followed with his eye the harsh steep rocks of the coast to where a narrow gorge came down to the sea. Beyond this a high barren headland fell, cutting off any further view. He decided that it would not be possible to climb the sheer white rocks of the far side of the deep gorge where it met the coast and looking inland he traced an alternative route up to a small wood on a col where trees promised water and where there might be possible access to the silver hills beyond. That was the way he should go; he guessed that the new palace site in the west was probably only just beyond the ridge, or, at most, a day or two beyond. Jasumatu imagined his people established in their new town, recognising him in the far distance as he came down from the hills. He imagined them rushing to meet him as he descended god-like and benevolent, welcoming him again as a beloved priest and leader, to be accepted and embraced by his tribe once more. Entranced by this image, Jasumatu resolved to follow his people into the west. In the late morning he set off confidently around the western bay and across the fractured limestone, climbing steadily towards the wood above him. The afternoon brought him to a spring on the col and he washed, refilled his flask and looked back on the distant bay beneath whose waves lay the wreck of his hopes and ambitions. In the hot sunshine he bid it farewell and with growing desolation turned again to his journey. Licking the salt tears from his cheeks he forced himself upwards through the thinning wood.

Now the great gorge opened under him and he had to scramble at an angle down its rough side to reach the bottom, fighting through tangled oleander and willow to a mossy spring where massive boulders blocked the downward route and where the sun disappeared behind the valley's edge. In the narrow valley there was a welcome coolness in the air and he sat for a while, refreshed. But the evening brought darkness in the gully and he feared its constriction and the lonely cries of unknown birds echoing from its walls; he thought he heard the vulture's call high above but he could not see it. Tired and lonely, he climbed a little way up a side valley to find a bed of juniper needles under a pile of boulders and made camp there for the night, wrapping his cloak tightly about him in the growing cold.

He had water but little food; the olives he had picked were early, hard and thin and the fish was dry; he tied to chew one but it tasted foul and its bones stuck in his throat. He lay back on the bed of needles and watched the stars drift westward across the narrow strip of sky between the steep valley sides. Exhausted by the trials of the day, he slept, his despair edged by a thin hope that tomorrow could bring him once again to his people.

At dawn he climbed to his feet stiffly and continued up the steep gulley to a gentler slope. There were plenty of olives here, bitter and green but refreshing; he ate some and climbed on up a tree-covered ridge hoping to see the coast.

Instead, to his dismay, he came to the edge of a new gorge and was forced to follow its edge ever upward. In vain he sought for a way down into the depths but the land drove him higher and higher as the afternoon wore on. This was a barrier which he had not foreseen, and, indeed, could not have known about. But it was leading him the wrong way, up into the white mountains above, away from the coast where his people had gone.

In the shade of the trees the journey had been easy, but as the forest thinned and the hot sun burned through Jasumatu grew lightheaded. He found another spring where he drank heavily and washed himself but the ice-cold water lay heavily in his stomach and made him feel ill. He stumbled on, legs torn by the scrub and with feet bleeding from the sharp limestone crags. Time either stood still or passed like the wind and the climb was without end. Sweat ran into his eyes and mingled with his tears, and despair tainted his mind. The pure white cones of unreal mountains rose spectral over the shattered landscape; the deep gash of the gorge was dark and ominous at his side; the everlasting ridge became a mounting passage to delirium haunted by great twisted trees with wild beckoning limbs. Weak and light-headed, wounded and desolate, the emptiness embraced Jasumatu and he grew small within it. Black birds circled a distant peak, unconcerned, dispassionate, alien. Evening mists crept along the floor of the gorge and called invitingly to him from the sombre depths.

Disillusionment, hunger, loneliness and loss were the burdens which Jasumatu carried across the mountain; sometimes Sirute came to help him with his load and they held hands and walked happily over the white hillside; sometimes Asumunde joined them with his cold wisdom, but as the sun sank, even they left him. Dark voices beckoned him from the swirling mists and the vulture called unheard on high blue air.

The sun was falling into the mountains in the west and the cold began to bite as Jasumatu came to a small spring at the foot of a cliff below the face of the mountain. He drank and washed his face and hands and shook droplets into the icy air, making falling diamonds in the golden light. He stood on the precipitous side of the gorge looking into the west and imagined the people of Phaistos happy and safe around campfires in the far, far distance. Sirute and Asumunde appeared again to stand beside him on the narrow path and to comfort him. As the sun touched the peak of a black mountain beyond the gorge Jasumatu took the hands of the ghosts of Sirute and Asumunde into his own. Holding on to them he stepped from the rock and fell soundlessly through the icicle air into the black depths.

On silent wings the vulture followed his fall and stooped over the broken body of the priest-king elect as it lay in the dark jagged rocks of the gorge. Climbing once again into the sunlight, it flew up over the black mountains into the west to resume its watch over the tribe of Phaistos.

Crete

Easter:
late 20th century AD

Chapter nine

Early morning, April: Iraklion, Crete

Crete in April, already warm to the traveller newly arrived from England, with just a hint in the breeze of the hot summer to come but still lush and green. Flowers everywhere, with a hum of insects, and a relaxing dryness in the air so different from the pervading dampness and drab colours of home. After a winter in the darkness and cold of Aberdeen, so delightful, so welcome, even at six in the morning on the bare airstrip at Iraklion. That first scented warmth is like magic, tantalising, ephemeral, promising a different life. The traveller's senses are teased already and he relaxes and starts the slow descent into the ease and indolence of the Mediterranean. The tensions of the north fall away. It will be many days before he is totally seduced but the process has already begun and will continue through his stay and will change him forever. Like the touch of an early love which is forgotten but fundamentally transforms, the scent of the Mediterranean opens senses to an exciting new landscape, a landscape peopled by dramatic characters in startlingly bright colours. Its tragedies are greater, its loves deeper, its stage wider. It is a world painted in impasto unlike the restrained pastel drawings of northern Europe.

Three young men left the plane in the dawn, yawning and stretching as they followed the line of jaded tourists down a steel ladder which bore the word 'Olympic' to scorn their stumbling arrival. The pretty air-hostess who watched them descend the steps into the warm grey light of Crete was sorry to see them go and followed them with tired eyes as they shouldered much-travelled bags and strode energetically towards the chaos of the Iraklion baggage retrieval. She looked up from the receding line of pale disorientated British to dark mountains newly touched by the rising sun, climbing pink-tipped into a clear sky. One day, she told herself again, one day she too would leave the damp-slicked plane and its cargo of empty bottles and half-eaten plastic meals and run away to the mountains and the unknown country around them. She shivered at the thought and turned glumly back to the banal routine of her life. So sad, she thought, to see rosy-fingered dawn touch the distant grey hills of Crete as she longed for her small crumpled flat in Hammersmith; that was a simile for her life. She shrugged and turned into the stale air of the aircraft. Putting on the artificial smile of her trade, she sighed and deliberately turned the temperature control down for the returning flight of tired, ill-clad and sunburnt tourists.

Two young Englishmen and a Scotsman walked quickly towards the customs barrier, holdalls over shoulders. Men clad in scruffy blue uniforms who glorified in the title of 'official' watched their approach with hostile stares. With grunts they indicated that the holdalls were probably crammed with contraband and should be emptied immediately. They stood back to watch suspiciously from a safe distance and were gloomily disappointed as a procession of shirts, socks and underwear slid across the scarred tin table. A face mask and a pair of rubber fins were eyed warily and fingered carefully; a couple of bottles of whisky were held up to the harsh white light and their sealing examined with care. Disappointed at their failure to find anything remotely questionable, the officials turned with renewed determination to eye the file of fragmented families which was beginning to emerge from the baggage retrieval area. Many recently arrived British would regret their first contact with Greek customs. The rapidly tiring rabble would be harassed well into the morning as the waiting coaches poured diesel fumes into the fresh Cretan air, and distraught young couriers sought to round up their charges and deliver them to barren rooms in concrete villages on the coasts. This new version of the Battle of Crete is always won by the Cretans no matter how numerous the invading foreigners.

Happily leaving the frantic tourists and their distraught shepherds behind them in the swirl of coaches and diesel smoke the three young men, Brian, Oscar and Robert headed for the taxi rank. Brian led the way as usual; the other two followed, side by side, holdalls swinging in unison, both tall, one black, shaven-headed; one white, short-haired; both strong, fit.

A khaki-clad porter sought to relieve Oscar of his bag but was repelled by a white grin. "It's OK, man. I think I can manage."

The porter found an urgent task elsewhere and Oscar watched him go, tossing his bag from one huge hand to another. "I think he understood English."

"It's not your English, it's your smile that puts 'em off. Scary, it is," Robert jeered, ever combative.

Brian, stern, important, frowned at their levity and led them to the first in the line of shiny Mercedes taxis.

"*Sto Iraklio, parakalo.*"

"*Endaxi.*"

Holdalls were slung into the cavernous boot. Brian joined the driver in the front seat; the others got in behind and assumed casual poses. In the growing heat of the morning the grey saloon left the panting coaches and their anxious occupants and joined the dusty road into the city.

Within minutes of checking in at a hotel in Iraklion, Oscar and Robert were asleep, oblivious to the awakening day around them, sprawled over the small beds, piles of discarded clothing on the floor. They would wake around midday, pee, scratch and sleep again through the hot afternoon. Not for them the excitement of a new town, new people; until hunger and thirst drove them out they were content to sleep dog-like awaiting their master's summons. When evening came they would wash and dress and wander in search of food, drink and girls. The same pattern would be followed whether they were in Athens or Aberdeen or Bangkok; to them the world was simple. Rarely did they stray beyond the animal outlines of their existence.

Brian was unable to sleep. He enjoyed the fresh warm air which drifted up from the harbour visible between the twin stacks of the high-rise hotel in front of him. He enjoyed the easy chatter that rose from the street below, punctuated though it was by the ripping howl of speeding mopeds. He smoked a succession of spindly cigarettes, rolled between stained fingers, flicking their stubs in bright arcs to the road. As growing shadows fell from the concrete balconies opposite he thought vaguely of the twenty-odd hours which had passed since they left the dull grey cold of Aberdeen. First to Heathrow by British Airways in quiet, expensive grey, then by the friendly crushed chaos of the charter flight to the pale blue sky of spring in Crete; the distance was not relevant, nor was the time. There ought, Brian thought lazily, to be recognition of a sort of senses-lag which was far more difficult to adjust to than any time difference.

Yesterday afternoon – or was it the day before – he had been tossing in a red rubber dinghy on cold steep waves from which the easterly wind had whipped a freezing spray, attempting to jump across to the slippery steel landing stage of a North Sea oil rig. Now he lazed, feet bare to the breeze, looking out over a gentle blue sea on which large white-sided ferries casually carried out manoeuvres which would have brought instant capsize off Aberdeen. It took time for the brain to catch up and to accept the reality of what the eyes witnessed, but before it caught up there was a feeling of rather pleasant remoteness, of being here but not involved, like watching a film.

The day before yesterday, in an already alien world, the three divers had been fighting to cap a rogue disused well which was leaking a nasty thick black gunge onto the storm-stirred sand of the Dogger Bank. Struggling in the ocean darkness, in heavy suits and gloves, and with badly focused headlights. Sweating despite the cold, breathing in short sharp gasps, the dirty end of the oil business. While lazy, salaried rig men listened by radio to their frantic efforts, the three tugged and levered the heavy lid on the old well back into place and then ascended in slow stages, shivering in the darkness, until they were pulled roughly onto the twisting red rubber of the dinghy. Better-paid men didn't do jobs like these, or, if they did, they took three times longer and cost ten times as much; the oil business needed cheap casual labour. Brian, Oscar and Robert provided it.

Brian grinned without humour on the shaded balcony; that was why they were here: to provide cheap casual labour. And skill and determination. And discretion.

He remembered the laconic telephone call from Theseus, taken in the dimly-lit hallway of the cold and draughty lodging house in Aberdeen while an easterly gale rattled the front door.

"Brian, my friend, *ti kaneis*? I need a job doing, on the south coast this time. Should take you a couple of weeks, not very deep, scuba should do. Interested?"

Brian had shivered in the draught from the door.

"Well." This was Brian's habitual response. "Anything to get us out of this bloody place. What is it? And how much?"

Theseus' deep chuckle had passed down the line. "You usually ask the price first, my friend, you are getting slow."

"It's the cold, it gets you. Even the Channel will be better than this."

"It's Sfakia, the south coast of Crete, not your England, and we'll talk about money when you get here. When can you come? No hurry, *siga siga*, but before summer if possible. And I'll get the explosives."

"What explosives? What are we doing? Come on, I need to tell the others something ..."

"No more now. Are you interested *ne i ochi*?"

Now, on the hotel balcony in the warm spring sunshine Brian

recalled the ill-fitting brown-stained door shaking in the wind. He pictured the scarred bare floorboards of his digs and the dim un-shaded lightbulb softly swaying in the draught, and recalled his delight at the prospect of the south coast of Crete in the spring. Warm water, blue skies, pretty girls and good money. He had taken a deep breath and tried not to appear too keen.

"Aye. We're on. But the money'd better be good and it can't be for four or five weeks. We've got a job to finish. And how did you know where to find us?"

"I know everything. Call me a week before you come. *Kalinikta.*"

Theseus had rung off abruptly, taking with him the warmth of the Mediterranean, leaving the cold wind of the North Sea.

Later that night the three divers had dodged the wind down to the pub, anoraks zipped against the cold. Brian had surprised the others. "Three pints of heavy, and three drams."

Usually the men bought their own, watching each other carefully to detect signs of unexpected affluence which might arise from a job the others knew nothing about. Tonight Brian bought without question and intrigued his two friends who knew something was afoot but would not ask for fear of losing face. But while Oscar was at the bar buying a third round, Robert could wait no longer.

"Come on, now," his soft Glaswegian accent was comfortable in the precise Aberdonian babble of the bar.

"What ye'er up to? It's not like you to buy the first round."

"It's more likely than you buying a round at all."

Brian rolled a thin cigarette and lit it with a cheap plastic lighter which carried the motto "Concorde" above a thin white streak which might once have been an airplane. "I'll tell you when Oscar comes back."

He blew thin grey smoke into the nicotine-streaked beams and stretched in the scorching heat of the fire, absorbing the warmth to take it back to his cold room. He watched Oscar coming back from the bar, three dark brown pint glasses clasped between big black hands, fingernails showing palely and shaved head reflecting the yellow lights above the bar. He set the pints down carefully and wound his way back through the throng to collect the whiskies.

"Well, man, what's this all about then? What gives?"

Oscar was like a beautiful black bronze statue draped with the contents of an Oxfam shop; the featureless clothes accentuated his body far better than any designer could imagine. Looking at him, and many women did, you could imagine him naked and shining, on a wide beach under palm trees. Even in an Aberdeen pub he suggested white sand and blue sea. He pulled his chair nearer the fire and took a deep gulp from the pint then picked up the whisky glass delicately between a huge finger and thumb and drank its contents in one swift swallow.

"What you got, then?" A white grin filled the black face. "Come on, spill it."

Around the fire, in the smoke-filled damp cold air of north-east Scotland, in the howling night, Brian spun a story of a sun-drenched island and the Sfakian pirate who had called them.

Chapter ten

Theseus Anopolakis came from a long line of Sfakian Cretans. His family had been engaged in robbery, piracy, sheep-stealing, rape, vendetta and murder from time immemorial; some said that they were the descendants of the Minoans, some said that they had come from Cyprus as part of the 'sea peoples' who traded across the eastern Mediterranean during the second millennium BC. But no matter what their origin the Sfakians had remained a fiercely independent race, never completely dominated by any invader whether Mycenaean or Roman, Byzantine or Venetian, Turk or German. Through all these occupations the Sfakians had carried on their own concerns, ignoring the incomers whose success in controlling this harsh and barren land rarely extended beyond tenuous footholds on the rocky shores. The landscape is riven by deep gorges, soars to desert peaks and descends precipitously to treacherous seas, and is not kind to the invader. The people – strong, proud and headstrong and savage – are not kind to the invader. Of all the tribes of Europe, this had survived longest, often threatened, never conquered. True, there were Roman ports scattered along the coasts and Venetian and Turkish castles up in the high passes which connected the north with the south of the island. But away from these, up in the mountains, was a land that had never felt the weight of an alien yoke. Here was a fastness to which the Sfakian could retreat in certainty that their enemies would not follow them; where the land was too high, too rough, too dry and too dangerous for any foreigner. When an invader appeared the Sfakians went up into the mountains and made brief and brutal raids to relieve the intruders of sheep and goats, wine and women. Sometimes they had been at the centre of Cretan rebellion and had been defeated, as against the Turks in 1770 and again in 1866 but although Crete itself was subjugated, Sfakia remained untouched. Even in 1941 the White Mountains remained free from German occupation

61

and the Sfakians were able to assist the escape of the some of the allied forces to Egypt, and the mountains and Sfakia became the lair of the resistance movement through the remaining years of the war.

This was the land where the Anopolakis family lived and these were the people whom they had ruled throughout the ages, and still controlled, even though the axe had been replaced by the chequebook. The growth of tourism had enabled the family to gain a stranglehold on development, travel, and roads. If a tourist slept, it was on an Anopolakis bed; if he moved it was on an Anopolakis ferry, or in an Anopolakis coach on a road built with the compliance of the family across land which it owned. Their empire was wide, and run and managed on modern business lines and few would have suspected that it was controlled by the gentle middle-aged man who spent most of his time on his launch in Lossos. Controlled with a hand as decisive and ruthless as any Minoan priest-king, by Theseus, a big man with a slow walk and hooded bright blue eyes and a vulture's nose, who loved to rise before dawn to fish, and who rarely smiled.

Theseus' father had died in 1949, just before the road connecting the north coast with Hora Sfakion was completed. He had overseen the hiding and evacuation of many of the ten thousand allied troops who had taken refuge on this coast in 1941. He knew the difficult descent of the Imbros gorge from Askifou down to the coast and had recognised the potential of the sea as a means of escape. By the end of the war he had control of the passenger and cargo traffic along the coast and had bribed the Greek government into funding the new road. Theseus had been only two years old when his father had been killed in a feud with the neighbouring village of Ahladha, and the family had lost control of the ships and of the roads.

When Theseus was sixteen almost the entire population of Ahladha was killed in a single night of revenge and since then the Anopolakis family have been undisputed rulers of Sfakia and have controlled the roads and the ferries on the south coast. Theseus grew into manhood working on the small boats which plied the coast and crossed the squally sea to Gavdos. He matured into a strong thickset man with a wiry black beard and bright blue eyes that hinted at his Minoan ancestry. His seamanship and strength earned him respect rather than love; he was volatile and unpredictable, sometimes kind, sometimes ruthless, a distant friend but an implacable enemy. He was made captain of the largest ferry, the *Anopoli*, when he was eighteen but was cold and distant to his crew and was tolerated rather than liked by them.

The onslaught of mass tourism in the sixties hit the south coast of Crete much later than it had struck the north but its impact was no less cataclysmic. Competition for control of the ferry services which were the only transport along the south coast grew and became bitter. More and more ships of all shapes and sizes sought the growing trade and it was not unknown for engines to suddenly seize, or anchor chains to be cut. The Anopolakis family forced out or bought out small operators, but a fast ex-torpedo boat named *Selino,* operating out of Paleochora, resisted every overture and guarded itself well against every attempt at sabotage. The *Anopoli* and the *Selino* fought a frantic battle of schedules, often leaving port half-empty in order to be the first to arrive at the next. Theseus tried to break the deadlock by agreeing timetables and sharing routes with his competitor but was repulsed; he tried to buy the ship but was met with a blank refusal. The game continued throughout one long hot summer, neither finding an advantage, neither weakening.

Theseus was now twenty; big and strong, hardened by the sea. His black beard was trimmed but still full and his blue eyes were bright and clear under the bushy black eyebrows. Although he was usually taciturn and remote he liked women and could break a girl's heart with a sudden rare smile. The women he loved discovered an unexpected gentle strength and a beguiling tenderness well hidden to the world, but could never claim his affection. He was the target and despair of ambitious mothers throughout the length of the south coast of Crete but showed no sign of settling down, preferring to take his pick of the black-haired girls who greeted the *Anopoli* in Sofia, Agia Rodhia, and Karave. Then, late one spring, he met Eleni.

Eleni came from Askifou where the Amoudhari family ruled the plain as ruthlessly as the Anopolakis ruled the coast. She was small and beautiful, her long black hair fell like a jet stream to her waist and her green eyes sparkled with spirit. She was just sixteen when she came down from the hills to work in a restaurant in Hora Sfakion and Theseus was totally captivated by her. He haunted the restaurant whenever he was not at sea, watching her, black and glowering, as she worked. At first she ignored him, which served only to increase his interest; then she took to glancing in his direction as she passed, green eyes glinting through a curtain of black hair. After a week or so of Theseus' constant attention, she met his eye and held his gaze, outwardly aloof but inwardly trembling. And he smiled at her. The dark brooding face was suddenly broken by a wide white grin above which blue eyes sparkled in admiration, and she in turn was captivated. That same night she came to his ship and they lay in the narrow cot as the sea rocked them to sleep. From then on Eleni was rarely away from the *Anopoli* and despite the battle with the *Selino*, Theseus was a happy and contented man.

Through the long summer their love grew and Eleni became as familiar a figure on the boat as Theseus became in the restaurant. Theseus mellowed through his adoration of the spirited black-haired girl and his dark moods were forgotten. His crew, now spared his volatility, ran the ferry with a happy and cheerful efficiency which gave the *Anopoli* an increasing advantage over its rival.

Eleni soon became a good sailor and grew to love the steep cliffs of the island, grey, green and orange during the day, a deep pink grey in the evening, and the white-fringed indigo of the sea on which they sailed that summer. In a white shirt and pale blue jeans, with her long shining blue-black hair flying in the wind, she became a familiar sight on the bridge of the *Anopoli* and an object of deep desire amongst the crew. She had made it very clear, soon after meeting Theseus, that she had no interest in any other man. Theseus had also made it clear that the man who showed interest in her would shortly be without a job, if not his life, and on this basis Eleni became a mascot for the *Anopoli* and had the crew eating out of her hand and vying for her approval at every opportunity. Her presence on board cheered the ship and made each repetitive journey into a cruise; the ship ran faster for her and the men worked harder; a smile from Eleni was a bonus greater than any payment. With her encouragement and Theseus' skill their advantage over the rival *Selino* grew with each trip.

As summer progressed the competition between the two vessels grew vicious as the *Selino* began to lose trade, not only along the coast, but also on the Gavdos run where its greater speed had made it most successful.

Although Eleni loved the mountainous coast of Crete her favourite voyage was to the barren sun-baked island of Gavdos. Two hours from Sfakia and the most southerly point of Greece, its mystery and remoteness appealed strongly to her independent spirit and she had already spent time there on her own, exploring the wide sandy beaches and the trackless heath of the interior. She had slept on the sand under the sea-junipers, sheltering under their twisted limbs which might have been growing when a storm swept St Paul past on his long journey to Rome. She had enjoyed a fierce *tsikoudia* with the owner of the café in Kastri, the lines of whose brown face matched the grain of the grey boughs of the trees, and had shared with him and his wind-bent wife tales of the high plains of Askifou and the stormy sea of Gavdos. But her delight in the grey island was still less than the joy with which she watched the hills of Crete grow above her as the ferry bucked its way across the Libyan Sea on its return to her homeland.

From the south Crete rises in four layers, successively orange-grey, green, grey again, and white. The sea cliffs are crowned with forested plains, and they in turn with cypress-spotted highlands above which soar the majestic White Mountains, the *Lefka Ori*; four strata distinct and yet part of the same land, each of six hundred metres height, all part of Sfakia. Eleni had not seen her land like this before sailing with Theseus and her love of her island grew with her love for him.

One night in early September when the nights were shortening and the early autumn squalls struck unexpectedly, the *Anopoli* was about to enter the small rocky harbour of Karave which is the only safe berth on Gavdos. They had left Crete in brittle daylight and had made good time across the darkening sea. To the west the sky was light and the island on the horizon was a dark grey with its two welcoming beacons flashing clearly in the growing gloom. The jetty at Karave is hidden from the northern approach; entry into it requires a tight turn to starboard about a sharp headland which guards the hidden quay. The steeply falling rocky promontory carries one of the two light beacons which act as guides to incoming vessels and which mark the turning point for ships entering the sheltered bay. The sky was light in the west between heavy clouds; the land was deep black against the brightness, the sea a dull slate grey.

Theseus was at the wheel of the *Anopoli*, watching the beacon carefully as he prepared to make the turn into the harbour, and Eleni was beside him on the small bridge, her white shirt crossed by the black band of her hair. Daylight was failing quickly. From the swaying ferry Theseus watched the beacon slowly move past and spun the wheel to make the right turn into Karave bay. As he did so he caught Eleni's bright eyes in the light of the instruments on the bridge and smiled at her, thinking of the night ahead in her arms. The *Anopoli* began its swing to starboard to turn around the headland and Theseus kept the flashing beacon in line with the bridge window. The ship gradually turned toward the lighter sky, the land now empty black before them but for a few scattered village lights.

From this distance the beacon on the jetty can usually be seen, making the final approach easy even in the darkness of the surrounding bay. But the jetty beacon was not lit, and that on the headland about which the *Anopoli* turned was suddenly switched off. With the bright sky ahead and the black land in front, Theseus was blind.

He knew that he had to turn away from the land, and swung the wheel wildly to port, reaching for the switch of his headlight in the darkness. His grasping hand found the switch and snapped it open, the wide beam cut through the night. The spot of light hit dark rocks which absorbed its power, and then, suddenly bright, struck grey steel with the word *Selino* ominous in black letters across it. At this moment the other ship turned its own spotlight on the bridge of the *Anopoli*. Blinded, Theseus spun the heavy wheel back to starboard to avoid a collision. The *Anopoli* turned away from the *Selino*, still travelling fast, and struck the sharp rocks at the end of the headland. The steel plates of the hull were torn apart like a twisted beer can and the black water rushed in. The momentum of the *Anopoli* carried it completely over the underwater trap and it sank rapidly in the entrance to the harbour, diving steeply under the waves. The cold dark sea swept though the ship trapping Eleni and the crew in the wreck. All but Theseus were drowned. He was torn from the bridge as it collapsed; the sea broke his arm and threw him to the rocks to survive bitterly, with a broken heart.

The *Selino* made a safe journey back to Crete, knowing nothing, it is said, of the dreadful tragedy which had occurred off the island of Gavdos.

Theseus did not sail again for many years; after the loss of the *Anopoli* he became a shepherd, a recluse in the White Mountains. When he did return it was as a quiet and reserved, unsmiling man, tolerant and gentle but with a cold steel in his soul and a touch of white in his strong black beard.

The *Selino* was lost at sea with all hands less than two months after the wreck of the *Anopoli*. The cause of its sudden sinking has never been discovered, but, after that, the Anopolakis family regained control of the seas, never to lose it.

Chapter eleven

On the balcony of his hotel in Iraklion Brian lit another of his thin cigarettes and idly wondered what to do about lunch. Poking his head back through the curtains he saw that Oscar was awake. "I'm going to change some money and grab a beer and something to eat. You coming?"

"Give me five, and I'm with you. I could kill a beer."

Oscar rolled off the bed as Robert stirred. "What time is it?" followed by "It's bloody hot", came from the crumpled bed and a long white body uncoiled itself from the sheet and a pale face capped by a thin fringe of gingery hair scowled out at the blue sky.

"So this is Crete," Robert surveyed the concrete blocks of his new world unimpressed. "It's like anywhere. But warmer," he conceded. "Did someone mention beer?"

"This isn't Crete; this is just another big town. Just you wait 'til you see the proper Crete. But there is beer and food here, if you're interested."

"I'm interested." Robert rubbed a hand over his ginger stubble and, going across to the half-open washroom door shouted through the spray. "Come on you big bugger, give a white man a chance."

Oscar, black and shining from his shower, emerged from the steam with a wide grin and a white towel which he flicked at the Scotsman. "You certainly need a shower. Don't think you've washed since you were in the North Sea."

Brian went out onto the tiny balcony and threw the damp butt of his cigarette down into the street below. One day, he thought, I will have space, away from the constant chafing of the others, one day I will be able to afford to have a room of my own, a big room, with a big bed, and beautiful girls to share it with, and champagne; one day.

A long black arm crushed his shoulders, "Where's this beer then?

Come on, I could drink a gallon."

"And you probably will," Brian shrugged. *Pame*, as they say here, let's go."

"What's this *pame*, then?" Oscar asked as they went down the narrow stairs.

"It's Greek, you daft sod. It means, 'Let's go.' You'll get used to it."

"Sure will, man," said Oscar happily, putting on his best Caribbean accent as they emerged into the street, and the hot sunshine hit them, "Ah reely will."

The three men climbed the slope to the beautiful Venetian loggia of the city hall then crossed the road through the stationary traffic into the tree-shaded Venizelou Square. Battered blue buses poured diesel smoke into the still air. Howling mopeds driven by disdainful girls wearing tight white T-shirts and designer sunglasses wove twisting patterns around them. Thin men in food-stained black trousers and false smiles tempted them to menus with expansive welcoming gestures.

"I 'ave very good table for you, jus' come an' look. You English? Maanchesta Yunited. Very good."

The three turned into the first café, were seated with elaborate ritual and then abandoned while the stained trousers returned to their everlasting patrol of the crowds which drifted through the square. A passing waiter dropped three battered menus on the table and went back to watching the girls with the cynical interest of the eternally disappointed voyeur. After a little while he returned and stood aggressively before them, pad in hand. "*Ti tha fate.*"

Robert and Oscar looked at Brian, "What you havin'?"

Brian thought. "How about pizza and beer? OK?" He turned to the stained jacket. "*Tris pizzes kai tris bires, parakalo. Kai mia salata horiatiki. Megali.*"

"Three pizzas, big salad, three beers? Which beer you want?"

"Amstel, please, big ones." Brian's attempt to speak Greek was soon abandoned but Oscar was impressed.

"Where did you learn to speak the lingo?"

"I had six or seven weeks here about eight years ago. One summer. Just back-packing and sleeping rough. Great time. That's when I met Theseus. Down on the south coast."

"Is that where we're going? What's it like down there?" Oscar poured beer into his glass where it frothed and soaked the thin tablecloth. "Christ, this is lively stuff."

Brian grinned at him. "It's not like a pint of heavy, you know.

You'll get to like it."

There was something appealing about Oscar's lack of pretension; if he wanted to know, he asked; if his beer spilled over, he grinned. Robert on the other hand would pretend to know, and would be embarrassed if his beer had not been poured correctly. But Robert also wanted to know about the south coast and was glad that Oscar had asked the question first. Now he wouldn't lose face by asking.

"What's the name of this place we're going to stay at – Lossos? What are we supposed to be doing there?"

Just then the pizzas arrived and saved Brian from having to admit that he did not know what Theseus had in mind for them down in Lossos. He had only spoken once more to the Cretan after the call to Aberdeen and that was merely to confirm their arrival date. He still had no real idea as to why they were here but didn't want to admit it. Luckily his two companions were not too concerned with what they did; as long as the money was good, that's all that mattered to them. And the beer and the girls, of course.

The three ate in silence for a while until Oscar called for more beer. "Not bad this stuff. A bit weak though."

"Wait and see if it's weak. You'll know after a couple of bottles, it gets you quietly."

The food finished, Oscar took a packet of Marlboro from the pocket of his loose grey jacket and Brian rolled and lit yet another spindly cigarette. Tiny wisps of tobacco drooped and then flared briefly as he lit it with the Concorde lighter. He chucked the lighter across the table and took a sip of beer.

"What's Lossos like? I can tell you what it looks like, but you have to be there for a bit to get to know what it feels like. It's isolated, hot, claustrophobic. You think that nothing ever happens there but under the surface there's intrigue and gossip and jealousy. And vendettas which go on for hundreds of years."

"Just like Scotland," Robert sneered, watching two young girls at the next table under the concealment of his sunglasses.

"But a lot warmer. And a lot quieter than here." Brian drank some more beer and reached across to get his lighter and steal one of Oscar's Marlboros. "You have to go by boat, or walk from Hora Sfakion. There are no roads into the village. And it's small; you can walk from one end to the other in ten minutes, round the bay, through the tavernas. And behind the town the cliffs rise five hundred feet. The colour is fantastic, white buildings and orange rocks and blue sea. It's a paradise."

"Sounds great," Oscar stretched. "Any girls there?"

"If there are I'm sure you'll find them. There's the village girls, but you've got to be careful or you'll find yourself dead. And there's the hotel girls, they're great, usually, just out there for the summer and sun ..."

"And sex," Oscar laughed, "I'll try to help them."

Brian came back to the reality of Iraklion and the noise and the diesel fumes. "Come on, let's wander a bit."

"*Parakalo! To logariasmo, parakalo.*" Brian paid and left a large tip which was accepted with a sneer by the waiter who wandered off to resume his girl-watching with a muttered, "*Endaxi. Efharisto*" and in hot sunshine they walked through the busy crowds up to Eletherias Square and across it to sit on the stone balustrade overlooking the harbour.

"It's certainly a change from Aberdeen," Robert remarked as he watched a large ferry edge its way out from the quay and then, free of the land, form a wide white wake as it started its twelve-hour sail to Piraeus.

"I've another shock for you," Brian looked at his friends. "Come on, a bit of culture won't do you any harm and it's too early to start drinking yet." He led them out of the square and towards the low long building of the museum with its curtain of pine trees.

"What are we going in there for?" Oscar wanted to know. "I haven't been in a museum since I was a kid."

"Let's give it a whirl, we've nothing else to do and besides, it should tell us a bit about Crete. We're going to be here for some time."

It was four o'clock and the afternoon was hot and the crowds and the lack of air-conditioning did not help; Robert was bored and led the way quickly through the stuffy rooms. Neither he nor Oscar found anything of interest until, in the third room, they found themselves trapped by a large party who were listening earnestly to a guide describing a single brown clay disk which stood in its own case, alone and unique.

The guide spoke first in Greek and then in English: "... most unique find yet made in Crete ... stamps have been used to impress characters onto wet clay ... strange that no other example of the use of these stamps has been found ... the symbols remain undeciphered ... only if further examples were found could a translation be attempted ... the disk and its inscriptions remain a mystery ..." Even Robert was impressed; he waited until the crowd had moved on leaving a powerful odour of unwashed bodies before going to the case and peering closely at the disk. The enigma gazed back at him

70

through the thick plastic screen. Thirty-five centuries old and still holding its secrets.

Robert, brought up like so many of his generation on a diet of ley lines and corn circles and pyramids built by Martians had never come close to something like this before. Something tangible yet magic. Weird. It blew your mind. He wandered through the remainder of the museum in a trance and if you asked him later what he remembered of it, it was only the Phaistos disk in its crystal case that lingered in his mind. And some immense and ominous double-headed axes like shadowy totems in the background.

* * * * *

Iraklion has the disadvantage of having three bus stations, only one of which actually looks like a bus station. It was to this that Brian led his two companions through the hot sunshine early next morning. It was the wrong one and by the time that they had visited the most westerly, from where buses leave to go south and returned to the centre of the city from where the west-bound buses depart, they were hot and resentful of his assumed leadership.

"I thought you knew where we're going. Didn't expect a tour of the bloody town. Brian's guide to the bus stations and back streets of Iraklion, only fifty euro. Not many takers even at that price."

"Sometimes, you miserable Scot, you're a real bloody pain. You never do anything, you just bloody criticise."

Oscar was used to this caustic exchange between his friends. "Stay cool man, we'll get there."

Greek buses invariably leave on time; tickets bought before departure carry seat and bus numbers and each bus is numbered and displays its destination. The display is in upper case Greek and difficult for the casual traveller to decipher. This stresses the tourist who will go from vehicle to stationary vehicle attempting to equate the number on his ticket with that shown on the bus and at the same time read a destination sign written in a three-thousand-year-old script.

The seasoned traveller, on the other hand, waits quietly, sitting on his bag in the shade, until one minute before departure time. He knows that a big green bus will emerge from the depths of the parking area at precisely one minute before it is due to leave. It will bear a number which corresponds with that on his ticket and will display a sign which can be translated as his destination. A friendly conductor will ask where he is going and will stow his bag carefully; he will climb on board to be greeted by a smart driver in sunglasses and white shirt. All will go well until he reaches the seat which bears the number shown on his ticket. Occupying this seat will be a large Greek wearing a black suit of heavy cloth and a white collarless shirt; his massive thighs and a cardboard box tied with string will fill the window seat and the one next to it. His malevolent glare will indicate clearly that this is his place by right; his black eyes challenge you while the beads click deliberately through the peasant-strong fingers. If the occupant of the seat is female then in addition to black skirt-clad thighs which not only fill but overlap the pair of seats, there will be parcels and carrier bags of all shapes, sizes and content draped about a heavy bosom of unfathomable and unsavoury depths. The stare will be similarly unyielding.

He with experience of Greek transport will note this without astonishment and will not challenge the native's proprietorial rights. He will immediately find an alternative seat acknowledging the unwritten law that no one will demand to sit in that place to which his ticket supposedly entitles him. If such a request was to be made departure would be delayed by some massively complex version of musical chairs. None make this request and the bus always leaves on time.

Luckily for him, in the light of his mistake about the bus stations, Brian knew the ritual. Bags were stowed and the bus headed west along the coast past grey concrete warehouses and anonymous office blocks. The men relaxed and watched the urban landscape slowly change to steep grey pine -covered mountains which sloped down to a blue sea where slivers of sand showed the solitude of silent beaches. Chattering passengers came and went; this was the stopping bus and a regular meeting place. A ticket inspector emerged from the shadows of a shaded *stasi leoforiou* to join the vehicle and moved gravely down the aisle scrutinising and tearing the strips of paper like one who practises origami. His job done, his face beamed with satisfaction and relief, he slapped the driver on the back and alighted at the next stop to retreat into the shadows to dream of his next fleeting minutes of consequence.

They changed buses in Vrysses for the climb up to Askifou where the mountains rise steeply above the village and the ruined Turkish castle perched on its conical hill dominates the plain. The dark wings and pale buff body of a griffin vulture could barely be distinguished from the grey limestone as it swooped over them at the highest point of the pass where the Imbros gorge plunged between its vertical limestone walls, the only way to the coast until Theseus' father had built the road fifty years earlier. Now Robert and Oscar took window seats to watch the tortuous twists of the road as it descended cypress-covered slopes to the coast.

"Wow, man, this is something. It's great – it's beautiful." Oscar was spontaneous in his delight.

"Yeah. This is proper Crete. Every time I come over here it gets better." Brian enjoyed the landscape and Oscar's pleasure in it. Robert, affectedly cynical, played his usual role. "It's OK. I suppose."

"You're a gloomy bugger, even for a Scot. Can't you enjoy anything?"

In Hora Sfakia the travellers descended and stretched; the heat of the south coast hit them as they retrieved their bags and started down the slope to the sea. The harbour opened out in front of them between the new marina on the left and an old stone jetty.

"So this is your famous south coast? It's bloody hot. And it's not exactly lively is it?" Robert surveyed the village which lay inactive, baking in the afternoon sun. A solitary waiter stood smoking in the shade of a taverna; behind him a glass-shrouded display of food looked unappetising. A thin cat lay in the shade with the very tip of its tail twitching. There was no wind and no sound. Even the waves lapped silently on the rocks.

"Siesta time – it gets a little more lively later. A little. Fancy a beer?" Brian led them to a table where the plastic covering sweated to the touch; the table bore a food-stained menu written in Greek, German, an indecipherable Scandinavian language, and misspelled English. A dirty ashtray stood in the centre; beside it was a small glass pot without water, in which a flower which had once been red drooped sadly. They sat on the sort of chairs which used to dominate the Mediterranean; strong angled wooden verticals supported a wicker base which sagged in the middle allowing the edges of the seat to form hard protuberant ridges to cut off the strongest circulation. The seat was too small and the back had two horizontal parallel rests perfectly positioned to strike the shoulder blades; the whole construction also rocked on its irregular legs. These chairs, now slowly being replaced by the ubiquitous plastic, are works of art and woodworking skill and appear to be agreeable to anyone born in these latitudes who use one chair to sit on, one as a foot-rest, and a third as an arm-rest. To the northern European they are exceedingly uncomfortable.

The waiter reluctantly left his cigarette burning in an ashtray and shuffled through the heat to their table. "Ugh?" he said, interrogatively.

"*Tris bires, parakalo.*"

"*Endaxi.*" He shimmered away to return carrying three brown bottles and three glasses which he dropped on the blue-check plastic. "*Oriste,*" he remarked to himself and went quickly back to retrieve the last embers of his cigarette. He stood, remote and smoking, surveying the world cynically; in an earlier life he had been the headman of a village, a person respected by his clan. Now the village was empty, following a bloody feud with another, and his kingdom was a dozen plastic-covered tables. He sighed in the heat. Silence smothered the small town. High above, in fresher air, the vulture watched.

Chapter twelve

The ferryboat which bears the name *Aradena* had replaced the *Anopoli* a year after the shipwreck on Gavdos and was already a veteran of the south coast. It was an unstable, high-sided ship designed for calm summer waters in the northern Aegean. It boasted a flat blunt prow which could be lowered to allow vehicles to drive into its depths; its height ensured that it would be possible to accommodate a double-decker bus but also made it vulnerable to the sudden squalls of the Libyan Sea and double-deckers are rare on the south coast. But it had been cheap and had survived ten seasons of boredom in carrying tourists between Hora Sfakia and Agia Rodhia, at the foot of the Ardos gorge. It now dropped its prow onto the pebbles of Lossos with a hushed crunch, dominating the village like a beached white whale.

From the bowels of the ship, Jonah-like ejections onto the shore, Brian, Oscar and Robert emerged into the comparative cool of early evening as the sun dropped below the high cliff behind the village. In the last of the sunlight a vulture cruised along the escarpment with wide wings pale against the darkening eastern sky.

A strong, heavy man wearing black trousers and a white shirt stood on the beach, arms by his sides, dark face edged by a black beard in which there showed just a touch of white. Despite his formidable appearance Theseus was welcoming and a smile nearly reached his blue eyes above a large hand extended in greeting.

"*Kalispera. Ti kanete?* How are you, Brian?"

Massive arms encircled the Englishman. "Introduce your friends to me! *Pame*, let's have a drink. *Harika*, Oscar. *Harika*, Robert. *Kalo taxithi?*" A large brown hand grasped a black, then a white as Theseus led the group across the pebble beach and up the stairs to the bar where Theseus rapidly reorganised the furniture and created an oasis at the end of the terrace.

"*Lipon. Ti tha piete? Bira?* Fiona! *Tris Amstel. Megalo!* How you like my home? Beautiful! *Poli Orea*! And our girls are beautiful too!"

As Fiona placed three bottles and three dew-coated glasses on the small table Theseus put an arm round the girl's waist.

"Thank you, *kirie Theseus*. I am not one of your girls." Fiona moved away from Theseus easily, unoffended, confident. Her dark blue eyes regarded him levelly, as equals might meet each other's glance. With a soft south Australian accent she turned to the newcomers: "Theseus, will you introduce me to your friends?"

Brian looked across the table at the girl, unnerved under her calm gaze. "This is, er, Robert, from Scotland," he stammered, "and this is Oscar …"

"… from Barbados, via Brixton." Oscar rose politely, offering a black hand. "Enchanté." He gave her a wide grin and Fiona could not help smiling back at the big man. She held his eye for a moment before turning to Robert. "Welcome to Lossos. I hope you enjoy your stay."

Robert, impressed, uncomfortable, half rose from his chair, thought of offering a hand, decided not to, sat down again sweating in the warm evening.

Fiona turned interrogatively back to Brian.

"And I'm Brian."

"Hello." Her smile faded a little as she met his eye. "Have we met before?" she asked.

Brian recovered, forced a smile. "I'm sure that I would have remembered." He was going on to say '… someone as beautiful as you', but did not have the courage to voice the platitude to this girl who, he was certain, would treat it with only lightly concealed scorn.

Fiona stood for a moment, tall, slim, firm breasts under a crisp shirt; long corn coloured hair tied in a neat ponytail, small black earrings accentuating a long brown neck. Fit and formidable; only her obvious intelligence stopped her from being conventionally beautiful. She considered Brian dispassionately for a moment then turned away. "Nice to meet you all. I'll put these on your bill, Theseus."

The men watched her in silence as she turned and made her way through the tables back to the bar.

"Well, well. What a cracker," Robert leered, leaning back in his chair, looking across Theseus to the bar. "Life here is going to be interesting."

Theseus suddenly seemed much larger and much less friendly as he intercepted Robert's look.

"Fiona has been here for several years now," he said. "She is well liked in the village and will soon marry a close friend of mine. Take care." Theseus met Robert's eyes in a hard cold stare which contrasted starkly with his earlier geniality and in the sudden silence the chatter in the bar seemed loud. Then Theseus was suddenly smiling again, recalling his position as host, and, possibly more importantly, that he had need of these three scruffy men. "Come, let us have another drink. More beer?" He raised a large hand and waved at the bar.

Jackie had come on duty looking, as always, as if she had just got out of bed. She was behind the bar, long earrings dangling across brown cheeks as she bent to retrieve glasses from the washing machine. She straightened as Fiona came round and stood beside her. "Who're they, with Theseus, then?"

Jackie had a deep voice which just avoided being attractive by possessing the nasal accent and lack of glottal stops of the true Essex girl. She was short and stocky with a full figure and good legs burnt to a beautiful brown, and wore battered white sandals with her toenails painted bright red. Her dark short hair revealed neat ears above a turned-up collar and the low square-cut neckline of a red dress.

Fiona smiled at her friend. "It didn't take you long to notice, did it? They're some diving mates of Theseus. Don't know why they are here, its not like Theseus to have friends here on holiday – maybe they're working for him."

The English girl leaned over the bar to see the new arrivals better. "I'll take those beers. You don't mind, Fi, do you? I want to get a closer look at that big black one."

"I'm sure he'll want a closer look at you, much closer. But he is rather nice; I think I might fancy him myself ..."

"Oi! I saw him first. Well, I know I didn't really see him first, but I thought of it first, I think. Did I? Oh well. Anyway, you're spoken for – I'll tell Dimitris." Pleased with this riposte, Jackie carried the tray with its cargo of four large brown bottles and bowls of peanuts through the crowded bar to the men at the end of the terrace.

Theseus watched her arrival with appreciation. "And this is Jackie, my favourite girl."

Jackie was delighted. "I'll tell Gillian." She giggled, not meaning it. She bent down over the table to lower the tray, well aware that Oscar had a front-seat view of two full brown breasts in the thin cradle of her red dress. She looked him straight in the eye as she stood up and smiled, full lips accentuated by small white teeth. "Hi. You must be Oscar."

"News travels fast out here. Yeah. I'm Oscar. Good to know you."

"It will be," Jackie thought. "Just wait."

Theseus was amused by the exchange. "Put him down, girl. He's only been here five minutes. Give the boy a chance."

"Oh, I will." Jackie bounced back to the bar to be met by a sceptical Fiona.

"You don't waste time, do you? Now get some work done and serve some drinks. You can have him later."

The bar grew quieter as visitors drifted off in search of dinner in the tavernas around the bay, leaving Theseus and the three new arrivals alone at the end of the terrace. Jackie and Fiona were collecting glasses and washing up, looking forward to the night ahead. Fiona wasn't working again until lunchtime and promised herself a long night alone with Dimitris as it was his last night before he went back to the bank in Athens. Jackie, in white halter-top and mini skirt would be down at Lakis' bar as usual, teasing the moths of the local men like a hot flame in the night.

After three beers Brian felt bold enough to ask Theseus the question which had been in the back of all their minds since their arrival on Crete. He lit another of his spindly cigarettes; the Concorde lighter briefly flared in the darkness, releasing a thin twirl of blue smoke into the still air. He leant forward. "Theseus, what are we doing here? What have you got planned for us ..."

"... and what are you going to pay for it?" Robert finished off.

Theseus leaned back in his chair and looked around the empty bar then out to sea. He was silent for a while, inwardly regretting that he had to use people like these English, but Greeks would talk and Greek ears would hear and that he couldn't afford. No one would take notice of these three, their language and behaviour would keep interested natives away. And, he shrugged to himself, if anything went wrong, well, they wouldn't much be missed.

"*Endaxi*," he said quietly, looking round at the intent and slightly apprehensive faces. "I will tell you what we are going to do. You can let me know if you need any money and we will agree payment later. In the meantime you can stay here in the hotel."

"Wait a minute," Robert was not happy about this. "I think we should know what we are supposed to be getting into before, you know, we start. I mean, it might be illegal or something."

Theseus looked at him coldly. "Would that matter to you?" he said quietly. "It hasn't mattered before, has it, like in that job lifting

78

heroin off that trawler off Mull?"

"What do you know about that? Nobody knows about that ..."

"I know. And I know what you were paid and who you worked for and how much you spent on that little blonde girl in Glasgow. Angie, was it?"

"Angela," Robert responded, already defeated. "Oh shit."

"So, my friend, you work for me here where it is only illegal if I say so. And I say this job is not illegal. It is not even very dangerous. And I will pay you well, very well. Now do we know where we stand? This is my land, this is my sea. If you do as I wish all will be well. If you do not, then the sea is deep. *Katalaves?*"

Robert threw himself back into his chair and looked despairingly at Brian. "What the hell have you got us into this time?"

Theseus looked out over the black sea to where the first light of the rising moon showed over the darker bulk of the cliff and turned back to watch Robert contemptuously, impersonally. He was continually amazed by the lack of self-control shown by the British. Greeks were supposed to be volatile and excitable but that was only superficial, an act played to an audience; underneath there was control. But the northerners lacked this skill; they were transparent, allowing their feelings to show, without dignity.

Oscar shifted on his sticky plastic seat, uncomfortable in the heat of the night and sorry that they seemed to have offended their host. He liked it here in Lossos; he liked the warmth and the gentle swish of the sea on the shingle; he thought that Jackie was splendid and the beer drinkable. He remembered the darkness of the North Sea and the cold of the water and had no difficulty in deciding that he would rather be here, Theseus or no Theseus, pay or no pay. He leant across and put an arm around Robert's shoulders. "Hey, man, stay cool, let's not balls this up, its great here and I'm gonna stay and do what ever Mr. Theseus wants." His grip tightened and Robert felt the bones of his shoulder crack. "Just loosen up, pal, eh?" He withdrew his arm and offered a huge black hand to Theseus. "Shake, man. Ignore my Scottish friend, I'm with you and with whatever you have planned. But I sure would like to know what it is."

Theseus relaxed and returned the handshake, noting its strength. "*Signomi,*" he said, "I have not been fair to you. Of course you should know what I would like you to do for me and I need your help and guidance in telling me how we should go about it." He put his hands on the table and looked at the three divers. "I want you to blow up a mountain, an undersea mountain."

He got up and stretched. "But before I tell you more, we must eat. Come, my friends, let us go and eat goat and drink red wine and get to know each other, and I will tell you what I have planned."

Theseus led the way down the stairs to the beach and crunched across the pebbles with Oscar at his side, Robert and Brian following. The black sea turned white at its edge as it met the stones and a wide silver avenue led to the rising moon.

Later that night the same moon, brilliant and four days from full, shone on two figures lying under a blanket gazing up at the pale stars. Dimitris and Fiona had first come to the restaurant roof in the very early days of their affair, sneaking up together for brief hungry sex before Fiona crept down the hillside and back to her room in the hotel, and Dimitris went back to work clearing dishes.

Now, although they had been together for four years, they still loved the starry isolation high above the village where the cool air chilled the sweat from their tangled limbs. They lay in that most intimate of positions, Dimitris on his back, half turned toward the girl with Fiona's leg between his and her soft breast pressed into his chest. Her pale golden hair drifted over him like a shroud in the moonlight and he spread and smoothed it with his free hand. A faint breeze gave a slight chill to the air and they snuggled under the thick blanket. Fiona kissed his nipple, teasing it with her tongue. "Don't go back to Athens. Stay here with me, like this."

"You'd kill me, my sweet, I have to go back to recover. It takes two weeks you know."

"Not always," Her fingers crept downwards and held him. "It's recovering already," she giggled.

"No more now, I have to get up early." Dimitris took her hand firmly and reluctantly she released him. He kissed her and turned to look up at the moon and the deep fire-black of the crags above the village. "Who was Theseus with tonight?"

"Two Englishmen, one of them black, and a man from Scotland. I think he said they were divers. They only came today, on the last ferry. Its funny but I think that I've met one of them before. Didn't like him then, didn't particularly like him now."

"Typical of you; just because they're British, you don't like them."

"No, it's not just that; I liked the big black one, but the others, no. The Scottish bloke, Robert, is just awkward, but the other, Brian, I think he's – well, shifty. He's creepy; you wouldn't like to be alone with him on a dark night." She shivered a little in the starlight. "I wouldn't trust him at all. I wonder what they're doing here? It's not like Theseus to deal with foreigners."

"You're a foreigner, my Ozzie girl. Theseus fancied you, though, didn't he? When you first came?"

"That was before I met you, love. Anyway I didn't give him a chance. And Gillian keeps a tight rope on him."

"When he's here, she does. But when he's away ..."

"Like all men." She thumped his stomach gently. "But why divers? There's nothing to dive for round here, is there?"

"You know there are some things I can't tell you, don't you?"

Dimitris worked for the Bank of Crete in Athens, where Theseus and the Anopolakis family had several accounts in various names, not all of them totally legitimate.

"But I will tell you one thing; it's to do with ships."

"Oh, great, Theseus and ships – there's a surprise, thanks a million."

"It's all I can give you, for now."

"Oh, no, it's not."

Fiona slipped down under the blanket. Her tongue and lips aroused him quickly and, with the blanket slipping from her shoulders, she eased herself onto him and sat in the moonlight like a mermaid on a large black rock. She stayed still with the moonlight glinting in her hair and lining the curve of a breast until her need and his rising desire caused her to move in increasing urgency and he arched beneath her and carried her up to the stars.

When Fiona awoke to the rosy-pink dawn, there was a bougainvillea blossom on the pillow next to her. She kissed it dreamily and went back to sleep.

Chapter thirteen

Theseus leant back in his chair and raised his glass; harsh light from the unshaded overhead bulbs refracted through the deep gold of the wine. Thin paper table-coverings were littered with broken bread and goat bones; a large earthenware bowl carried the remains of a country salad. An empty decanter, standing beside another which was less than a third full, showed how much *krasi* had been drunk. Theseus belched comfortably in appreciation of the meal and drained his glass.

"*Yamas, poli orea*," he remarked to no one in particular. He turned and beckoned to Yannis who was drinking *tsikoudia* with two black-bearded fishermen while his wife and son loaded dishes, plates and glasses into an enormous and ancient dishwasher. "*Kafe, parakalo. Tesseris kafedes kai tessera koniak.*"

Theseus looked around the taverna. Apart from a young couple at a table at the water's edge who were holding hands and looking out into the white band of moonlight and the three local men chatting quietly at the back all Yannis' customers had gone. The clatter of pans and the clanking of the dishwashing machine came through the open windows of the kitchen mixed with quiet bouzouki music from the radio. Theseus turned his chair to the sea, stretched and placed two large hands on his black-trousered thighs; he looked at his companions. "The first thing you must learn," he said, "here in Sfakia, is that there are ears everywhere. And if you are with Theseus, the ears are big, very big. If I am to work with you, do not forget this. All that I do, all that I say, is watched and heard. As friends of mine, all the village will watch you and listen to you also. You must not betray me. You should always remember the ears and always take care."

He turned his clear blue stare on each of the three men in turn. The British had had a long day and now, after several bottles of beer and half a litre of wine each, were tipsy and relaxed. Theseus' words cut through the haze. Brian shivered despite the warmth of the night and suddenly felt alien. This was not the friendly fringe of Europe he had looked forward to; here on the south coast of Crete the Levant was close and Theseus' admonitions held something of the sinister flavours of the east.

"You, Brian, have been here before and you should know how it is in Lossos and along this coast, and in the mountains also. Not only do the walls have ears, but the very stones in the walls listen. Whatever I do or my family does is of interest in Sfakia and you must respect that and be careful. Now you are to work for me we must make a story about what we are doing and why you are here."

Theseus looked around the quiet terrace. The three villagers were drinking coffee with their *tsikoudia*, smoke from their cigarettes drifting in the soft breeze off the sea. The kitchen was quiet and the warm charcoal glowed dully, spasmodically lit by small flashes as droplets of fat dripped from the spit; the young couple sat bathed in moonlight, arms around each other, lost in the romance of the night. Across the bay, white cubic buildings stood scattered in the moonlight, separated by deep rectangular shapes of shadow. The sound of music from Lakis' bar could only just overcome the swish of wavelets on the shingle and the subdued slap of the sea on the tethered fishing boats. The cliffs soaring above the village were grey against the blackness of the sky and the ancient olive trees stood in deep dark pools of shade.

Theseus leaned forward and spoke quietly; the others drew their chairs towards him, hooked like fish who had taken his bait. "This is a harsh land under the dry mountains. It is a land where my family have ruled for years. No one knows how many years, maybe a few hundred, maybe a few thousand, we cannot know. But my people have always been here. Enemies have come and we have repulsed them; enemies have come and defeated us and ruled by the sword for a year or two but when they left we were still here, waiting in the hills. We have many enemies but my family overcome them; we will always survive. Nothing will defeat us."

The big man looked at his audience, silent and spellbound in the high harsh light of the moon. It was possible that the same moon had looked on the same group three thousand years ago, making plans in the night; the scene would have been little different.

"Drink more *koniak* my friends; you will be a part of the history of this island. Here in Crete you cannot escape history; here in Lossos you cannot escape the power of my family. It is as real as the rocks, as wide as the sea, as dominant as the cliffs."

Oscar broke the long silence which followed Theseus'declaration.

He was in a dream, totally seduced by the warmth and the wine and the romance of the place, and Theseus' piratical appeal. To him this was a fairy story and he wanted to be part of it; he could not act the indifference of Robert or the wariness of Brian, he was completely enthralled. Like a child asking what came next in a bedtime story, he said quietly, "What do you want us to do? I don't mind what it is, but I really would like to know."

"I will tell you now." Theseus liked the big black man and his easy ways; they would get on well together. "But before I do, I must tell you a little more history and show to you why I want to do these things. I have said that my family has always had to fight for this land; in the past it was by sword and gun but now we fight with money and politics. Our aims are the same, to control the land and the sea, but the means are different."

Yannis came to stand beside him and coughed apologetically; Theseus slapped him heavily on the back. "I know, my friend, you wish to be paid and to go to bed with your beautiful wife. *Poso kani?*"

"*Trianda euro, parakalo, kyrie Theseus.* Was the goat good?"

"*Poli orea, Yanni*, very good. *Ekharisto poli.*" Theseus gave Yannis a fifty euro note. "The tip is for your wife. She looks after me well, thank her for me. Now go to her but we will stay a while if that is right with you."

"*Endaxi. Kalinikta.*" Yannis left, winding his way between the tables. The fishermen got to their feet as he returned and, shaking his hand, made their way out into the night.

The lights from the kitchen went out, leaving the terrace stark in the moonlight; the four men were alone, the twentieth century ebbed away.

"My father built the road over the mountains to Hora Sfakia fifty years ago. Before then there was but a narrow path, a *kalderimi*, which came down the gorge to the coast, suitable only for mules. The south coast was isolated, home to my family, the kri-kri and the vultures, and little else. With the new road came people and they wanted to travel along the coast and out to the far islands." Theseus looked out over the black sea towards Gavdos. He was silent for a while and unconsciously stroked his beard where the streak of white caught the moonlight.

"And we helped them to travel; we had small boats and built bigger ones. The villages on the coast grew and needed supplies and we served them. The tourists needed places to stay and we built those too. Our ships became a lifeline to Sfakia and when people came

84

along and wanted to build roads along the coast we stopped them because we also owned the land. And our investments had to be protected."

Robert stretched and drained the last of his brandy. "How did you stop them, Theseus? How did you stop them building the roads?"

Theseus looked at him and then out to sea to where the beacon which marked the western extremity of the bay flashed its constant warning. "Things go missing," he said quietly, "and men take fright. Bridges are built at high cost and are found to be too short. Bulldozers fall down steep cliffs. These things happen, and the roads fail."

"Nothing to do with you, I suppose?" The drink made Robert bold.

"No, it has nothing to do with me. I am never involved."

"But you benefit, don't you?"

"Understand this, my Scottish friend. I am never involved and neither is my family. These things happen and we take advantage of them. That is all." Theseus' face was carved in moonlight, cold. "But," he went on "the three branches of my family have prospered, running the ferryboats, owning the hotels, and controlling the land. And when tourists started to pour down the Ardhos gorge in their thousands, whose boats carried them home, whose buses took them across the hills to the towns in the north, whose tavernas did they eat and drink in? This is my empire. And this is where you come in."

Theseus got up from the table and stood tall over them in the darkness, spot-lit by the moonlight against the dark background of the cliff.

"At last," Robert thought to himself, not daring to say it openly. He had taken a deep dislike to the arrogant Sfakian, a dislike which was tinged with mistrust and possibly a little fear. His usual brash confidence had deserted him and was replaced by resentment; he had begun to feel out of his depth in this alien place. Brian felt his growing animosity and put a steadying hand on the Scotsman's arm. "OK, boss," he said quickly, to Theseus, "this is what we are here for, let's have it. Where do we come in?"

Theseus relaxed and grinned without humour.

"I want you to blow up a mountain," he said, "an undersea mountain. I want to be able to bring big ships into Maranes bay to pick up the tourists who will come down the Amores gorge. And I can't do this because there is a big piece of rock in the way. I want you to take that rock away."

Robert snorted. "That's all, is it? Just like that, take a rock away? How big a rock is it? Doesn't sound very difficult to me."

"It is not difficult, not for experienced divers like you." Theseus frowned at Robert. "And it is not very big, not very deep; I will show you tomorrow. I am sure that you can do it. But it has to be done carefully and as quietly as possible."

"Sounds OK to me, no problem." Oscar didn't want to find any difficulties.

"I didn't know many people came down that gorge," Brian remarked thoughtfully.

"They don't, yet. But they will when we make the walk easier, and when we can take them to the top, to Amores, in coaches. That's what we are going to do. And now all we need is a cover story for your work, some story to tell the villagers so that they will not ask too closely what we are doing."

Brian got up and walked to the water's edge. He looked up at the moon. "I know," he said. "If you can arrange for a permit, we'll be archaeologists, underwater archaeologists. Like the people I worked with in Turkey. It's a good cover. Tell the village that we are looking for old wrecks and they won't be a bit interested. Come on now, I'm going to bed."

* * * * *

Theseus was nowhere to be seen when Brian joined Robert and Oscar for breakfast on the hotel terrace next morning. Brilliant sunlight reflected from the mirror calm of the sea and drenched the village in a blaze of light. Behind the white buildings grey and orange limestone crags reached up into a blue sky like the ramparts of an immense castle. Perched on top of the ramparts the chapel of Agia Katerini caught the morning light on its white walls. Higher yet above the crags the vulture floated on light winds, endlessly, effortlessly patrolling the skies.

"Where were you all last night?" Jackie asked, addressing the group but looking directly at Oscar, "Didn't see you down at the bar." She wore a long blue denim skirt with a red shirt and dangling red and gold earrings. Possibly in haste but probably deliberately, she had fastened too few of her shirt buttons. Gillian would scold her later but in the meantime she would enjoy teasing the men and annoying the women guests as she served rolls and strong black coffee.

Without waiting for an answer from the divers she disappeared back to the kitchen well aware that three pairs of eyes were watching her. She rewarded them with an extra flick of a firm buttock as she turned the corner.

"Well, what do you think of it, then?" Brian finished his roll and took a sip of the hot dark coffee.

"She's great ...", Oscar watched the kitchen for Jackie's return.

"Not her, you randy sod. The job, I mean – what Theseus told us last night."

"Oh, yeah, that. It's OK. I'm staying anyway, and I'm going down to the bar tonight. You two can please yourselves." He lit one of his Marlboros and leaned back in his chair, nearly dislodging a middle-aged English lady who was sipping tea at the next table. He grinned at her in apology; she smiled back uncertainly and edged her chair closer to her own already cramped table. "I like this place, and I don't mind what we do. Compared with our last job this is paradise."

Robert watched Oscar from behind dark glasses which reflected the bright sunlight and concealed his eyes. "Don't you ever think, you black bugger?" His Glaswegian accent was strong. "I'm not sure that I trust this Theseus, he's a hard man and I don't know about the job either. It sounds too easy and I can't see why the locals can't do it. Why does he need us?"

Brian waited to see which way the argument was going before deciding what he thought, and came down on the fence as usual. "Why don't we wait and see? We're here now and it's not costing us anything and it's a pretty good place to be in for a few days. Why not see how it goes? Theseus said that he would show us the job later; we might as well check it out, you know, while we're here?" Brian's statements always ended in an interrogative upturn as if seeking reassurance. He rolled a thin cigarette in his fingers and lit it with the Concorde lighter; the smoke was invisible in the strong light. He looked at Robert for reaction. They had been together for a long time; it sometimes seemed that all they had in common was a mutual contempt woven into a taut tie of tolerance. Brian found Robert selfish and bitter; Robert thought that Brian was weak. But they stayed together out of familiarity and laziness and, possibly, because they were both fond of Oscar. Oscar needed them because they found the jobs and provided the money and they, in turn, needed his genial uncritical dependence and his great strength.

Robert shrugged. "Aye, I suppose you're right, we may as well see what our Cretan friend has to offer since we're here. But if we do stay I want a place of our own. I don't want to be in the hotel. I want somewhere where we can get away from Theseus and I want to be paid for what we do – I don't want to live on his charity."

"Who's talking about my boss, then?"

Jackie had served breakfast and took advantage of a quiet moment before she had to start cleaning up to come over to the divers' table and steal a cigarette from the red and white packet in front of Oscar. Taking Brian's Concorde lighter she lit up and inhaled deeply; the strong smoke hit the back of her throat and made her cough. "Christ, how the hell can you smoke these things?" she gasped.

Oscar patted her on the back. "You get used to them in a year or two, if they don't kill you first. You've got to work at it. Come on, tell us about Theseus."

"Oh. He's OK. Bit of a pirate, really," Jackie enjoyed the attention. "He's the sort of boss around here and it's best not to cross him but he's all right if you're straight with him. There's all sorts of stories about him but I don't know if they're true." She thought a little, drawing on the cigarette and repeatedly tapping its ash onto a plate.

"Dimitris is the one who could tell you, they're very close and Dimitris is his right-hand here and in Athens. But I don't know much about it. Fiona might tell you a bit, she's been here a long time, but she's very faithful to Dimitris. It's all pretty complicated really, I try to stay out of it, it's safer." Jackie looked round at her now devoted audience. "Just do your job, that's best here, that's what I do. And then you can enjoy yourself. Don't get mixed up in anything. And stay quiet. Everyone listens and watches, there's nothing else to do."

Robert said, "We've only been here a few hours and you're the second person who's told us to keep quiet. What is it about this place?"

"It looks good," Oscar surprised his mates by this contribution. He usually just sat and listened. "Don't spoil it for me," he went on, "I like it here. You'll have to look after me." He grinned at Jackie who treated him to a slanted smile and held his eyes.

"I'll look after you, don't worry, big boy."

The others were forgotten for a moment; it was just the two of them, the big black man with his wide smile and the dark-haired gypsy girl with the tempting lips and shining eyes of a Carmen. A silent promise was made.

"Jackie, where are you?" An authoritative English voice came up the stairs followed by a scruffy black and white mongrel dog which, coming on to the terrace, immediately did the rounds of the tables seeking scraps of jam-covered bread roll which he ate with slavering enjoyment. "Where's that damn girl?"

"Oh, Christ, it's Gillian. I'll see you."

Jackie piled plates and cups quickly onto a tray and shot off towards the kitchen.

An attractive English woman whose forty-something years were belied by her easy walk and her tan came onto the terrace and stood for a moment, hands on hips. Her light brown hair was pulled sharply back from her face to reveal neat ears with large pearl studs. She wore a well-cut white shirt over jeans from which the lower legs had been hacked; shoe-less brown feet with chipped red-painted nails completed the incongruity. Her practiced eye swept the terrace before turning to her guests "Good morning. *Kalimera*. How are you today. Everything all right?" she said to no one in particular. Without waiting for a reply she turned back to Jackie. "Get those tables cleared quickly, and wiped clean. Come on, girl, what have you been doing all morning?"

Gillian had little love for Jackie who, in her first season in Lossos, was becoming a little too popular with the local men and, possibly, her husband. She suspected that Theseus had been tempted, and had quite likely already succumbed to her gypsy charms. She turned again and called to the dog. "Raki, stop it, come here."

The mongrel raised a black ear and carried on searching for bread, unimpressed by his owner's threat. Gillian came across the terrace and took the dog by its collar. "I'm sorry," she said, smiling vaguely in the direction of her breakfasting guests, "He shouldn't be up here, really."

She cuffed his head affectionately and led him over to the divers' table and looked at each man closely, deciding where to place them in her attentions.

"I'm Gillian. I believe you kept my husband out late last night." Before they could answer she went on, "You must be Robert and Brian, welcome to Lossos. And you must be Oscar; Theseus liked you."

Brian was going to say "Does that mean he didn't like us?" but he didn't dare as she continued, "I'm sorry that I couldn't join you last night. What are you doing here anyway? No, it's all right, you don't need to tell me. He keeps these things to himself. Likes to be secretive. He thinks I know nothing."

All this was said, without a break, in the sort of English voice which used to be known as "well-spoken", the clear and confident tones of someone who was used to being obeyed, as Gillian scratched the dog's ears and watched Jackie closely. It was entirely due to her diligence that the hotel flourished as it did and she gave the accurate impression that she missed nothing. Without appearing to be interested she knew everything which went on in the hotel and most of what went on in the village. She was respected by her staff; if a little arbitrary at times, she was also scrupulously fair and kept a motherly eye on the girls. She was liked by her guests whom she flattered with attention while her mind was elsewhere. She was accepted with distant respect by the native women of the village who could find no fault in her other than her occasional rowdy behaviour in the tavernas. Even this they excused on the grounds that she was English and had a lot to put up with as Theseus' wife. Her husband was both feared and respected within the community and Gillian was simultaneously sympathised with and envied.

Things had been different twenty years ago when she had first arrived as the young foreign bride who spoke little Greek and who dressed, to Sfakian eyes, outrageously. Gillian had earned her respect in the village by hard work, by quickly learning to speak Greek and by showing herself devoted to her saturnine husband. The birth of her three children in the village and their Greek education had shown her determination to be a good mother, and this had helped her to gain the respect of the local women.

Gillian's achievement was that she was now a sort of honorary Sfakiani, slightly eccentric, slightly noisy, slightly mistrusted, but accepted for what she was.

She had been keeping an eye on Jackie; now, seeing that the washing and cleaning had been completed satisfactorily, she was free to move on to other responsibilities. She nodded dismissively to the British. "See you later; enjoy your day. Come on, Raki." The dog bounded down the steps, leading the way.

Jackie watched her go and went across to steal another cigarette from Oscar.

Chapter fourteen

The morning was hot; most of the visitors had opted for sunbeds and umbrellas on the beach. A few ventured into the cool sea, others had left on foot or by the early ferry to explore further along the coast. In dark kitchens black-clad women and their daughters prepared food for lunch and dinner. In the shade of tamarisk trees men sat smoking, drinking strong coffee and endless glasses of ice-cold water, arguing about the world. The village drifted into the lethargy of mid-morning and the vulture continued its distant patrol high above the cliff. The sea was a mirror of molten steel distorted by fading ripples left by a small fishing boat. Jackie and the divers talked quietly on the shaded terrace and Fiona, cool and damp from her shower, stood in her window looking down on the village, thinking of Dimitris. As she brushed her hair she pictured him shirt-sleeved in his office in Athens and remembered with a secret smile last night's love under the stars of Lossos. She tied her hair into a ponytail and slipped on a long pale green dress and salt-stained sandals and walked slowly down the steep concrete steps into the village and into the heat.

Most of the supplies for the village came in on the eleven o'clock ferry; its arrival brought the busiest time of day for the small community as down the ship's ramp came water and wine, beer and bread, tomatoes and toilet paper; all the stores necessary to feed and entertain the villagers and two or three hundred tourists. Anxious restauranteurs counted loaves and disputed over fruit; orders which had been telephoned to Hania or Hora Sfakia were checked and carried off in small boats or on wheelbarrows across the rough pebbles. For ten minutes there was a scene of frantic activity focused on the yawning steel mouth of the ship; villagers and tourists alike gathered to watch, the former in heavy black dresses or dark serge trousers, the latter in colourful and scanty swimsuits. Sweating men and women tugged at cardboard boxes of tins and bottles, stacking

91

them on the hot stones before disappearing back into the dark hold for more. After ten minutes of madness in the morning sun suddenly it was over. The ferry closed its steel jaws and withdrew to the placid sea, growing rapidly smaller as it turned to resume its journey to the west. Small boats laden with stores, lying low in the water, returned carefully to the further tavernas. Wheelbarrows bumped over the shingle to disappear into dark kitchens. Then all was silent again, and the village turned and went back to sleep, back to sunbathing, back to the tamarisk trees, quiet again under the heavy hand of the heat. There was a collective sigh and a relaxation but high in the sky the vulture circled and watched.

Visitors read, swam, talked. Villagers worked and talked, the girls gossiped. Through the town, currents of conversation ebbed and flowed. The currents flowed but did not mix. On the surface was the chatter of the holidaying classes, comparing experiences, claiming affluence and travel-weariness, hinting at exotic plans for next year, implying that a few weeks stay, spread over several years, gave them an intimate and unique knowledge of the village. Beneath this came the gossip of the hotel staff: who was sleeping with whom, who had drunk too much last night, who had been found in bed with two local fishermen. Scandalous, cheerful, salacious, this gossip was invaluable to Gillian who found it not only highly entertaining but very useful when it came to dealing with suspicious villagers or supercilious guests. Since she lacked intimacy with the native villagers, she made sure that she was at least as well-informed as they by encouraging her girls to pass on to her what they knew.

Then came the deeper currents of the villagers and the tavernas; cynical about the foreigners and scornful of their ways, plotting a neighbour's downfall, complaining about the price of vegetables. Dark currents, moving slowly, with many mutterings through black headscarves and the shaking of heads and the frowning of lined faces.

And deepest of all, the secret plans of the landowners and the shipowners. These rarely surfaced, but when they did, they struck like a tidal wave through the ripples of the sunnier, lighter levels above.

Unlike the other summer staff, Fiona did not gossip. Her relationship with Dimitris gave her entry into two levels of village life and she had decided early on that she could only be trusted if she was known to be discreet. So, on meeting Andreas, Dimitris' father, as she crossed the terrace of his taverna on her way to the hotel, she was immediately invited to drink coffee under the tamarisks. Her relationship with Dimitris' family was complex; Andreas was secretly delighted by his son's choice, finding the girl both charming and deferential, not to say beautiful, and he had chosen to treat her with a gruff kindness which masked his admiration. His wife, Katrina, on the other hand, would have preferred Dimitris to have married a nice Cretan girl who would have helped in the kitchen and produced a string of strong olive-skinned black-haired children. Both parents had been critical of the relationship in its early days, but they had to accept that the Australian girl had been constant and faithful to their only son during the four years in which she had worked in the village. She was polite and friendly without being familiar and Andreas and Katrina had become secretly quite proud of her, feeling that she brought distinction to the family.

"*Kathise, pedi mou*. Sit down and drink some coffee with me." Andreas ushered her with a stiff formality to a table covered with a crisp red-checked tablecloth and Katrina brought two small cups of black coffee and two frosted glasses of water. Andreas was a big man without a neck; his enormous shoulders and immense arms ended in large fisherman's hands which continually twisted about each other in attempting to please. His round face, fringed with wiry grey hair, seemed too big for two kindly blue eyes. He spoke English poorly, knowing little more than the names of the dishes of food displayed in the glass-fronted cabinets in front of his kitchen. Nevertheless he always attempted to speak to Fiona in her own language, a mark of respect which he offered to few others.

"The day is beautiful, *poli orea*? *Pou pate*, where do you go?"

Fiona answered him in Greek. "It is a beautiful day, *kyrie* Andrea; I am going to work in the hotel. I am working at lunchtime and in the evening today."

Her Greek was slow and pedantic, lacking in the inflection of the native, but clear in her low voice. "Tell me, have you been busy in the restaurant? There are not yet many visitors in the village. I hope that there will be more in the summer."

They talked of the village for a little time until Andreas suddenly turned to her, now speaking Greek.

"I knew that there was something I had to tell you. This morning, before Dimitris left, Mateo came to see him and they talked for some time before the ferry sailed. He asked of you and hoped that you would visit him at Lavris soon. He will be there for the summer, working with Yorgos and climbing in the mountains."

Fiona had been introduced to Mateo soon after she and Dimitris met and when their relationship was meeting the disapproval of the

93

villagers. Dimitris had taken her over the headland from Lossos to Lavris to seek the older man's advice. From then on Mateo had been a kind and supportive friend and had helped her through those difficult times and it was mainly due to him that her friendship with Dimitris had survived. On the shaded terrace under the vines of Lavris she had fallen under the spell of his dark compassionate eyes in a walnut-wrinkled face under a riot of white hair. Fiona admired his love of Crete and his delight in the country in which he had found a home and envied the way in which he had become accepted as a Cretan. She became a regular visitor to Lavris and often spent time with him learning the paths of the mountains and the properties of the plants which grew in them, when Dimitris was away in Athens.

Mateo had been born in one of those mid-European countries which had been precariously independent before being swept on the tides of war and politics into German and then Russian hands. He had trained as an engineer and then at the age of twenty had found an escape to the West, leaving family and friends behind. He had wandered until the start of the North Sea oil boom had led him to work and marriage in Norway and for a few years had lived a conventional domestic life and produced two striking daughters who had adored him. Then oil lost its bloom and he had to find work elsewhere in the world and, after illness in Indonesia and redundancy in Venezuela, he had returned to Norway to find that his wife had disappeared. He had searched for some time and eventually discovered that she had married again and that a solid reliable German had provided her and his daughters with a good home and security. Mateo had watched in secret for a while, willing the girls to recognise him, and then left sadly and never returned. His wanderings had brought him to Crete and he had lived a lonely life as a shepherd in the Lefka Ori, learning the ways of animals and the lore of plants. The short winters he spent on the south coast with Yorgos and his father Manolis and helped in their taverna and with the fishing.

During this time he had met the young Dimitris and become mentor and tutor to him and taught him English and engineering and tolerance. He had moulded a primitive Cretan boy into a sophisticated European man, and, he hoped, a mate for his favourite Australian girl.

For her part, Fiona had high regard for him and she promised that she would lose no time in going over to Lavris to drink wine with him under the stars. She thanked Andreas for the coffee and crossed the hot pebbles to the hotel, back into the western world and lunch for the visitors who, as usual, would drink too much and waste the afternoon in sleep. Fiona found Jackie and together they listened to endless comment on the heat, made countless sandwiches, opened crates of wine; all with the attention and sympathy which Gillian demanded of her staff. And, really, quite enjoyably. After all, as Jackie had once said, "It's better than Margate in the rain."

Lunch was over; the first heavy heat of summer pressed the village into lethargy. Jackie and Fiona were stacking the dishwasher when Theseus' launch swept into the bay at the end of a creamy arc which spread and died over the steel blue of the sea. He tied the boat up and jumped onto the jetty swinging a heavy bag of fish before him and ambled down the rough wooden planks to cross the pebbles and disappear into the kitchen. A brief flurry of action then silence again; the heat settled more heavily; the vulture, pausing in its patrol to note the boat's arrival, resumed its watch.

The girls had finished their work when Theseus appeared in the bar. "Where are the Englishmen?"

Fiona said, "Good afternoon, *kyrie* Theseus, how nice to see you." She smiled up at the big man and for a moment there was a suggestion of a returning smile in his cold blue eyes.

"*Signomi*, I am sorry, I was thinking of something else. Good afternoon, *kyria*. Would you please tell me if you know where our new guests are?" He paused for a moment. "I am sure that you will have already become acquainted with them."

Fiona grinned. "Jackie has."

Jackie reddened under Theseus' knowing look.

"Well, yes, we've met them," she flustered. "I think they've gone for a siesta, about half an hour ago."

"I'm surprised that you haven't joined them."

Jackie recovered with spirit, "They said that they were tired – I can wait. I am sympathetic, you know."

"Sometimes. Get them for me, will you. We're going for a sail. Tell them to bring swimming gear. Ten minutes, on the jetty." Then, unexpectedly, "Do you want to come?"

Fiona was working again at five, but Jackie jumped at the chance. "Oh, yes, I'll come. I'll go and get them now." She dashed off down the stairs, breaking the peace of the day with her clatter.

The launch curved out of the bay, past the rocky island with its iron-framed beacon; tourists and villagers watched, the former envying the romance of the boat and the open sea, the latter with conjecture and comment. News spread around the village quickly; on a quiet afternoon any unusual activity was bound to raise comment and Theseus was not known for his hospitality to visitors. Small boys were dispatched to the headland to plot the launch's route; Jackie's presence on the boat implied a pleasure trip but the villagers wanted to make sure.

The small boys reported that the launch had turned the far headland and had slowly sailed round Lavris bay before heading to Maranes. It had lingered a while inshore near the small pebble beach and then turned back out to sea where it put down an anchor. It was reported that Theseus had stayed on board while the others swam. It was obviously a swimming excursion and the watchers lost interest and started to throw stones at goats and to climb on the sharp white rock; wiser heads, knowing Theseus, were not completely convinced, and reserved judgement.

When the launch anchored Jackie, not too reluctant to display her amply filled leopardskin bikini, dived clumsily in first. Oscar and Robert followed quickly. To demonstrate their skills to Theseus and to impress Jackie each made elaborate dives, swimming deeply underwater in competition.

Theseus held Brian back. "If you were to take a bearing on the Maranes beach from here and swam some forty or fifty metres, you would meet our underwater mountain. Do that, and tell the others, but not the girl. Explore a bit; let me know what you think."

The water was cold but calm. Jackie splashed about happily, she was not a good swimmer and stayed close to the launch, reluctant to follow the others as they swam away towards the land where the cliffs rose steeply from the narrow strip of beach. Slightly disappointed by the apparent indifference of the men, she soon gave up and dragged herself like some exotic and slightly plump fish on to the boat to flop, streaming water, at Theseus' feet. He looked down on her. "You're getting fat," he said, factually.

She glared up at him and shook the seawater in a spray from her dark hair. "But you still fancy me, don't you? You've got to be nice to me or I'll tell Gillian."

Theseus looked at her as she stood rubbing her hair in a rough red towel and accidentally pointing two full breasts at him. He had a brief memory of that full body sitting astride him in the hot afternoon darkness, teasing him with her eyes and with her movement and felt a passing lust. But that was in the past, and he didn't need the risk. There were plenty of other girls, both here and in Hania, who enjoyed his attentions and posed no hazard.

"If you tell Gillian, you will not see England again; you will live with the fishes here in Lossos. Do you understand me?" His cold eyes made her shiver in the hot day and made her teasing seem pathetic and she quickly covered herself up in the towel and turned away. "Yeah, OK, just joking, no problem."

"There will be no problem," he said quietly, "not for me." The hot afternoon turned cold. Jackie couldn't wait for the divers to return.

When they did return they pulled themselves up onto the boat with the ease of long practice, two slim white fish and one strong black one against Jackie's colourful flounder.

"Wow, that was great; some improvement on the North Sea, eh?"

Jackie's mood improved quickly as she watched the young men dry themselves. She was particularly conscious of Oscar whose wet black skin shone with the sheen of a bronze statue. She shivered again, but not from cold or fear, and her nipples strained the smooth contour of her bikini.

Now Theseus was relaxed and the mood brightened. He produced cheese and olives and a large flagon of golden wine. Robert poured too quickly and drenched himself and had to be thrown into the sea again to wash and the outing soon became the happy pleasure jaunt it purported to be. Theseus turned the launch out to sea in a wide sweep to the west and showed them the coast to Agia Rodhia where the mountains came down to steep cliffs covered in cypress and pine. Above the cliffs a vulture floated on silent wings and above him the White Mountains turned pink as the sun set.

Back at the jetty in Lossos a happy swimming party climbed off the boat and made its way up to the bar. The mood was only slightly jarred by Theseus' curt dismissal of Jackie. "You've got work to do, I think."

"Oh. Yeah. Well, see you later, boys," was all she could manage as he ushered the men up the stairs. She stood abandoned on the beach then went angrily to find Fiona and complain about men in general and Theseus in particular. Fiona was very interested to hear how the afternoon had gone and to read between the lines of her friend's complaint. She knew that Theseus was up to something and the more she knew, the better. If Dimitris wouldn't tell her, she would find out for herself.

Up in the bar, Theseus called for ouzo.

"Let us celebrate the start of our project. *Yamas!* Now tell me what you think – what did you see down there? Is it possible, do you think?"

97

Brian rolled and lit one of his spindly cigarettes and poured water into the ouzo, watching the cloudiness caused by the first drops fade away as he added more. He took time to reply, the others waited for him; in diving matters he was the most experienced and even Theseus would have to defer to him in this. He savoured his moment of authority. He would have liked to have presented a long considered statement, dwelling on the difficulties, on his brilliant solutions, on the logistics and timescales and techniques, but, as so often in his life, he missed the occasion. "Well," he said, not a good start, "I think it should be OK, it's a big job, but ..."

Theseus was already irritated; he wanted answers. "So you can do it. When will you start? I have all the gear you might need here. How about tomorrow? Just tell me what you want."

Brian tried to re-gain the initiative but Robert broke in. "We want your launch and some scuba gear. I think we will have to go deep to place the charges and it's very difficult to tell what the effect might be when they go off. And it's dangerous." He took a gulp of ouzo for courage. "How much are you going to pay us? That's what it's all about, really, as far as I'm concerned." He looked round at the others for support but found little. Brian was intimidated by Theseus and had some idea that this was not the way to deal with Greeks, not powerful ones anyway; Oscar was happy to go along with anything provided that he could stay in this delightful place and close to Jackie. He had one or two ideas in that direction and thought that they might be reciprocated.

But Theseus surprised them yet again.

"I hoped that you would mention that. This is what I have done. There is an account in the Bank of Crete in Athens, in your joint names, with a balance of twenty thousand euros. When the job is done to my satisfaction, the money is yours. In the meantime you can live here at my expense; but I will not pay for your drinks. That would be too much, even for me." He laughed loudly, disturbing early guests. Gillian heard the laugh from below and wondered. Her husband rarely laughed, and when he did someone usually suffered. She guessed that it was the young men who were the target of her husband's mirth and felt momentarily sorry for them, then shrugged and carried on with her grocery list. They could look after themselves; if they couldn't, well, that was their problem.

"Twenty thousand, that's fantastic. Hey, that's great, man. You've got a deal." Oscar was ecstatic. He leant over and offered a big black hand. "Shake, boss, it's on."

"Its euros, not pounds, you idiot," Robert sneered. "But it's not bad," he conceded, "It's about twelve grand. But what I don't like," he went on, turning to Theseus, "Is why in joint names? Why can't we each get paid, separately?"

"You're in this together. I don't want three individuals, I want a team who work together and get the job done. Anyway, that's how it is. Do you accept?"

The men looked at each other. "Yeah. OK. It's on," Brian said, at last, "But this is what we need."

Theseus drained his glass, suddenly impatient. "Write me a list. You'll have it all in the morning. And you will get your own boat, I don't want to be too close to this, and besides, I need the launch."

He got up. "*Kalinikta sas*. And I like your idea of being archaeologists. I'll talk to people about the permit. And one last thing. I will give the go-ahead when you are ready to make the explosions. No big bangs to scare the natives before I say so; these things must be planned, even here in Lossos. Good night."

He left the terrace, ignoring the murmured greetings of his other guests; his launch left the jetty with a low growl, heading out into the darkening sea towards the lights of Hora Sfakia. In the west the sun set behind the White Mountains; in the east the glow of the rising moon showed ominously over the black bulk of the hills. The vulture made its last pass of the day and the red of the dying sun painted its wings crimson.

Chapter fifteen

Theseus had lost no time; in the early morning a large rigid inflatable dinghy was at the jetty complete with three sets of scuba masks and fins and a number of full bottles of compressed air. Fiona brought Brian a hand-written note at breakfast; it was from Theseus. "The boat is yours until the job is done. You can keep the gear. I want a report every night. Remember your cover story. I will back it up. *Kalos taxidi.*"

Fiona said, "I didn't know that you were archaeologists. Sounds interesting. What are you looking for here, have we got sunken ships filled with gold? It must be good to interest Theseus."

A few years ago Brian had done some work on the coast of Turkey where a tenth-century galley had been found at Ulu Burun. He had only worked as a recovery diver but he had picked up enough to convince Fiona and his friends that he knew what he was doing. He would enjoy the opportunity to impress this girl who had treated him so far with a very thinly-concealed scorn. "There have been reports," he began pompously, "that an ancient ship may have sunk off this coast. We are here to investigate, have a preliminary look at possible sites."

Fiona broke in. "Doesn't sound like Theseus to me. What's he got to do with it?"

"Well, he's sort of funding it, you know how he takes an interest in these things; and it's on his patch, really."

"Never heard of Theseus taking an interest in anything that's not to do with money, or girls," she added absently. "OK, if that's what he wants you to say, why not? It's a good story." She wandered back to the bar.

"That didn't go very well," Robert said.

"We're going to have to do better than that if anyone is to believe us. Did you really work in Turkey? If you did you must have learnt something, even you. You'd better tell us what you know so that we can sound convincing," he ended dismissively, "like you did then."

"Well, I tried didn't I? More than you lot did. It's that bloody girl; she always seems to know more than she lets on."

" Yeah, gets to you, anyway, but that's not difficult. Anyway, maybe she does – know more, I mean. I wouldn't trust her an inch. We'd better be careful with her, tell her nothing you don't need to. Walls have ears, as our Greek boss would say. Be canny."

Oscar wanted to stick up for Jackie. "The other one's OK though, isn't she? She doesn't like Theseus much, from what I see."

"Think with your head for once, not your big black dick. Don't tell anyone anything – got it? Not a thing, and certainly don't tell Jackie, it'd be round town in a flash."

"Come on, you two, drop it. But I agree with Robert, not a word to anyone. We don't want to upset the boss. And remember the bonus; that makes it all worthwhile."

Brian stood up, walked to the end of the terrace and looked down on the inflatable. "Let's go and play with our new toy. It's a great morning for a swim," and with a rare attempt at humour, he added, "On the way I'll teach you all about underwater archaeology."

The Lossos morning was still and warm as the new craft left the bay. A few tourists watched idly; the villagers were always aware of the movement of boats and watched with more care. Word had spread quickly through the town that Theseus was using the newcomers to hunt for lost treasure and had provided them with a new boat to do so; fishermen who knew the sea intimately tugged at thick black moustaches in thought. Where could the treasure be? What was it? Rumours of gold and ancient jewels grew and spread and multiplied, became elaborate, turned back on themselves, tangled with others in the shade of the tamarisks. Many a fishing trip would take a new direction in the early morning. How did you look down deeply into the sea? Fishermen look for fish and the signs of fish, the birds dipping over a flurry scarcely discernible on the surface. They did not look down into the depths, except when setting a new mooring or freeing an entangled net. Now they would start, early in the morning, scouring the deeps as never before. Arguments rose as to the most likely place for a wreck; it must be close to the shore for it was a precipitous coast, and the route of Theseus' launch yesterday was analysed over and over again. Attention centred on the Lavris bay and Mateo and Manolis over in the Lavris taverna would be surprised to see so much fishing in the area next day. In the meantime small boys were again dispatched to the ruin of the Turkish fort on the ridge to keep a lookout and to report.

The tales from the bored spies brought nothing new. The British had anchored where they were yesterday and swum about a bit. Then they had eaten and drank and sunbathed; nothing interesting. More stones were flung at annoyed goats, more rocks climbed. Boys get bored quickly when there is little to see and the exciting role of watchers soon lost its appeal to them. There was an early return to the village where the boredom of the day was relieved by the butchering on the beach of a small shark caught accidentally in a fishing net. In this new excitement the divers were quickly forgotten, but older heads remembered and would continue to watch.

On the inflatable the divers were relaxed and content. The exploration of Theseus' undersea mountain had been done; it was a big lump of limestone, possibly part of an ancient headland which had disappeared under the waves. Although extensive, it had only a few points which would be dangerous to ships. These could be removed quite simply by a few well-placed charges. All in all, an easy job, a week at the most. The mood on board was relaxed.

"We mustn't make it seem too easy," Robert said, lying in the sun and eating grapes, "After all we want to be seen to earn our money, don't we? Otherwise the bugger will probably split on the deal."

"Yeah. Mustn't leave too soon, I've things to do." Oscar planned to meet Jackie that night in Lakis' bar.

"What we'll do is this," Brian said. "First we say that we need more time to explore, two or three days. Then we need to fix all the charges, that'll take a week or so, then we have to wait for Theseus to agree when we blow them. Then we need to go down and check, and possibly set some more charges to shift the debris. We can spin it out to a good two weeks, if not a bit more."

"Sounds good to me." Oscar was dreaming in the sun. "As long as you like."

"Right, let's show some activity. We might be being watched; we must remember that we are looking for wrecks or something."

"Tell you what," Robert roused himself, "Let's swim back across the bay, with the gear, it should look right to anyone watching what we're up too. Like exploring."

"Do you want to drive?" Brian asked Oscar, "I wouldn't mind a swim. Just follow us up to the point, we'll take our time."

"OK, you're the boss. I'll pick you up over there, in that little bay under the headland, don't hurry."

Oscar stretched out in the sun and dreamt of Jackie.

Brian and Robert donned the gear and fixed bottles, jumped overboard and started a leisurely paddle in the direction of the Lavris point.

Much later in the cool evening as the moon, nearly full now, rose over the eastern hills and turned the dark water into silver the three men were sitting over the remains of a moussaka and salad. The last of the wine had been drunk. Oscar was getting restless as his appointment with Jackie approached. He had shaved with unusual care and splattered himself in unlikely places with a pungent aftershave which challenged the soft scent of early bougainvillea drifting on the still air. He had drunk far less than the others who had started on ouzo with Theseus when they made the first report and now were feeling the effects of the wine and the sun. Theseus had been relaxed at their meeting. "No hurry, take your time, see how it goes." He had even been affable to Gillian who had joined them for a glass of wine and they had talked of Lossos and Sfakia, Gillian adding salacious gossip to her husband's stories of the town and laughing about the stories of sunken treasure which now gripped the village.

When Gillian left them to talk to other guests, Theseus said, "It was a good idea, this archaeology cover, but I think it's become a bit centred on Lavris bay. Tomorrow we had better go a bit further along the coast, show that we are casting the net widely. We don't know what we are looking for or where; go off towards Agia Rodhia, that should distract them a while."

Brian had asked what the cover for the explosions would be.

"Ah, yes, the explosions. I have some friends in the navy who will help me. There will be a Greek navy ship here when we make the explosions, they will be removing old shells from the war which were dumped hereabouts – it's an old story but it will satisfy the locals. And the local fishermen are accustomed to using dynamite to catch fish so explosions are not unusual. Trust me."

Now as the last drops of wine were drunk, Brian thought of what he had said. "He can pull some weight, that Theseus. Fancy bringing the navy in, that's impressive."

"I just hope the buggers don't sink us accidentally," Robert was cynical. "You can't trust any of those braided types, especially the Greeks."

"Theseus will look after you, trust him."

"Like hell I will. Trust is not a word I'd use where he's involved. Be canny, that's what I say."

Oscar grinned at him in the dark.

"That's what you always say. I'm going. See you later."

"Be good, see you."

Oscar left the taverna, a striking figure in white trousers and black T-shirt.

"Fancy another bottle?" Brian stretched out and watched a small fishing boat cross the long silver reflection of the moon.

"How about an ouzo instead? I've taken a liking to that stuff."

"Never trust ouzo, it gets you."

"Just like our boss, eh? Anyway I'll have one."

The men were silent for a while, listening to the quiet chatter around them.

"Brian?" Robert said, deep in thought. "What would happen if we did find something, a wreck, I mean? That would complicate things a bit wouldn't it?"

Brian stubbed his cigarette out in the full ashtray. "Don't worry, mate, it's not going to happen."

Robert leant forward over the table. "Don't be so sure. When we swam to the point today, I dived down, do you remember?"

"Yeah, so what?"

"You know it's steep there, the rocks look like old cliffs, and then there's a flat bit, and then there's another bit of cliff, down to the sand; it's twenty metres or so to the bottom."

Brian rolled another cigarette. "So what? You see a mermaid or something?"

"You're not going to believe this; I thought I saw the top of a mast, just the top, sticking out of the sand, below the lower cliff."

"Come on, you're having me on. Don't be daft – just because we are supposed to find a wreck, it doesn't make it happen. Don't get carried away with this archaeological nonsense."

"The story could be true. I'm certainly going down there again to check, anyway." Robert's facade of cynicism seemed to have deserted him and his face looked unusually serious in the gloom of the sparsely lit terrace. He was not gifted with imagination and in their long acquaintance Brian had never heard him voice an original idea; now in the balmy, still night, with lights across the bay twinkling on the black sea and dull mysterious shapes of moored boats barely visible against the shore, he was seduced by the thought.

"Bloody hell. That would be something, wouldn't it? That'd teach bloody Theseus. We'll have a look tomorrow." He blew a long stream of smoke at the moon.

A planned early breakfast was delayed by Oscar who eventually turned up looking, as the phrase goes, as if he had just got out of bed, which indeed was the case. He rapidly demolished a large yoghurt and fruit and several rolls well spread with jam and two cups of coffee with only a grunt in reply to the crude questioning of his friends. When he had finished he tilted his chair back and lit a Marlboro. "Morning, beautiful day. What are we going to do? I'm ready for anything."

Before Brian could answer, Gillian came over to their table carrying a cup of coffee and took one of Oscar's cigarettes. "Who didn't come home, then? Sleep well?"

Unfazed, Oscar put an arm round her waist and squeezed. "Thank you, marm, I slept like a baby."

"Let's hope you don't make any, eh, I can't afford to lose waitresses, you know. Now put me down and go to work or Theseus will be angry, and that's not a good thing for everyone, and for me in particular."

"OK boss, we're off. See you."

"Didn't take long for Gillian to find out, did it? About you and Jackie, I mean," Brian remarked as the inflatable crossed Lavris bay and headed west past Maranes in cool, fresh morning air.

"Walls have ears, let's hope they don't have eyes as well. Not a pretty sight," Robert leered. He went on, "A strange place, this Lossos, you'd think it was just a little holiday spot, sort of idyllic, like in a brochure. But it's not like that at all, when you get to know it. It's a bit sinister."

"That's the longest speech you've ever made, what's got into you?" Brian was intrigued by this new side to his friend who had made a career of bored disinterest.

Robert pointed back down their wake to the long finger of the cape resting on the horizon with its knuckle slightly raised. "Look at that. Its like it's pointing at something, accusing. The finger of fate, you know; how about that for a sunny morning?" He laughed without much humour. "It gives me the creeps." He shivered in the chill of the morning wind and the vulture soared overhead on wide wings.

They worked along the coast during the day, conscious all the time of being watched. They dived diligently and often for the unseen eyes, enjoying the clear sea, finding its kaleidoscope of colour refreshing after the drab grey of the North Sea. In the late afternoon they sailed slowly back to Lavris, getting to know the land and to recognise the coast. The white tavernas of Lavris and Philikas were becoming familiar below the nearly deserted village of Liridiana where the disfiguring scar of an unfinished new road cut orange across the grey limestone of the cliffs.

"It's difficult to imagine a Roman town there, and a port," Brain remarked, pointing to the Lavris headland. "A lot of people must have lived there. And then the Turks came. What a place to be garrisoned. Must have seemed a long way from home with the Sfakians raiding down from the mountains and no way to get supplies, except by sea. Must have been pretty hard. And then St Paul was supposed to have stopped here, on his way to Rome."

"Didn't know you knew so much about it. The history, I mean. Where did you pick it up? I'd like to know more about this place."

"There's books in the hotel. I read them when I was here before. When I first met Theseus and Gillian. No Jackie then, unfortunately." He looked at Oscar who grinned happily back at him.

"Tough."

Robert asked, "What were you doing here, anyway?"

"I did a backpack around Greece, some time ago; spent three or four weeks here, Theseus had a mooring problem in the bay and I helped. That's how we got this job."

They drifted in towards the headland. Oscar was content to sleep in the sun when Robert suggested that he and Brian should make a last dive. "We've only got about thirty minutes of air, won't be long."

They went over the side and swam slowly to the land side of the headland, Brian leading. The underwater cliff fell below them, down to the sea bed where dark green weed patterned the golden sand. There was no more than fifteen minutes of air left when Robert signalled that he was going down. Here the cliff fell for three metres before levelling to a sharp rocky ridge parallel to the shore; to the left of the ridge the cliff resumed its fall to the sandy floor. They followed the spiny ridge for a while until Robert indicated that he was going deeper down the cliff and Brian followed his bubbles downwards.

The cliff ended in a scree slope against which sand had drifted to form a steep ramp; there were clumps of weed and much broken stone. The sun's rays slanted down; distorted by the waves they made ripples of light on the sand and on the slowly waving weed.

Brian, above and behind, followed Robert's black fins and the line of silver bubbles which rose in a delicate chain to the surface.

Robert was down the sand slope moving slowly through patches of weed until he stopped and signalled that Brian should join him. The inflatable threw a dark shadow on the gentle slope of the sandy sea floor to their left, comforting in its presence.

Where the scree met the ramp of sand there was a scattering of recently fallen rocks which had disturbed the slope, creating sharp-sided channels as they rolled to the seabed. One channel was deep and new, obviously caused by the large boulder which lay at its end in a clump of flattened weed. At right-angles across the channel lay a broken length of wood shattered by the fall.

Robert put out a hand and the wood crumbled to his touch. With Brian hovering close by, he moved more sand to reveal a round length stretching diagonally down the slope. He dug feverishly, surrounded by a cloud of sand, to expose two or three metres more and came to loops of rope which disintegrated under his clumsy fingers.

Brian joined him and they dug together by touch as the sandy cloud enveloped them; they knew that they were doing irreparable damage but their excitement, and their rapidly depleting air reserve, drove them on. More mast became uncovered as they followed it down the slope until Brian felt the hard sharp edge of broken pottery; he waited impatiently for the slowly settling cloud to clear, then, by putting his mask close to the sand he was able to see the curve of a large earthenware jar. Carefully now, he smoothed the enveloping sand away from the vessel which lay on its side with a substantial part of its lip broken away. He put a tentative hand inside into a space where the sand had not settled and encountered a small round shape. Working entirely by touch he felt the loop of a small handle; the goblet came easily into his hand. With a thrash of his fins he backed away and headed up to the surface, resentful of the need to take his time to acclimatise to the reducing pressure. When he finally broke the surface he tore his mask off and lifted a double-handled black and grey cup into the first light which it had seen for thirty-five centuries. He treaded water and rubbed its lime and shell encrusted surface with a wet finger. The grey coating cracked away to reveal a rim below which a horizontal white band was decorated by sinuous curves in black. Below the band and the two handles the vessel tapered then swelled to a delicate base.

Brian held the goblet up, dark against the late afternoon sky and the vulture swooped down to admire it.

Chapter sixteen

The report to Theseus that night was vague in content and unspecific in detail. Work had been done, Brian reported, in a number of situations chosen for the underwater configuration of the land, and as such likely to have been possible wreck sites. These had ranged from west of Maranes to east of Agia Rodhia and had yielded nothing of value other than a quantity of empty and broken amphora of uncertain age at the narrow steep- sided inlet below the small chapel at Agios Pavlos. It was probable, he remarked expansively, that these had been lost from a quayside rather than from a wrecked craft. They had, nevertheless, brought a sample back as evidence, and as justification, of their activities. This artefact lay below in the inflatable awaiting Theseus' decision whether to reveal it or not. Brian thought that such a decision was best taken by him in his understanding of the complexities of the village situation; other than that, Brian continued, with a deference bordering on obsequiousness, they regretted that they had little to add. What were their instructions for next day?

Normally Theseus would have been alive to the inadequacies of their tale and to the overplayed subservience. Tonight he was distracted. Dimitris had called during the day to report problems over the funding for the new ferryboat, provisionally called the *Ioannis*, and the likely failure of the EC grant application for its construction. Consequently Theseus had resolved to go to Athens the next day to consider the problem with Dimitris before meeting the EC Under-Commissioner responsible for the difficulty. He had instructed Dimitris to find out what he could about this official and was confident of finding some leverage, but for now was understandably preoccupied. He listened to Brian's presumption and Robert's whining with only half an ear and dismissed them without further questioning; taking a bottle of malt whisky to the end of the terrace he sat alone, watching the moon rise.

Oscar joined his friends for an unexpectedly expensive fish meal and wondered why they had chosen to go to the very end of the village to dine. He was content with the story about the goblet which Robert and Brian had spun him on their return to the boat. They did not want to deceive him and intended to tell their friend the whole story later, but each needed time to collect their thoughts. Consequently it was with a slightly guilty relief that they waved the black man off to his date with Jackie.

"Well, then," Brian said as Oscar left. They watched him making his way through the tavernas and across the shingle towards the other end of the village where windows reflected moonlight and buildings were white blocks scattered at random on darkness. Taverna lights made sparkling stars on the ruffled black sea and the regular repeat of the beacon threw sharp daggers of gold towards them.

Brian had run out of his tobacco and now opened a packet of Marlboro begged from Oscar. He rummaged for his Concorde lighter and lit a cigarette and inhaled deeply; the night was shattered by his cough.

"Christ," he wheezed, "Jackie was right. How can he smoke these things and live?"

"And dive," Robert added, "which brings us back to the problem in hand."

"Theseus is away tomorrow and the next day. I think we should explore a bit more but we're going to have to do it quietly and we are going to have to tell Oscar." Brian stubbed out the cigarette. "What do you think?"

"Aye, you're right, but he'll have to keep it to himself until we decide what to do. Best tell him tomorrow, on the way out."

"What do you think we should do, really, I mean, if we find anything valuable?"

Robert looked at his friend across the table and flicked an olive stone which disappeared soundlessly into the ink-black sea. "Depends what it is and what you mean by valuable; who would own it, anyway?"

"As far as I know it all belongs to the State; the Greeks are very strong about that, they've had too much pinched in the past. And there's the problem of getting rid of any bits you might keep. It'd have to be very valuable to make it worthwhile risking. The State's one thing but Theseus is another. He wouldn't be too pleased if we stole bits off his patch."

"But a nice little bonus would be very useful, and I wouldn't mind getting one over our Greek friend, the arrogant sod."

Brian thought for a while, turning the lighter over and over on

109

the torn paper tablecovering; the nearly full moon lit the bay in front of them as if it were an empty stage awaiting the arrival of nocturnal assassins. "It might be interesting to know what would be valuable. When I was in Athens I came across a Greek who did a bit writing about archaeology, bit of a shifty bugger, seemed to know a few people in the market for antiquities. He was asking me about the Turkish job, said he could shift a few pieces for me. Never used him. Didn't like him much really, too oily for me, big belly. Married to an English girl from what I remember."

"Could be useful; you still in touch?"

"Think I could find him if I wanted to, through the Press Club."

"Tell you what; we'll have a good look tomorrow. If we find anything good, we'll give your oily friend a ring. What's his name?"

"Nikos, I think, Nikos Kontos; wife's called Jenny, nice girl. Well brought up, Oxford type." He thought for a while. "Now I remember. Do you remember that air crash at Athens – ten, eleven years ago? Those fantastic pictures of the plane on fire and the girl rushing towards it? That was her. Her father was on the plane. He was with the British School of Archaeology, in Athens. Then she met this Nikos and married him. Haven't heard of her since – she would be about thirty-five now." Brian lit another Marlboro and looked around the empty stage of Lossos, awaiting its players. The cold spotlight of the moon turned slowly overhead, the actors were gathering in the wings.

Brian and Robert were becoming accustomed to Oscar's distraction at breakfast and didn't disturb him until he had finished his second cup of sweet black coffee and had lit the first Marlboro of the day. As he chucked the packet across to a waiting Brian the sound of a powerful engine came up from the jetty as Theseus left to meet his driver in Sfakia for the journey over the mountains to Hania and the 8.40 Olympic flight to Athens. Gillian and the dog Raki were on the jetty to see him off and came up to the terrace as the launch dwindled to a speck on the sparkling eastern sea, the dog bounded ahead and did his rounds of the tables. Robert gave him half a slice of toast which Raki carried off into the shade and ate noisily to the horror of a fastidious English couple who had only recently arrived and had not yet appreciated the priorities in Lossos. Gillian sat down and took another cigarette from Oscar's quickly diminishing stock. "Two days of peace," she remarked to no one in particular, "Well, two and a half, really."

She hugged Raki who had come to sit beside her and was annoying Robert by dribbling onto his bare leg. He in turn tried to dislodge the dog and only succeeded when he stole a small piece of roll from the next table and threw it surreptitiously across the terrace where it came to rest under the English couple's table closely pursued by an enthusiastic animal. In the ensuing commotion the icy reserve previously shown by the English was thawed and later they became some of Gillian's most regular and devoted guests. On such small things futures turn.

Fiona came over to the table. "God help Athens," she said, ruffling the dog's ears, "when he gets there. I pity that poor Commissioner; he doesn't know what's going to hit him."

"He'll manage. They're going to get him to sort the new boat out, are they? Theseus doesn't tell me a thing these days. Anyway, two days of peace."

Fiona thought that Gillian didn't look too upset at being left out, smiled drily at her and looked out across the bay to where the distant smudge of Sfakia showed under a pale purple peninsular. "Two long days," she said quietly to herself.

"Two short days," Gillian responded acidly. "Come on, let's get to work."

It was still early in the day when the divers' inflatable put down an anchor just inside Lavris bay, close under the headland. There were no other craft in sight and the sea reflected the grey and orange of the cliffs. Oscar had been told of the discovery and insisted on being in the first pair to dive. He and Brian went down together into the translucent turquoise, deep to the sand slope where the parts of mast which they had uncovered yesterday now lay under a thin patina of fine sand. The clear water revealed their earlier excavations and a number of amphorae scattered down the slope beneath. Brian signalled to Oscar to follow and dropped slowly down to the sea floor, disturbing as little silt as possible. There was a bunch of crushed weed where a clean white limestone boulder lay at the end of its scarred passage through the sand. Brian tugged at a handful of weed which came easily up in his hand, leaving a thin spiral of sand to drift gently down. He reached down into the hole left by the roots and felt metal. He pulled at it gently, freeing it from the grip of the sand. A long dagger came out and the gold on its hilt caught the sun.

* * * * *

Every morning should be like an early spring morning in Lavris; quiet and fresh, with shafts of hot sunshine striking through a latticework of shadow formed by the overhead vines. Small transparent waves lapped at the water's edge and the sea stretched beyond the horizon and became the sky, the cliffs over Maranes made a theatrical cut-out against the intense blue. In the silence there was only the soft sibilant shush of the sea; cool air stirred the stillness with a whisper as it teased the vines. Early blocks of shade moved awkwardly in corners and were slowly conquered by the mounting sun. Argus, an old German Shepherd dog, lay with twitching nose on the cool stones beneath a table suddenly aware that Manolis was in the taverna doorway, scratching his chest through his thick shirt. The old man's smell reassured the dog who sighed deeply and slept again. Manolis shuffled across the patio to spit into the sea and to survey the horizon. A morning like so many before it, quiet, peaceful, undisturbed. And yet it was disturbed. That boat was out again, under the lee of the Lavris point, the alien orange of its rubber floats vivid against the dark limestone ridge. Its presence was an affront to Manolis, an intrusion into his peace and his domain; he stared out at it in resentment, willing it to go away.

Mateo joined him at the water's edge and Argus, unwilling to be left out of this meeting of his pack hauled himself stiffly to his feet and came to stand beside the two men. He stretched and yawned noisily then sat between them staring out at the foreign boat. As if aware of this distant scrutiny, the inflatable's engine came to life and disturbed the silence of the bay; the craft turned through a wide arc and motored slowly towards Maranes, its three passengers clearly visible against the sea. It crossed the bay and then came to halt again off the headland. Three splashes were clearly heard across the water as the divers dropped into the sea and disappeared under the surface.

Manolis, Mateo and the dog watched a little while longer and then turned back to the terrace; the old man sat at his usual table at the back and Argus lay at his feet. Mateo went into the building and brought a small cup of hot black coffee and a glass of water for Manolis; taking a broom from the wall he started to sweep the stone floor, raising a light dust which drifted towards the sea. Peace returned and the dog snored softly. Having re-distributed the dust to his satisfaction, Mateo came to stand beside Manolis' table and leant on his brush, looking out to sea. "I wonder what they're up to?" he remarked, as much to himself as to his companion. "They go here and there, they go off to Agia Rodhia, but they always come back to those two spots. They seem to be trying to lead us away from what they are interested in, but they do it badly. They have no feel for concealment, no understanding. By their actions they draw attention to what they wish to conceal. But what, what is it that they are seeking, out there?"

Manolis' Greek was musical with the sibilance of the south. "They are working for that pirate, that Anopolakis brigand. There is no good in anything which he or his accursed family do. They intend to rule Sfakia and will not let anything stand in their way – they are ruthless. Whatever they touch they destroy, like they destroyed Ahladha." He spat drily on the hot stones.

Argus, disturbed by the old man's sudden anger, got to his feet and put his muzzle reproachfully on the dirty black serge of Manolis' trousers. His master patted the matted fur under his ears in apology. "I am sorry," he said confidingly to the dog, "It's that man, he always upsets me. But he destroyed my village and I will never forgive him for that. And now what is he up to?"

Mateo looked at the bright orange boat stationary on the flawless sea. "I don't know," he said, "There was some story about them looking for treasure, seeking an old shipwreck, but I don't believe it. It's more likely to be something for Theseus, but what, I don't know. I will go to Lossos tonight and ask. Dimitris will know."

"But will he tell you? He is Theseus' man now, working in Athens." Manolis hissed at the thought. Athens lay distant and alien to him, a big evil city, a suitable lair for a confederate of the detested Theseus. He crossed himself and clicked his beads through his scarred brown fingers.

"Maybe not," Mateo frowned, "But I will ask, anyway." He turned and went into the cool gloom of the kitchen; the dog watched him go and put a paw comfortingly on the old man's bare foot.

Under the dinghy, in the clear sea, the three divers were working around Theseus' underwater mountain deciding how to place the charges. The rough limestone had many holes in its eroded surface and there was no shortage of natural sites for the explosives. The aim was to ring the rock with enough to ensure that the top was blown off by a simultaneous firing; any remaining points could be removed later by more precisely placed small charges. A straightforward job requiring less skill than it appeared to demand; Theseus could be told on his return that all was ready and would, they hoped, be impressed. This gave the divers two days in which to explore the wreck but brought a problem: how could they work on the sunken ship without revealing too much to the watchers on the shore? During their early dive that morning Brian had suddenly felt exposed and vulnerable and had insisted that they leave the site quickly; he had not seen any watchers but remembered Theseus' admonition that there were eyes everywhere. His urgency had been transmitted even to Robert who had not yet dived and was impatient to go down again, and persuaded him that they should leave. And away from the wreck, free from the frantic need to continue to search, they had time to consider what they were doing. Recovering from the dive to Theseus' reef, drying and warming in the sun, they talked thoughtfully, with many silences, about what they should do. Each accepted that they had already gone too far in disturbing the wreck, but each acknowledged how difficult it would be to stop now. The urge to explore further was hard to resist despite Oscar's misgivings, although they all knew that sooner or later they would have to reveal what they had done.

Robert summed it up. "We shouldn't have gone on. We should have stopped before. So why stop now? We get shot anyhow. I say we do another dive each and then decide what to do."

Even Oscar, usually so reluctant to take any risks, had been caught by the excitement. "One more dive, that's all, each of us with full bottles. If we leave the boat here we should be able to swim back to the site, spend twenty minutes or so down, and swim back, without any one knowing where we are."

"Yeah, that's it," Brian didn't want to be left out. "If there are two of us in the dinghy over here, who's to tell where the other is? Let's go for it. But leave whatever you find down on the bottom, say against that big rock; don't try to bring anything back unless it's very small."

Robert went first, swimming fast on a compass bearing, small fish riding his slipstream. The bubbles from his mask left a trail on the silken ruffles of the sea, marking his passage. Down on the wreck he dug deeply beneath the mast to feel wooden planking disintegrate in his fingers. In the space beneath was a pile of heavy metal plates each about the size of an open book, with small rings on the four corners. Robert pulled one out with difficulty and laid it on the large boulder where it caught the light and the copper glinted where it had been scratched; Robert brought out three more ingots before looking at his watch; only three or four minutes of air were left allowing ten for the return to the inflatable. He went back to the hole in the planking and dug around beside the remaining ingots with both hands pulling and tugging to reach beyond them. In the sand mist his fingers found a flat plate with a sharp curved edge. With care he worked below and round it and moved it slowly from side to side to release it from its ancient grip. Reluctant at first, it suddenly came into his hand and he raised it through the filtered green sunlight. A double axe head of bronze, its broken shaft still visible in its socket, each blade the size of a man's hand, showed through the water-born cloud of sand. With reverence Robert reburied it beside the boulder and carried the indelible image of it in his mind and its cool touch in his hands on the long swim back to the reality of the dinghy.

Brian dived deep well before the site of the wreck and trawled along the sea floor, skimming over the yellow sand and weaving through the beds of green weed. He came to the foot of the ramp of sand which ran up into the scree and the cliff above, and swam slowly to where the silt disturbed by Robert's hasty digging still hung in the still sea, bright against the deep green of the depths behind. As he swam he ran his fingers through the sand surface leaving parallel runnels below spiral smoke-trails of sand.

Cruising like some large fish just over the bottom through the waving fronds of weed gave an impression of speed as he homed in on the wreck site and he had to stop suddenly as his hands encountered something hard buried under the surface. With fins building a sandstorm behind him Brian ran his hands over a large encrusted pithos which lay at the foot of the slope with its upper curve almost hidden by the sand. To anyone approaching down the ramp it would have been hidden from sight; from the flatlands of the sea bottom it appeared to be another fallen stone but the seeking hands found the rough curve and explored it. It was a large jar, lying on its side, tapering to the base and with a sharp shoulder from which sprang a short neck. Brian hovered in the water as he felt around the neck, gently freeing it from the silt. The top of the jar was unsealed; now working entirely by touch he put his hand inside and as promptly withdrew it as a sharp point cut a finger. Small fish gathered to taste the blood as he examined the wound through his face mask. Satisfied that it wasn't a bite or an urchin spike he explored, more carefully this time, within the open mouth of the pithos.

A pile of broken shards of fine pottery lay inside; aware but unrepentant, Brian's questing fingers sorted through these seeking something whole. Broken cups and jugs littered the jar but under them was a larger vessel which seemed intact; backing away with fins thrashing and bubbles stretching in a gaseous chain from his air valves, Brian turned to allow both hands to enter the open neck of the pithos. He pulled gently at the shape inside the pithos and it moved in his hands. With infinite care he eased it from its grave and carried it to clearer water.

The jug raised its dark spout and showed the striped pattern painted under its throat three thousand years ago; the handle curved elegantly to return to the full body which bore a stylised leaf pattern in dark swirls. With difficulty Brian resisted the temptation to carry it to the surface in triumph; carrying it carefully in both hands to the erratic limestone boulder, he reburied it with reverence. He laid a cross of small stones above it to mark its position and swam quickly back to the inflatable.

Oscar came down to the ramp of sand from the cliff face and stopped for a while to try to work out how the craft had sunk and fallen. Presumably it had hit the sharp spines of rock at the top of the cliff and could have been stuck there for some time before falling down to the sandy slope. If this had happened, he thought, the mast would have broken away during the fall, leaving the hull to roll down the ramp to the bottom. If that were the case the bulk of the cargo would be at the foot of the slope, not on its flank. Oscar followed the slope down and started to dig. Pieces of rotted timber disintegrated under his attack, then a smooth triangular shape of stone with holes in which could have held ropes yielded to his search. He buried the ancient anchor with scraped sand beside the big rock and swam back to where he had found it. Where the stone had lain were two swords, their broad flat blades encrusted with the concretion of ages of sea creatures, the gold on their hilts unblemished. These too he buried. Desperate for time now, he dug furiously in the open hole into which sand was already beginning to flow.

Suddenly his hands found a large jar which had been cracked open and lay on its side in a triangular space protected by thick wood beams from the hull; he reached into it. Like a fallen pile of coins a number of round clay disks lay in a frozen cascade, the upper layer covered in sand and sediment which had secured it in its ageless disarray. Oscar prised at one of the disks which broke into three pieces which he threw away in haste. He could now release others from the cascade and carefully prised one free. He swam up to the surface and turned the disk to catch the light of the refracted evening sun. A spiral of impressed pictographs showed through the crust of lime.

Oscar swam breathlessly back to the inflatable, grabbed at the rope and pulled himself strongly up over the side. Water streamed from his skin and froze in droplets which caught the sun and sparkled like stars. He reached into his pocket and tugged the hard clay free of the wet cloth. He held it up to the dying sun and the vulture came steeply down from the high cliffs on a wave of cool air to see.

"Bloody hell," Brian touched the roundel gently as it lay in Oscar's charcoal-drawn palm.

"It's the Phaistos Disk."

The vulture swooped down over the inflatable then soared up into the darkening evening sky to resume its endless patrol.

Chapter seventeen

The headland beyond Maranes was dark against the brittle blue of the early evening sky when Mateo came down the hill behind Lavris and crossed the plateau where seas of red earth lay vivid between white islands of limestone clints. As sure-footed as a kri-kri, he strode over jagged rocks and harsh green scrub and descended the rocky path to the taverna where Manolis sat at his customary table. The old man nodded and the dog Argus raised his head and beat a heavy tail in the dust of the patio in greeting as Mateo leant his staff against the taverna wall and wiped the sweat from his forehead with a black cloth neckerchief. He went into the building and came out drinking from a dewy bottle of cold water. He drank most of it and poured the dregs onto his hair where it disappeared to re-emerge as tiny streams in the gullies of his walnut face. He combed his fingers through his hair and threw tiny droplets into the setting sun.

Mateo walked to the wall at the edge of the patio and looked out at the bright anonymous surface of the sea. The sea was not familiar to him as were the mountains and the bay looked threatening; there was a suggestion that fearful things lay in wait, ready to strike from under the protective mirror of the sky. He turned to where Manolis was shuffling an ancient pack of cards in the course of his endless games of patience. The old man grunted and pointed across the bay. "That boat has been there all day. It sailed a short distance early this morning from under the point and has moved no further."

Mateo returned from the seawall and sat down at Manolis' table, scratching Argus' belly with his bare toes. The dog stirred and groaned softly, content to be with his two masters; he licked his nose with a long wet tongue and turned on to his back in the dust, dangling heavy paws in the air. Mateo rested two callused brown feet on his matted fur. The evening breeze stirred the leaves on the vine, making a soft rustling sound to contrast with the shush of small waves on the shore. "I wonder what they are doing, out there all day."

Manolis grunted in acknowledgement of the question and

resumed his game, dealing long lines of grubby cards across the wooden table in the fading light. Mateo stared thoughtfully out across the enigmatic sea, toes comforted in fur, and the dog made quiet sounds of contentment.

That evening in Lossos the inflatable dinghy lay silently on the black water and moved imperceptibly on unseen currents, tugging tentatively at its mooring. On the slats of its damp floor a pile of wet towels hid a clay disk from the palace of Phaistos. A rising full moon threw a pewter sheen onto the sky behind the cliffs and one or two stars struggled against its challenge, scarcely twinkling in the still night. The beacon on the island sent a coded signal over the water to the crowded tavernas. In a corner of Andreas' restaurant, isolated as if already ostracised, the three divers sat over the remains of their dinner. Empty beer bottles formed a defensive palisade between them and the rest of the relaxed and chattering crowd of tourists. Brian and Oscar smoked tobacco-sparse cigarettes which flared like tapers when lit and expired as quickly.

"So what are we going to do now?"

For active men the silence was unusually reflective and long. After a while Brian broke the quiet, "There is a tide …", he muttered.

"Tide, what tide? There's no tide here."

"Not that sort of tide, I mean a sort of choice, it's from some play, I think, maybe Shakespeare. We have to decide, and when we've decided, well, that's it. There's no going back. The moving finger and all that."

"What finger, where the hell do fingers come into it? You're talking rubbish."

"No I'm not," Brian was stung into defence. "I mean it; we've two choices. We either tell everybody or we don't. If we tell then we'll be slung in gaol for disturbing the wreck; if we don't, then we're stealing the stuff and we'll probably get shot by Theseus and dumped in the sea. We're in the shit both ways. And if that's the case, we may as well go for the money. But it's bloody dangerous." He looked gloomily out to sea to where the dinghy with its purloined cargo tested its painter as if contemplating escape.

"What about that bloke you spoke about, the one in Athens?" Robert seemed less daunted by the choice than the others. "Do you think it's worth talking to him? From what you said he may be the sort of bloke we need. I don't think we should just give this chance up, without finding out what's possible – I mean, it's not often things like this come up. There's a chance of making some real money here."

The others thought for a while. Oscar fidgeted and looked at his watch.

"Let her wait for a bit," Brian said, "Let's just try and sort this out before you go off shagging. Concentrate on something else for once."

Oscar was hurt. "I don't think we should do this, it's not right. People have been good to us here and it's a good place, I don't think we should steal the stuff."

"You don't think at all, that's your problem. Do you want to be penniless forever? It's old stuff, doesn't belong to anybody. We wouldn't hurt anyone. Just cash in while we can. And cash there will be, if I'm right. Those disks will bring millions. Want to miss out on that?"

"Oh, the cash would be nice but – I don't know – it just doesn't seem right. Look, I've got to go. If it makes you feel better, ring your bloke in Athens and see what he says. I'm off now."

"Christ, she's really got him tied up, stupid sod," Robert sneered after the tall figure as Oscar crossed through a patch of lamplight on his way to the bar, "Can't think straight. So," he went on, looking hard at Brian, "are you going to ring him, or not? If you're going to, you'd better do it now, before it gets too late."

Brian had drunk enough to arrive at that state when stupidity mixed with greed seemed rational and when thought was clear but skewed. It seemed logical to ring up a man he hardly knew in the middle of the night and ask him if he would help them to steal some ancient treasure. He was certain to help, Brian had no doubts. "OK, then," he said, and got up from the table. Beer bottles rattled dangerously. "Have you got a phonecard?"

120

Chapter eighteen

The area north-west of Omonia in Athens is a concrete maze of rect-angular building blocks through which runs Liossion, a wider diago-nal road. The buildings are five or six storeys high and the narrow streets hold the heat and smog of a traffic-strangled evening and reject the bright sky. Dusk sets in early as the darkness is attracted by the dust and gathers in the deep canyons, spreading slowly upwards to eventually overcome even those who live on the upper floors. It is an area of flats and apartments made barely tolerable by crowded balconies on which families congregate to catch the last of the light and the tail of the brief evening breeze. Caged birds sing plaintive songs and struggling plants strive upwards from these balconies, pro-viding a reminder of natural things forgotten in the urban desert. Families gather to seek escape from stuffy rooms and to gossip with those who perch on similar balconies nearby. In the darkness televi-sion sets talk to empty rooms and strange blue light travels slowly through the hot stale air. Heavy men clad in white singlets spread their legs widely on flimsy chairs and smoke and drink beer; their wives, in thin black dresses, perch on the edges of chairs and sip bitter teas, perpetually suspended between tasks. The balconies slowly empty as the night deepens and the sky becomes one with the turgid dark of the streets; families retire to airless rooms and restless love-less nights and the late traffic makes a subdued sporadic growl, more intrusive than the constant roar of the day.

In clubs and bars men and girls smoke and sweat, heat excites the night and sex stirs the darkness. Bright lights and music trap people in oases of dance and lust but outside the streets are empty save for the cats and the rubbish.

Most of Athens is asleep but on isolated balconies lonely men sit, torn between the need for sleep and a hunger for the lights and the girls.

One narrow balcony, on the fourth floor of a six-storey block of flats, faced north and was lit by the garish light from an enormous revolving advertising sign on top of the building opposite. Its occupant smoked a small cigar and appeared red or blue or white with the change from Marlboro, to Ouzo 12, to Wonderbra.

Nikos liked the changing colours and blew smoke into each as its turn came; he had lived under its rainbow for twelve years and had become completely inured to its impact. Rare visitors to the flat wanted curtains drawn despite the heat, unable to stand the awful regularity which altered faces from alien to florid to sick within as many minutes, but Nikos rather liked the effect. It made him feel that he was still part of the colourful action of the city around him without having to do anything about it. He missed his sign when he was away from Athens and, under it, never felt alone. In fact, he thought as he blew blue smoke which changed to white in midstream, he was really less lonely when Jenny was away. He could sit out here and smoke, and he could, if he wanted to, go out and drink with men or pick up lovely girls; it was all possible, whereas, when Jenny was here, it wasn't, and he felt trapped in his multicoloured flat.

The telephone rang in the dark room and he pictured his beautiful wife sitting on the moonlit terrace in Sounion thinking of him and missing him, and felt guilty.

He imagined her slim tall figure, simultaneously dressed in her white trouser suit and naked with uplifted tight breasts pointing small nipples at the moon. He tried to recall her face as the red light shone through the thick dusk of Athens. He could remember the sun-bleached blonde hair as it fell from the pale forehead to curve on her neat shoulders; he could recall the thin rising line of her eyebrows and the soft pale lips, he could picture her patrician, English beauty. But he could not, try as he might, recall her eyes. He knew that they were blue, but, for the life of him, he could not see into them. It was as if there was a veil across her gaze; he could see her shape and colour but not her spirit. After twelve years of marriage this remote English girl was still a mystery to him; she shared his bed and his life and yet remained an enigma. Possibly, he thought, throwing the cigar end down to the street below, this was why he was, well, happier, when she was away. Nikos felt that he knew less of Jenny now than when he had met, courted, and married her, all in six months. She had been twenty-two then, beautiful in a remote, sexless way; pale and thin in contrast to the dark Athenian girls he was used to. He had been, still was, he reminded himself on the coloured balcony, a promising writer, knowledgeable on the affairs of Athens and particularly on archaeological matters. He contributed articles to the *Eleftherotypia*, to *The Times*, to the *International Herald Tribune*, to *Le Monde*. 'Our Athens correspondent'; 'Our archaeological representative'; 'A close associate of the British School'. These had been his bylines. Nikos Kontos had been at all the parties, all the soirées, his saturnine good looks were matched to a strong body which he kept fit by regular workouts; popular and sophisticated, witty and well-dressed, he was the target of many an Athenian mother.

And then the whirlwind marriage to the tragic English orphan. The newspaper photographs were imprinted on people's minds, images dramatic and terrible. The stark flames of the crashed aircraft lighting the night and, against the flames, the black outline of the young girl, running, arms outstretched in horror, to the funeral pyre of her father. These images had affected a whole world. And Nikos had caught the young girl in her grief and carried her away.

Alone in the alien world of Athens, an alien also in her own country, Jenny had been easy prey to the world-wise Nikos. Although she had loved her father, Gerald Winchester had not been the easiest of men, regarding life as a duty to be borne rather than to be enjoyed. His role as the Head of the British School of Archaeology in Athens had been executed with authority and not a little talent, but in an unbendingly anachronistic manner. He was the sort of Englishman who wore a tweed suit while digging a desert site in forty-degree temperatures. To the orphaned Jenny, Nikos and the delights of Athens were refreshment, a colourful exciting contrast to her earlier life, and she embraced it eagerly. Their contrasting good looks, he dark and she fair, and their transparent if sometimes brittle happiness made them welcome in the fashionable bars and clubs of Kolonaki where they were popular guests. Nikos introduced Jenny to the boisterous young Greek society of dance and drink and good food and she introduced him to the intellectual ex-patriot society of which her father had been an unbending leader. She was popular for her innocent good looks, he for his apparent success and style. They had seemed a talented and happy couple and their marriage in the Anglican church on Leoforos was attended by a glamorous mixture of Greek and foreign society.

Jenny had been only six when her mother died, shortly after her father had been appointed to his job in Athens. She had been taken from her safe and familiar school in Alcester and sent to the British School in Athens. Terrified by the alien city she found a surrogate mother in Mary, the wife of Kenneth Ashworth, the School's expert on ancient scripts. Mary had guided her through the difficulties of childhood and under her gentle direction the girl had become a beautiful and polished young woman. They had also become firm friends and when, in Jenny's last year at Oxford, her father had died in the Athens aircrash, she had moved into the Ashworth's flat in the leafy enclave of the British School. At her wedding she had been given away by Kenneth despite Mary's unspoken reservations about the union.

Kenneth Ashworth had been an unexpected appointment as the new Head of the British Archaeological School in Greece. His was an academic rather than administrative background and his speciality in deciphering ancient scripts clashed badly with the chores of management. His inability to fill both roles made him increasingly unhappy to the point where he was seriously considering returning to a university job in England when Mary, lonely after Jenny's departure to go up to St Hilda's, decided to get involved with the School administration. She found that she had a talent for management and a taste for the politics of archaeology. Under her new-found enthusiasm and interest Kenneth was released from the tedium and constrains of management to enjoy again his academic role. Mary now ran the School with an efficiency which it had not experienced for years and thoroughly enjoyed the responsibility. She also enjoyed her husband more. Free from the worries of management he relaxed and became once again an entertaining companion and lover; their marriage had never been happier than in these last few years.

Mary had been encouraging in the early days of the relationship between Jenny and Nikos, glad that Jenny was joining in the young Athenian society and finding new interests. But when the romance deepened and Jenny talked of marriage, she was not so sure. With her new efficiency Mary started to make enquiries about the Greek and found that he was not quite the well-connected success that he liked to pretend. The published work was sparse, the connections tenuous, the wealthy family non-existent. Mary dug deeper and unearthed Nikos' tentative and amateur involvement with the underworld of stolen antiques where he appeared occasionally useful rather than profitably participant. She had smiled wryly to herself while debating the merits of success against failure in illegal activity. The further she dug, the less she admired the man, and the more careful she had to be in her relations with Jenny. Mary did not want to lose the younger woman's affection and trust and yet she feared for her future. It was almost a relief when Jenny announced that she and Nikos were getting married; the time for confrontation had passed and Mary concentrated on the details and the arrangements and kept her disquiet to herself.

And for the first few months all had looked well; Jenny blossomed in her new love and threw herself into the role of an Athenian house-wife with pleasure. She and Nikos moved into a new flat, admittedly not in one of the best areas of town, but appropriate to a young and mobile couple. The flat was furnished with an eclectic mix of old English intellectual, and cheap, popular Greek. One wall bore a torn poster of Santorini and an original early Matisse; a graceful Queen Anne table contrasted with clumsy, sombre Greek furniture. The bookcase contained a pile of football magazines and a beautiful set of first edition leather-bound Thackeray. A cheap modern earthen-ware jug bearing a crude ink drawing of a satyr with an enormous phallus stood next to an elegant Waterford glass vase. Contrasts abounded, two cultures brought together and not at ease.

Socially, their life was busy and Jenny and Nikos showed an open affection which impressed the reserved Athenians. They enter-tained well and were popular guests and their many commitments put a strain on Jenny's friendship with Mary. The two English women met infrequently and had now incompatible interests; Jenny was im-mersed in the trivialities of her social life with her husband and Mary was busy with the administration of the School. A gulf opened be-tween them which neither could bridge; Mary could not condemn Jenny's life, Jenny could not admit to the growing difficulties in be-ing married to Nikos.

In the late summer of the year after her marriage, when Athens was sweltering in a heat wave and the smog-laden streets grew more stifling day by day, Jenny received a rare phone-call from Mary. "I'm in Sounion, at the villa; there's a breeze from the sea and fresh fish and a cold Chablis. Why don't you come down for a few days?"

Nikos grunted and sweated in the heat. "I am happy here, this is my town. I do not wish to leave." He took a cold beer from the fridge and drank noisily. "Why don't you go by yourself, you'll enjoy it?" He was pleased by his own magnanimity. "Yes, take a few days off, I can look after myself. Don't worry about me." He caught his breath at his sudden lust for freedom and had difficulty in not ap-pearing too enthusiastic. "You must go; Mary will be disappointed if you don't. I'll miss you; it will be the first time that we have been apart, but it will be good for you to have some fresh air and a bit of exercise." Nikos almost choked on his duplicity, treading a fine di-vide between his suddenly acknowledged need to be free of her and his false solicitude.

And Jenny was not blameless, either. She wanted to go to Sounion, and she wanted to go without Nikos.

"Are you sure? You'll be all right, won't you? I'll make some meals for you so you don't need to cook, and I'll catch up on the washing, and go down to the supermarket and get some things in. You'll be all right. I won't be gone for long. And I'll miss you, too."

And already her heart was singing like a newly-released bird, revelling in the thought of freedom, of swimming in clear fresh water, of being free from that night-dominating sign and its relentless revolving colours. And, dare she admit it, free of his coarse sweaty lovemaking and the smells and oppression of his gross black-haired body. And the boring frantic evenings surrounded by smoke and drink and noise through which they stumbled in a desperate attempt to remain together. In those few moments, they took the first steps on the slope to the betrayal of their marriage, and there was no way back.

At Sounion, the first night she had spent apart from her husband in a year and a half, Jenny cried endlessly, regretting the loss of her old friends and her frantic attempt to share Nikos' life through the bars and clubs and the alcohol. Now Mary had reminded her that there was a life apart from Nikos. She realised how much she hated life with him.

On the same night Nikos realised how much he had missed the bright lights and the girls and the music and cigarette smoke as it swirled across the dance floor. How much he missed the knowing kiss, the tantalising hand on his thigh; how little he missed the cold thin blonde woman who was his wife. Each celebrated their first night apart in their own way; she in regret, he in lust.

From then on they spent more time away from each other and as her ties with Nikos weakened, Jenny's friendship with Mary recovered. Now Nikos found excuses to be away on business and Jenny found new reasons to be with Mary and at the School rediscovered her dormant interest in archaeology. She blossomed again, becoming the clear-eyed contented girl she had once been, free from the late nights and the desperate drinking.

The telephone rang in the dark room and Nikos immediately felt guilty. He got up quickly from his chair on the balcony in the hot Athenian night and stumbled through the gloom of his cluttered room to answer it. "*Ne.*"

It took him a long moment to adjust to the fact that this was not Jenny; the beer and the heat made a fog in his mind.

"*Ne. Nikos K ....*"

"Hi. This Brian, from England; we met some time ago, in Athens, and in Turkey; I'm a diver, do you remember? We talked about antiques and selling them and stuff ..." Like all Brian's questions the statement ended with an upward inflexion, seeking reassurance. Nikos had a good memory for voices and the inflexion recalled a tall thin pale youth who smoked thin cigarettes. "*Ne*. I remember. One moment." Nikos put the phone down and went to get another beer. He sat down in an uncomfortable armchair and lit a cigar. He picked up the phone again. "Yes. I remember. *Ti kaneis*? What can I do for you?"

Brian stood on pebbles under a lamp-post on the beach at Lossos with a dog-fight of insects circling the naked bulb above his head; the newly-risen full moon poured a metal pathway to his feet. Robert cast a clear grey shadow against a white wall as he threw small stones to form circles in the velvet black sea.

"Yes. I remember. What can I do for you?"

Brian always disappointed himself in his responses. He wanted to be quick and clear and dominant, but always failed. "Well," he said, never a good start.

Nikos blew out a stream of smoke towards the open window where it suddenly turned Marlboro red. "Yes?"

"We've been doing a job, down here ..."

"Where's that?"

"Oh, yes. Down here, in Lossos, in Crete ..."

"In Crete, *Endaxi*. What job?"

"Well, it doesn't really matter ..."

Already the initiative had slipped away. "Anyway, we've been diving and found some stuff, you know, treasure and things ..."

"And what has this to do with me?"

Brian made a valiant attempt to recover the initiative, aware that Nikos had taken charge and that Robert was sneering impatiently. "When we last met I was working on the Ulu Burun wreck and you asked if I could help you ..."

"I remember it well, and I also recall that it was you who needed my help. But, never mind, what have you got this time, who knows about it, what do you want me to do?"

"Well ..." Brian disliked this barrage of questions; he was supposed to be in charge. "Well, we have some swords ... and a jug. I think it's very old."

"Come on now," Nikos relaxed and took a deep drag on his cigar, "Tell me the story and I'll do my best to help. Start at the beginning." He leaned back in his uncomfortable chair and drank from the bottle; patting his stomach he burped quietly into the telephone. He would listen to the Englishman for a while, it couldn't do

127

any harm and would pass a little time. Brian's tale poured out into the hot Athens night and was coloured red, white and blue by the revolving sign. Nikos listened without comment, except to ask again if anyone else knew of the discovery. At the end of the disjointed tale he was not impressed and was more than slightly irritated by Brian's rather plaintive claims about the quality and quantity of his finds. He yawned noisily into the mouthpiece. "Ok. *Katalava*, I understand. What I want you to do is to fax me a drawing of each of the better pieces, then I'll decide what to do. Ring me tomorrow night, say about seven? *Kalinikta*." He put the phone down and took another beer and cigar out on to the balcony, pleased with the way in which he had handled the call. He had shown little enthusiasm and yet had left the door open in case anything really interesting turned up; that was professional, he told himself complacently, scratching his stomach under his dirty singlet.

Oscar drew well and responded with enthusiasm to Brian's fatally imprecise request to draw 'a few of the better things'. His sketches of the swords and dagger, of the double-headed axe and the elegant ewer were clear and detailed. His ingots and cups were good in outline but it was when he came to the disk that he excelled himself and drew a perfect likeness. The others had gone for a shower and a beer; he did not show them what he had done and used Gillian's ancient fax to send the drawings to Athens where they fell to the dusty floor in Nikos' apartment to await his return. Oscar had begun to feel excluded by the others and, although still uneasy about their aims, he was pleased with his contribution and glad to be involved again.

Hot dusk was already filling the caverns of the city's streets when Nikos picked up the curled sheets. Taking them onto the balcony, he smoothed them out over the small dusty table where last night's beer bottles still congregated. He had decided that he did not want to become involved in this messy business with people he hardly knew and couldn't trust; besides there was no money in archaeological finds these days, there were too many professional gangs involved. These gangs, like the *Clandestini* in Italy, made it virtually impossible for the amateur to operate and anyone foolish enough to try found that the rewards were small and difficult to collect. As in all walks of life it was big business which thrived, and, if he annoyed the big operators, the small man was eliminated, totally.

Nikos had decided not to be involved; he unravelled the spirals of paper and placed them face down on the table, using an empty bottle to stop them curling. Going to the fridge he took a fresh bottle of beer, opened it with a practised flick and returned to his chair on the balcony. He put a foot on the table and took a long drink, enjoying the cooler draughts of air which crept down from the rooftops. He lit a cigar and reached across to lift the bottle from the faxes which immediately resumed their curvature. With one hand he held the top of the papers and unrolled the sheaf with the other, still clutching the damp bottle. A nice jug, he thought, probably Minoan if the pattern was accurately drawn, not a bad piece. Two swords, difficult to tell the shape and form of the hilts from the drawing, could be interesting if they were reasonably intact, some cups with Middle-Minoan decoration. The third sheet rolled back into its tight coil before he could see the drawing on it. Nikos put down the beer bottle and straightened out the sheet and Oscar's drawing of the Phaistos disc unravelled. He held it up, annoyed and slightly disappointed that this was turning into a hoax, that the British were laughing at him. Angrily he crumpled the drawing and went to throw it over the balcony when he was suddenly aware that something about it wasn't quite right. He went to his bookcase and found a sketch of the disc found by Professor Levi at Phaistos in 1910 and compared it with Oscar's drawing.

Hours passed slowly as Nikos sat in the deepening darkness willing the phone to ring. "Brian. *Ti kaneis*. How are you? I am pleased that you have rung again. Thank you for the faxes. Did you draw them yourself? Oh, it was Oscar. He's very good. I look forward to meeting him."

Nikos' oily charm slid down the wire into Brian's receptive ear. The Englishman had had a bad day in Lossos not knowing what to do and on the pointed end of Robert's cynicism. They had not returned to the wreck, preferring to take Jackie on a swimming trip down the coast to Rodhia. Jackie had thoroughly enjoyed the sail and the company of the three men although she felt that Brian and Robert were a bit quiet. But Oscar more than made up for his friends by being his usual cheerful self; his affection for Jackie was growing and they were glad to have a whole day together instead of a few snatched hours of drink and sex.

"So," Brian said to the telephone, flatly and pessimistic, "What do you think, then?"

The handset spoke back to him; there seemed no connection with anyone at the other end of the line. He could not picture Nikos and had no concept of the dingy apartment and its changing illumination;

129

the words were mechanical comment from the instrument alone. "The swords are good, and the jug is beautiful; I think it's Minoan, probably around the end of the second palace period. They could be valuable. What do you really want me to do? I could find out if there is a buyer for this stuff, if you like? The disk could be particularly interesting to the right person."

Brain froze. "What disk?"

"You know, the one Oscar drew, very unusual stuff. Could be really valuable."

Brian put his hand over the telephone. "Oh shit!" he hissed at Robert, "Bloody Oscar, he's sent the bastard a drawing of one of the fucking disks. Oh, hell. What do I do now?"

"Oh, Christ. What a dick. What a bloody stupid thing to do. Didn't you tell him not to?" Robert thought rapidly. "OK, look, keep him talking, say it was Oscar being daft, having a joke. Don't tell him anymore."

Brian laughed into the phone, falsely, even to his own ears. "Sorry, Nikos, thought I'd lost you for a moment. Disk? That's just Oscar, having a joke, I didn't see the drawings; there's no Phaistos disk."

"Joke, *ne? Endaxi.* Pity. It would be good if there was anything like that. OK." Nikos grinned to himself and slurped his beer. Cheerful, discursive, informed, competent, he played Brian like a fish on the telephone line, dragging him in. Stupid British, of course there was a disk; Oscar wouldn't have drawn it if there wasn't, not in all that detail and showing new symbols. So that was their game, trying to get him to help them to shift the ordinary stuff and keeping the best for themselves. He'd ignore it for the time being, pretend he was convinced. He went on to talk about the wreck, his tone interested, affable; much warmer than on the previous night.

Brian relaxed and grinned at Robert, wiping his brow dramatically.

Nikos finished his cigar and threw it to fall like a meteorite through the murky dust of Athens to the street beneath. "OK, I need to make arrangements. I'll call you back when I know what I can do. I'll be in touch soon. Take care." He lit another cigar. "Brian," he said, "Just one more thing – if you didn't see the drawing, how did you know Oscar had sketched the Phaistos disk? *Kalinikta.*"

He put down the phone and went to get another beer.

Returning to the balcony, he looked out at the steamy Athens night, deep in thought. Another Phaistos disk, how about that? After all this time. It would be worth millions, and he wasn't talking *drachmes.*

At the other end of the suddenly dead phone, Brian tightened his grip on the sticky plastic, slimy with his sweat and his sudden realisation of what he'd said, trying to crush it in his dismay. First bloody Oscar, and now he himself had given the game away. He looked blankly at Robert. "Oh, bloody hell, now I've really cocked it. That bloody Oscar." As usual, Brian wanted to blame someone else.

Robert looked at him coldly in the moonlight. "It was you who said it was a Phaistos disk. I didn't know Oscar had drawn it. What a fuckin' balls-up. The disks were going to make our future and now you and that stupid black bugger have given them away. What a cock-up."

Brian stamped off along the beach throwing angry pebbles into the black sea. Robert followed him across the shingle and caught him up, "Shit," he said.

Brian's anger ebbed. "Yeah, shit." He threw another pebble at the moon. "OK. OK. I know I should have checked what Oscar sent. I'm sorry."

"Yeah, OK. Shit happens."

Brian stopped. He couldn't be too hard on Oscar, or on himself, it wasn't in his nature. "Look," he said, "I suppose you could look at it this way. It might have been better to mention the disks, to bring him in, you know? Nikos knows what he wants and how to get rid of it. We need him. All we have to do is to get some more gear up, particularly swords, daggers, jewellery, that sort of stuff, and he'll be happy. Then we hide it somewhere and our Greek friend will come down and take it off to Athens, maybe with one of the discs. So we'll know the contact and can flog the rest of the disks to him without Nikos knowing. Come on, it's not so bad." He shrugged. "Let's get some beer."

Robert spoke quietly against the shush of the sea. "Yeah, we'll talk our way out of it later. But believe me, there's no way that Greek bastard is getting his hands on those disks; no bloody way." They crunched across the pebbles in the calm moonlit night and drank to an uncertain future which became more probable with each bottle.

Back on his perch under the revolving sign in Athens Nikos patted his stomach complacently; he had, he thought, sown the seeds well, concealed where his real interest lay. Let the Englishmen have the baubles; if that disk, and there could be more, was what he thought it might be, it was beyond price and as soon as it was in his hands, well, *adio* English. They couldn't complain – who would listen? He'd give them a few thousand, enough to keep them quiet, stress the difficulties of disposal, and then cash in. The kudos would be his and he had no doubts about the value. There were collectors in England and the United States who would be desperate for such a prize, provenance or not. He rubbed his hands and pictured a nice villa on Aegina and a good flat in Kolonaki, that would show Jenny. But, then again, he thought, why Jenny? Time for a little freedom. She would be stuffy about it, anyway. So he substituted a couple of blondes and a redhead instead. What a delightful prospect. He would start to make a few enquiries. He picked up the phone again and dialled.

Many beers later, with the moon high and bright over Lossos, Brian looked up and blew smoke-rings in the still air. "We'll have to do it tomorrow. What do you think?"

"Theseus comes back tomorrow night, so we've got to do it tomorrow, no alternative. I don't fancy trying to steal stuff with that brigand around."

Robert was drunkenly adamant. "So we take what we can find, hide it somewhere from where we can shift it later, and then return in triumph to Lossos to announce our fantastic discovery."

"Yeah, that's it," Brian was impressed, "When did you think of that?"

"Just now," Robert admitted, drunkenly. "D'y like it?"

"It's great, we get the gear and we get the credit for finding the wreck as well. Great stuff. And we must take the disks, as many as we can. That's where the money is; they're our jackpot."

"Well, we'll see about that. If that Greek bastard doesn't get his hands on them; we'll have to keep a tight watch on the bugger. Be canny, that's what I say."

"Oh, come on, give the bloke a chance."

"Oh, yeah, but he gets no chance from me. I say we stick to him like glue until he's done the deal and we see the colour of his money, and if that means going to Athens with him, we'll go to bloody Athens. This is our job and I'm not going to let some Greek welsh on us." Robert hiccupped quietly, "Come on, let's have more beer, I'm thirsty." He grinned to himself, "Did you like that, by the way? Greek welsh?"

"You must be pissed to make jokes like that, it's not like you. This place is certainly getting to you."

They raised their glasses to the moon. "Disks for us, pay off Nikos, and Theseus can have the wreck to do what he likes with. I'll drink to that. Not a bad day's work."

The moon was not impressed.

Chapter nineteen

A new day. A new dive. But different, this time with a clear purpose and with determination. An early start. The inflatable was under the lee of the headland before Mateo, brushing the uneven stone of the Lavris taverna floor in the fresh morning, woke Argus. The dog stretched front legs then back legs, tail quivering, yawning widely. Mateo went to sit on the low sea wall and Argus came to sit beside him, resting his matted head on the man's knee. Mateo scratched his ears and they both looked out across the bay.

"They're there again," Mateo remarked to the dog. "What are they up to?"

Argus yawned again.

"That's not very helpful. You'll have to do better." Mateo cuffed the dog's head, got up, and finished the brushing. Argus went back to sleep under Manolis' table. The morning was silent and still again.

In the cold, dark green sea depths of early morning three divers worked around the wreck. Oscar was taking disks from within the large pithos and placing them carefully in a plastic tray borrowed from its more prosaic purpose of holding tomatoes. The upper disks of the cascade were cemented together and had to be prised apart with care. This was difficult work in the near darkness and it took Oscar three dives before he could be sure that he had recovered them all. The filled tray was too heavy for him to move and, after covering it with weed, Oscar climbed wearily into the dinghy and sat drying in the sun.

Robert worked on the upper part of the wreck; he had been able to move some beams and was searching by touch alone through a pile of broken storage jars which appeared to have been thrown together in the ship's hold when it turned over in falling down the sand slope. A torch was useless as the fine sand rose to form an impenetrable mist and hung in the water. It was hard work and unproductive; at lunchtime Robert had only a small earthenware plate, a couple of small cups, what might have been a milk bowl, and three coloured glass ingots to add to his best find of the day, a short sword with a broad blade. The blade of the sword was badly corroded but seemed to have a pattern incised along its length. Robert buried it with care in the soft sand near the big white boulder, and marked its grave.

The plan was to move as much as they could salvage from the wreck to a safe hiding place in a small sea cave between boulders at the apex of the bay. Once in the cave the treasure would be split, the first and smallest part they would take to Lossos as evidence of the discovery. The disks and the most valuable of the rest they intended to keep and would be left in the cave. At the end of a hard day's work they had accumulated a couple of swords, the dagger, the axe-head and several ingots of copper and glass together with a collection of bowls, jugs and a few larger pithoi. And, of course, the collection of disks. Ferrying the finds into the cave during the afternoon when a number of walkers and tourists used the path around the bay made the task more difficult than they had imagined and as evening came on Brian called a halt to the diving. They wearily raised the anchor and motored slowly across the bay and round the Maranes headland.

Mateo had watched the dinghy all day. He had no doubt about what they were doing, it was clear even to a landsman that they were working hard underwater; a diver would come to the surface, climb into the dinghy, change his air bottles and fall back in to reappear forty minutes later. So much was obvious. But it was not clear why they were diving; Mateo used Manolis' ancient German binoculars to watch the boat but they didn't help and he became more intrigued as the day progressed.

Manolis passed the day playing patience at his table under the vine and Argus lay asleep at his feet, their tranquillity a foil to Mateo's restlessness. When the dinghy finally moved off, Mateo came to Manolis' table and sat down and put his bare feet on Argus. The dog lifted its head to check, recognised his master, sighed and went back to sleep.

"What are they doing out there?"

Manolis played his last cheating card, completed his tattered columns in triumph and raised his lined face to look at Mateo and then out to sea. He scratched his head through the black net of his headband. "They're diving."

"I know they're diving, but what for? That's what's important."

"Why is it important? Does it matter what they are doing? All foreigners are mad. They do stupid things all the time, they have no sense of peace. I have watched these three work through the day, and yet they have brought nothing to the surface." Manolis grinned his gapped smile at Mateo. "And they have taken nothing down into the sea."

Mateo looked at the old man. "I thought you were not watching," he said.

"Oh, I watch; and I think. And I think, if they take nothing into the sea, and bring nothing up and yet work hard all day, then they are moving things under the sea. They hope not to be seen. But it is obvious, to me."

The old man yawned widely and patted Argus. "It is clear. Now you must find out what they are moving and where they have put it." He put both hands on the table, on the tottering columns of cards, and moved them slowly in opposing circles to shuffle.

Mateo looked at him in surprise, "I didn't think you were interested."

"I am not. But I thought you were."

The old man assembled the cards into an irregular stack and put four from the top of the pack down on the table; not liking them, he replaced them with a further four which he preferred and continued his solitary game.

Mateo looked out across the silver water to the headland opposite and followed the bay round with his eyes; "That's where I would go if I had to hide anything," he thought. "There, under that pile of big boulders where there are small caves. That's where it will be." He turned back to Manolis. "I will go to look, tonight."

Back on the dinghy the discussion was subdued. The divers were disappointed with what they had found and Robert wanted to keep it all. "What's the point in letting your friend and Theseus have any of it? I say that we should keep the lot and get out of here before Theseus gets back. If we go directly to Sfakia we could be in Iraklion in the morning and Athens by tomorrow night, sell the gear and be in England the next day. Why not take our chance now?"

Brian sneered. "So we take Theseus' dinghy to Sfakia, and what do we do with it then, sink it in front of the quay? If we don't sink it Theseus will know where we went, so what else do we do? And then what – get a bus to Iraklion with all this stuff in a plastic bag? And there aren't any buses now until tomorrow anyway. And we'll probably pass Theseus and Dimitris on the way. Then if, just if, we get to Athens, how do you sell stolen antiquities?"

Brian hadn't impressed himself as much with his logic for a long time and sat back, looking pleased.

"Aye, well, mebee, but ..."

Oscar butted in, "I think we should take all the stuff and give it to Theseus. He'll know what to do with it. I don't like the idea of stealing it at all. And I don't want to leave like that. Let's be sensible."

"But it's not sensible to give up the chance of making some money, is it?" Robert sneered at the black man. "You're just thinking with your dick as usual."

Oscar looked at the Scotsman who shrank away from his glare. "Sometimes you are a right shit, aren't you; a nasty little sod. Do what the hell you like with the gear, but leave me out, got it? I don't want anything more to do with it."

"Come on, you two, drop it," Brian cut in quickly. "I'll tell you what we'll do. We mustn't offend Theseus so we'll give him a few bits. But we'll let Nikos make the arrangements for selling the rest; we should make a few bob out of the jugs and swords and so on. And we keep all the disks for ourselves and flog them later. OK? Any better ideas?"

Robert grunted and Oscar was silent.

"OK, then. Let's go back, get the things we are going to keep and then sail back to Lossos in triumph. Come on, this way we win all the hands. Cheer up, you miserable buggers."

Those pieces which they were going to keep and the plastic tray with its priceless cargo of disks were buried in soft sand in a narrow sea cave between big boulders at the head of the bay. Brian, fully in charge now, had selected the items which they were going to admit to finding. In the bottom of the dinghy were two small cups painted black with white chevrons on a band below the lip and an earthenware plate about twenty centimetres across. There were two copper ingots and two of coloured glass and three large pithoi. And the item over which there had been the greatest argument, the double headed bronze axe which now lay wrapped in two wet towels under a pile of empty air bottles in the bottom of the boat.

The sun had fallen behind the Maranes headland leaving a slight chill in the air as the dinghy left the bay and Brian looked back to where their booty lay buried. He watched a couple of tourists make their way slowly along the coastal path which lay just above the cave.

"I think we should move everything as soon as possible," he said thoughtfully. "Find somewhere up in the hills to store it. We don't know how long we will have to leave it and I'm not sure how safe it is there in the cave. If somebody doesn't find it, the sea will wash it away, or uncover it; I'd be happier if it was on dry land."

He looked up at the great grey cliffs and followed the line of the *kalderimi* to Liridiana which slowly climbed across their lower slopes. "I think I know where to hide it." He pointed to a narrow gully which turned and climbed up into the cliff before petering out in a vertical chimney.

"I once explored that gully, there's nothing in it apart from the bones of goats. No-one ever goes into it and there is a shallow cave on the left, just above a steep step, which would be ideal. I think we should move the stuff there, soon, probably in the dark. What do you think?"

Robert sulked. "Yeah, sometime."

Oscar said, cheerful again now, "Anything you say, boss. Night would be best. There's a good moon now. Why not tonight? If we're going to do it, it should be soon."

"If t'were done 'tis best done quickly," Brian murmured. "OK," he said, "We go tonight. About twelve. We'll need a couple of rucksacks, and torches, and some rags or towels to wrap the stuff in. And wear dark clothes."

Oscar grinned, "Just like playing pirates."

Robert looked at him glumly. "Pirates end up dead," he said.

Chapter twenty

Theseus and Dimitris had not had a good day in Athens. Being forced to wait an hour for an audience with the Under-Commissioner had not improved Theseus' mood and when the 'mealy-mouthed little prick', as Theseus had described him to his face, had found convincing reasons to decline their request for grant assistance, Dimitris had only, with difficulty, smoothed feathers and contrived a dignified exit.

"I'll get that little sod. I'll get the bugger. Find out everything you can about him and I'll get him. Probably fancies little boys, *to malaka*." Theseus' anger had persisted throughout the journey to the airport and had reduced even an Olympic Air hostess to tears. Only in the car, climbing the long bends from Vrysses, did he start to relax. Yorgos, his driver, known as Mercedes George to distinguish him from the other twenty-seven men named Yorgos in Sfakia, was long experienced in his boss's moods. He watched Theseus carefully in the driving mirror to judge the right time to break his silence.

"How was Athens?"

Theseus snorted and loosened his tie. "Bloody awful, I hate the place; and I hate everyone in it, particularly little *malakas* who work for the EC."

Yorgos grinned at Dimitris through the mirror.

"Slow down for God's sake, Yorgo, I want to get home in one piece. Let's enjoy the journey."

"OK, boss, whatever you say. The launch is at Sfakia so there's no hurry."

Theseus leant back and took off his tie, carefully rolling it into a tight coil. He opened a window and the cool sweet air of the mountains of Crete swept in. With a great throw Theseus flung the tie out into the evening; it slowly uncoiled as it fell down the mountainside. "That's what I think of Athens and all its wankers. Now let's enjoy ourselves." The big man closed the window and settled back in the grey Mercedes. He grinned at Dimitris.

"Don't look so glum, Mitso, we'll win in the long run."

Dimitris looked at Yorgos in the mirror and winked. He took his own tie off and threw it out of the window as the car snaked down towards the distant blue of the Libyan Sea. "I never doubted it."

* * * * *

Lissos was like a theatre at all times of the day: the sea was the stage; the beach and the canopied restaurants and bars; the stalls. Above these rose the rooms and houses forming the circle, boxes and balconies; even the gods were there, looking down from the cliffs. The audience was sometimes sparse, often numerous, and at times the theatre was full. Sometimes the stage was empty; a few tethered boats bobbed on it, tourists in canoes crossed it, the lighting changed slowly; sometimes, when the ferries arrived or a storm struck, great casts performed impressive dramas and the cliffs made dramatic backcloths.

In the early evening as the stalls filled with early diners and the lower balconies with those enjoying the ever-varying colour of the sea with a glass of wine and a bowl of olives, the audience was always at its most numerous and attentive. They watched as a large ferry crossed to the front of the stage to discharge a straggle of late travellers onto the beach. They watched as small children swam in the wake as it left and the ripples of the boat's departure expire slowly as it rounded the island beacon and headed to the west. And now the stage was empty except for a few late swimmers and an old woman in a black dress sitting bare-legged and cool on a chair in the sea. The sky darkened and the sea-stage became silver; the lights from the tavernas brightened; evening crept in quietly.

A fast launch appeared in the east, stage right, a black point on a widening arrow, carrying two men in white shirts, lit by the last of the sun.

From stage left a second craft entered the bay; it was moving more slowly than the first as it circled the island and turned to head down to the landing stage. There were three men in it. Gillian appeared on the terrace; Jackie joined Fiona on the jetty. The audience watched from above.

The theatre lacked a sound system; the audience had to guess the dialogue from the actions of the players. The launch swept in on a steep wake, picked up its mooring with practised ease and drifted to allow its occupants to jump out onto the pier. Fiona hugged Dimitris and kissed Theseus briefly on both cheeks. Two overnight bags and two briefcases were handed up from the launch; the men shouldered the bags, picked up the cases and walked down the jetty to meet

Gillian who had descended from the terrace in her starring role. She kissed her husband respectfully and Dimitris with affection.

At the same time Robert brought the inflatable up to the other side of the pier and cut off the outboard; Oscar jumped on to the jetty and tied up before swirling Jackie around in his arms. He kissed her as Brian climbed up beside him.

The audience saw rather than heard Brian call to Theseus who clearly indicated his displeasure at the summons. They saw Theseus hesitate then put down his bags and walk back along the jetty, followed by Gillian.

Robert was seen to pass a number of objects up from the inflatable to Brian who appeared to be showing them to Theseus and Gillian. Brian handed Theseus the double-headed bronze axe and Theseus raised it high above his head and marched down the pier and across the beach to the hotel entrance. As he and Dimitris entered the wide arch the ancient axe caught the light and shivers of gold flashed around the theatre. The audience were entranced; a breath of air drifted down from the mountains and a cold and ancient hand touched the village; and the vulture floated unseen across the night sky.

The scene drew to a close and the audience turned their attention to drinks and food; the first act was over and they spent the rest of the night discussing what they had seen and guessing what the next act might bring. The actors retired to the bar, as actors do, to discuss their performance and to rehearse their lines for the next act. The props of the play, the axe and pithos and the other trophies, lay on a table between Dimitris and Theseus as the Cretans questioned Robert and Brian. The Cretans were not interested in the circumstances of the discovery or the archaeological problems or in Brian's story of how the wreck had been found. All they were concerned with was the problem of who knew what; Theseus had been initially tempted to conceal the finding of the wreck but he soon accepted that already too many people knew of it as the whole village had been witness to the dramatic arrival at the jetty.

The divers were dismissed with a curt admonishment not to return to the wreck. Disconsolate and disappointed that their role in the discovery had been so poorly appreciated, they slunk off to Georgio's taverna to drink beer and eat a rather sad moussaka. Theseus and Dimitris, with the aid of a bottle of Glenfiddich, spent the rest of the evening considering the consequences of having an archaeological site on their coast and how to turn the discovery to their personal advantage.

* * * * *

There was no sound save for the conspiratorial crunch of footsteps on pebbles as Brian and Robert crossed the beach at Lissos where the village and the sea were drenched in a progression of paler greys and deeper blacks on which a few pale lights showed. The divers left the shingle and climbed a concrete staircase which brought them into deep darkness beneath Jackie's open window; Robert threw small stones which clattered alarmingly onto a marble floor. A dim light showed like a halo around Oscar's head; only his teeth and eyes showed like holes in a mask.

"Bugger off," Oscar said quietly as Jackie squeaked in the background.

"Come on, you randy black sod, there's work to be done," Robert hissed, sibilant in the stillness, suddenly jealous of Oscar and the girl in the dark crumpled bed. His quick anger stung Oscar into action.

"OK. I'm coming. I'll catch you up; get going."

Brian and Robert emerged from the shadow and followed a stone-grey path around the headland to where the white walls of a chapel reflected the moonlight. Each bright rock of the rough track lay in a pool of shadow, making their progress difficult and, despite the cool night, they were soon sweating, partly from the exertion, partly from a feeling that a threshold had been crossed, a threshold of legality. From tonight none of the three would ever be free of guilt. This nocturnal journey was long and hard and only one- way.

Oscar caught them up as they came to the sea cave; in its depths what had been a translucent green sea during the day was now transformed into an ominous slapping black wetness. It took resolution to lower oneself into those cold depths in the dark and the light from Brian's small torch served only to emphasise the fears which lurked beneath the surface. Everyone was reluctant to make the first move until Oscar took the lead; he slipped off his sandals and his baggy trousers and, jumping noisily into the water, splashed into the cave. What had seemed an easy place to store the artefacts during the day had been transformed into a labyrinth in the dark and it was a very wet Oscar who eventually found where the treasures were buried by treading on one of the swords. He was soaked and tired by the time they had found all the pieces and set off to carry the booty up to the narrow gully in the hills above Lavris. The track was not easy in the dark and they did not dare to use a torch until Philikas was well behind them; there was a hint of dawn in the sky as the last of their illicit trophies was stored in the shallow cave and a few boulders moved to conceal its entrance. Fishermen were astir as Brian and Robert came down from the headland into the village and climbed, exhausted, the stone steps to their room and a welcome bed.

Oscar chose to return to Jackie's room and, taking off only his shoes and trousers, he collapsed into bed beside her. The girl woke and turned and snuggled up to him then recoiled in distaste. "Ugh, you smell horrible, and you're all wet. Where have you been, for God's sake?" She sat up and pulled the sheet up under her chin. "Go and get a shower before you come to bed, and get those grotty clothes off. What the hell have you been doing?"

Oscar climbed wearily up again and stumbled across the cold stone floor to the shower leaving a salty trail. The shower was cold and he emerged shivering to find Jackie sitting in the window dressed in one of his shirts under which the cool dawn air tightened her nipples. "So, what have you been doing? What drags you from bed at one in the morning and brings you back smelling like a dead fish?"

This, from Jackie, was not a casual enquiry; a contented and phlegmatic girl, she did not allow the world to worry her too much. If she was concerned she shouted; otherwise she accepted events without reaction or comment, doglike. Now she was frightened and Oscar knew that she would not let go until she had a satisfactory explanation. He did not want to tell her what had happened, about the treasure and how they had hidden it; he did not yet know how he really felt about it. But he was tired and felt a tenderness for her and a desire to be open which overruled his reticence. He felt a need to confess and be comforted. He sat up in the crumpled bed and put a pillow behind his back against the cold rough wall and told Jackie how they had found the wreck and plundered it. Through the long tale she sat judgemental and featureless, outlined against the coming day and blowing smoke from a chain of Marlboro like a small, erotic, and angry dragon. The story came to an end on an apologetic and plaintive note, failing to convince both its narrator and its audience. There was silence for a while until Jackie shook her head and came to kneel on the bed. Oscar reached out for her but she evaded his grasp and sat back on her heels unheeding of how her gaping shirt tugged at his senses.

"You are stupid. You're a bloody idiot. You're all mad. Why the hell do you want to do a thing like that, here of all places?"

Oscar had never seen Jackie like this; angry, scornful and dismissive, but despite his dismay, clung at a straw of comfort. If she was as angry as this, he consoled himself, she must feel something for him.

"This is not England, this isn't even Greece, this is bloody Crete. This isn't the place to start annoying people. This is not the place to steal things. This is Sfakia; if you steal from Sfakians, they kill you." Jackie kept her voice low but could not hide her anger and dismay; she beat the mattress with small despairing fists. "If I were you I would be out of here now. There's no way you can get away with it. And even if you had gone and they found out, they'd come after you. You don't do this to Sfakians; you certainly don't do it to Theseus unless you want to die." Jackie sobbed, eyes bright with tears and anger.

"Oh, you stupid sod. What a crazy thing to do. You take a man's hospitality, you take his money, you take his job and then you steal from him. You steal from Theseus, of all people. I can't believe you're that stupid."

Jackie lunged forward in the dim room and slapped Oscar's face hard before bursting into tears and throwing her arms round him. He held her firmly for a while, until her sobs diminished and she sniffed noisily and turned onto her back. Together they watched the sun come up over the cliff top.

"Oh Jackie, love, what are we going to do?" he whispered quietly.

The girl turned towards him and kissed him and a heavy breast rested on his chest comfortingly. "Go to sleep now," she said. "We'll think of something tomorrow. Well, today really." Jackie giggled sadly, "At least you smell better." She put a plump brown arm across his chest and they slept for a while before Oscar dragged himself wearily away to go fishing.

In contrast to Jackie's worries, Robert and Brian felt happier in the sunlit morning than they had for some time. Somehow the events of the previous day and night had clarified their situation and both were relaxed now that the big decisions had been taken. The discovery of the wreck was already public knowledge among both tourists and villagers and despite Theseus' warnings not to talk too much, they found it difficult to resist the interest which their discovery had aroused. At breakfast on the hotel terrace they were the centre of attention and soon were spinning stories of how they found the wreck and uncovered its treasures, enjoying the unaccustomed attention.

Gillian's arrival was heralded as usual by an exuberant dog doing its rounds of the tables in search of scraps. She, in turn, performed her ritual visit to each breakfasting group, exchanging gossip and banter in the half-familiar, half-distracted fashion which was her trademark. She gestured to Fiona that she would take her coffee with Brian and Robert and arrived at their table as it was served. She flopped on to a chair and Raki collapsed at her feet, energetically chewing a dry bread roll; she reached over and took one of Brian's Marlboro and lit it with the Concorde lighter. Blowing smoke out and gulping coffee almost simultaneously, Gillian leaned back in her chair. "Now tell me what you have done."

The phrasing caught Brian unaware. Others had asked what they had found, where they had found it; Gillian asked, innocently enough, what they had done, and a fleeting glance of guilt passed between. It was there and so faint that even Gillian, who was adept at reading faces, nearly missed it and it was only later when she recalled their subsequent conversation that she remembered it. It left a faint question mark in the clear morning.

Brian laughed. "What have we done?" he said, reaching across the table for his lighter. "What have we done? We've found a shipwreck, that's all. But the ship is probably over three thousand years old and that makes it pretty unusual. And there's going to be a lot of interest in it, and lots of people will come to Lossos." In his elation Brian nearly went on to say "and you will make lots of money," but luckily didn't. Gillian took advantage of his mood to lead him on. "What will happen now, to the wreck, I mean, and to the treasure?"

"The last time I was involved in something like this," Brian began expansively, "was in Turkey."

"Oh, I didn't realise that you were an expert," Gillian encouraged him, sneering inwardly and taking another cigarette.

"... and it was a big job, and it went on for years." Once again one of Brian's stories missed its opportunity, lost in the indecision between mind and voice. Conscious of the lack of impact, Brian attempted to recover. "Over ten years, I think ..."

But he had already lost his audience. Gillian was getting up, Raki jumping to his feet, other guests competing for attention, Fiona clearing the table. The moment had passed and could not be regained. The centre of interest moved away and was never to be regained. From now on the divers were history.

Chapter twenty one

Jackie got up early and climbed up onto the headland, feeling an unusual need for solitude. She came to the ruin of the round Turkish tower and climbed the unprotected spiral stair to the rampart from where she could see the twin bays as described in the Acts of the Apostles where the ship carrying St Paul took refuge on his voyage to Rome. The village of Lossos nestled under the cliff to her left and the dark blue water in the bay to her right covered the wreck which Oscar and his friends had discovered and plundered. Holding tightly to the parapet Jackie turned further round to her right to trace the line of the Liridiana path to where, unknown to her, an insignificant gully held Minoan swords, pottery and disks. She felt lost and insignificant and inclined to cry, but what good would that do? Tears weren't going to help Oscar. She took a deep breath, wiped her eyes and sniffed. She came down the ruined stair daring herself not to touch the wall and followed the old track down into the village, feeling grown-up at last. She would go and talk to Fiona.

While Brian and Robert were holding court on the terrace and Jackie was worrying about Oscar, Fiona was washing up and listening to Gillian with one ear. Her boss's remarks were familiar and on one of her most consistent themes: the inadequacies, incompetence, perfidiousness and total unworthiness of men. Fiona had heard it all before and didn't agree with the generality although she had her own reservations about specific individuals of the sex. She knew from experience that the only course of action when subject to one of Gillian's tirades was to continue to work and to mutter expressions of muted agreement from time to time. This she did while the rest of her mind was free to enjoy memories of the previous night's lovemaking on the roof with Dimitris, and in contrast, her total dislike of Brian and his sneering Scottish accomplice. Only when she heard Gillian mention Dimitris did Fiona concentrate on what the older woman was saying.

"And now they've gone off again together, just when we've so much to think about. When you really need them, they always disappear …"

"What do you need them for, anyway?" Fiona asked, as much in the hope of diverting her employer as with any particular interest.

"To talk about the wreck and the treasure, of course; we've got to make plans. What do you think will happen now? To the wreck, I mean?"

Fiona dried her hands and poured them both a cup of coffee; she went to sit at the edge of the terrace and looked out to sea. A distant boat which could have been Theseus' launch appeared to be travelling slowly towards the village from the general direction of Sfakia but she could not be sure.

Gillian sat down beside her and Raki flopped panting into the shade of the table.

"I don't know really." Fiona pulled her sunglasses down against the dazzling reflection from the sea. "From what was said last night and those fantastic things they've found I think that it might turn out to be very important, you know, like Phaistos and Knossos. I'm sure that lots of people will be interested and will want to come and see it. And work on it. That horrible Brian might just be right, it might take ten years; and that would change things a lot around here."

"Some people might make a lot of money out of it," Gillian mused, finishing her coffee, "But what shall we do next?"

"I don't know how these sites are developed and under whose authority but I bet that Mateo does. I'll go over and talk to him later."

Fiona got up and stretched, completely captivating a young, rather pink Englishman who had recently arrived and who was taking a solitary late breakfast whilst his new wife was in tears contemplating the problems of walking over hot pebbles in the expensive high-heeled shoes she had brought. By the time he had recovered, Fiona had cleared and wiped his table and was pouring the remains of his coffee down the sink. The young man enjoyed his stay in Lossos, his wife hated it; they were divorced six months later; she returned to mother in Middlesex and he became a diving instructor in Roatan. Lossos does things to people.

Fiona decided to change before setting off to walk over to see Mateo but on her way back to her room she met Jackie coming down the steps from the headland path. The two girls had never been close friends and had little in common other than a love of the sun and Lossos, and a distrust of Theseus; they had spent time together because they were both aliens in Sfakia and were doing the same job.

They had become distant friends, supportive and sympathetic, but not close. They had shared tights and make-up and occasionally clothes, but never boyfriends and rarely ideas. They had become companions by contact rather than compatibility. But it was clear to Fiona as soon as they met on this early summer morning that the English girl was upset and needed a shoulder to cry on. Her first guess was that she and Oscar had split up, and to encourage Jackie to talk Fiona told her of Gillian's breakfast dissection of men and Theseus in particular. Usually this struck a chord with Jackie who would respond with her own delighted stories of how badly she had been treated by whole regiments of manipulative men over many years. But this morning the chord did not resound and Jackie sat moodily chain-smoking in the window.

Fiona changed into cream shirt and light trousers and was sitting on the edge of her bed tying the laces of her trainers and wondering how to get rid of her friend when Jackie suddenly turned from the window. "Fi, I've got a problem, or at least Oscar has, and he doesn't know what to do and I don't either. It's all a terrible mess and what Theseus will do when he finds out I hate to think, and I know it's stupid but I don't want anything to happen to him – Oscar, that is, not Theseus. Oh, it's all such a mess. I don't know what to do, and I can't think of anyone to talk to, other than you, of course, you're all I've got. Apart from Gillian, of course, but she's bound to tell Theseus ..."

Fiona finished tying her laces, wryly amused by being grouped with Gillian, and sat back on the bed. "Jackie, what the hell are you talking about? I can't follow a word of it. Start again at the beginning; I can't help if I don't know what the problem is. Come on now, tell it as it is. And don't look so miserable, nothing's that bad." She patted the bed and beckoned. "Come over here."

Jackie came to sit beside her. In a rare tenderness Fiona put her arm round the English girl who promptly burst into tears. "Oh, what would I do without you?"

Fiona held her until the sobs subsided. "So, tell me."

Jackie told the story, slowly at first and then angrily. She told how the divers had discovered the wreck and hidden the treasures. How they had contacted the Greek man in Athens. How they had decided to keep some of the finds for themselves. How frightened she was for Oscar if Theseus found out what they had done. She didn't know what they had kept, but it must be valuable. She didn't know where they had hidden the loot. She wished that she had never got involved. And what should they do now?

Fiona listened in silence. She felt for Jackie and consoled her as well as she could. She had no sympathy for the divers; they had dug their own graves. But, for the first time, she realised how deep Jackie's feelings for Oscar had become. "Don't worry, mate. We'll sort it out. The best thing is to do nothing. Not that there's much you can do, anyway. Tell Oscar to keep his head down and stay away from anything to do with the treasure, like moving it, or giving it to *malakas* from Athens. Who was it, from Athens, do you know?"

Jackie didn't, but felt happier already; her troubles were not very deep, once they had been shared she recovered quickly. "Do you mind if I use your shower?" she said inconsequentially and stripped off. She came out of the cold spray glowing and happy, grabbed Fiona's towel. "I enjoyed that. Oh, and thanks. Thanks for listening, you're a great mate." She dried herself quickly, watching herself in Fiona's mirror. "Do you think I'm getting fat?" she asked. She lifted her breasts and pulled her stomach in and grinned at her image, "I'm not so bad, really." She towelled her hair into an attractive mess and tugged on a dress. "Right, I'm off to work now, see you later."

Fiona picked up the wet towel from where her friend had dropped it and hung it in the sun in her window. Looking across the bay she saw the launch with Theseus and Dimitris aboard drift into view with barely a wake showing on the placid sea. She watched Gillian walk down the beach towards it, preceded by a bouncing dog. By the time Dimitris had tied up Gillian had dragged Theseus off, presumably to discuss the wreck, leaving Dimitris to ward off Raki. He threw stones into the sea which Raki sought enthusiastically but unsuccessfully as Fiona came out of the tamarisks to meet him. She put her arms around him and kissed him, and the dog, feeling left out, embraced them both in salty soaking fur.

Dimitris threw another stone for the dog, who tore into the sea in pursuit, and turned back to Fiona. "You look serious," he said. "What's the matter?"

"I'm glad you've come back, I want you to come over to Lavris with me, to see Mateo. Now. Please. Will you come? We can take Raki."

"I want to see Mateo, too. *Endaxi. Pame.* You can tell me about it on the way. We'll take the boat, it's quicker."

As they backed away from the jetty a wet dog jumped on board, shook himself and sat on the prow; a companionable, damp, canine figurehead.

* * * * *

Mateo and Manolis, Fiona and Dimitris and two dogs were sitting on the terrace of the taverna in Lavris in sunlight filtered by a lattice of bamboo and vine. A breeze from the sea brought a taste of salt and seaweed overlain by the smell of strong coffee from the table. In the quiet the slap of waves against the hull of Dimitris' launch was clear and sharp.

Dimitris told his tale first, admitting that the divers were employed by Theseus and what they were doing for him. Fiona added what Jackie had told her that morning. Mateo described what he had seen during the last two weeks and told how he had been along the shore of the bay to try to discover where treasure might have been hidden, but had not been successful in the dark.

Manolis blamed it all on Theseus and his accursed family and grumbled angrily at the plans for the development of Maranes, his bay. The Anopolakis family had driven him out of Amores and now were intent on driving him out of Lavris. He, Manolis, would not permit it; he would fight to the last man to defend his territory. No one pointed out that he was the last man, but Dimitris offered the thought that the discovery of the wreck would almost certainly interfere with Theseus' plans. Manolis subsided into fierce mutterings and Argus raised his tattered head and watched him with concern, unused to such anger.

There was a long, thoughtful silence, broken at last by Dimitris, who said, "It seems to me that there are two questions." At his voice Raki raised his head from the dusty concrete in reprimand, sighed deeply and resumed his interrupted sleep. "First, what do we do about the wreck and its treasures? And, secondly, what do we do about the divers?"

Manolis spat on the floor and his bright blue eyes glared around the table. "They are foreigners and friends of Theseus; they should be punished," he growled.

Mateo said, "But they cannot be punished until we can prove them guilty. I know that Fiona has told us of what the other girl has heard, but that is not sufficient in my view. We must have stronger evidence, particularly if we are going to involve the police."

"Theseus would want to avoid involving the police," Dimitris broke in. "Despite the opinion of Manolis, he is not a bad man and loves his land. He would wish to deal with the matter himself."

"And to his own advantage, no doubt." Manolis was not

149

convinced.

"Whichever way, there must be more evidence," Mateo rejoined, "And, speaking for myself, I think that this is more than a crime, more than breaking the law. The action of these British is an affront to Theseus, who invited them here. It is an insult to the Sfakiani who offered them hospitality. And it is an injury to Crete to which the wreck belongs. I am not a Cretan but I feel the injustice of this action as strongly as any native. If they have done this thing then these men should be punished. It is right. But," he finished emphatically, "we have got to be sure that they are guilty."

Dimitris smiled across the table at his former mentor. "Well, you made that quite clear. But how? How do we find them guilty?"

"You catch them, red-handed," Fiona said quietly. "Look, we know that they've taken some things and we know that they have hidden them somewhere in the hills. We don't know where because Jackie wasn't told, or didn't understand. But they have contacted the man from Athens, so they have to hand the loot over sometime. When the man comes we start to watch; there's no point in doing so before, because the divers won't move anything until they know what to do with it."

"I will watch," Manolis was excited. "It will be like the old days, I will go into the hills with Argus, and we will watch. I will whistle in the old way." He blew between his thumbs to produce an ear-shattering shriek which brought both dogs to their feet barking loudly, and ended in his own wracking cough. Mateo patted the old man on the back, "Careful, *yero mou*, don't die on us yet, we need you. But where will you watch?"

"The treasure can't be far away," Fiona thought.

"Why?"

"Because we know it was last night when it was moved and we know that they were in Yannis' restaurant until twelve, and that Oscar was back with Jackie before dawn, say five hours at the most."

"Five hours to pick up the stuff, carry it in the darkness, hide it, and get back to Lossos."

Dimitris followed the argument. "Well, say three hours walking, an hour and a half each way, from Lossos, and they are divers not runners. It can't be more than, say, an hour from here."

"You know," Mateo came in, "I think that from the top of the scarp above here you could cover all the possibilities, with one man only."

"And his dog," Manolis said proudly, "We'll do it, Argus and I. Like we did in the war."

"*Endaxi*. That's what we'll do. Just as soon as you tell us that the man from Athens has arrived, Fi, we'll start the watch. And we'll catch the *malakas*."

Fiona looked at the three men, "What will you do with them? I don't want you to hurt Oscar, he's OK."

Manolis drew a dirty gnarled finger across his throat and Mateo nodded; Dimitris shook his head. "We'll think of something, don't worry, *agapi mou*, leave that to us."

Fiona's skin prickled in the hot morning and high above the vulture stooped to approve.

The latticework of shadow had moved around and now crossed a plate of freshly cooked sardines and a large salad. Sunlight dappled the glasses and a small carafe of wine making the dark red scarlet by refraction, and chunks of bread lay on the checked cloth.

"The next question is," Dimitris said, "What do we do about the wreck itself? We've got to tell someone officially, but I would prefer it to be someone we know and can trust, who would be sympathetic to Lossos."

"I know a man who would be perfect for the job." Mateo surprised them. "He's just about the best there is, but I don't know where he's working now. But he's American," he said slyly, glancing at Manolis, who snorted but remained quiet, lulled by the wine.

"Who's he?" Dimitris asked, "If he's the right man, I'm sure Theseus will get him."

"You can't buy this chap," Mateo laughed, "Not even Theseus can buy him. But if he's free, he'll come; he loves wrecks and the older they are the better. He runs the American School of Nautical Archaeology; his name's Slinger, Brad Slinger."

"How do we get him?" Dimitris asked, "Where can I find him?"

"You can't, my friend. But I can. If we're lucky, he'll run the whole thing for us, well, for the Ephorate of Antiquities, anyway. They'll have to ask him."

"Leave that to me, I'll make sure that they ask him. Theseus and I have a few friends in Athens and more in Hania, and those we have are good. If this Brad is available, we'll get him."

The afternoon relaxed into chatter and wine; Manolis and the two dogs slept, Fiona and the men talked quietly of Lossos and the coast, of the coming summer and the expected influx of tourists, both desired and dreaded. At length Dimitris brought the talk back to the problem which had brought them together.

"I have been thinking," he said, "There can be no advantage in our doing anything about the divers and their stolen treasure until they show their hand. After all, we do not know much about what they have done, or are supposed to have done. We only have what Jackie told Fiona, and she is not a very reliable source, and what Mateo and Manolis have conjectured. These are not good grounds for taking any action at the moment. But we must remain aware of the possibilities and we must make sure that we miss nothing."

He paused for a while and thought. "Fiona can let us know if and when this mysterious Greek turns up in the village; Manolis and Mateo can watch the hills and the paths. I will make sure that the divers stay in Lossos. I don't think that they will leave until they are paid, and I will arrange for them to be moved to live somewhere where they can be watched. I will also see if we can arrange for this Brad Slinger to get the job of managing the excavation of the wreck and I will discuss with Theseus how we should inform the authorities in Hania." Dimitris drained the last of his wine and stretched back in his chair.

"I don't think much will happen quickly. This man from Athens will not be able to make arrangements for some time and will then have to plan how to get his ill-acquired gains out of Lossos. That won't be easy. It could be a month or two before we see things happening and it may also come to nothing in the end. We must watch and wait."

Manolis woke, dislodging Argus who was asleep on his foot. "Eh. I will watch and wait, just as we did in the Resistance. Watch and wait and do not be seen." He went back to sleep again and Argus settled at his feet.

Dimitris got to his feet and smiled down at Fiona and Mateo and the snoring Manolis. "Come *glikia mou*, let us go back to Lossos. You have to go to work and I have to talk to Theseus." He walked to the seawall and looked out across the bay. He spoke quietly, to himself. "Who could have thought that the Minoans came here, all those long years ago? How many men died in that shipwreck? And how many survived? And are they still here now?"

He turned from the sea and looked back at his friends. "Maybe Theseus really is a Minoan, a Minoan priest-king. Maybe I am also a Minoan. Who knows? This is going to be an interesting summer."

Crete
September

Chapter twenty two

Two telephones rang in the overpowering heat of a late August evening in Athens.

Nikos Kontos turned red then white then blue and red again as he drank a bottle of beer in the glow of the rotating sign above his balcony. A muted roar of traffic rose through hot air from the deep canyon of the street to meet the pall of smog which had hung over the city for weeks. Heat and fumes spread across the town, stifling thought and action; those whose work kept them in the city managed two or three hours in the early morning before succumbing to the universal lassitude. Those who could escape had fled to families in the country or to laze on beaches, others sought the fresher air of the mountains or the islands. Tourists outnumbered the natives in the city; indomitably they emerged daily from their air-conditioned hotels grasping cameras and guide books and wearing improbable hats to do battle with the heat and the taxi drivers and the formidable guardians of the ancient sites.

Those natives who stayed in town perched on balconies like caged birds awaiting the release of the autumn winds and rains. Nikos was one of these, only leaving his balcony and the company of the revolving sign to buy more beer or cigarettes, or to eat a *tiropita* and salad in a corner cafe. He resented being tethered to the city by the telephone wire while Jenny was at Sounion in Mary's cool and airy villa. He felt that he had been abandoned by his wife and he took revenge by drinking too much and spending money which he could not afford on bar-girls too lethargic to leave town or too ugly to expose themselves to the light of day.

Nikos was waiting for a phone call from London from an underworld buyer whom he had discovered in the weeks of searching since Brian's call from Lossos. By posing as a reporter wishing to write an article about the trade in stolen antiques his tortuous enquiries had led from Athens to Albania to Rome and now to London; the expected call should connect him with someone who knew the market well enough to dispose of, and pay adequately for, a number of Minoan antiquities and one or, possibly more, Phaistos disks. Nikos had spent hours rehearsing the anticipated conversation and how he would lead it convincingly from the cover of a reporter's enquiries to his true purpose. Not an easy transition but he was confident that he could make it. The call would make worthwhile the waiting and the discomfort of an Athenian August.

The telephone rang in the dark heat of the apartment; Nikos struggled out of his chair and flicked his cigarette over the balcony rail into the night. Beer bottle in hand and heavy-bellied he left the balcony and picked up the phone. "*Ne?*" he grunted.

* * * * *

At the same time another telephone rang in the hot Athens night.

Kenneth Ashworth also sat on a balcony, but a balcony refreshed by the cool breeze which drifted down from the heights of Likavitos Hill into the steep narrow streets of Kolonaki. Away to his left the floodlit Parthenon stood upon its rocky plinth above the haze and in front of him the streets fell down through leafy squares to the university. From his flat in the British School, the Archaeological Museum was hidden by the tree-clad slope of Likavitos and far away beyond the city the distant hills of Attica showed black against a deep red sunset. Even the traffic noise was reduced to a murmur here; if one had to be in Athens in August there was no better place than this.

Kenneth swirled ouzo around the ice in his tall glass and thought idly that a refill would prolong his enjoyment of the day. If Mary had been here she would have frowned; she hated ouzo. Although she would never say the words, a zephyr of disapproval would make her thoughts clear and Kenneth would not have a second drink. But Mary was in Sounion with Jenny. He would have another mild one before strolling down to his favourite restaurant for a fish *mezes* and salad and a cold dry wine from an earthenware jug.

Kenneth missed Mary when she was away; he missed her constant chatter and her interest in the world. She found fascination in everything she encountered but what could have been a naivety was tempered by her sharp mind. She made the day brighter, heightened the colours, focused the interest. They had been married for twenty-six years and had enjoyed all of them. But Kenneth was not lonely when she was away, he was a man who was happy with himself; he enjoyed his work and would often go on late into the night, free of domestic constraints, missing meals before wandering into town to drink a beer while watching the world go by. Occasionally on these nocturnal jaunts he would catch a woman's eye. He was fifty-two, fit, lean, and smiled easily; the girl would join him and they would talk, but at the end of the evening he would say goodnight and climb the hill through the soft warm air to his flat. Without regret, although sometimes a little flattered.

Kenneth drained his glass and went across to the cabinet to replenish it. The phone rang; he picked up the receiver. "*Ne?*" he said.

* * * * *

In his fetid, strobe-lit flat Nikos took a gulp of beer and burped quietly into the phone.

"Nikos?" Brian spoke uncertainly with the habitual question present in both voice and enquiry. "Brian here, in Lossos. You remember?"

Why did he do it, he asked himself as the words came out? Why did he always have to put himself at a disadvantage by requiring recognition and reassurance? Annoyed with himself he continued quickly, "I think that we might have a problem down here. You know that the archaeological team are working on the wreck now, surveying and photographing and so on. They haven't started any digging yet, they say that might not start until next year and we haven't been near the site for ages since that American, Slinger got here. Don't like him, he's too clever by half. Hadn't been here five minutes before he almost accused us of, well, irresponsible damage he called it."

Nikos grinned to himself in the darkness and lit a cigarette. "But that's just what you did, isn't it? He was spot on, the chap obviously knows what he's talking about whether you like it or not. Now get to the point. What problem?"

"Well, they've found a disk."

"Found a disk? What sort of disk?"

"It's like a Phaistos disk, you know, like the one in the museum in Iraklion."

"Like the one that Oscar drew?"

"Well, yes …"

"The disk you weren't going to tell me about?"

Brian fumbled for words, "Well, yes, but we were going to tell you, I mean, later, when we met. You know, surprise you."

157

"Some surprise, another Phaistos disk. Didn't you think that I'd need to know, to help me make the arrangements? 'Oh, by the way, Mr Buyer, we've got a Phaistos disk here; just give me a million for it.' This isn't bloody easy, you know." Nikos was enjoying the other's discomfort; he went on, "What about me, how do you think I feel about it now, now that you have already tried to cheat me? I think I'll drop the whole thing."

"Nikos, wait, wait a minute; look, I'm sorry. We'll sort this out later. But, there's more ..."

"What, more stuff you haven't told me about?"

"No, more disks. About fifty altogether."

"Fifty Phaistos disks? Come on, I'm not that stupid ..."

"Look, it's right, we've found fifty or more, but ..."

Nikos gulped at his beer and hunted for a cigarette, prowling his balcony in the night as if it were his cage. The *malakas*, they really were on to something, and were trying to cheat him as well. Bloody British, they'd pay for this. "But, what now?"

"They've found another, the archaeologists, I mean, they've found another disk, a broken one – we thought we'd got the lot. It broke when Oscar was digging it out, and he threw it away. And now it's been found ..."

"... and they now know what you've got, or at least they might guess. That'll intrigue them."

Nikos knew enough about archaeology to guess the questions that would be raised by finding a second Phaistos disk, underwater, freshly broken and out of context. It wouldn't take professionals long to come to the obvious conclusion that the wreck had been tampered with and to surmise that there could have been other disks; he thought quickly. "Where are the others?" he asked, trying to guess what Brad Slinger and his team would do next.

"Well, they're hidden in a gully, about a couple of kilometres away."

"Are they safe?"

"Well ..." Every utterance from Brian started the same way. "Well, pretty safe. It would have to be quite a search to find them."

"Are there any other clues to lead people to them? Did anyone see you, at any time?"

"No." This time Brian was more positive. "No. I don't think so. And we haven't been back since to check them."

"*Endaxi*. I'll tell you what we'll do."

Nikos paced the balcony of the dark flat changing colour like a nocturnal chameleon as the sign above him revolved. The telephone

158

cord got tangled around heavy furniture as he walked, adding to his agitation.

"*Ena lepto.*"

He put the receiver down and went to get another cigarette before attempting to untangle the cord from a forest of chair legs. He picked up the receiver again and took a deep drag on the cigarette. "Brian, are you there?"

"Yeah, but hurry. I'm running out of money."

"I'll come to Lossos. The day after tomorrow. On the late boat. I'll stay in the hotel, but you don't know me. We'll talk later. We'll try to get the stuff out quickly. Think about how we could do it. OK?"

"But what …"

The phone went dead; Nikos put the receiver down thoughtfully and, getting another Amstel from the fridge, went out onto the balcony. If he leant out and craned round to the right he could look up the length of the traffic-filled gorge under him to where the chapel of Agios Yorgos stood like a beacon on top of Likavitos, clear of the city smog. His thoughts followed the road upwards and past the hill and on to Crete and the clean air of the White Mountains. With a flutter of excitement and shiver of apprehension Nikos raised his bottle to the future; restless now, he showered and changed and went out into the steamy night. As he went down the echoing stairs the telephone rang unheard in his flat. The call from London had come at last but Nikos was not there to answer it.

* * * * *

"*Ne?*" Kenneth Ashworth expected to hear his wife's voice and guiltily put his drink down.

"Hi." A soft American voice. "I'd like to speak with Ken Ashworth?" An upward inflexion again, but requiring compliance rather than approval.

"Kenneth Ashworth speaking."

"Mr Ashworth, Brad Slinger here, Dallas Nautical Archaeology department. We met in Paris last year."

Kenneth remembered the American and recalled his lecture on the final stages of the Turkish excavation which had set new standards in underwater archaeology. The excavation had lasted a dozen years; its careful execution had extended knowledge of Bronze Age trade to an extent inconceivable only a few years previously.

Meticulous work and rigorous analysis had spread Brad Slinger's reputation through the archaeological world and ensured that the best jobs would come his way.

Kenneth had heard of Brad's appointment to the Lossos excavation. "Yes, of course I remember. I enjoyed your lecture greatly. I saw that you got the Lossos job, how's it going?"

"*Siga siga*; you know how the Greeks work, but it's early days yet."

"I know how the Greeks work: slowly," Kenneth laughed, "Mr Slinger, how can I help you?"

"Brad, please," the American replied, "I think we're going to get to know each other well."

"I certainly hope so, but my work is academic, you know. I don't often get my hands dirty like you chaps. Or wet, for that matter," he added drily.

"But what I've got is right up your street. And you don't need to leave Athens."

"That's a pity; it would be good to leave Athens in this heat. So, what can I do for you?"

"We're doing the preliminary work on the Lossos site, the surveying and site exploration. Nothing serious yet. But we've found something which might interest you."

Kenneth took a sip from his ouzo and carried the glass and the phone out onto the balcony. The lights of Athens twinkled hazily below him; he could not see the stars.

Brad Slinger chuckled over the line. "You may not believe this but we've found another Phaistos disk. Now wait. Before you sneer, just go and look at your fax; I've just sent you a photograph."

Kenneth was disappointed; so many had found Phaistos disks, so many had attempted translations. It had become the laughing stock of archaeology; every nut understood it, every amateur could translate it, every academic was at best mystified, at worst dismissive. He put his ouzo down on a small table and crossed the room to the fax machine. There were two sheets in the tray; he picked them up and took them across to the shaded light on his desk. Each sheet bore a photograph of one side of a clay disk which had been broken into three roughly equal pieces and had been re-assembled. The breaks were clear as was the spiral of pictographs. Kenneth recognised the symbols as being identical to those on the infamous disk in the Iraklion museum, but there were one or two omissions and one or two additions which he did not recognise but which appeared to be formed by similar dies. If this was a hoax, it was a good one; it certainly deserved investigation, and Crete would be fresher than Athens.

Kenneth picked up the phone. "Mr Slinger," he said, somewhat formally, "do you think that I might be welcome in Lossos? It is rather hot here and I would enjoy the break. And I would rather like to see what you have found."

"Ken, you would be very welcome. Fax your arrangements and I'll meet you off the boat. I promise you an exciting summer."

Kenneth poured himself another ouzo and added a lot of water. He took the two faxes out onto the balcony and studied them in the light flooding out from the room behind him. The reproduction was poor; the disk had obviously been placed on a photocopier and the resulting image had further distorted by passing through the fax, but it was clear enough. The disk, which had been unique for nearly a hundred years, now had a twin. But not an identical twin. Kenneth's mind raced with the possibilities. If there was a twin there might be brothers; with enough of these a decipherment might be possible. And the new disk had been found near a shipwreck on the south coast of Crete, not very far from Phaistos. Surely there was a link. He shivered in anticipation; this was going to be interesting. The phone rang; he picked it up and answered it absently.

Mary said, "You sounded miles away, what have you been up to?"

"Oh, hello, love. Yes, I was thinking. Would you like to come to Crete? I'm going the day after tomorrow … Yes, of course you can bring Jenny, she'll love it. I'll book the morning flight, nine o'clock; you can come straight up from Sounion. Good; love you."

Kenneth finished his drink. The great thing about Mary, he reflected, was that she never asked why, or what she should wear; she just said yes, with enthusiasm.

* * * * *

Tuesday, 10th September: 1200 hrs

Nikos slept until midday in the airless flat, waking with a headache after a restless night. A momentary feeling of wellbeing was quickly overcome by recollection of the excesses of the previous night, and subsequent guilt. Too many cigarettes, too many drinks, too much money spent; in an attempt to ease his conscience he tried to phone Jenny in Sounion but there was no answer. Unfairly resentful that she was not available, he took a cup of coffee and a cigarette out onto the balcony where the glare hurt his eyes and increased the pounding behind his temples. He turned back into the stuffy darkness and took two aspirin and showered and lay naked, sweating unpleasantly on his tangled bed, listening to the noise of the city around him and contemplating the tantalising prospect of lots of Phaistos disks. But that was later; for now the long afternoon and night loomed depressingly ahead.

Tomorrow he would be in Crete, but today was bleak. So – the thought struck with a bolt of guilty excitement – so why not go today? An afternoon flight would get him to Iraklion in plenty of time for a leisurely dinner and then there was that nightclub down near the harbour where he had enjoyed himself so much last year. Suddenly the day was bright again. Nikos phoned Olympic and struggled through a tangle of indifference to book a seat on the six o'clock flight. He stuffed a few shirts and underclothes into a bag with some light trousers and, as an afterthought and recalling the harsh Cretan limestone, a pair of trekking boots.

Nikos showered again and changed; he rang Jenny; she was not in; he picked up his bag and left the flat as it was, littered with empty beer bottles and overflowing ashtrays. With a re-discovered sense of adventure he ran down the stairs and out into the blazing street in search of a pizza and beer before getting a taxi out to the airport. It was going to be an enjoyable night after all.

By nine o'clock Nikos was eating a rather good *stifado* washed down by *ena miso kilo kokkino krassi* at a restaurant just off the Platia Venizelou in Iraklio and looking forward to a long and lecherous night. He planned to take the midday bus to Hora Sfakia and the early evening boat to Lossos and could have a long lie-in in the morning. He finished his meal and relaxed in the warm evening; lighting another cigarette, he took a sip of wine and watched the girls go by with the appreciative eye of a connoisseur.

Wednesday, 11th September: 0830 hrs

Kenneth Ashworth sat in a corner of the Olympic terminal of the old Athens airport shielded by the thin pages of the overseas *Times*, and pretended not to notice Mary and Jenny as they crossed the lounge towards him. Mary was leading as usual, confident, swinging her leather cabin bag. Her brown hair was well cut and short, greying a little at the temples; sunglasses concealed the laughter wrinkles around her eyes. She carried the light brown jacket of her trouser suit over one arm and her cream blouse did little to conceal her full figure.

162

Red painted toenails completed the picture of a mature, sensuous and happy woman. Kenneth loved her, hiding behind the obituary column, pretending indifference.

The swinging bag hit *The Times* and destroyed his composure.

"Mary, my love." In creased khaki suit, with crumpled *Times* in one hand, he put his free arm round his wife and kissed her with an Englishman's embrarrassment at public displays of affection. He looked over his wife's shoulder in apology at Jenny who was watching them with amusement.

"Sorry Jenny, lovely to see you, glad you could come," Kenneth struggled free of Mary's embrace and offered his hand to the tall girl who ignored it and kissed him on each cheek completing his discomfiture to the entertainment of all in the departure lounge. Jenny was wearing a white trouser suit and white sandals with high heels. Her hair was severely swept back from her face revealing small ears and beautiful pearl studs. Her sunglasses were perched on top of her head, making her appear even taller. She wore no make-up and no other jewellery and a faint sadness misted her dark blue eyes.

Kenneth finally got them both settled and they watched him with a bogus diffidence as he struggled to refold his *Times* while holding his boarding card and ticket between his teeth and his battered leather travelling bag between his feet.

"So," Mary said, "Why are we here?"

"And why are we going to Crete," Jenny joined in. "What are we going to do there? It can't be just a holiday, 'cos you never take holidays ..."

"It won't be a holiday, that I know," Mary said. "And why so suddenly? That's not like you at all. Come on, tell us." She smiled at him. "What's happened to drag you away from your beloved Athens?"

Kenneth grinned at the pair, delighted that he'd asked them to come, revelling in their excitement.

"First," he said, "We have to go to a museum ..."

"Iraklion," Mary guessed. "It's stuffy and full of earnest Germans."

"And it has the Phaistos disk," Kenneth finished. "That's all I'm going to tell you for now."

There were squeals from the women, but Kenneth was saved from further pressure by the announcement of departure and the consequent Greek rush to the door.

As she came to the departure gate Jenny pulled her sunglasses down to cover a sudden fear, and half turned back, reluctant to face the brightness outside and her recollection of the fire on the runway beyond. Understanding, Mary took her arm and squeezed. "Never mind, love. Be brave." Only she knew Jenny's vision of another airport gate and a burning plane and the darkness and flames of her father's death. "I always hate this bit, too," she pretended. "Come on. I understand. It'll be OK on the other side. Just think, Crete and a whole new life are out there.".

Mary could not have known how accurate her prediction was going to be.

Kenneth sat apart from the two women during the short flight to Iraklion and finished reading his *Times* while Jenny enjoyed the aerial view of the Cyclades, brown and grey and fringed in turquoise in the blue Aegean. The arc of Santorini was beautifully clear in the early morning with the white sprawl of Thera edging the dark shadow cast by the high cliff over the caldera. It was easy to imagine from the air the steep-sided volcano of which only the rim was now left, before it exploded three and a half thousand years ago and contributed to the end of the Minoan civilisation.

Following the explosion a tidal wave travelling as fast as the plane would have raced across the sea to strike the north coast of Crete which was already visible as a smudge across the southern horizon. Minoan coastal settlements would have been destroyed as the wave raced inland but it was hard to imagine that the sea would have reached Knossos, six kilometres from the coast and one hundred and fifty metres above it. And even more difficult to argue that Phaistos, which was sheltered by high mountains from the wave, could have been affected at all.

Certainly the sea was calm today, its deep blue filled the window as the Olympic 767 banked to make a bumpy landing in Iraklion and to discharge its passengers into the shimmering heat.

They took a taxi directly to the museum and Kenneth disappeared into its underground depths to look at some recent finds of Linear A script from Malia. Jenny and Mary wandered off into the public museum which Jenny had not seen before. It was still quite early and the coach trips of bored tourists had not yet arrived from the big hotels at Rethymnon and Agios Nikolaos. The rooms were quiet, free from the strident tones of the museum guides, and the two English women were able to spend some time looking at the Phaistos disk in its finger-smeared glass case. It was here that Kenneth joined them.

"That's what has brought us here," he said, glancing at the enigmatic clay roundel.

"Come on, I'll take you to lunch and tell you what it's all about. Well," he added quickly, "as much as Brad Slinger told me, anyway."

"Who's Brad Slinger?" Jenny wanted to know.

"Oh, you'll like him. He's a contradiction, a civilised American. And very bright. And good-looking, too. He's about the best underwater archaeologist in the world."

"And, I suppose, he's happily married, with four beautiful children with perfect white teeth," Jenny laughed

"No, I don't think so. He was married but his wife died in a diving accident some years ago, on one of the wrecks he was working on. Bad business. He gave up diving for years afterwards."

"Poor man," Jenny said thoughtfully, "Sounds interesting, though. I look forward to meeting him."

"Are we meeting him, then?" Mary looked across at Kenneth as he led them down a narrow pedestrianised street lined with expensive clothes shops which were distracting Jenny.

"I'll tell you at lunch; I promise. When Jenny can give me her full attention."

He grinned at the tall girl who, distracted by the smart shops, looked back at him with such a brilliant smile that made him wonder, not for the first time, how the oafish Nikos had managed to hold on to her.

The narrow street which they were following suddenly emerged into a noisy traffic-filled road where a number of cafes spread under the trees beside the beautiful stone Venetian fountain. Turning right, Kenneth pointed to the elegant building in front of them.

"That's the best building in Iraklio, its one claim to fame. That and the fountain. Venetian. Beautiful." He paused for a moment in contemplation before turning right again into a small quiet square where a few early diners were already sitting under elegant umbrellas. Kenneth shook hands with the waiter and waved to the white-haired patron in the kitchen before settling the women at a check-clothed table. A whisper of the *meltemi* found its way up from the harbour and tempered the heat of the day. Before sitting down, Jenny took off her suit jacket to reveal a thin strapped top which showed off her brown shoulders perfectly. Several diners and the waiter watched this display with a delight of which Jenny was unconscious, and returned to their companions and tasks with an a collective sigh. Mary smiled up at her, "Careful, darling, you're distracting the natives."

Jenny hadn't noticed.

"Oh. I'm sorry, I didn't think."

She sat down quickly and was about to stretch when she caught Mary's eye. "Oh, shit. What is it about men? You can't do anything."

"Yes, you can, love. Just know that you're doing it, that's all. Use it, don't just give it away."

"Nikos always says that I flirt, but I don't really, I just don't think."

At the mention of her husband Jenny lost some of her sparkle and a shadow crossed her face.

"Come on, let's forget Nikos for a bit," Mary leant forward and patted the younger woman's arm. "Let's enjoy ourselves."

"That's what I feel sometimes. But it's wrong isn't it? I'm his damn wife and I shouldn't think like that."

"Nikos can stand it," Mary said firmly. "He's probably enjoying himself in Athens while you're away. He'll have forgotten about you already."

Jenny relaxed and gave Mary a rueful smile. "I'll remind the sod. I'll ring him tonight."

Kenneth came back to the table and sat down. "Ring who tonight?" he asked.

"Oh. Nikos. Don't worry, no problem," Mary said quickly. "Where have you been?"

"Paying my respects, and ordering our lunch. See that old woman in black in the corner? She's boss round here. The three cafes are run by her sons, but she owns them. Nothing happens here without her knowledge. A useful person to know."

A frosted jug of golden wine and three tumblers arrived at their table followed by a larger jug of iced water and a cut-glass fingerbowl. The waiter poured wine and water scarcely taking his eyes from Jenny, and retreated to the depths of the kitchen, to be replaced by the patron himself carrying an enormous platter of mixed fish crowned with three large crabs. Salad and bread followed; the patron retired to a discreet distance with a graceful "*Kali orexi*" and a questioning eye at his mother.

"How about that, looks good enough to eat, doesn't it? Let's start. *Kali orexi, kyria.*" Kenneth raised his glass, delighted with their company and not unaware of the jealous looks he was getting from fellow male diners, young and old.

The fish was fresh, the bread crisp and crusty. The golden wine complemented both. There was an appreciative silence while the three enjoyed the food and the peace of the square made precious by the muted rumble of traffic only a street away. The heat was dry and comfortable and the gentle breeze brought a welcome freshness after the stuffiness of Athens.

Kenneth dipped fishy fingers into the lemon acidity of the fingerbowl and wiped his hands. He leant back in his chair and grinned at Mary and Jenny. "Thank you for coming," he said, "and for being tolerant. Now I'll tell you why we are here." He told them of the call from Brad Slinger and how he had received the fax of the photograph of the disk. "As soon as I saw that," he said, "I just had to come and see it for myself. It's what we have all dreamt of for years, the Phaistos disk was always an enigma and it was impossible to believe that it could be the only one of its kind. But nearly a hundred years have passed since it was found and it was still the only one. And now it may not be. And we can be part of this, this opportunity. We can make history. It's as big as that."

"So where is Brad Slinger working?" Mary asked, "I didn't know he was in Crete."

"At Lossos, of course, you remember? On the wreck. That's where I think the disk was found."

"So what's the Phaistos disk doing on a wrecked ship at Lossos?" Jenny wanted to know.

"That, my love, is what we're going to find out. But, disk or not, you're going to enjoy Lossos. It's a beautiful place. Mary and I stayed there a few years ago with Gillian who runs the hotel. She's a great character. You'll like her a lot, she knows everyone and everything. But stay clear of her husband, Theseus, he has an eye for beautiful girls."

Wednesday, 11th September: 1800 hrs

When Jenny phoned Nikos that night there was no reply because Nikos was already in Crete. And in Lossos.

Gillian had lived in Greece for more than twenty years, becoming familiar with and tolerant of her adopted countrymen, but there were certain types of Greek who she disliked intensely. Nikos was an excellent example of that kind. They had not met before and yet each had identified the other and exchanged glances of mutual hostility before Nikos had crossed the ferryboat's ramp to the beach. He noted a casually dressed, middle-aged, good-looking and very confident foreign woman; negatives in all but one context as far as his preferences were concerned. She saw, and instantly disliked, a tall man carrying his full belly like a regimental drum before him, olive-skinned, with thick black hair, and full lips under a black moustache.

He carried a clumsy dark leather holdall and wore soft shoes which slipped on the rough pebbles. Gillian watched him stumble up the steps to the hotel, drop his bag, and wipe his sweating face comprehensively with a dark handkerchief.

She chose to greet other arriving guests with impressive enthusiasm, leading them across the beach into the foyer chattering all the while, ignoring Nikos. Such was her welcome of the new arrivals that they were totally captivated by her and would return every year, allocating to themselves, quite wrongly, the status of 'very favoured guest'. This was an honour greatly aspired to in Lossos but rarely bestowed. There were guests who had presumed to the status of 'very favoured' for years to their own immense pleasure and whom Gillian had never needed to undeceive. Of such was one Duncan, a disappointed schoolteacher from Swindon, in England. For three weeks every year this heavy-bellied man with splayed feet fulfilled his fantasies. He pottered about the hotel doing odd jobs badly. He bored anyone who came within the range of his piercing school voice. But he lived in his own eyes a life, so unlike the reality of Swindon, in which he was universally liked and appreciated. For three weeks, increasingly brown and salt-stained, he gloried in the image of hedonistic beachcomber, unshakeable in his belief that he was adored by all and treasured by his hostess. A hard man of the sea, knowing of currents and weather, familiar with the shepherds and the fishermen, respected for his knowledge of the wider world; these were his delusions. The reality was that he was forgotten within five minutes of the boat's departure on the first leg of the journey back to England but the image sustained him through the long northern winter until he could once again waddle across the sunlit pebbles.

There were other guests who would never presume to the accolade but who were nevertheless greatly appreciated by Gillian for their courtesy and style; Brad Slinger had already become one of Gillian's favourites. Always polite, always charming, she welcomed him every evening to her alfresco soirée on the terrace. He drank white wine and she always had a cold bottle awaiting his arrival; Fiona adored him like a favoured uncle and even Jackie, whose taste in men was rather more robust, thought him 'cool'. Like any good hostess, Gillian shared him with her other guests but she was always glad when Brad arrived early and they could share a couple of convivial glasses and she could catch up on the gossip from the excavation site. Tonight she had been delayed by the arrival of the new guests and was impatient to get up to the terrace to tell the American the news of the imminent arrival of Kenneth and Mary.

By treating the new arrivals with such warmth, Gillian contrived to ignore Nikos for a good ten minutes during which he became increasingly annoyed. When she finally chose to acknowledge him, with an interrogative "*Ne?*" he reacted with an overplayed coldness. Ignoring her Greek, he asked in his heavily accented English if there was a room available for him. This was a mistake. Most men would have left five minutes earlier in search of a warmer welcome. Nikos had not only stayed but made himself vulnerable to Gillian's extended perusal of her booking schedule. She had decided immediately which room he should have but deliberated for ten minutes before telling him, reluctantly and in Greek, that she could spare a room for a few days. His acceptance gave her victory and he endured a further few minutes delay before Jackie could be persuaded to leave the bar to show him to his room.

His spirits revived a little as he followed Jackie's tantalising bottom up the steep stairs, only to be dashed again as he surveyed the room. It was small and narrow, leading to a meagre terrace entirely shrouded by the thick foliage of a small tree. Jackie followed him onto the terrace and brushed dry leaves from the table.

"It's OK on a hot day, very shady, and you're not overlooked."

Jackie's closeness on the tiny balcony destroyed any protest.

"Thank you, *agapi mou*," he fumbled sweatily for money. Jackie waited until he had found a tight roll of notes before ignoring his offering of a crumpled twenty, and closing the door behind her more forcibly than necessary.

Nikos showered sadly, wondering why he had bothered to come to this alien place. To an Athenian, he thought, Iraklio was just about possible, but Lossos was dead. He foresaw the long night stretching ahead. His dreams of sunshine and pretty, willing girls under a star-filled sky vanished in the gloom of the shrouded terrace.

At length, hungry and thirsty, he dressed and went down to the bar in search of drink and company. He took a seat overlooking the bay and lit a cigarette. Jackie brought him a beer then went back to sit with Gillian who was talking to a slim sandy-haired man dressed in a dark shirt and well-cut cream trousers who fidgeted restlessly as he talked, his hands emphasising every word. Nikos strained to hear; the man appeared to be American and Nikos envied his manner and the easy way in which he seemed to be entertaining the two women. When Jackie brought a second beer he was going to ask her who the American was but didn't have the courage. Instead he found himself asking if she knew Brian.

"An Englishman, a diver; about thirty years old."

"Sure, he's around somewhere, lives up there." She pointed vaguely up the hill behind the town. "How do you know him?"

Disconcerted by her direct response Nikos made up a story of meeting Brian in Athens which quickly lost Jackie's attention. With a casual "If I see him, I'll tell him," she went back to join the others at the other end of the bar.

Nikos sat alone on the terrace, smoking and drinking. Just like back in Athens, he reflected, but cooler and quieter. And back home he could go out and enjoy himself, whereas here … Oh, well, at least he could have a rest and get some exercise; he finished his beer and wandered sadly off in search of food.

Gillian watched him go. "I wonder why he's here," she said. "Did he say anything to you when you took him up to the black hole?" she asked Jackie.

Brad laughed, "What's this black hole thing?"

"I've put him in our worst room," Gillian pointed up at the tree, "Behind there. It's dark and stuffy and full of dead leaves. I reserve it for people I don't like."

Fiona looked across at her boss. "I'm surprised it's not always full."

"Any more of that and I'll put you in there with him, that'll teach you."

Fiona shuddered. "OK, I take it all back. But who is he? He doesn't look like a tourist. I wonder what he's doing here. Do you think he might be a journalist?"

This was another of Gillian's pet dislikes: travel writers on expense accounts who spent little and who went away to write trite, spiteful and superficial articles in the manner of a theatre critic. Or a food critic. But Lossos wasn't a single performance, just a meal, it was a life. Not to be destroyed or mocked in a few clever words which would be thrown away on Monday morning but might leave a lasting and inaccurate impression.

"If he is, I'll throw away the key and he'll perish in the black hole; *malaka*."

Gillian took a gulp of wine and stole one of Jackie's cigarettes.

"Looks too pale to be a travel writer," Brad remarked. "They're usually bronzed if they do vacations and weather beaten types if they do adventure. This chap was neither; seemed a city type to me."

"He did ask if I knew Brian," Jackie remembered, "You know, that diver chap? I said I did and I asked him how he knew him, if you see what I mean. He, the Greek that is, said he'd met him in Athens. That's all."

170

Brad smiled at her, "Facts at last. After all this conjecture. Well done, Jackie."

Jackie adored him and forgot Oscar for a moment.

"So, what does he want with Brian?" Gillian mused. "They're certainly two of a sort. Two *malakas*."

Fiona said nothing. Since the discussion over at Likkos with Mateo and Dimitris they had been waiting for something to happen to indicate what the divers' plans were. A week had passed, a month, two months. Nothing unusual had happened; visitors came and went; the village grew busy with the start of summer and with the disclosure of the finding of the wreck and the arrival of the team coming to work on it. But the British divers had done little to further their plans. Oscar had got work with Vasilis at the fish restaurant; Brian and Robert helped the archaeological diving team with surveying and mapping the site but these are technical skills and they were reduced to the status of labourers. They found it difficult to be part of a co-ordinated team having been used to an independent and freelance existence. Most of the people working on the wreck were there for experience and for fun and found the British divers poor company, and Brad Slinger was reluctant to pay Robert and Brian for work which the others did for free.

They had also helped to shift stores and equipment round the headland from the quay at Lossos to the diving camp but one day found that the dinghy which Theseus had provided had gone.

"*Filos mou*, in Sfakia, he has it. It may come back soon. When we can finish your work, *ne?*"

No mention was made of the bank account in Athens and Theseus was dismissive when Brian broached the matter with him.

"You are happy here, *ne?* You live free and you have work to do and there are many beautiful girls to work with. What more do you want? *Endaxi*. If you wish to leave, then we will talk about money, but until then enjoy the summer."

But the British divers could not leave; they were tied to the place by the stolen treasures and the long awaited phone call from Nikos.

At Dimitris' suggestion Gillian had found them a single bare room in a partly finished house high in the village. When they were not working Brian and Robert sat endlessly on the rough concrete of the terrace looking down on the town and making vague plans; feeling increasingly alienated, they only ventured down to the beach at night to eat sparse meals. The credit they had been given in the village was quietly withdrawn and Brian had had to go to Hora Sfakion to squeeze more cash from his exhausted credit cards.

Jackie was busy now that full summer had arrived and spent less time with Oscar. He was the only one of the three who was working regularly and being paid a wage, although a small one, but at the cost of getting up before first light to sail into the dawn in search of fish for the night's tables. He was often just setting out to sea when Jackie left Lakki's bar to fall into a drunken and exhausted sleep and their lovemaking was brief, sweaty and unsatisfactory and snatched in a few minutes between Oscar's return from his fishing and Jackie's afternoon stint in the bar. She was still in love with his body but did not rush back to their room for his company when Lakki's bar was filled with lustful and sometimes exciting men at the end of a drunken evening. She was a party girl and her relationship with Oscar was becoming slightly domestic and boring.

"So what does he want with Brian?"

Fiona thought she might know what Nikos and Brian had in common and longed to escape to tell Dimitris what she had discovered. But she could not leave yet: Gillian had more news for Brad. "Those friends of yours from Athens, Kenneth and Mary Ashworth, will arrive tonight. Theseus has gone to Sfakia to meet them in the launch. They should be here soon. They're lovely people; how do you know them – is Kenneth going to work with you?"

Brad thought quickly. The discovery of the broken disk was not exactly secret but its rarity was concealed among the many finds from the wreck and its possible significance was recognised by very few. "We've found a lot of bits with some sort of script on them and I thought it would be a good idea to get a first-rate man like Ken Ashworth to have a look at them. Get him out of Athens, give him a break; he's an academic, you know, doesn't like to get his hands wet."

Gillian, more concerned with personalities than artefacts, was already on to her next thought. "And Mary is with him, and a girl called Jenny. Mary said that they intended to do a bit of walking while Kenneth was working. They're all good walkers, although it's still a bit hot for the coast."

"Who's this Jenny?" Jackie was clearing up the empty glasses from the bar tables.

"Don't know. Mary said that she was a friend of hers from Athens, married to a Greek, poor girl."

Brad smiled at Gillian. "It hasn't done you much harm," he said.

Gillian blew smoke from yet another stolen cigarette into the still evening air. "There are Greeks and Greeks. I was lucky. Mine's not so bad, sometimes. When he can keep his hands off the staff."

172

She glared at Jackie who smiled back innocently.

"And here they come, if I'm not mistaken." Brad defused the sudden tension between the women by pointing to where the red and green lights and white wake of a fast boat could be seen on the dark steel blue of the sea.

Wednesday, 11th September: 1930 hrs

Nikos sat alone over the remains of a charred but otherwise undercooked chicken in a restaurant round the curve of the bay and nursed a three-star Metaxa contemplating the empty night ahead. He heartily wished he had stayed in Athens. What a dead place this was; did nothing ever happen here? He lit yet another Marlboro and looked gloomily out to the dark bay and the bright lights of the tavernas on the opposite shore. The dark finger of the hotel jetty pointed at the beacon which replied in light dashes of Morse. As Nikos watched there came the sound of a powerful engine and he turned to watch. Any event was welcome in helping to lift the boredom of this awful place.

A launch was travelling into the bay, fast, its long white wake spreading an echelon of urgency behind it. It headed towards the hotel pier, slowing quickly as it approached. A silhouetted figure on the jetty caught ropes and steadied the prow. Squinting through the darkness Nikos saw a woman, recognisable as his tormentor from the hotel, Gillian, and followed by a man and a fair-haired girl, come down the hotel steps and cross the shingle to the pier. A big man in a white shirt jumped from the launch to the wooden slats and assisted a short woman and a taller man carrying a briefcase. From their awkwardness they were obviously not used to the sea. Suitcases were handed down. The big man turned again to the boat to help another passenger, a tall slim woman in white whose hair caught the light as she jumped across the narrow strip of black sea to the pier.

From where Nikos sat in the brightly-lit restaurant it was hard to see clearly. The lights on the opposite shore made it difficult to detect detail and the figures on the pier appeared only as silhouettes except when they caught the light from the hotel, but there was something about the white-suited woman that made his heart skip a beat. He strained to see; surely it couldn't be, Jenny should be in Sounion with Mary, how the hell could she be here in Crete?

That would make things bloody difficult. He strained to watch.

As the group climbed the beach and came into the light which streamed from the hotel foyer the figures became clearer and confirmed Nikos' guess, and his fears. It certainly was the Ashworths and his wife who were now being introduced to the American who had come down from the bar to meet them and who was bending over Jenny's hand in his confident manner. Nikos hated him as he watched Brad ushering the party up to the bar. He lit another cigarette and ordered another brandy; he needed time to decide what to do, and courage to face it.

So, what were the Ashworths doing here? No mere coincidence surely that it was in Lossos, there was a Minoan wreck nearby and Kenneth Ashworth was an archaeologist and a specialist in ancient scripts. It was an easy step then to guess that the Englishman was involved in the wreck, but why? As far as he, Nikos, was aware, none other than the three divers knew of the disks. Brian had told him that they had collected all there were from the site and that they were safely hidden. But it could just be that Kenneth had been told of the broken disk. He remembered Brian's grovelling admission that they had taken the disks and that Oscar had thrown one away. It was possible, of course, Nikos argued with himself, that other examples of script had been found which had attracted Kenneth Ashworth, Linear A or B for example. In which case there was no problem and no urgency. But it could be the broken disk which had brought Kenneth Ashworth from his desk in Athens.

The thought worried Nikos and he began to regret that he had not acted more quickly to get the disks out of Lossos. He had earlier decided that he would have plenty of time and that it was better to have arranged the disposal of the loot before removing it from the safety of the south coast. But this strategy was now looking false as Lossos filled with archaeologists, divers and reporters, and facts and tales were cross-checked and investigated.

Nikos gulped his brandy and beckoned for a refill, urgently lighting another Marlboro from the stub of the first. So what he had intended to be a leisurely reconnaissance and a carefully planned and discreet removal of the stolen trophies had now become an urgent task. He could not trust the divers to stand up to the interrogation of newspapermen and the questions of the professionals for long. What should he do? He needed to talk to the man from London: without an outlet for the loot the whole thing was pointless. He needed to contact Brian and the others to find out where the treasure was and to warn them against giving anything away. He needed to discover a way to get it all out of Lossos, and quickly.

That wasn't going to be easy; every boat and ferry would be watched, he knew something of the concern that the professionals had for security on a site such as this. If he hired a boat he would be noticed, and how heavy were the damn things, and how much other stuff was there; could he carry them himself? Carrying a heavy load in his adopted role as a journalist would draw unwanted attention; writers travel lightly.

He smoked and drank in the warm still evening while the sounds of laughter drifted over to him from the brightly lit hotel terrace, and turned over possibilities in his mind. If, he mused, travelling publicly was difficult, then why not go secretly? Was it possible to smuggle the disks out of Lossos any other way? By now Nikos had drunk enough to arrive at that state of mind in which reality and unreality, practicality and impossibility, became merged, and mere possibilities become solutions. The ferries would be public, he thought, and would be watched; the taxi boat was out of the question. He didn't have the local contacts to bribe a fisherman, so escape over the sea was out. So if it couldn't be by sea, then it must be by land; and the land was coast and mountain. The coast led to Rodhia or Sfakia; there was nothing after Rodhia but more coast. Sfakia would be busy and buses full. Taxi drivers talked. So why not go over the mountains?

Nikos conjured up a map of Crete in his mind: it could not be more than fifty kilometres from Lossos to Hania, possibly only thirty to the villages north of the mountains from where it would be possible to get a taxi or bus which would not be subject to the surveillance probable in Sfakia. Thirty kilometres, say two days, at the most three. And there were old paths, he was sure, paths used by shepherds which had been the lifelines of Cretan resistance during the war and were now used daily by trekkers. That was the way to get the loot out and over to the north coast from which Athens could be reached in a day or two by ferry or plane. Brilliant. Nikos was so pleased by this radical solution that he ordered yet another Metaxa and drank to himself in congratulation.

From being a drunken conjecture, the escape over the mountains became the only, the romantic solution, to his problem, and Nikos never again questioned it seriously. It appealed to his imagination and his immaturity; he saw himself striding over the hills in triumph, leaving his enemies behind. The fact that the journey to Theriso, north of the Lefka Ori, would take a fit and experienced mountaineer at least two twelve-hour days even if he knew the route and where the wells were, was ignored; Nikos just prided himself on his forethought to bring his boots. That was planning.

And now to more immediate and practical problems. Nikos had to decide how to meet his wife and the Ashworths. They would not expect to see him here; in that respect he had the advantage. He could choose whether to get it over with tonight or to leave it until the morning. With the confidence of the alcohol he decided that he would do it tonight, playing the role of international newspaper reporter intent on an 'in-depth analysis of one of the most important archaeological discoveries of the late twentieth century. From our Special Correspondent, in Sfakia, Crete.' The words rolled across his mind. He liked the role, would play it well, with authority and conviction. He would, he decided, actually write the article and thus benefit twice from his involvement. A good cover for his other activities.

He imagined meeting Kenneth and Mary: 'Good evening, Professor. Mary, how are you? How lovely to see you. And to make my pleasure complete, my darling wife, looking as beautiful as ever!'

At this last his imagination stumbled. Even drunk he could see Jenny turning to him with those cold eyes which saw through him, and his resolution faltered. Oh shit, why did she have to come here and spoil his fun, it wasn't going to be easy with her watching him all the time in that cool English way she had. But he would have to be nice to her to get as much freedom as possible. He called for a fifth brandy and his bill before staggering out into the darkness and the treacherous shingle which rolled under his feet, adding to the effects of the brandy.

Nikos paused at the foot of the stairs up to the terrace to compose himself. He hitched up his trousers around his stomach and tucked his shirt in tightly; holding on to the stair rail he carefully wiped each black and now scarred shoe against a trouser leg. He rubbed his face with both hands and smoothed his moustache and started up the steps to be met by Jackie bouncing down. She shot past him, calling, "I'll be back in a minute," and disappeared into the darkness. Nikos continued the climb and prepared his face to record astonishment. But the terrace was bare, empty; in the few minutes that it had taken him to stumble across the beach, Brad and Gillian had led the Ashworths and Jenny to Andreas' restaurant where the big man was already displaying his dishes with anxious enthusiasm.

Nikos dropped into a chair on the terrace and lit yet another cigarette, torn between relief and disappointment; part of him wanted to go in search of the group, part felt tired and drunk, and sleep called. The latter won and by the time Jackie returned he was unconscious on his bed, sweating in the stuffy black hole behind the tree. Jackie climbed the steps and looked around the empty terrace, relieved that the Greek had gone; without giving him a further thought she poured herself a vodka and lots of tonic and ice and went to sit on the wall and watch the nightlife of Lossos unfold beneath her feet. Another hour and she could finish, five minutes after that she would be in Lakkis' bar and the night would start.

Nikos awoke disorientated and still drunk to the sound of voices and laughter from the terrace. He showered and cleaned his teeth before going to sit on his small leaf- covered balcony wearing only a thin pair of shorts. He lit a Marlboro and coughed and blew smoke at the dry leaves through which the quiet conversation of the returned Ashworths and Jenny filtered from the bar. Once again he was undecided as to whether to introduce himself or not and sat straining to hear, but the soft crash of the sea on the shingle covered the words. He had just decided to get dressed and go down when he heard the scraping of chairs and the unmistakable intonations of "Goodnight", "*Kaliniktasas*", "Sleep well", followed by the sounds of people descending the stairs. Nikos cursed his tree and resolved that if he had to suffer it, at least it could be pruned tomorrow to allow him to see out, undetected.

The last sounds passed away but the lights on the bar remained; thirsty and in need of another brandy, Nikos slipped on a shirt and trousers and shuffled barefoot downstairs to the bar. The clatter of glasses showed that Jackie was still on duty and if she was surprised to see him, she did not show it. "I thought you'd gone to bed."

Unable to resist the response, Nikos leered at her. "I went to bed but I was lonely ..."

"Tough. That's your problem. Here's your brandy. I'll bring the water over in a moment. I'll just nip down and get some big bottles."

She looked at him levelly as she came out from behind the bar, still polite, for he was a guest, but totally dismissive. "Please have a seat." She waved a hand at the empty terrace.

But the terrace was not completely empty. At the far end where there was less light a figure in a white dress leaned, with hands on the low wall, looking down along the beach. As Nikos scraped a chair across the floor, Jenny stood up and turned towards him. A look of horror crossed her face, fleeting but clear, to be replaced by a more acceptable incredulity.

"Niko? What the hell are you doing here?"

Their marriage had come to an end. Each had shown to the other their true feelings in that snapshot on the terrace. Lovers would have been astonished and delighted. Jenny and Nikos both showed horror

177

and disappointment and could never forget their own response mirrored in the reaction of the other.

Chapter twenty three

Jackie served Nikos with more brandy and Jenny with a cold white wine and stood uncertainly at the bar. A tape of Greek music ran quietly and repetitively; one, two, one, two, emphasising the regularity of the waves on the shingle. A gust of distant laughter crossed the bay from one of the few tavernas which were still open; a nearly full golden moon rose through wisps of thin cloud and a few stars bravely fought its pale light. Silence. Stillness.

Jackie was unsure, oddly reluctant to leave the terrace to the tense couple at the far end. She had finished her shift and Lakki's bar beckoned; the last few glasses and ashtrays could wait until morning but she remained fascinated by the mime of antipathy between Jenny and Nikos. If one had taken a dagger and plunged it into the other, blade flashing in the moonlight, she would not have been surprised. The hostility was screaming into the night from Nikos' growls and Jenny's responding caustic yelps. Jackie knew nothing of the history of the actors but the pantomime told the story of ten years in ten minutes and the audience of one was fearful of the end. She was not a particularly empathetic girl but would remember later the awful coldness between the two, a coldness contrasting with the warmth and beauty of the night.

At length Jackie broke the tension. She lit a cigarette for courage and ventured a little way across the terrace towards the discordant couple. Nikos sat with his back to her, crouched over the table and his brandy glass; Jenny was perched on the edge of her chair at right-angles to him, feet on the low wall, arms about her knees, looking out to sea and the long golden path to the moon. Jackie coughed quietly and Jenny turned and smiled at her, relieved that the tension between her and her husband had been broken.

"Do you want anything else? I'm going to close the bar now if you don't mind."

"No, thank you."

"I'll have another brandy," Nikos grunted, unmoving.

"Nothing for me, *efharisto poli*. Thank you. I hope we haven't kept you too late."

Jackie smiled back at the older woman, "I'm used to it. No problem. I'll close up then, if that's OK."

"That's all, thank you. *Kalinikta*."

Nikos muttered unintelligibly and lit another cigarette.

Jackie took Nikos' brandy and put it beside his slumped elbow. "Good night, sleep well."

Jackie locked the bar shutter and turned off the lights; with a last look at the silent couple she went down the stairs and into the night.

In silence Nikos smoked and Jenny watched the moon climb higher into the sky. Jenny shivered despite the warmth.

"I'm going to bed now. I'm tired. It's been a long day." She stood up and looked down at the slumped figure in front of her. A sudden nostalgic tenderness made her stroke Nikos' thick black hair as she passed his chair and he caught her hand and brought it to his lips in a clumsy kiss.

"No, Niko, it's too late, now; it's all over. I'll see you tomorrow." Jenny gently withdrew her hand from his and left him on the moonlit terrace.

As Jenny walked slowly down the stairs, Nikos stood up and drained the last of his brandy in sudden loneliness. He pitched his cigarette out into the still night. She wasn't going to leave him like this; she had brushed his hair and hadn't totally rejected his kiss. She was beautiful and she was his wife and he wanted her. Waves of lust swept the brandy aside and he stumbled down the dark stairs after her. Where had she gone? A light suddenly flooded another staircase and he caught a glimpse of her white dress as she closed the door to her room, returning the stairs to darkness.

Nikos stood for a while at the foot of the staircase, caught between his lust and his fear of almost certain rejection. He remembered her fingers on his hair and climbed a step. He remembered her words 'It's all over' and retreated again. He imagined her slim body and her small breasts and her pink nipples. She was his wife; she would not, could not, refuse him. Taking a deep breath he stumbled up the dark stairs. He knocked quietly and there was silence within the room; he knocked again more loudly. Jenny opened the door and a wedge of light dazzled him.

"Go away, Niko. Be quiet," she hissed.

"Just let me come in for a moment."

"No. Go away, go to bed." Down the corridor another door opened and a dark silhouette peered out.

Jenny was horrified. "Oh, all right, come in, but don't make any noise. Only for a moment."

Nikos stumbled into the light, pushing the door noisily shut behind him.

Jenny stood at the far side of the twin beds wrapped in a white towel. She had let her hair down and looked smaller and vulnerable. Simultaneously tempted by her beauty and repelled by her disdain he moved round towards her with a greasily ingratiating smile. She glared at him.

"Stay where you are. Don't touch me. What do you want anyway? I told you it was all over."

"Jenny, *agapi mou*, I didn't want it to be like this. I don't want to fight with you."

"I won't fight you any more. It's finished. Everything. It's all over. I told you. Now, please, go away."

"No, you're my wife; you can't throw me out like that. You can't do this to me."

Nikos sat on the edge of the bed and lit a cigarette.

"You can't do this to me, you loved me once."

Jenny sighed.

"Yes," she said sadly, "I loved you once. But I don't love you any more. Don't you see, Niko, it's finished, I don't want to be married to you any more."

Nikos stood up suddenly and moved around the end of the bed, anger turning his florid face a deeper shade of red. He made a grab for her and sparks flew from his cigarette. Evading his grasp, Jenny retreated towards the window.

"I won't let you go; you're my wife, I won't let you." His voice rose, echoing around the small bare room.

"Oh, go away you drunken slob. And be quiet, for God's sake."

"So it's drunken slob, is it now? I'll not be quiet; I'll wake up your precious English friends and make you look stupid. I'll say you invited me in and then made a fuss. Nobody will believe you."

Jenny was silent for a moment facing him and fearless now, blue eyes blazing at his arrogance. She stood straight, her composure only slightly marred by having to hold the towel in place with one hand. She pointed at the door. "Get out now or I'll scream." She spat at him like a cornered cat.

Nikos grabbed the outstretched arm, pulled her towards him and flung her across the room onto the bed. Jenny fell awkwardly on her front and hit her head on the wall. Nikos stood panting by the window and then hurled his cigarette out into the night and walked back to the bed to stand angry and dangerous above her. Reaching down, he pulled the towel viciously from under her and she rolled over, a thin red trickle of blood falling diagonally across her white forehead. He knelt in sudden apology. "Jenny, I'm sorry. I didn't mean to hurt you."

Jenny kicked out hard and her foot caught him on the side of his head. Nikos rocked on his knees then recovered and hit her shoulder with a backhand blow which knocked her back onto the bed. She lay naked and tempting below him, her innocence betrayed by the scarlet blood on her face which gave her an appearance of unconscious depravity. Excited by her body and the blood and his violence, he ripped his shirt off the dark-haired sweating rolls of his chest. Jenny's eyes dared him, almost tempting. She kicked out at him again but he caught her ankle in a sweaty fist. Holding her with one hand despite her struggle he ripped his trousers open and dragged down his shorts. He dropped heavily on to her and thrust his knees between her thighs. Overwhelmed by his sweating bulk and terrified by his violence Jenny, arched against him and unmoving, submitted and allowed him to enter her.

Her tightly shut eyes filled with tears and pain and humiliation as he thrust roughly, endlessly, grossly, panting to his climax. At his final, grunting gasp she lay still then shuddered her horror and slipped from under him. She stood naked, looking down at him in contempt, white with shock but cold and calm. Her voice was sharp and hard like an icefall.

"You pathetic Greek bastard; you arrogant, incompetent, greasy shit. You can't even fuck properly. You are a nasty, dirty *malaka* with no talent; you're an arrogant boorish peasant. Now go to hell, you dirty bastard. I don't want to see you or speak to you again. Now get out and stay away from me. For ever."

She picked up the towel and covered herself from his gaze for the last time. "I'm going to shower now; I don't want you here when I come out."

But he did not leave. When Jenny came from the shower, refreshed but with a trickle of blood from the scratch on her forehead and a crimson wheal on her right shoulder, rubbing herself in a large white towel, he was sitting on the bed, back to the wall, smoking again, wrapped in a damp sheet.

She looked at him in loathing. "For God's sake, Niko; I told you to go."

Nikos looked at her with hate tempered by a little residual lust and a hint of remorse. "So that's it, is it?" he sneered. "Goodbye Nikos, is that it? I'm not good enough for you any more. Not up to your clever English friends. A poor Greek boy, with no money and no talent. But I will be good enough, you'll see; better."

He got to his feet and glowered down at her, his erratic gestures no longer frightening; part grotesque, part pathetic.

"You wait till I get the disks out and make all that money, then you'll know how clever I am. Then you'll be sorry. You'll be sorry that you're not still with me when I've got my house in Sounion and my new flat and I'm going off round the world. Then you'll be really sorry and you'll want to be with me again."

Jenny walked to the window with the towel wrapped tightly round her shoulders and stood for a moment looking out at the night. She turned to the angry and sullen man on her bed, indifferent now, and dismissive.

"Niko. The only regret that I shall ever have is that I met you. Now get out or I will wake the hotel. And remember this: our marriage is over. I hate you and I despise you, and I don't want to see you again, ever."

She wanted to cry but wouldn't let herself. "Now go to hell and leave me in peace."

Chapter twenty four

Jenny awoke from a deep sleep to the soft rustle of waves on shingle. Patterns of sunlight were reflected across the ceiling of her room, highlighted by occasional prismatic diamonds, erratic, irrational, entrancing. There was an early freshness in the air which drifted in through her open window and the heat in the elongated rectangle of sunshine lying on her bed promised a hot day ahead. She stretched catlike and sensuous under the thin sheet then grimaced as the bruise on her shoulder reminded her of Nikos; she felt the dry scar on her forehead and felt sick as she recalled the weight and thrust of his heavy body. But at the same time she felt a tremendous relief, out of the shadow of Nikos at last; liberated and free. She stretched again and wondered how it was that the events of the previous night had so little effect; had passed like a cramp, painful for a moment, then gone, to leave only a faint memory. There was nothing left but a slightly bruised shoulder, a scarred forehead and a glorious sense of escape.

From the window she watched a fishing boat etch successive triangles into the grey steel of the sea which promised a cleansing and rebirth, a baptism into a new life. Jenny scattered clothes from her suitcase to find a black swimsuit; within two minutes of leaving her room she had dived from the pier and was swimming a fast crawl down the brilliant path of the sun.

A few weed-entangled buoys littered the bay, moving erratically to the tug of invisible currents and the lift of small waves. Jenny swam towards one of the bigger ones, intent only on her breathing and the pleasing regularity of her strokes and the cool water on her body. She was just about to grab the buoy when she realised that there was already someone holding onto it and came to a splashing clumsy stop.

"Oh, I'm sorry, I didn't see you." Jenny treaded water and swept her hair away from her face with one hand. "I didn't think that there would be anyone else here."

Fiona grinned at her, "I'm always here, at around this time, I do this every day. You were in a bit of a hurry."

Jenny held onto the buoy and they both looked back at the village which lay open and innocent, lit by the low morning sun behind them.

"Yes. There are some things you want to leave."

"And some people?"

"Yeah. And some people. Well, certainly one."

"Tell me more. I'm Fiona, by the way, I work here."

"Oh, right. I saw you in the bar last night, early on. I'm Jenny." She was going to say 'Jenny Kontos' but suddenly decided that it was no longer appropriate. "I'm with Mary and Kenneth Ashworth, we only arrived yesterday. Kenneth has come to work with Brad Slinger on the wreck. We had dinner with him last night, he's nice."

Fiona smiled at Jenny; she was four or five years younger but felt matriarchal in the face of Jenny's innocence. "He's unusual. So who were you rushing away from?"

It was a long time since Jenny had had anyone other than Mary to talk to. There was something about this clear-eyed Australian girl which invited confidence. Something about the isolation in the middle of the bay with the village spread around them peacefully in the morning sun. Jenny held on to the chain of the buoy and turned to look at the hotel and its white reflection on the blue sea.

"It's my husband. Ex-husband-to-be. I hate him." She unconsciously raised a dripping hand to brush the scratch on her forehead. "I hate him and I'm leaving him. Forever. He's foul and horrible and fat; he makes my flesh creep. I hate him to touch me. And he smells. And he smokes too much. And drinks. And he's fat."

Now the tears came, salty to mix with the salt of the sea.

"Is that all? You said 'fat' twice; that's bad," Fiona said quietly. Jenny sniffed and sobbed again, wanting to laugh and cry together.

"You poor thing. He's only a man, you know. They're like that. You mustn't be too hard on him."

Jenny was glad of the dry Australian humour and could not resist a weak smile though her eyes glistened with tears. "He's not a man, he's a shit. I didn't like him much when he was poor and I certainly won't like him if he's going to get rich, like he says. He'll be even more horrible then."

"Well, let's hope that he doesn't get rich, then. I'm sure there's not much chance of that here in Lossos."

"Oh, that's why he's here, I think. He's got some plan or other, something to do with the wreck, some disks or something."

Jenny had not yet linked the disks of Nikos' ravings with the Phaistos disk and Kenneth Ashworth's visit to Lossos. Fiona, more used to intrigue, spotted the connection immediately. She needed to know more. "Come on. I'll race you back to the pier and you can tell me all about it over breakfast. OK!" She shot off like a fish through the water. Jenny blew her nose in an unladylike fashion and set off after her.

It is impossible to climb gracefully from the sea onto a beach of pebbles. Most stagger and fall, slip and splash like some sea creature in a distant geological age venturing for the first time on to land. Fiona watched Jenny's emergence from the waves with amusement and chucked a towel at her as she groped for her sandals.

"It's not easy, is it? I keep telling Theseus to put a ladder up onto the pier, but he's an idle sod. Come on, let's eat; I'm hungry."

Fiona led the way up the stairs to the empty sun-soaked terrace which sheltered behind huge tilted umbrellas. "Tourists always miss the best parts of the day in Lossos," she remarked. "The best parts are early in the morning when the air and the sea are fresh, and very late at night when the stars shine. Those are my favourites. What do you think?"

"This is my first time here, so I don't know yet. But this morning is so good, I feel reborn."

Fiona gave Jenny a sidelong glance. "Lossos changes people. It seems to be working on you already."

"Mmm. I feel so relaxed and yet I've only been here twelve hours. God, it seems a lifetime already. Athens seems so far away."

"Athens is a long way away, but your husband is here. You don't seem too happy about that."

"I'm not happy about that, I didn't expect him to be here, and I know it sounds bad, but I was so …" She hunted for the word. "So … hurt, so disappointed, that he was here. As if he'd done it deliberately."

"So, why is he here, and why didn't you know he was coming?"

For ten minutes Jenny talked without stopping as if a broken dam in her mind had suddenly released ten years of repression. She told Fiona of her mother's death and her time at school in England, of coming to live with her father in an alien Athens, of his death in the plane crash. She told of her love and admiration for Mary and Kenneth and of how she felt that she had betrayed them when she married Nikos. She told of the happy days of her early marriage and her hopes that she would have children, and then how she had drifted away from Nikos and the partying society of Athens, and how she came to resent his grossness and drunkenness.

Throughout it all, Fiona sat silent; receptive, sympathetic and attentive.

Jenny's tale came to an end at last. "I'm sorry, I haven't talked so much for years. I'm boring you, you don't want to know my problems."

"I told you, Lossos changes people. You, no one, is the same here as they are anywhere else. I loved hearing your story. But tell me one more thing: why is your husband, if I can still call him that, here in Sfakia? Do you know?"

"Not really, but last night, after ..."

Fiona had guessed that something nasty had happened to her new friend last night which had caused this outpouring of confidences. "Yeah, I understand. So he was trying to justify himself to you. Yeah, I know, they do. Wankers, most of them. So what did he say?"

"Well, he said something about getting rich. Something about selling some disks, I didn't take much notice. But I thought that selling computer disks in Lossos was a bit unlikely. But he's always had silly ideas."

"I don't think it's computer disks. Did he mention the wreck?"

"No, I don't think so. But he did talk about some divers he knew, who were here. Do you think that's something to do with it?"

Fiona thought rapidly. She did not want to exploit the confidences of this charming, naive woman, but was not yet sure enough of Jenny's allegiances to be totally open with her. "Maybe it is," she said, "Oh well, we'll see. Don't worry about it. Now let me tell you a bit about Lossos."

Fiona chattered inconsequently about life in the village and the hotel, all the time desperate to escape to find Dimitris. She had to tell him that the time had come when the disks were going to be moved from their hiding place and that the watchers should be ready.

Thursday 12th September: 0930 hrs

Nikos felt uncomfortable in Lossos; neither native nor tourist, and dressed inappropriately for either role, he stumbled along the pebbles in the heat, his black leather bag swinging clumsily, sweating already. He resolved to buy something more suitable than the dark trousers, white formal shirt and black leather shoes which he had brought from Athens and which now set him apart from the black-clothed locals and the bright beachwear of the visitors. He was accustomed to the anonymity of the big city and hated the feeling of exposure and interrogation which followed him as he climbed the steep and narrow passages to the upper regions of the village.

Nikos had not had the courage to face either breakfast or his wife after the excesses and activities of the previous night and had slept late and badly. The cheap brandy still soured his stomach and his mind churned with a succession of recollections of his behaviour with Jenny. These memories had a powerful underlying theme of remorse decorated with brief rhapsodies in which he saw himself as dominant and even heroic. He refused to accept that what he had done was wrong. Rather, he argued, Jenny had been wrong to refuse him and in denying him had brought the violence upon herself.

And now she wanted to finish their marriage, well, he'd see about that. It was not easy in Greece and Greek lawyers were reluctant to represent foreign girls against Greek men. He would hold on to her and she would eventually come to realise that she would be better off with him. And he would be nice to her and treat her well, and she might come to love him again. But, of course, he would be in control, and he would not let her influence him. With a house in Sounion and the new flat in Athens, he would have plenty of time for freedom. And plenty of money. With such thoughts he stumbled uncomfortably up the steep concrete staircase, his sweat turning his white shirt grey. Now to face Brian and the others.

Oscar was down on the beach bringing in the morning's catch of small shining fish whose lustre was visibly dying in the air and heat. He would come up at about twelve, shower and sleep for a couple of hours before going back down to the village to find Jackie.

Brian and Robert sat on their bare terrace shielded from the sun by a tattered umbrella which had once been blue and on which the words 'Martini – *ciao!*' appeared faintly. Brian was smoking a meagre cigarette, feet up on a tilted chair. Both turned at the sound of Nikos' panting arrival which contrasted with his brisk "*Kalimera.* Good morning, gentlemen." Nikos was not going to let his physical discomfort detract from his wish to be in control. "Good morning, Brian, and I presume that you must be Robert. I am pleased to meet you and I look forward to working with you."

Brian's astonishment turned to a belated recognition. "Nikos, good to see you, when did you get here? You should have called, I would have met you. Yes, this is Robert."

Robert did not bother to get up and offered a casual hand. "Hi. Good to see you. So you've come to give us a hand. About bloody time, I'm sick of this place. So, how're you going to do it, then?"

Brian was embarrassed by his friend's hostility. "Nikos, let me get you a coffee, will you have a cigarette? I'm afraid we've only got these."

"*Efharisto*, Brian, I'll smoke my own. But I would like a coffee, if you don't mind."

Robert's truculence and Brian's apology had already given Nikos the advantage he sought and he settled back comfortably in his chair and talked expansively of his journey and his work in Athens. Robert was bored by this and felt that Brian was being overly polite with this gross Greek. After all, he thought, they had discovered the wreck and had done the difficult part of taking and hiding the treasure; all this man had to do was to get the gear out of Lossos and sell it. The sooner the better as far as he, Robert, was concerned. The earlier instinctive distrust of Nikos which he had felt during the telephone discussions with Brian had already hardened into something stronger. He wasn't going to let the initiative pass completely from their hands, even if Brian seemed intent on letting it do so. He got up, noisily scraping his chair back on the rough concrete, and went to sit on the low unfinished balcony with his back to the sun and looked down on Nikos.

"So, what's the plan then, and what do you think we're going to make out of it? I suppose that you've got it all in hand or you wouldn't be here. And before we start, let's decide what your cut is going to be."

Nikos moved his chair round so that he was out of the sun and looked blandly up at the Scotsman. Brian could not see his eyes through the dark glasses. "Yes, of course I have made the arrangements. As you say, I would not be here if I had not," he lied readily. "But, first, let us clarify the matter of the disks, which you tried to conceal from me. That is not the way I wish to do business. I wish to be sure that there is nothing else which you have not told me. Without this, I regret that I cannot help you."

"Well, yes," Brian gave a weak smile, "That was a mistake. I'm sorry, but we had only just found the things, and we didn't know what they were ..."

"And you thought that an ignorant Greek would not recognise the value. That was another mistake, my friend. The disks could be quite valuable, as I am sure you have now realised; in fact, without them I would not be here. The rest of the stuff is not worth my effort." Nikos leaned forward and stubbed out his Marlboro; he was enjoying this. "So," he went on, "How many disks are there?"

Brian looked at Robert fidgeting on the balcony. "How many are there?"

Robert didn't like being put in the spotlight, his preferred role was to say little and criticise later. "Aye, well, there's a few ..."

Nikos suddenly stood up and walked slowly across the terrace to stand between Robert and the sun. His dark glasses revealed nothing and his girth and height dominated the Scotsman. "Let us understand one another before we go further. You will tell me all there is to know about what you have stolen, now. If you do not, I can easily become the investigating reporter who discovers the true facts about the Lossos shipwreck and who reveals all, as his public duty, to the Greek police. Do I make it clear? You are foreigners here, *xenoi*, and the Greeks do not like people who steal their treasures. Greek prisons are unpleasant, *ne?*"

Robert glared at Brian, "See what you've got us into again, you bloody idiot." He looked up at his reflection in Nikos' sunglasses and shrugged at himself. "Yeah. Ok. Point made. But remember that we both have this problem. We have to trust you as well."

Nikos laughed and went to sit down again in the shade. "Of course. You can trust me. We will do this thing together; we cannot have, what do you say, quarrelling among thieves, *ne?* Now tell me what you have got and I will tell you what we will do with it, and we will be friends."

Under Robert's sullen gaze and Nikos' calculating stare, Brian told the story of what they had found. At the end of his recital, Nikos was silent for a moment and then gave a great laugh. "*Poli orea. Endaxi.* It is good. Now we are friends and we do business together." He grinned at the two British and opened his arms wide. "*Signomi.* I am sorry. But you will understand that I had to come to meet with you and to see how the land lies. You two have done the main job, getting the artefacts out of the sea and on to dry land. And hiding it, of course. By the way," he looked at Brian, "where is it hidden? I should like to know so that I can finalise the plan for getting it off Crete and to Athens."

"Wait a minute," Robert interrupted, trying to regain some initiative, "I don't think that you need to know that yet. We'll tell you when it's necessary."

Brian was embarrassed again. "I'm sorry," he grinned weakly, "I think that Robert is right, really. We can show you later – it would be difficult to explain, anyway. But it's not far from here, up on the cliff." He waved vaguely up at the escarpment behind the house.

"*Endaxi.* That is no problem, you will show me later. First we should get to know each other better, become good friends. We are going to have to work together so it is better that we be friends." Nikos reached into his bag and pulled out a half litre of '12' ouzo.

"First we must have a drink together, so I have brought you a small gift. I hope that it is to your taste." He looked at Robert, "I am sorry that I did not bring whisky; if I had known that you were a Scottish man, I would have done so."

"It's 'Scotsman'," Robert muttered ungratefully, "But don't worry, we drink anything these days. I'll get some glasses. We don't have any ice, so it'll have to be water. This place doesn't run to a fridge."

Nikos poured the drinks, making sure that he gave himself less than the others, partly out of consideration for his stomach and partly to keep the advantage which he had gained. After a couple of glasses each during which Nikos told tales of Athens and salacious stories of his escapades whilst his wife was away, the British were more re- laxed and Nikos grew more confident.

"Now I tell you my plans, *ne*? I hope that they meet with your agreement. I have made contact with a man in London who is a buyer for an American who makes a collection of these things, a private collection. No, I do not know his name, it does not matter, but I understand that he pays well and in whatever currency you like. The buyer will be in Athens for two or three days from the eighteenth of this month and if he likes the goods he will arrange for them to be placed in a – I do not know your word – *to fortigo*, yes, a lorry, which will then go to London. The American will come to London to see them and to make payment. Easy, *ne*? All we have to do is to get the things to Athens in good time. This gives us about a week, a little more."

This fiction rolled off Nikos' tongue like a well-rehearsed story and he was secretly delighted with his invention. He had no inten- tion whatever of letting the treasure out of his hands and, once in Athens, his town, he would have no difficulty in separating it from the British forever.

Brian was impressed; Robert, on the other hand, had more prac- tical considerations. "So there's your commission, the buyer's cut, payment for the transport – what's in it for us? You must have agreed a price."

"I am sorry, my friend, no price can be agreed until the goods have been seen and approved by the American. And, besides, I have only just learnt about the disks, which does not help. If he likes what we produce, he will give us a fair price, that is the way things work in these matters, you should understand." Nikos challenged Robert to disagree, "Unless you have any better ideas?"

Robert hadn't, but wasn't satisfied. "Sounds bloody dodgy to me," he grumbled.

"We give up the stuff to you and your buyer and then sit and wait till some bloody American coughs up. What guarantee do we get that it all works? We haven't a chance."

"Look, my friend, I am a man of honour," Nikos leaned back in his chair and patted his stomach in confirmation. "You will be paid, and paid well. You will have to trust me. Sometimes there is no other way."

Robert subsided, muttering. "Well, I suppose so, but how long will it all take?"

"If, when the American comes to London, he likes the goods and is satisfied by their authenticity," Nikos confirmed with confidence, "he will make the arrangements to get the goods to the US and pay the buyer. The buyer will then pay you, wherever you want, and you should think about this," Nikos added irrelevant detail to make his story more plausible. He went on, "Some countries are more tolerant than others. You should have your money in, say, a week after we get to Athens. And then, my friend," Nikos leaned forward and slapped Robert heavily on the knee, "You will be free, and the world, and all the girls in it, will be yours for the taking. You will enjoy, *ne*?"

Midday. Hot sun moving across the sky, shadows moving in counter balance. Ferries coming and going with their loads of tourists leaning over the rails enchanted by the small village nestling under the orange-grey cliffs and its air of peace and tranquillity. Three conspirators, milky white glasses of ouzo, the smoke of cigarettes drifting out over the balcony.

"It's not going to be easy getting the stuff out of here, everyone watches all the time; can you imagine getting onto a ferry with the disks in your rucksack and a couple of Minoan swords in your hand? Not easy, not easy at all." Brian watched the town beneath the terrace. "Theseus said that there were bloody ears everywhere; he should have said eyes. And we have got to decide what to tell Theseus, about our leaving, I mean. Any thoughts?"

Nikos stubbed out his cigarette and took a sip of his ouzo. "I have thought about this and I think I know how we could do it. First, a question. How heavy is it, all together?"

"Well, it took three of us to carry the lot to the hiding place, I suppose about ten, twelve kilos each. Something like that."

Nikos mused, "So it's going to take three of us again next time; I had hoped only two but three is OK." He sat forward in his chair, a big man, hands on knees, dominant now, his eyes still concealed by the dark glasses. His smile was humourless, with a touch of complacency. He took a cigarette from the nearly empty red packet on the small table, lit it and blew smoke. He finished his ouzo and leaned back, tilting the chair on its back legs so that its back came to rest against the wall. The others waited. Nikos was in control.

"This is what we are going to do. We are going to carry the things out over the White Mountains, to Theriso. We will go by night, soon, as the moon is still good. Now wait –" Robert was snorting his derision as Nikos continued, "I know it sounds difficult, but we are strong. It is only about thirty kilometres and there is a hut on top where we can get water. It will take two days. We will get out of Lossos while it is still dark and then stop somewhere until dawn and then go on again. We should be at the hut by nightfall. Then down to Theriso next day, Hania the day after, and Athens the day after that. We'll sail, I don't fancy getting on a plane with stolen Minoan treasure going through the scanner."

He stopped and looked at his sceptical audience. "OK, you do better."

"Bloody hell," Robert sneered, "What a crazy idea. Leave me out of this, I'm a diver, not a bloody mountaineer."

Nikos shrugged, unimpressed. "Right, we leave you out; that means we must take your other friend, what's his name, Oscar?

Some decisions are taken accidentally. What should have been a discussion of whether it was possible to carry fifteen kilos each over 2000m mountains in the night, rather became an argument about who should go. No talk about the route, no discussion of rations, no thought about clothes or footwear, but whether it should be Oscar or Robert who was left behind. Robert's initial derision had weakened to a faint optimism under the influence of the idea and, possibly, the ouzo, and he had also decided that he would need to go to keep an eye on Nikos. His mistrust of the Greek had not been mollified by Nikos' glib plans; it all seemed a bit too easy, a bit too plausible, and if Brian was going to be his usual gullible self, then he, Robert, had better be wary. Be canny, he though to himself, be canny.

Somehow the matter was resolved. No real decision had been taken, nothing had been agreed, but they would do it. Nikos, Brian and Robert would carry the Phaistos treasures over the hills en route to the riches of the United States.

One final question. When? Today was Thursday; the village was busy on Saturdays so their absence might not be as noticeable. They would go on Friday night, using tomorrow to sleep and to buy food and water and an extra couple of rucksacks. Midnight on Friday. Friday, the thirteenth.

Chapter twenty five

As Nikos was struggling up the alleyways of Lossos to his meeting with the divers, Kenneth and Mary were eating a leisurely breakfast on the sunlit terrace, shielded from the early sun by tilted umbrellas segmented in blue and white. Jenny came to join them as Fiona left, making the excuse of having to return to work but actually going to find Dimitris and to tell him what she had learnt from Jenny. The time to alert the watchers had come.

"Sleep well, dear?" Mary smiled across at Jenny. "What have you done to your forehead? You've got quite a scratch there."

"Nikos is here," she said flatly, "We had an ... argument. I'm leaving him, it's all over. He's a shit and I hate him."

Tears welled in her eyes again but in her new-found resolution she held them back. She would not cry over the bastard again.

"Nikos here, in Lossos?" Kenneth and Mary spoke almost simultaneously. "What the dickens for?"

"What's he doing here?"

"Oh, you poor thing, did he hurt you?"

Jenny said, quietly, "It's all over; I don't want to talk about it, or him, any more."

"OK, love, tell me about it when you're ready." Mary patted her arm, frowning at her husband who was about to ask further questions. "Don't worry, we'll sort it out. Forget him and enjoy yourself."

Kenneth got the hint and decided to change the subject. He wondered why Nikos was in Lossos; he knew that the Greek was interested in archaeological matters and was intrigued as to why he should turn up now, just as the new disk had come to light. Possibly news travelled faster than he thought. "Did he say anything about what he was doing here? And why now?"

"Oh, he said something about some disks, but I didn't really

195

listen. He's always going on about his great plans and they never come to anything."

"Disks? Now there's a thing – I wonder what he's up to. Did he say anything about meeting anyone here?"

"No. You know what he's like …" Kenneth did; they had little in common and he had realised that at an early stage in their acquaintance, "… a lot of waffle and few facts. I'm sorry, but I don't listen to him any more. It'll be something shady, no doubt."

Gillian, preceded as usual by her dog, interrupted them, Raki going round the tables seeking scraps and ignoring his mistress's admonitions.

"*Kalimera*. Did you all sleep well? Rooms OK?"

"Very comfortable, thank you."

"And you, Jenny; sleep well? That's a nasty bump on your forehead."

Jenny was discomfited by the question and wondered whether her fight with Nikos had gone quite unnoticed; that would be a bit embarrassing to say the least. She wondered how much had been heard.

"Well, yes, thank you. I just caught it on a rope when I was swimming …" She sought to change the subject quickly, and scouted round for something to say. "Oh, and I met Fiona this morning and had a good chat with her, she's nice."

Gillian looked at her with her knowledgeable, somewhat cynical glance. OK, if the girl didn't want to talk about it, fair enough, but she would have to keep a careful eye on Nikos. Lock the sod in the black hole for the duration.

"Fiona's a good girl, the best of the lot. She's been coming here for a lot of years now. Have you met Dimitris yet? He's her boyfriend, lover, whatever. He works with my husband Theseus in Athens but we see a lot of him in the summer when she's here. I'll introduce you later."

Kenneth broke in, "Sorry Gillian, to butt in. Do you know where Brad is this morning? I'd like to see him. Got to start work sometime."

"He was in earlier. He said that you would be welcome over on the headland, at the site base, whenever you like."

"I think I'll go over now. Do you fancy a morning stroll, girls?"

The site base, a badly insulated, and therefore baking, hut surrounded by a growing accumulation of equipment had been erected on the shore side of the headland overlooking the wreck and facing across the bay to Lavris and Philikas. Young divers, boys and girls beautifully browned by the sun, were constantly in the water in the task of creating the one metre-cube grid which would be the reference against which the excavation would be carried out. The site was complex because of the steep and interrupted fall of the undersea cliff and the wide area over which it was presumed that the lost ship and its contents were scattered. Anything that was recovered would be precisely located according to the grid to ensure that its relationship to other discoveries could be noted and to enable a detailed picture to be built up. Eventually a computer picture of the sea cliff and the ship would be created and would serve as the record of the site, but in the meantime all the measurements on which that picture would be based had to be taken by the divers. Working underwater at depths of no more than twenty metres was not particularly difficult but even an experienced diver could not stay down for more than forty minutes and, in coming back to the surface, would have to wait around five minutes at five metres depth to acclimatise to the pressure change. The survey alone would take all the first summer and would have to be completed before anything was taken from the wreck. In the meantime it was hard meticulous work and the young team needed skill and accuracy as well as the physical strength to dive four or five times a day.

Brad emerged sweating from the stifling hut as Kenneth and the two women approached along the well-trodden path which wound round the seaward side of the headland from the quay at Lossos past the tiny white chapel of Agios Theodoris and the ruins of the Roman town. Kenneth showed them where the cave chapel of Agios Adonis lay hidden in the rocks below the path, and pointed out what might have been a tiny Roman harbour which was now well above sea level, made redundant by the rising land. The noise of the compressor for the air tanks met them with a muffled mutter as they approached.

"Hi, everybody. Nice of you to come out to see me. Glad to get you out on site, Professor; it will be good for you to see how the workers live at the sharp end of the job. Might make you appreciate us a bit more when we can't find all the bits for you."

Laughing and expansive, the American led them towards the hut, winding through piles of bottles and ropes and beached dinghies. "Any of you got a certificate, to dive, I mean? I'd like to take you down to the wreck sometime."

Jenny had taken her certificate some years earlier but it had lapsed. The others had only snorkelled.

"Never mind," Brad said, "I'm sure that Jenny will soon come up to scratch again and you, Ken, and Mary will be able to see quite a lot from the surface. I, myself, don't dive much these days; prefer to leave it to the youngsters."

A passing shadow dimmed his smile as he turned and looked across the blue bay. Jenny was fascinated by this charming man, and caught the fleeting change. He had his own ghosts; she sympathised, she had hers too. She gave him a smile of such disarming freshness that he was in turn captivated. He had thought last night at dinner that she was attractive but had rather dismissed the English girl as somewhat superficial. Today her happiness and enthusiasm were infectious and the few questions she asked showed that she was not as empty-headed as he had thought; his delight in showing her around was distracting him from the real purpose of their visit.

"I'm sorry, Ken. I am ignoring you. My apologies. But I do have an excuse. It is not every day that I have such a charming lady as a visitor to my site." He corrected himself quickly. "Ladies, I should of course say. Dear me. I plead the excuse of the heat. I am sorry, Mary; ladies, of course."

His embarrassment at this social hiccup was so obvious that Mary took pity on him. "Brad," she took his arm, "it's a delight to be here and it is so kind of you to show us around. Now what else have we got to see?"

Mary was inwardly amused by this slip and its revealing of Brad's interest in Jenny. Now that was something she would encourage. She took a sidelong glance at Jenny who was focusing so much of her unconscious good looks on the American that Mary sympathised with him. The poor man wouldn't have a chance.

Brad recovered quickly and with an un-American grace ushered them into the hut.

"I'm sorry we haven't had air-conditioning installed yet, that may take a little time, in Greece and over here. But we don't need to stay long."

He reached under a bench cluttered with a bizarre mix of modern tools and shards of Minoan pottery and pulled out a battered tin box. He opened it with care and lifted an old piece of towelling.

He stood back. "This, Professor, is what you have come to see."

The clay disk lay in a plastic envelope, its three segments apart. Brad lifted the envelope and the pieces slid out onto a clean paper on the bench. Kenneth leaned over to see and fumbled for his spectacles. He took a stylus and gently urged the three segments together to form a whole and peered at the disk which now lay cracked but complete before him.

Unseen by those in the hut, a vulture circled high in the intense blue of the sky above the headland.

Kenneth was silent for some time, following the spiral of script with a practised eye. "Fifty different symbols, five more than the Iraklion disk, four of them on this side not found on the original disk and in sixty-three groups on this side," Brad said quietly in the background. Two hundred and forty seven signs in total on the two sides."

Mary and Jenny crowded in to see but Kenneth remained still and silent. "Well, well, well," he murmured to himself. "Well, well. I never thought I would see this."

He straightened at last and wiped beads of sweat from his face with a handkerchief. The women crowded in to look more closely as he turned to Brad Slinger and offered a damp hand. "I think that we have to congratulate you, Mr Slinger. We'll have to age test it of course, but I think that you have a second Phaistos disk here. What a remarkable thing. Well done. But," he wondered, "why here? How was it found, what was the context?"

"You have to congratulate Chris, the diver who found it, it was not my doing, and you will want to talk to him. But let's turn it over first, so that you can be sure."

Brad folded the paper over and revealed the second side. "Fifty-one different symbols this time, five new ones including one not used on the other side, in sixty-one groups."

Kenneth adjusted his spectacles and looked closely again, his eyes following the spiralling script. "Yes, I see the new characters. We'll have to recalculate the probable total of dies again," he remarked, "You know the theory that says that for any piece of work the number of total symbols available must be some twenty per cent greater than those used?"

Brad did. "I leave that to the experts," he grinned. "Come on now, you can play later." He took the segments and replaced them in the envelope in the tin box. "I'll have to find somewhere safe to keep these things, I suppose, although there doesn't seem to be a problem yet out here."

He led the way out into the sunshine and the breeze which seemed cool after the heat of the hut. "Come on, we'll go and find Chris, he's usually down there somewhere."

He pointed across to the temporary wooden jetty which had been constructed to allow easier access to the boats and on which a few young divers lay resting in the sun.

As they walked down the new track, Kenneth recalled his

thoughts that morning.

"Do you think that there could be any more, of the disks, I mean?"

Brad laughed, "I give you one and you want more, just like an academic. We can't be sure of course, there's going to be a lot of stuff down there, and we won't know for some time. But this was found out of context, you know, so it might have come from somewhere else altogether. You know what the nuts are like; they would say that it might have been dropped from a passing spaceship. Come on, there's Chris down there."

Chris was a young American, fit and brown, his long limbs sprawled over a damp towel. He looked up as the four approached, shading his eyes from the sun, and jumped to his feet. He shook hands quickly with Kenneth and Mary, and gave Jenny a look of intense approval. "Wow," he said, "If you wanna dive, beautiful, I'm the man. With a buddy like you I could search the whole Atlantic."

Jenny shook his hand, laughing, "I'll think about that."

Brad said, "OK, kids, back to work. Chris, Ken is the expert I told you about, the script man. I want you to tell him how you found the bits of disk."

Chris grinned ruefully at Jenny, "Yeah, OK, back to work. But remember. I'm your man if you're gonna dive, or anything else, for that matter …"

"I'll remember …" Jenny smiled at him, "if I want to dive."

Chris told them how he had been carrying out some general photographic work. "Just covering the site, for the record." He had been out over a patch of weed, some distance from the main wreck site, not expecting anything of interest; the sun had caught a bit of pottery and showed it bright against the dark green weed. He had gone down to look, photographed the thing as it lay and, assuming it would be modern, picked it up.

"Against all instructions," Brad didn't like this admission of unprofessionalism.

"Yeah, well, at least I didn't pick up the second bit." Chris had found, photographed and marked the second piece and then sought others. The third segment was lying only a few metres away, on the weed bed, like the others. "It was as if they had just been thrown there, carelessly, recently."

Chris had searched the area closely but had not found any more pieces. He had not disturbed the weed bed, knowing that this might disturb more contextual evidence, and had brought the three pieces back to the dinghy. "The boss told me off, of course."

Chris grinned his wide white smile at Brad, "But that's what they do. Anyway, I brought them back, job done, balls up, damage done. Anyway when he'd calmed down he got quite excited. I suppose that's why you're here, Mr Ashworth; what do you think of it, is it another Phaistos disk?"

"Can't be certain, of course, and it might just be a late twentieth-century hoax, put there by some idiot who has an odd idea of fun. But it's promising, to say the least. Very interesting indeed." Kenneth shook Chris's hand, "Well done, you might go down in history for this. I'll talk to you again later, and ... I'm sure that I would have picked it up." He turned away and then back. "I don't suppose," he grinned, "that there are any more under there – what do you think?"

"I'll sure keep my eyes open. Nice to meet you." Chris shook Mary's hand and then Jenny's, holding on to hers for longer. "Don't forget, if you want to dive, let me know."

Jenny laughed again, "I will."

This brought a stern comment from Brad. "I decide who dives, and with whom. Now back to work."

"OK, boss, will do." He called across to his buddy, Mike. "Time to go again, you ready?" The two started to sort through their equipment.

Mary had watched the two Americans and their brief exchange. There was no doubt who was in charge, but had Brad not been a little too quick to step in? He was showing interest already. She would watch carefully.

Thursday, 12th September: 1030 hrs

Fiona went straight from the terrace to Andreas' taverna to find Dimitris stacking cases of empty bottles ready for removal by the next ferry. He looked up as she came into the storeroom. "You look serious, today, my love. Where's that usual happy smile?"

"Dimitris, I think we should go to talk to Mateo, now. I think the time has come." She told him what had happened that morning and how she thought that the newly arrived Nikos had come to help the divers to get the looted treasure away.

"I suppose it's possible, but we still don't know if anything was stolen. And it's going to be pretty difficult for them to get it out if it was. Let's wait and see how it develops." He lifted a case of bottles onto the stack and reached for another. Fiona came round to stand in his way and put a small, determined foot on the red plastic crate. "No, that's not right, I don't trust the divers, and from what I hear, this Nikos is no better. We agreed that we would watch them and we can't do that properly without Mateo's help."

Dimitris reached for the crate but Fiona stood her ground, unwilling to give way. "Please, Dimitris. We've got to do it. We've got to stop them. If we don't, who will?"

"OK, OK, we'll do it. Later. You win. Now let me finish this job." He grinned at her.

Fiona was angry, "I don't want to win, I want to watch them because it's right to, and because I don't want these *malakas* to get away with it. It's not a matter of winning, it's a matter of doing what's right, and I really believe that they have stolen some of the things from the wreck. It all adds up, with the divers staying here when there's nothing for them to do, and now with this Greek turning up and asking for them. We've got to do something now or it will be too late."

Fiona's conviction finally reached Dimitris and he began to regret his earlier scepticism. "Ok, ok, you're right. We did agree to do this and from what you say, it is possible that the time has come. We'll go and tell Mateo. Give me five minutes and I'll be with you. We'll walk over to Likkos and decide what we are going to do. Get ready, and I'll pick you up from your room."

They walked fast in the hot morning, climbing through the ancient olives behind Lossos, over the ridge and down to Philikas, then following the rough clints and the red soil of the trail to drop down a limestone staircase steeply into Lavris. As they came down the steps to the taverna, Argus jumped to his feet and came to greet them, heavy tail swinging widely and low. He put two dusty paws on Dimitris' white shirt.

"*Mavros skillos, kleiste, kleiste.*"

The dog turned and barked his warning of their arrival, drawing Mateo from the taverna and Manolis from his everlasting game of patience. Mateo offered coffee and Manolis struggled to his feet to offer a hand to Dimitris and, unusually in an ancient Cretan, also to Fiona. "Please, sit down; tell me, Dimitris, of Andreas, my old friend, and of your mother, are they well?"

Dimitris shook the old man's hand and put an arm around his shoulders. "They are well, indeed, and they send to you their best wishes. They hope that one day you will find it possible to visit them in Lossos."

"Ah, Lossos." Manolis frowned as if the proposition had referred to Athens or even New York. "Lossos, it is far." He lifted his eyes as if to peer over the two intervening ridges. "But, maybe, one day, I will go."

Manolis squared his shoulders in resolution, bracing himself against the unknown dangers of the wide world outside Lavris. A proud memory of his only visit to Hania, twenty-five years ago, crossed his mind and re-enforced his determination. "Tell your father that I will visit him soon, maybe next spring, and that I send him my regards."

He sat down again and shuffled his cards with the air of one who has taken a great decision and is somewhat apprehensive of the outcome. Argus looked up at him sympathetically and put a heavy paw on the old man's dusty black trousers.

Mateo brought coffee and tall glasses of water and sat with Dimitris and Fiona under the twisted latticework of the vines. The sun threw sharp shadows of leaves, tendrils and bunches of grapes across the table. Beyond the sea wall small waves teased the pebbles.

The peace of the morning and the polite exchanges of the men irritated an impatient Fiona who broke into the conversation at the first opportunity. "Mateo, I think that the time has come, they are going to take the loot away, soon."

Mateo took a sip of water and smiled at the girl. "I thought that you had something to tell us, but remember this is Greece and there is always plenty of time. It is not good to be too hasty. Now, if you will, take your time and tell us your tale."

Fiona told her story again and there was silence for a little while when she finished. The sun moved rectangular patterns clockwise over the table until they fell soundlessly to the concrete floor.

Mateo broke the thoughtful quiet with a sigh. "So the game has started. I had hoped that it would not come to this." He spoke quietly and sadly and turned away from the table to look across the bay to where the archaeologists' camp disfigured the headland. The thump of the compressor came across the water in a persistent subdued beat. He turned back and spread his wide-fingered hands over the table, white hair catching the sun and throwing his lined brown face into deeper shadow. He frowned up at Dimitris and Fiona with eyes bright and resolute in the shade of his bushy eyebrows. "But we must now act. We must not let them get away. It is in our hands, and ours only, and we must be determined. If they have stolen anything we will stop them. We will not let this happen, it is an insult to Crete and to Sfakia. Are we agreed?"

The others nodded; Manolis cheated his cards.

"It is well, then. We will stop them." He thought a little. "But when will they go? That is the question."

"Not today," Fiona was sure. "They have not had enough time to plan anything yet and they've got to get the treasure from where they've hidden it."

At the adjacent table, Manolis agitated his cards violently and his sibilant Greek revealed his excitement. "We must watch, like in the old days. I will go to the mountains and watch. Argus and I will go and we will call to you. I will make the old whistle to warn you that the Germans are coming." He got up stiffly from his chair and Argus came to stand proudly beside him. "We will go now."

Dimitris smiled up at him. "They are not Germans now and you do not need to go yet, old man. Later, perhaps, and possibly Mateo should go. He has younger legs."

Manolis was offended. "He may be younger but I am strong and these are my mountains. I will defend them."

"*Endaxi.* You must go, of course," Mateo tried to pacify Manolis who was standing straight and twirling his moustache. Wearing his *sariki* head-dress and his high black leather boots he needed only two pistols tucked into his waistband to complete the picture of the old Cretan warrior.

"But," Mateo went on, "I will go tonight and you can take over from me tomorrow."

Manolis was not happy. "I should go now."

Mateo said, "Look, they will not go at night, they are not mountain men and do not know the land. I am sure that they will go by day, so you will be the one to catch them."

Manolis sat down again reluctantly and shuffled his cards vigorously, muttering to himself. Argus, with a clear expression of relief, resumed his horizontal position at the old man's feet. "*Ne, pame simera. Endaxi.* But it will be I who catches the brigands."

Fiona was practical. "But what are you going to do when you catch them?"

The old Cretan was excited again. "I will take my gun. I will shoot them."

"*Oxi, oxi.*" Dimitris got up and stood beside Manolis' table. He put a hand on the old man's shoulder. "I understand what you feel, but we cannot shoot them. This is not like the old days. There are laws, now."

Manolis sniffed his contempt for the law; he produced an ace of spades from nowhere and banged it down on the sun-crossed table.

Dimitris went on, "We will take them and the stolen treasure to Theseus, he will know what to do."

204

Manolis hissed his dissension. "I do not trust that man, he destroyed my village." He shuffled his cards violently, but the ace stayed on top.

There was silence for a while as the vulture circled and the surge of the sea syncopated with the beat of the compressor. Two uncertain and polite tourists crossed the patio, following the trail to Phinikas, unsure of whether to stop. Argus watched their passage unblinking until they had climbed the stone staircase, before resuming his interrupted sleep. Crickets called from the tamarisks. An aircraft drew a remote white line to divide the intense blue of the sky into unequal halves.

"That is what we will do." Mateo agreed with Dimitris, looking up at his protégé whose white shirt showed distorted shadows of vine leaves. He nodded in confirmation to himself. "But I think we should tell Theseus first what we propose, so that he can think about what he will do. He may decide to tell the police and leave it to them." Mateo looked at Dimitris for confirmation that this was improbable.

Dimitris shrugged, Fiona smiled a small smile, Manolis scowled. "He may do," Dimitris said, "But, somehow, I do not think it likely. We shall see. That's all we can do for now."

Mateo brought freshly-fried small fish and a tomato salad through the chequered squares of sunshine and placed them on the table. He returned to the kitchen to fill a small carafe with golden wine from the immense wooden barrel in the kitchen and set it in the sunlight where it refracted golden triangles. A perfect lunch of simple ingredients counterpointing the complex concerns of those who enjoyed it.

Lunch finished, Dimitris summed up: "Mateo will watch from the top of the scarp from, say, seven o'clock tonight, through the night. Manolis will relieve him at midday tomorrow, Friday. If, and when, we catch them, we will persuade the men to return to Lossos, with the loot, but there will be no violence. Are we agreed?"

Manolis grumbled his disappointment; Fiona and Mateo nodded.

"There will be no violence," Dimitris repeated. "No one needs to get hurt, but we must be sure to catch them red-handed. If they have stolen anything we must let them collect it and start their journey before we stop them. *Endaxi*. Fiona and I will return to Lossos now and tell Theseus what we propose. If anything happens, you will telephone me at Andreas'. Are we all agreed?"

Manolis muttered under his breath; the other two were silent.

"OK, then. It is resolved." Dimitris turned from the two men and the girl to look out at the sea and the Lossos headland beyond. The water sparkled and a soft wind whispered down from the cliff barely moving the ceiling of vine leaves. The call of the vulture came clearly through the silence. History was in the air, rising from the land, evaporating from the sea, stirring the sparse trees on the hillside, caressing the stones. The Minoan stones; the Mycenaean stones; the Hellenic stones; the Classical stones; the Roman stones; the Byzantine stones; the Arab stones; the Venetian stones; the Turkish stones; the Cretan stones of history.

Dimitris watched the sea and spoke only to himself. "How many men have sat here under the vine, and wondered and planned? Over how many years? There is something timeless about this. Who knows? We may be Minoans, after all." He got to his feet, a big strong man, his black curly hair and beard emphasising the intense blue of his eyes. The dog watched, scenting the hunt.

Dimitris' mood lifted and he smiled in the speckled light at Fiona. "Not you of course, my girl. Australians had not even been thought of then."

Fiona looked at the three men; the tall strong man who was her lover, the small white-haired man with the brown face of wisdom, and the old man with his black shirt and trousers and the swept moustache of the Cretan. She followed the wild and rugged coast beyond them with her eyes; time disappeared, the twentieth century faded and the hand of history held her. Fiona looked at the three men whom she loved more than any, with affection and respect and a touch of envy.

"I think that you three are the brigands; Minoan or not, this is your land."

The vulture circled high in the intense blue of the sky and the sun caught the pale underside of its wings at it turned against the wind.

"*Pame*. Let's go. Take care. We will go back to Lossos now and see Theseus."

But when they got back to the village, Theseus had left to go Hania and would not be back until Saturday night.

Chapter twenty six

On leaving the divers' house Nikos dropped down through the village to Vasilis' taverna and enjoyed a plate of fresh *calamari* and a *miso kilo krassi* before returning to his black hole under the tree and a new crop of dried dead leaves on his small terrace. He showered and dropped off into a deep sleep. Gillian had seen him arrive and was glad that Jenny and the Ashworths had not yet returned. She would make sure that Jenny was aware that he was back; possibly a new room, closer to Kenneth and Mary might be appropriate. A word with Jackie, who obviously shared her views about Nikos, ensured that any wanderings by the Greek would be noted.

Oscar climbed the concrete stairway to the divers' retreat tired after an early start and reeking of fish. His arrival was greeted by an unusually subdued reaction from Brian and Robert. Normally his return would be met by cries of "Here come the workers," and "For chrissake, get a wash," but today the others were preoccupied.

He came out onto the terrace drying himself with a thin towel and took a sip of Robert's ouzo. "What's with you guys today, drinking this early? Didn't think you could afford ouzo any more." Oscar draped his damp towel on the terrace railing and crossed the concrete towards the kitchen, "God, I'm hungry – anything to eat?" He glanced at Brian as he passed. "What's up with you? You look cheerful today, for a change. What's happened, win the pools or something?"

Robert looked at Brian. "Well, maybe. Look, just sit down for once, and listen. Nikos has been here."

"Nikos?" Oscar had forgotten the name for a minute. "Oh. The Greek guy. The bloke from Athens, what's he want?"

"Well, basically, he's come to help us get the gear away to Athens and then to London, where he hopes to sell it to an American. Just like that."

"What do you mean, hopes? Is he going to sell it or not? And how are you going to get it out of Lossos, have you worked that out?"

"Yeah, course he has; well, we have. We're going to take it over the White Mountains, it's the only way. Obvious, really."

Oscar pulled on a pair of shorts and off-white trousers which had been drying in the sun. He picked up a wooden chair, twirling it round like a match, and sat on it open-legged, with his arms folded across the top of the back. He rested his head on his arms and watched his companions without smiling. "Come on, I'm not that bloody stupid, how are you going to do it?"

"That's what we're going to do, tomorrow," as always Brian asked for agreement with a touch of uncertainty in his voice.

"You've got to be joking, come on, now, don't piss about."

Robert was suddenly angry. "Listen, you great black plonker, that's what we're doing. Tomorrow. Over the mountains, to Hania, then to Athens. Too clever for you, eh?"

He sneered, "You wouldn't have thought of that, would you, you thick bastard?"

Oscar rose suddenly and picked up his chair. For a moment Robert thought that the big man was going to hit him with it and flinched. Oscar stood silent for a moment, the chair dangling from his hand, forgotten. He sighed, walked to the edge of the terrace and set the chair down gently. He turned back to face the others. "How lon' we bin together? Six, seven years, somethin' like that?" He sounded alien to his companions. "And wi've bin friens, well, for most o' time. An' now you've reelly fuck'tup."

He turned and pointed up to the ridge above the village. "Have you seen what's up there? Have you really looked at it? Those mountains are big, real big. You go out in a boat and you see them, going up and up and up. There's a lot of land up there and not a track on it. And you crazy buggers are goin' to carry all that gear over those hills and down the other side. No way. No bloody way." He shook his head in disbelief. "Of all the crazy things you've done, we've done together, this tops the lot. It's mad."

The others said nothing; they had agreed with Nikos without thinking and now Oscar's scorn was making them realise what they had committed themselves to. But what else could they do? The silence continued.

Oscar got up, shrugging, raising his arms, palms outermost. "OK, you do it. But count me out. This is stupid, totally bloody daft. It's not for me. I'm off. I'm goin'." He went into the flat and came out a moment later carrying his holdall into which had been stuffed as many clothes as he could lay his hands on. He carried two pairs of trainers and a wash bag in the other hand and had draped a blue shirt over his shoulders. "If you're really goin' to do this, then I'm off. Thanks for the ride."

Brian sat looking sadly out over the town, saying nothing; Robert glared up at the big black man. "Piss off, then, fuck off. But ye're not going to get any of the cash. Sod you. If you're not doing the job, you're not gettin' anythin' from it. Just piss off."

Oscar looked down on him with contempt. "You really are a horrible little shit. Do your thing; I want no part of it. Even niggers have consciences." His changed accent suggested his moral victory. "But I hope you fail and get what you deserve. This is a beautiful place and it has good people in it, and you and that wanker," glaring contemptuously at Brian, "have spoiled it with your daft ideas. We could've done well here, but you two've balls'd it up." He swung the heavy holdall lightly. "I'm going. I feel better already." Oscar disappeared down the steep staircase.

Brian looked over at Robert. "You fucked that up. I liked that guy. You shouldn't have done that. He won't come back now."

"He can fuckin' well stay away. Sod the black bugger. If he won't come with us, then, sod him."

"Serve you bloody right if he went straight to Theseus and told him everything."

Robert was suddenly anxious, "You don't think he'll do that, do you?"

Brian looked out over the bay. "No," he said sadly. "He won't. He's too loyal for that."

Thursday, 12th September: 1800 hrs

Mateo climbed the shattered limestone of the scarp behind Lavris to cross the Liridiana path and headed for the steep crags beyond. The sky to his right was already dark but the setting sun gave enough light to allow him to climb to a ledge which gave him a clear view of Philikas and Lavris and the rough country behind them where, they had guessed, the cache of stolen treasure from the Phaistos wreck was hidden. If, Mateo shrugged to himself, any had been stolen. A doubtful premise on which to hold a night's cold and uncomfortable vigil; still, he decided, it was better to make sure. To his left, reflecting the last of the fading light, the Venetian castle and Turkish watch-tower above Lossos were distinct against the dark sea beyond. Below the ruins the land fell to Philikas and its bay and turned out to the headland on which the lights of the archaeologist's camp still glared. Slowly, one by one as Mateo watched, the lights were extinguished as the day's work was completed and the divers returned to camp or followed the path around to the beckoning nightlife of Lossos.

As the floodlights went out, Mateo's nightsight returned and he was able to follow the line of the path to Lavris and Liridiana as it divided, one branch to drop to the coast, the other to climb tortuously to the scattered lights in the village on the ridge to his right. The land was dark but the sky in the west was still bright as the vulture made a final pass of the day before soaring to his eyrie in the broken cliff to join Mateo's lonely vigil.

Now the land and sea beneath him were matt-black and Mateo settled himself in a blanket and watched the slow emergence of the stars in the east. The sky was filled with a crystalline scatter until the night wheeled above him to bring Saturn first, then Jupiter, untwinkling up from the velvet black of the cliff, their brilliance dwarfing the stars. The reign of the two planets in the night sky was brief and soon overcome by a silver glow announcing the birth of the moon which suddenly spilled diamond light from between high crags. In moments the whole disk climbed to drench the land in a cold spray of silver, and the shape of the landscape changed before Mateo's eyes. The moon's low angle threw a strange relief over his familiar land and there was no sound; the whole land was sleeping.

And yet there was change, the stars moved across the sky, the silver path of the moon on the sea shortened and lengthened again as it passed the end of Cape Mouros and swung into the west. As Mateo watched, a tease of light etched the crags behind him and a shiver of breeze came down from the plain. Soon the white walls of the chapel of Agia Katerina caught the light of the rising sun and directed it down on to the still sleeping coast, and night was over. The moon hung, incongruous and redundant, in the west, its glory swiftly overwhelmed by the deepening blue of the eastern sky.

Mateo rose and stretched, drank water and ate olives and cheese and resumed his watch as the warmth grew and the land beneath him became familiar once more. With the early light came the vulture, soaring on the strengthening thermal over the dawn-bathed plain. Man and vulture watched through the morning; watched small boats cross the sea and small men cross the land. Watched birds take spiders in dew-drawn cobwebbed shrubs and lizards come out to bask in the sun. Watched eagles play over the cliffs and mists rise from the gorges. But the watchers did not see what they anticipated; the cache of Phaistos, if such there was, remained untouched.

Friday, 13th September: 1200 hrs

At midday Mateo climbed stiffly to his feet; staff in hand he climbed down to Lavris and the waiting, impatient Manolis. Like a relay runner taking a baton the old man and his dog took Mateo's place; mounting the cliff like goats, they continued the watch.

Friday, 13th September: 2000 hrs

Manolis watched the sun dip over the bare western flank of the Amores gorge away to his right as Argus slept at his side. During the afternoon both man and dog had been alert, Argus sensing their role as watchers and growling quietly whenever he saw any movement on the tracks beneath them. But there were a lot of walkers at this time of the year and the novelty soon faded and the old dog fell asleep leaving Manolis to watch alone as the afternoon passed into evening. When the sun touched the ridge a touch of cold air trickled down from the Anopoli plain and on it came the vulture, so close over the man's head that he heard the wind sigh over its widespread wings. The rush of wind awoke the dog who stretched and drank a little of the water which Manolis poured for him in a cup of limestone. Manolis cut roasted goat from a bone which he ate with olives and dry bread and the cleaned bone kept Argus occupied as evening stretched into night. There was no movement on the trails as the old man drew his blanket tight around himself against the chill of the darkness, and fought an urge to sleep.

In Lossos Jackie and Fiona had a busy time in the bar. Friday night brought many visitors into the village which seemed to wake from its sleep in expectation of the weekend excitement; the terrace was full of guests and visitors. Both girls were distracted. Jackie's siesta had been broken by Oscar who had rambled on about Brian and Robert and how he couldn't work with them any more, before falling asleep leaving her awake and worried. Fiona constantly watched for the signal from Dimitris in Andreas' taverna across the bay which would alert her to the expected phone call from Lavris. Both worked hard and efficiently but with little of their usual affability.

Kenneth and Mary had met Brad on the terrace for early glasses of white wine and had later been joined by Jenny who had spent the afternoon walking to Sweetwater Bay. Her odd mix of sophistication and naivety made her tales of the antics of the nudists at the bay hilarious, and Jenny responded to her own sense of freedom and her

211

receptive audience to produce increasingly outrageous stories. Mary and Kenneth had not been to Sweetwater and found it difficult to imagine that the sight of totally brown German men doing handstands in a metre of water was anything other than ridiculous, but Jenny's description produced, as Mary remarked, "a whole new angle on things".

A second bottle of wine encouraged a final story: Jenny had met, while climbing a stone stair, an aged man clad only in a dusting of sand and an orange cycling helmet, thus coming face to phallus with a shrivelled, shaven member. She had, she said, looked him in the eye and passed on. The laughter echoed around the terrace and Fiona looked across at her, thinking how the English girl had relaxed since their meeting in the sea that morning.

Mary and Kenneth had not seen Jenny like this for years and had forgotten how quick and caustic her wit could be; Brad Slinger even forgot to fidget as he fell deeper under her spell. As they left the terrace in search of food, Mary held Kenneth back to follow Jenny and Brad across the shingle as they walked side by side, hands and shoulders nearly touching. She sought her husband's hand and held it tightly. "This could be good," she whispered, "if only we could get rid of that Nikos, Jenny could be happy and I wouldn't need to worry about her any more."

Later in the evening Mary pleaded tiredness and dragged Kenneth away for a coffee in the hotel, leaving Jenny and Brad to each other and the warm star-strewn night. Brad told laconic stories in his relaxed soft mid-American accent then encouraged Jenny to share her tales; each found the other receptive and understanding and the stories became more personal. Jenny spoke of the death of her father and her disillusionment with Nikos; Brad told her of his wife's accident and how he had retreated into his work. As he recounted the tale he started again to turn the empty cigarette packet over in his fingers on the table and Jenny put her hand on his, stilling and comforting. They left the taverna and followed the path through the village to the Turkish fort on the headland and Jenny, outlined in silver, looked up at the moon. She turned to Brad and took his face between her hands and kissed him, at first tentatively, unsure, then with growing desire and urgency. Brad gently returned the kiss and led her back down to the village and through the tavernas and to climb the steep stair to Jenny's room. She shut the door behind him and came again into his arms. Their mouths explored each other and Brad's fingers tangled Jenny's hair as it fell from its restraining clasp.

Breathless, Jenny broke away and opened the shutters. The soft sound of the sea swept in as she stood outlined against the moonlit night. She crossed her arms and edged the straps of the white dress away from her shoulders. As it fell away the moon caught one breast in a halo of cold light and splintered off a taut nipple. She opened her arms to him and Brad came to her and kissed each breast gently. He picked her up and carried her to the bed and bent to kiss her toes and then to follow the long line of her leg with his tongue. Jenny squirmed in urgency and delight as his tongue crept over her stomach and his lips tugged at her nipples. Her hands reached down and held him and in aching need directed him into her. She melted into a demanding urgent movement which flowed over her in waves of desire until she exploded in a fountain of delight and clawed and bit Brad in his own simultaneous climax. She held him tight for a long moment and then relaxed. She kissed him on his damp forehead and giggled happily. "So that's what it should be like. I often wondered what all the fuss was about, but now I know. Do you think we could do it again, some time?"

Brad grinned in the moonlight, "I think we might, I just think we might."

Friday, 13th September: 2100 hrs

At the end of the village Nikos, Brian and Robert raised glasses over the remains of a *stifado*. "Here's to tonight and to Athens and to the American. *Yiamas, kalo taxithi.*"

They clinked glasses and drained the last of the wine.

"Another carafe?" Nikos urged.

"Well, OK, but only a half, we've work to do tonight. Are we still going at twelve?"

Nikos said, "*Ne*, at twelve, and I think we should leave the village separately, and meet at the top of the path. Have you got enough supplies, plenty of water?"

"Yeah, we're right, but it's going to be quite a load when we pick up the gear." Robert, for once, sounded unsure. "I've got a feeling about this trip. I'm with you, of course, no problem, but I'll be glad when we get going."

Brian punched him on the shoulder. "Not like you, that, what's happened to the hard and canny Scot?"

"Yeah, well, like I said, I'll be OK once we've started." Robert turned in his chair to look moodily out to where the beacon flashed intermittently on the unseen island. He felt cold in the warm night and the sounds of the busy village nightlife seemed distant. He poured

213

himself another glass of wine and drank it in one gulp, knowing that it would do nothing to lift the darkness from his mind. He watched Brian and Nikos, wondering how they would fare together. If only he trusted the Greek a bit more, that would help, it was going to be hard enough without having to watch his step every inch of the way. He looked at Brian, enthralled by Nikos and trusting, and sneered to himself. He wouldn't get caught, he'd stay canny. And friendless. Unwilling to face any more doubts, Robert jumped to his feet. "I'm off. I'm going to kip for an hour and get my stuff ready. See you on top at quarter-past."

The long journey had started with that single step.

Saturday, 14th September: 0100 hrs

Argus growled in the night, bringing Manolis back from a shallow and uncomfortable sleep. For the first time the old man regretted his enthusiasm for the watcher's role; what had been easy and exciting sixty years ago did not hold its appeal to old limbs in the cold and dark and he groaned softly to himself as he rubbed his legs to get the circulation going again. He pulled the blanket more tightly about his body to fight off the chill which was spreading through his bones. Below all was quiet but the dog growled again and got to his feet. Manolis peered down into the darkness, wishing the moon was higher to reduce the depth of the pools of blackness which broke the grey landscape. He strained to hear, but there was no sound other than the whisper of the night air in the limestone clints. The dog growled again; he had heard, or seen, something. Alert now, Manolis put a restraining hand on the animal's collar to reassure and quieten him. Argus turned his head to look into the old man's eyes and then back to his intent watch, ears fully forward and nose teasing for a scent.

Man and dog and moonlight. Manolis did not feel cold any more, years dropped from him and he imagined the steel helmets and the glint of German firearms and remembered the bitter adrenalin of the ambush.

Argus growled, a long rumbling noise from deep in his chest, and quivered under the old man's hand. Manolis caught the brief flash of a torch beam as it struck the white rock before dying in the red soil. There was someone on the path; he strained to see more, unable to hear now over Argus' rumbling warning. He tightened his grip on the dog's collar.

The flash came again, two flashes moving erratically, then three, three people at least, moving quickly along the Liridiana trail. Manolis watched from above, remembering that he should wait to see if Nikos and the divers, if indeed it was them, collected anything en route. He followed the progress of the torches along the familiar track in the night, knowing every turn, every step. As they passed beneath him the moonlight showed three figures, packs on backs and with torches in one hand, sticks in the other. Argus trembled under Manolis' hand and the moon climbed slowly up the sky.

The progress of the torches stopped at a tight bend in the trail where Manolis knew that the path made a left turn to climb a ridge beside a long narrow gully. The beams of light pointed up the gully as if questioning it and then back up the path. The grey-black figures were stationary for a moment and then one jerked upward as if climbing a step and slowly entered the gully. The others followed and disappeared into the gully; Argus stopped growling but sat intent, unblinking, watching the ridge behind which they had gone. The wind sighed and the moon reached its zenith. Man and dog watched and waited, Manolis now convinced that the three men were those they sought. Anyone else would have climbed the path to Liridiana; the gully led nowhere. If anybody entered the gully at this time of night, it was only to retrieve something hidden, there could be no other reason. He would wait until they reappeared and then would make the signal down to Lavris that the quarry had been sighted. Mateo would then phone Dimitris who would come to Lavris in the outboard, having alerted Theseus to the chase. A good plan, intended to recover the stolen artefacts and at the same time confront the culprits with the authority which Theseus wielded.

A good plan. But Theseus was not in Lossos and Dimitris awaited his return in vain. And further tragedy was about to strike.

Manolis and Argus watched for the re-emergence of the torches from the gully, both silent, still and intent. Argus saw the lights first and gave his warning growl, the old man strained his eyes to see the three ghostly figures climb down from the lip of the rocky valley to rejoin the trail. There was a pause for a minute before they set off, climbing the ridge towards Liridiana, zigzagging across the hillside. Their progress seemed slower now, possibly because of the steeper gradient, possibly because their loads were heavier. Now was the time to give the signal. Manolis struggled to his feet, stiff with the cold and his inaction. He edged out on to spur of rock and took a deep breath to power his whistle. The gulp of air made him suddenly light-headed and he stumbled. His cold limbs reacted too slowly to prevent him falling. He put out a hand to save himself and felt only air as he toppled off the spur to fall into a cleft of deep shadow in the white rock. His falling body twisted his leg and he heard the bone snap in the quiet before feeling the shocking impact of his shoulder on the clint. His head came forward and his temple struck the stone with a dull, flat noise which echoed through his mind as he lost consciousness.

Argus came to him, uncertain and frightened, and whimpering softly, licking the old man's face and smelling the blood from his forehead. The dog nuzzled Manolis' free hand, urging it to move, then stretched out beside him and howled in the night.

Some time later Manolis stirred and groaned, opening his eyes briefly before sliding back into sleep. Argus watched intently for further movement then impatiently licked his face, urging Manolis to respond. The man's eyes flickered again and the dog scratched sharply at his arm and Manolis groaned and tried to move. Argus scratched harder, somehow sensing that the pain which he was inflicting was helping his master. Manolis opened his eyes again, "*Stamato, skillos, stamato*," and pulled his arm away from the dog's heavy claws. He tried to move his leg and the pain swept over him again and the moon circled in his vision, swooping across the sky. He concentrated on making the moon stop and slowly came to realise that he was lying on his back. He turned carefully on to his side. His shoulder hurt more but the intense pain in his leg diminished a little and he breathed more easily. The dog licked his face again then sat, dark and wolf-like against the moonlit sky, watching him as if wondering what to do.

Manolis slept again and when he awoke there was a hint of light in the sky and he felt cold with the dawn. His thirst was terrible and he licked his cracked lips. Argus got up and came to look closely at him; Manolis felt his hot breath on his cheek. As if reassured, the dog went to stand at the edge of the spur, looking down the scarp to where Lavris was beginning to take shape in the growing light. He looked back at the man and then down the hill again and knew what he had to do. Argus licked Manolis' hand in farewell, then bounded away down the steep slope, leaping from clint to boulder in a frantic rush through the dawn. The overwhelming urgency which the dog felt leant wings to his flight and his speed matched that of the vulture which stooped above him like a guardian in the cold air.

Within the hour the rescue helicopter from Agia Rodhia had lifted the old man from his high ledge and was carrying him, wrapped in blankets and with a little refreshing water on his lips, over the White Mountains to Hania. As he drifted off into a deep sleep in the starched white sheets of the new hospital, he murmured. "*Pou ine, skillos mou?* Where is he, my dog?"

The nurse smiled to herself as she smoothed his sheets; "That's nice," she thought, "the old chap misses his dog, I wonder where it is?"

Argus was lying under Manolis' table in the Lavris taverna, awake and watching for his master's return.

Chapter twenty seven

Fiona and Dimitris had spent the night on the roof above Andreas' restaurant as they always did when Dimitris was in Lossos, but it hadn't been the happy, loving time it usually was. They had gone to bed late, then spent a few restless hours unable to sleep anticipating the expected call from Mateo.

At around seven o'clock Dimitris decided to phone Lavris to seek news. There was no answer to his call. He went into the kitchen and made a *Nes* coffee and took it to a table overlooking the sea and the mist-shrouded hillside beyond. The sun had not yet risen; although the air was bright with its promise, there was a chill in the air which hinted at autumn, and a touch of dew on the blue-painted balustrade. Dimitris held his coffee cup in two hands, enjoying the comfort of its warmth. The village was quiet and nothing disturbed the placid pale sea; a kingfisher made a sudden dash across the bay towards him, then, as if sensing his presence, banked steeply showing brilliant blue and gold, to return to the mists hovering on the far shore. The chapel on top of the upper ramparts of the cliffs appeared like a fairytale illustration above a veil of wispy cloud and higher yet the wings of a vulture showed dark against the dawn sky.

Dimitris took a sip of hot coffee, enjoying its bitter stimulus, willing himself to enjoy the peace of the morning yet nagged by the thought that he should by now have heard from Mateo in Lavris. What had happened? If the divers and Nikos were going to go today, they would surely have started by now, avoiding the heat and the Saturday crowds. If they had gone last night, Mateo would have phoned. Did this mean that they were not going to go today, or, indeed, were not even involved, and the whole thing had been 'a figment of the imagination proceeding from the heat-oppressed brain?' It certainly had been hot enough during the last few days to produce hallucinations and, really, what did they have to go on? What were the facts underlying the assumption that an Athenian and some British men were actually attempting to steal Minoan treasure from underneath the noses of the Sfakians, the most dangerous men in Europe? And from under the noses of archaeologists who were similarly keen on holding on to things which they had found?

And, what grounds were there for the assumption that the thieves, if they were such, would attempt to escape by carrying their loot over the White Mountains? In the calm of the quiet dawn these conjectures appeared ridiculous; imagination gone wild, borne on inference and born of guesswork. Based on gossip and built into an unstable edifice which would not stand the cold analysis of day. Dimitris finished his coffee and decided that he would be much better off in bed with Fiona than in such pointless considerations. How did he come to be so persuaded? He was a mature and balanced man, his life ran on the logical lines of a businessman; the romantic imaginings of Sfakia were a thing of the past. He got up from the table and carried his empty cup into the kitchen and rinsed it; he glanced at himself in the mirror and smoothed his hair and stroked the black curls of his beard into life. The thought of Fiona, curled up under the rough blankets, tempted him and he turned to the staircase which would take him back to the roof.

But as Dimitris came to the foot of the stairs he met her, in jeans and a dark blue sweater, and barefoot. Her long hair poured a golden waterfall over her left shoulder and ran down the slope of her breast. She looked beautiful and vulnerable, and anxious.

"I thought you might have gone, without telling me," she had just begun, when Jackie clattered, noisily and breathless, through the doorway. "They've gone; I thought I'd find you here; Oscar went up to get some stuff, and they've gone, and I think Nikos has gone, too. His door was open and there was no one there and he hasn't paid. I thought I ought to tell you first, you'd know what to do, after what I'd told you about them stealing that stuff." She panted heavily but this did not stop her from pulling a battered packet from her jeans pocket and lighting a slightly bent cigarette, blowing the match out with a stream of smoke. "What are we going to do? Theseus isn't here and I can't find Gillian and no one else knows anything about it."

Dimitris treated her to his big, slow grin. "I think we should have some coffee, that's always a good start. And five minutes isn't going to matter anyway, not now. Go and sit down and I'll bring the coffee to you." He turned to the stove and poured hot water over three spoonfuls of Nescafe in a battered tin jug and took a tray and carried cups and milk and sugar out to a table on the terrace.

As he was about to sit down, the phone rang. It was Mateo.

"They've gone."

"I know."

"They've gone, and Manolis is hurt. He's gone to hospital, in Hania."

"Oh. Hell. What happened, did Nikos and his gang hurt him?"

"No. He fell, and Argus came down to tell us, and I found him and got the helicopter out. He's got a broken leg, I think. He'll be all right. But the British got away, I don't know how many of them, and I don't know if the Greek has gone. Manolis could only tell me that he'd seen three of them, some time in the night, possibly around one-thirty or two."

"Nikos has gone," Dimitris confirmed, "and the two white men. Oscar is here, he's not part of this."

"OK. Right. I'm going after them," Mateo's voice came down the wire, determined and angry. "I'm going because it's my fault that they escaped. I shouldn't have let the old man do it."

"You mustn't blame yourself for that; you didn't seem to have much option, from what I remember; he was pretty determined to go."

"Anyway, I'm setting off now, it's certain that they are going to try the mountains and there's only one route from here. That's through Agios Ioannis and on to Zerankephalo and Melindaou to Therisso, unless they go to Omalos. But that's probably too busy for them. I'll stop them somehow. I'll leave a note with Eleni in Ioannis and she can ring you."

Fiona had heard the phone ring and had come into the kitchen to hear most of what had been said. She took the heavy black handset from Dimitris. "Mateo, this is Fiona, hold on a minute."

She put a hand over the mouthpiece and spoke to Dimitris. "Kenneth Ashworth is here, he's just been over to the camp but Brad isn't there. I've told him everything and he's a bit upset, to say the least. He seems to have assumed that the British have stolen lots of the disks, and now he wants to go after them."

Dimitris was unconvinced. "He's not a climber; he'd have no chance on his own. Anyway he'd never catch up with them. They've got six hours start or more. We'll have to leave it to Mateo, he's fast enough to catch them."

"Wait, I know how we can do it," Fiona lifted the phone again. "Hold on, please, Mateo."

Jackie and Kenneth came into the kitchen; Fiona waved the phone at them. "We can't leave it to Mateo alone to follow them. How would he stop them? You've got to go, Dimitris, and if Kenneth wants to go with you, well that's better still. Three against three. So you've got to catch up with them. Now listen to me for once."

Fiona held the phone close to her mouth and spoke clearly to enable Mateo to hear. "Nikos is going to have to rest sometime, say for three hours or so. He's got six hours start, so you have three hours to make up. Mateo can go twice as fast as them, so he can catch them up in about six hours from now. But Dimitris and Kenneth can't go that fast so they have to cheat. This is what we are going to do."

Saturday, 14th September: 0900hrs, Lossos

The outboard flew across a flat sea throwing a spray of diamond drops into the air. Dimitris and Kenneth sat at the stern, close to Fiona who was steering, to keep the prow up for maximum speed. Hora Sfakion lay ahead, still in shadow; the journey from Lossos took less than fifteen minutes and the grey Mercedes waited on the ramp, engine running. Yorgos the Merc stood importantly by the open driver's door and watched the speeding boat approach. He had been awakened by Fiona's call and had not had breakfast but was alert and excited by her unusual request. "Be on the quay at Sfakion, in the car, in ten minutes. Dimitris will explain."

His awakened wife had complained as he dressed.

"Be quiet, woman, I am needed on important business. Go back to sleep." How he had enjoyed that. He brushed his moustache with a tobacco-stained finger, left then right. This tale would guarantee an audience in the *kafenion* tonight.

The boat came to the edge of the ramp, slowing quickly as its prow dropped. Dimitris kissed Fiona as Kenneth chucked haversacks on to the jetty and both men jumped out on to the wet concrete. Within a minute Fiona was heading back to Lossos and the Mercedes was climbing the hill through the quiet town. Dimitris sat in front with Yorgos, Kenneth shared the back seat with the two heavy haversacks.

The road to Anapoli from Hora Sfakion is twelve kilometres in length and climbs over six hundred metres from the sea to the plain, twisting back and forth over the bare hillside. Its hairpin bends are tight and in one or two places the tarmac is frayed at the edge; it is not an easy drive and possibly a large saloon car is not the most suitable of vehicles in which to attempt the hill-climb speed record. But there is no doubt that Yorgos took the record that day. His instruction was clear and brief, to get to Agios Ioannis as quickly as possible, and he rose to the challenge, passing through Anopoli after only fifteen minutes and hitting the long straight before Amores at over 120 kilometres an hour in a storm of dried leaves.

The straight stretch of road gave Yorgos time to brush his moustache again before taking a zig-zag leading to the gorge with tyres squealing and they crossed the wooden planks of the bridge with a roar which could be heard in Libya. The remaining five kilometres of dirt road took only five minutes and left clouds of red dust hanging in the still air. Within three quarters of an hour of leaving Lossos, Dimitris and Kenneth were greeting an astonished Eleni outside her house in Agios Ioannis. The first part of Fiona's plan had been accomplished. Kenneth and Dimitris were already ahead of Mateo but were still some two hours behind Nikos. A long day lay ahead.

Saturday, 14th September: 0900 hrs, Lavris

Mateo put the phone down with a reluctant approval of Fiona's plan to stop Nikos recovering the treasure and he made his preparations in haste. He quickly packed a small sack with a light sleeping bag and bed roll and added fruit, bread and cheese, and water. As he worked, with Argus watching him warily, he began to try to calculate the logistics of the chase. He knew that Nikos and Robert and Brian would have heavy packs and were not accustomed to the mountain trails. On the other hand they would be desperate to make good time, but they would have difficulty in route-finding and would tire quickly after the night start. Manolis had thought that they would have left Lavris at around one or two o'clock. If they had not stopped, and knew the path, they could be in Agios Ioannis in three hours, say five o'clock. But the route in the gully up from the Ahladha gorge was difficult; they would surely have to wait until it was light before attempting it. A rough guess suggested that they would be in the village at around nine o'clock, in which case they would by now have already passed through the last habitation before the high mountains. Short of the helicopter, which was in Hania with Manolis, there was no other way in which the villains could be stopped. He would have to catch them on foot. Even with the start that Yorgos' drive would give Kenneth and Dimitris they would have to go quickly to catch up by nightfall.

At a little after nine he was climbing the long curves of the ancient footpath towards Liridiana, past the dry gully where the stolen treasure of the Minoans had spent a summer. By eleven-thirty he was eating Eleni's sweet cake in Agios Ioannis and reading the note left by Dimitris an hour earlier.

'10.30. The quarry is ahead, by an hour or so, but they must rest sometime. Catch us quickly but take care. D.'

Chapter twenty eight

The night air was cool as Brian, Robert and Nikos climbed, separately and secretly, out of the sleeping village, through the grove of ancient olive trees, onto the plateau where the Venetian castle loomed like the overdrawn scenery of a Gothic play. The moon's light left gulfs of impenetrable shadow in which traps of sharp unstable boulders lay hidden, and torches helped little. By the time that the men had reached the gully where the Minoan treasure had been hidden they were sweating and thirsty; by the time they had climbed up to Liridiana with the extra loads they were tired and hungry as well. Their progress in the dark village was slow and they did not dare to use torches. With relief from a fresher breeze they came up to a white moonlit chapel and turned north to leave the village and cross dry fields where the going was easier.

The track wound over a ridge at an easy gradient before dropping down steeply into the Amores gorge through oleander and ash. In the dark depths of the gorge torches could be used but it is difficult to climb over big boulders whose upper surfaces are drenched in white light and whose lower parts disappear into Stygian black. It is even more difficult with a fifteen-kilo sack on your back. The three men were getting more and more tired and dispirited as the enormity of the task ahead of them became clear. They were, after only two and a half hours, already exhausted and hungry, and had two thousand metres yet to climb before the day was over. Nikos thrashed ahead through the gloom with Brian following, shoulders already bruised by the sack he carried; somewhere behind a cursing Robert could be heard stumbling through the oleander. They turned up into the gully which climbs to Agios Ioannis at four o'clock and Brian called a halt to the slow progress.

"Look, this is bloody difficult and we're all tired. Why don't we kip for an hour or two, until it gets lighter? There's no one following us, and they won't notice that we've gone until well into the morning,

224

if they notice at all. And we don't need to do this in two days – if it's three it doesn't really matter."

For once his leadership triumphed; five minutes later they were all asleep on beds of pine needles, rucksacks under heads in case any one of them made off with the treasure during the night. A restless sleep, each aware of his vulnerability to the others, each tired, each vowing to stay awake longer than the others, each failing. Such is the trust amongst thieves that even sleep cannot be enjoyed.

There had been much discussion in the gully where the cache had been hidden over the distribution of the artefacts between the three of them. Nikos had suggested that he, being the biggest and strongest, should carry the heaviest load and it therefore made sense that he should take the disks. This philanthropic view had been hotly resisted by Robert who had insisted that the weights should be equal, as should the mix of articles, thus, he argued, lightening Nikos' load, which was only fair. Consequently they carried sacks of comparable weight and each had daggers and swords and cups and disks, to show how little they trusted one another.

They awoke stiff and cold in the damp chill of the dawn. The sun was below the high eastern side of the mist-filled valley up through which the upper branches of trees grasped at the light and over which the vulture skimmed. They had no stove; cold water from the flask gave little comfort and only helped to wash down an unpalatable breakfast of biscuits and chocolate. It was a slow start to a long day; the first hour of climbing was unrelenting and without pleasure but slowly the gradient eased and the sun came up and its warmth improved the mood. They were strong young men, possibly not as fit as they could be, but nevertheless active. The enjoyment of the challenge of their task and their self-belief grew; the slanting sunlight and the scent of the pine woods lifted their spirits. Nikos, Brian and Robert made good time through the early morning, sharing plans for the future and hopes of success; enjoying the trail. They had the treasure, they had made a good start to their escape over the mountains, it was a beautiful day and, as they climbed and the air became fresher, their confidence rose with the sun. They knew that pursuit was likely but there was no sign of it and they felt secure. Had they known, as they entered the village, that Mateo was only then rolling up his sleeping bag in Lavris, eight hundred meters below and seven kilometres behind, and that Kenneth and Dimitris had only just started the journey to Hora Sfakia, they would have believed that their venture would be successful. Even without this knowledge they felt safe and they grew ever more confident as they came through the small village and started up a dry winding valley toward the wells in the wooded plateau above.

They saw nothing but a few cats and a single tethered but silent dog as they passed between the stone buildings of the apparently deserted settlement. Somewhere in the back of the village a mule brayed and chickens chuckled but otherwise there was silence. The vulture circled, infinitely high in the bright blue morning.

Agios Ioannis was like many other villages throughout the world, deserted and watchful, peopled by eyes only, and the men were glad to leave the last of the houses behind. Eleni alone had watched their progress, sitting with her old brown dog and its long-legged pup in the shadow of a fig tree in her courtyard. Behind her the long Cretan arch of the old building framed the doorway and a water trough; in front of her was the cooking range, built into a retaining wall beyond which the land dropped over gullies and woods to the distant sea. This was her house and had been her father's house and his father before that; now she was alone with her two dogs, her husband long dead and her three sons away in distant places, her story typical of the people of the White Mountains.

Little happened in the village and any stranger was watched with curiosity and, if possible, was lured by coffee and cake to sit a while under the fig and tell stories from the world below. But some passers-by were foreigners who could not or would not communicate and whose passage through the narrow streets was watched silently and warily. Eleni sat in cat-like stillness and the old dog gave a low growl to warn its pup as the three strangers carrying heavy sacks passed her courtyard in the mid-morning. She made no attempt to speak to them but watched which route they took. She looked at the shadow of the old tree and noted the time. It was about half-past nine o'clock.

Out of the village Nikos called a halt under a cypress. "We're going well, time for a break, rest the legs a bit."

Brian agreed, "That's the worst part over, should be on our own now. If we were going to be followed, we would know. Obviously nobody's noticed, and no-one knows where we've gone …"

"Except Oscar," Robert reminded him, unwilling to be convinced.

"He won't say anything, and anyway, he's no idea what time we left. Even you must think we've done all right."

"So far, aye, so far," Robert glowered. But even he could not resist a little satisfaction as he relaxed in the warmth of the morning sun. "Not so bad, so far."

Nikos watched the exchange without comment then lay back on a bed of pine-needles to enjoy the heat and to consider the situation.

So far they had been favoured. They had made good time and were unobserved and now only the mountains lay ahead. They had plenty of supplies and could fill up the water bottles at the well on the plateau above. His plan was succeeding and he had no doubt that he could give the divers the slip once they were in Athens. Until then, they might as well carry the treasure for him. He closed his eyes and the bickering of the British receded. All three slept and dreamed of riches as the sun shifted cypress shadows across them.

Saturday, 14th September: 1030 hrs

Dimitris, Kenneth and Yorgos the Merc arrived in Agios Ioannis in a noisy cloud of white dusk. Eleni recognised Dimitris immediately and hobbled out to greet him; Dimitris introduced Kenneth and Yorgos to her. Delighted by their visit she ushered them to eat her sweet dark cake and drink coffee under the fig tree. She looked forward to a long gossip with new arrivals but was quickly disappointed by Dimitris. "I am sorry, *Kyria*, that we cannot stay with you, but we have to take the path over the mountains, to Melindaou. Tell me, have any passed this way today, any strangers?"

Eleni was excited and the dog came to stand beside her, tail wagging in corroboration. The pup brought an old bone and laid it carefully at Kenneth's feet. He ruffled its ears and watched Eleni, trying to follow the soft Cretan Greek. "Three men came through here about an hour ago. One was a big man, a Greek; the others, *xenoi*. They carried heavy bags and looked, *lathreos*, furtive, hunted. They climbed up the valley to the wells. They were going slowly. Do you want them?"

"They are bad men, Eleni, do not talk with them, but if you see them again, remember where and when, and what they did." He got up from the bench and drank the remainder of his glass of water. "Now we must go, but Mateo from Lavris is following us and may be an hour behind. Give him this note and tell him that Nikos is in front of us by another hour or so, and is going up the valley to the wells." Dimitris turned and pointed up to the cliff high above the cypress-dotted grey foothills in the north where it appeared that an old man's face had been drawn on the white stone, frowning over the western hills.

"Tell him that I think that Nikos will go on to Zeranokephala and Melindaou by the shepherds' path, and that we will catch him up but stay behind him. Tell Mateo that we will leave a mark if Nikos leaves the path. Wish him *kalo taxithi*." Dimitris kissed Eleni,

"*Adio*, take care, I will visit you again when this is over, and tell you all of what is happening. *Herete.*"

He turned to Yorgos and took him by the hand. Pulling him close, he wrapped the little man in a big hug. "Thank you, my friend, you did well, very well. Now go home to your beautiful wife, and give her my apologies for taking you from her bed. Drive carefully." He looked at the grey Mercedes, streaked in white dust, and imagined Theseus' reaction to its condition. "It might be a good idea to give it a bit of a wash, before the boss sees it?"

Yorgos the Merc smiled proudly, "First I take a photograph, only then I wash it."

Kenneth and Dimitris hoisted their sacks on to their backs and set off across the stone-girt fields to the foot of the dry valley as Yorgos turned the big car round and started back down through the woods to Amores. Eleni, feeling very important, carried her chair out to the edge of the village and sat staring fixedly down the path up which Mateo would come. Her old dog and its pup came to sit, upright and alert to her excitement, beside her. She would not miss him. In her mind she was a young girl innocently playing in the dust but set as a sentry to look out for the searching Germans. She was the one entrusted with vital information; even if she did not quite know what it was for, she would not fail.

Saturday, 14th September: 1130 hrs

Brian awoke with a start as a long-legged spider walked over his hand; he watched it for a moment and shivered to its touch; with an abrupt movement he shook it off and lay back to enjoy the heat of the sun. So far so good. Just a few more hours then it was downhill all the way to Athens, they should be in Hania easily by Sunday night and Athens by Tuesday at the latest. Then a few more days wait before the money came through. He shifted a little on the hard stones, unable to rid himself of a niggling doubt about Nikos' intentions; the Greek was very plausible and friendly but would have to be watched. He'd have a word with Robert soon to make doubly sure that they would not be duped; he wished that they had some further hold on Nikos now that the treasure had been lifted from its cache. His mind drifted inconclusively over the problem then, Brian-like, sought refuge in the much easier and attractive consideration of the money and how he would spend it.

Robert lay awake watching the lazy circling of a large bird, also thinking about Nikos but with much more specific intentions. He had been as friendly as possible towards the Greek during the day, listening uncritically to Nikos' flatulent boastings and contrived stories, and encouraging the Greek to relax. After their first sleep during which each had held on to his haversack, Robert had been obviously more casual during subsequent breaks, leaving his sack unattended in the hope of persuading Nikos to do likewise. Robert hoped that in the dark of the night he could separate Nikos from his sack permanently and began to consider how it might be possible to leave the Athenian to his fate in the mountains. With the value of the treasure escalating in his mind, he had to think of everything; it was no good leaving it to Brian.

Nikos sat up and retied his boots. He took a drink to finish his bottle of water then poured the few remaining dregs over his thick black hair. "*Pame.* Let's go. Next stop the well; let's hope it's still fresh." Shouldering his sack he stepped out into the hot sun and started slowly up the winding track through screes of grey limestone and the pink-grey resinous trunks of trees; Robert and Brian followed him, each in a cocoon of thought. Each now believed that they had escaped with the treasure. The gods of the mountains sought their thanks and the vulture came to circle the plateau to receive them. But Brian, Nikos and Robert had only thought for themselves; how they would outwit each other and how they would spend the proceeds for their own selfish enjoyment. Such thoughts offend the gods and alert the ancient Nemesis.

Dimitris and Kenneth were only half an hour behind now, having caught up during the complacent rest by Nikos and the others in the valley. Thirty minutes is only a kilometre in such terrain as this and the followers were fresh and going well. Behind them, still over an hour away, Mateo quickly approached Agios Ioannis like a small white-haired avenging angel, staff in hand and ready to strike.

Chapter twenty nine

The three wells above Agios Ioannis mark a change in the landscape of Sfakia. Below them the land is richly forested in oak and cypress and Cretan pine; barley and olives are to be found in fields and enclosures, small birds flit though the maquis. Below the wells the country is never entirely free from the signs of human habitation. Walls and tracks, terraces and buildings and ruins show the influence of mankind on the land.

But above the wells is a different world, a world of white rock and prickly oak and the silver wind-twisted boughs of the wild cypress with its small tough dark green leaves, a world little touched by men, where golden eagles and griffin vultures and ravens hold their sway. Men pass through this land, they camp in it with their flocks in summer, they climb its mountains, but they change it little and never tame it.

The only man-made changes to this wild land which do survive are the tracks, the *kalderimi* which cross it in erratic meanders from well to well and pasture to pasture, skirting cliffs and crags and gorges. These tracks are ancient, maybe four thousand years old, maybe five thousand or more. Ever since mankind came into these hills these paths have been used because they are the only possible routes. Over many years the tracks and paths have been improved; possibly armies devoted time and effort to their construction, more often than not it was a solitary shepherd who whiled away a day by building a step or two, or a short wall, from the scattered limestone blocks. These tracks have been used by Minoans and twentieth-century resistance fighters, by goat-herds and soldiers, and now, today, were used by men in pursuit of the prey of other men and a purloined Minoan treasure.

Above the wells the path climbs over rough scree until it comes to the head of a dry valley whose steep end it mounts in a succession of angled bends. This is the worst stretch; limbs are already tired, the altitude is beginning to tell, the view lies behind and the way ahead is unclear, the landscape is featureless. Those who know the route console themselves with the promise of the magnificent country which lies ahead, the extensive views, the beauty of the twisted trees. Those who do not, become depressed by the everlasting slippery scree of the trail and the lack of apparent progress with which their strenuous effort is met.

Brian trudged ahead, Robert trailed behind, Nikos stumbled sore-footed and heavy. The euphoria which each had felt on the way up to the wells was fading rapidly into gloom as the afternoon passed. Men on hills are usually companions sharing the enjoyment of their endeavours, happy in reminiscence and observation, solicitous of one another. Brian and his companions found no pleasure in the countryside, no delight in its plants or the shape of its rocks. These three had little in common other than greed and guilt; each watched the others out of fear of betrayal rather than concern for well-being. The trail was hard and everlasting.

By contrast Dimitris and Kenneth found both enjoyment and purpose in the beautiful afternoon; enjoyment in the trees and the birds, the stark drama of the landscape, their shared experiences and knowledge; purpose in the task which they had set themselves of recovery of an ancient treasure. The trail ahead was, to them, a continuing challenge; the hunter has conviction and confidence; the hunted only fear.

And behind them came Mateo, moving from stone to stone with such lightness of foot that he seemed to fly, *ambelitsa* staff across his shoulders for balance and driven by a cold-hearted determination. He knew the land and loved it; he knew its flowers and its herbs, its oaks and its cypress and where the eagles nested on the great limestone walls but today had no time for contemplation, today he was a hunter, as primitive in his aims as a wildcat. He was driven by two emotions: firstly, as a foreigner who had been accepted by this harsh country, he felt that the British and Nikos had betrayed Crete and its people by the theft of the treasure; and, secondly, there was the injury to his old friend Manolis; illogically, perhaps, Mateo blamed the old man's fall on the men whom he was now following.

At the wells Mateo was only half an hour behind his allies; he spotted them high up on the valley head ten minutes later and the sight spurred him on.

Above the valley the land changes again, here is the edge of the high desert, a clear line beyond which only ancient wind-stretched cypress boughs coil over the limestone. The oak has gone, the maquis

231

too; only low clumps of endemic herbs and flowers cling to thin soils in hollows where the dew might collect or the snow linger. Across the bare white rock ahead there is a well-engineered track which ignores the high prow of Zeranokephala in front and instead angles left, climbing gradually beside the gorge which deepens below it, and turning to the north to follow the gorge rim.

Here three and a half millennia before had come Jasumatu, hungry, thirsty, lost and light-headed, in the late afternoon. Distraught at his failure to rescue the disks from the wreck of the Phaistos flagship, desperate to rejoin his tribe which had sailed away into the west under Turusa and Ramati, he had wandered along the flank of the gorge until at length, at sunset, he had come to the small cave and its spring at which now Nikos intended to spend the night. Then, in hunger, despair and loneliness, he had taken the hands of Asumunde and Sirute in his own and stepped out into the icy air of the gorge.

And now, thirty-five centuries later, the disks were about to return to him; Nikos, Brian and Robert with their loads of treasure took ten minutes rest at the end of the maquis as countless others have done before them, then started up the solid stone pathway which wound across the shoulder of the mountain. As Mateo caught up with Dimitris and Kenneth they saw the three dark shapes of their prey on the skyline.

Saturday, 14th September: 1600 hrs

"Well, you took your time, I must say," Dimitris hugged Mateo in his great bear arms. "Thought you would have overtaken us hours ago, you must be getting old."

Mateo, who had climbed over two thousand metres in under six hours, smiled sadly. "It is true; I am not as fast as I used to be. But, then, I am surprised to see that you townsmen made it at all." He drank and poured water over his wiry grey hair. "And, more to the point, not bad for the robbers either. They're carrying heavy loads and they are even less accustomed to the mountains than you are. They've done well but they must be tired now."

The three sat and ate, looking out over the desolate gorge to where the bay of Rodhia glinted under the grey shadows of the Volakias ridge. Kenneth tossed an apple core to fall, spinning slowly, endlessly down through the sunlight. The steepness of the gorge wall allowed it to drop into the shadow before they lost sight of it. As it disappeared Kenneth sat back and stretched. "What now?" He looked along the trail to where the others had passed over the skyline. "What are we going to do now? We've caught up with them. Now comes the difficult bit – how do we stop them?"

Dimitris said, "I suppose they will spend the night in the cave, we could surprise them then. Bit difficult to creep up on them in the dark, though."

"Difficult to creep up, either in the dark or in the light. I don't fancy a chase across this country, too unpredictable by far. Come on, Mateo, what do you think?"

Mateo looked along the track and then turned to lift his head to look up the flank of the mountain which towered above them. He was silent for a while; the others followed his gaze.

"Oh, no, not that way, not likely. There's no way you're getting me up there."

Kenneth was adamant. "I'm not a goat. That way is for the kri-kri only. What do you say, Dimitris? Tell your old friend. No way."

Dimitris punched Mateo on the arm, nearly knocking the small man over. "No, my old friend, not even for you, not even for all the treasure in Phaistos. Just look at it, it's another four hundred metres and damn near vertical. Then how do we get down, and where, and how long will it take?"

They all looked up at the white layers of limestone climbing steeply into the intense blue of the sky. Kenneth shook his head. "Come on Mateo, think again. You can't get us up there."

Mateo lowered his gaze to the two faces in front of him and smiled his long slow smile. His teeth shone white in the lined brown of his face and his eyes creased in amusement under his wild grey hair. "Not you two, I know that you couldn't make it, being city men. Not you. But I will. I will climb Zeranokephala and come down the far side, to the path beyond the cave. You can take the easy way and we will trap them between us. There will be no escape for them." His smile faded and his lips closed firmly over the white teeth; the humour had gone to be replaced by an implacably steely, almost animal contemplation. "There will be no escape."

The words chilled the air and Kenneth felt the hairs on the back of his neck rise. The day moved from the twentieth century to a primitive time long ago; there were no nuances, only absolutes. There were no greys, only unchangeable blacks and whites. What had begun as a sort of game had taken on a deadly reality. A cloud crossed the sun and took all the colour from the landscape and the warmth drained from the air.

Kenneth glanced at Dimitris to see if he had felt the same cold touch but the big man was finishing a sandwich without an obvious care. Possibly all Sfakians were at one with primeval forces, the patina of their civilisation thin. Kenneth remembered a phrase he had once heard to the effect that Greece is an outpost of the east, treated as western in error. At times like this he could believe it to be true.

"OK," Mateo was saying, "this is what we will do. The thieves are going slowly now, they do not fear discovery. It will take them about an hour to the cave, then they must settle, say an hour and a quarter in total. I have to climb four hundred metres and come down three, say about the same time. You have to cover a couple of flat kilometres, but quietly, say forty minutes. And the sun sets at about six. OK? So we'll meet at the cave at six, gives us all plenty of time. Any problems?"

Simultaneously Dimitris said "No" and Kenneth said "Yes."

Kenneth looked carefully at them both. "Look," he said, "It's all right making these plans, but what are we going to do when we surprise them? We can't just jump on them and throw them off the edge. And then there's the treasure, we must make sure that we get that, that's the most important thing of all. We can't let the disks slip out of our hands now we've got this far. Whatever we do we've got to make sure of that."

Dimitris got to his feet and offered Kenneth a hand. He pulled the older man to his feet. "Don't worry, we won't do anything rash. You'll get your disks. Now get something to eat and some rest before we go on."

Kenneth would not get any reassurance from Dimitris beyond that.

Saturday, 14th September: 1700 hrs

As the trail turns north around the shoulder of Zeranokephala and the path follows a rough terrace under the face of the mountain, the Eligias gorge opens up beneath it. Gullies from the limestone cliffs plunge to the depths of the gorge. Spurs to which the occasional twisted cypress clings spring from the face to stand in a line of diminishing minarets before they also fail and fall. Over spur and gully, in and out of the face of the old man, the trail winds, up and down, and all the time the awful gorge deepens beneath. In the gullies there is a false sense of security; on the ridges the exposure grows. Tired limbs increase the vertigo, making each step a greater effort, a greater hazard. If you have not passed this way before the trail seems to go on for ever; the promised refuge in the cave, the fresh cold water of the spring are mirages.

Nikos stumbled down the sharp edge of one of the limestone spurs, avoiding looking down into the gorge, concentrating on the path as the terrace turned into the face of the mountain around the head of a wide gully. He followed it with his eye to where it rose again to climb another ridge, and shifted the heavy rucksack on his aching shoulders.

"Christ, it goes on forever. I'm buggered, let's take five minutes."

"Can't stop here, I'm going on."

There was an edge of desperation in Brian's voice which prompted Robert's sneering bravado. "Getting scared? Come on now, just watch this." Robert stood on top of the sharp ridge and peered down into the indistinct depths below him. He looked back at Brian. "It's easy, if you're not scared."

"I'm not scared, just tired. I'm going on, it can't be much further." He set off, moving slowly, rucksack hanging heavily from one shoulder, feet sore. Nikos and Robert watched him go until he had reached the gully head then started after him. The late afternoon sun bathed the cliff in a deepening golden glow, turning the white to bronze and emphasising the depths of its gullies. The three men had been going, with only brief stops and little sleep, for seventeen hours, and were coming to the end of their endurance. At moments like this distance ceases to matter, only time is relevant, time and the shifting stone beneath the feet. Concentrating on each step, searching for the easiest way to cross the next metre, avoiding sharp rocks which hurt aching feet, avoiding unstable stones which jar tired limbs, these are the priorities, the only concerns. Time stretches endlessly ahead in a blur of weariness; there is a goal but hope of achieving it recedes. The only realities are the path and the stones and the feet and the heavy load. Thirst withdraws; hunger recedes; only pain is left.

And then all these things come to an end; crossing a final ridge, looking into the mountain face, suddenly there is deep green vegetation clustered around a copious spring of fresh cold water. Suddenly the cave is there, promising warmth and respite. The last fifty metres curve around the upper edge of an immense gully which falls from under the face for over a thousand vertical metres. But the exposure is forgotten, the rough sliding stones are forgotten, the heavy sack ignored. The last fifty metres are covered quickly and easily; the rucksack slides to the ground, cupped hands fill with water and raise it to parched lips, pour it over unkempt hair. Droplets thrown from hands and hair hang like small diamonds in the golden sunlight before falling into the depths. Three tired men stand, noticing for the first time the glory of the sky to the west as the golden sun slips through strata of shining cloud, progressively lemon, orange, gold, down towards the black jagged ridge of Volakias. Sunbeams spring, as crisp and clear as in an icon, from the splinters of cloud, and the vulture sweeps by, black and ominous above the gorge.

Saturday, 14th September: 1800 hrs

Mateo had climbed to the very summit of Zeranokephala and stood for a moment to survey the magnificent view which encircled him. To his north he could see the lights of the refuge at Kallergi, to the west Volakias' long ridge drops down to the bay at Rodhia, to the south the trail falls back to Agios Ioannis through the forest, to the east the land is dark except for where the sun struck the high grey point of Psiloriti and the peak sanctuary which Jasumatu built, and picked it out in a diminishing triangle of gold. This was his country, he loved every centimetre of it, but tonight his thoughts were elsewhere. Three hundred metres below him, Nikos, Robert and Brian were taking their last tired steps down the slope to the spring and Dimitris and Kenneth were watching them from the ridge. Mateo turned and dropped like a mountain goat down the steep slope, jumping from rock to rock, staff held before and above him in balance as he went, down, down to the path above the gorge.

Kenneth had now completely entered into the spirit of the hunt; he was no longer the civilised academic, content in his cerebral considerations. He was the hunter, intent on the chase, conscious only of the need for stealth and silence. Behind him came Dimitris, equally intent, equally careful, equally determined. The wild landscape and the intended kill have combined to eliminate reason. All that remained was the chase, the hunted and the hunter; there was no longer any concept of right or wrong.

The hunted had drunk their fill. They pulled their sacks up on to sore shoulders and got stiffly to their feet. They followed the trail up to the cave and stood at the edge of the path looking out at the sunset. The gorge fell almost vertically from their feet, fringed only by a line of spiny hedgehog plants. Above them the trail climbed steeply to cross a rib of limestone which threw a deep shadow.

Nikos, Brian and Robert were silhouetted against the dark shadow beyond them. To their right rose the steep spine of the limestone ridge, dark and jagged against the fading sky. There was no wind, no noise as the vulture flew by on widespread wings and disappeared behind the ridge.

Dimitris watched the sun sinking over the peaks of Volakias and glanced at his watch. The time was a few minutes before six. Kenneth suddenly saw Mateo's head, hair catching the light, above the ridge. He whispered to Dimitris, "He's made it. Time to go."

They started up the path towards Brian and his companions, moving quickly and quietly over the scree-laden slope. Mateo dropped back down to the trail, out of sight for the moment.

Kenneth and Dimitris were in deep shadow within three metres of their prey, there was only a primitive instinct, to kill. Kenneth was ashamed of it, later, but not now.

As Nikos, Brian and Robert watched the setting sun and its lower rim touched the top of the highest peak of the black Volakias, Kenneth stumbled over a loose stone in the sudden twilight and Dimitris grabbed his arm. The robbers turned, incredulous, at the sound, their eyes dazzled by the sunset. "What the hell …"

Instinctively they turned again, to seek escape up the path. In front of them, outlined against the sky, stood Mateo with his *ambelitsa* staff raised above his head. The last sunlight splintered in his grey hair to form a halo of fire. He looked like Nemesis.

Time froze.

Turning from Mateo, Robert caught his foot in the spines of the prickly plant at the edge of the gorge and fell. His flailing hand caught the strap of Nikos' sack and Nikos tried to slip the strap from his shoulder as he was pulled over the edge. He succeeded, only to recall, in that last moment, that the rucksack carried his share of the Minoan treasure. He grabbed for the sack as Robert fell. They fell together over the edge of the path, down into the dark gorge. There was a single, strangely plaintive scream, and a sob from Brian who stood frozen, one hand outstretched, on the path. The sun set suddenly and the light went. There was a rush of air as the griffin vulture stooped to follow the falling bodies to the sharp rocks a thousand metres below.

Nikos and Robert and two rucksacks carrying priceless Minoan treasure struck scree and bounced, struck again and rolled, falling through the dark mist to drop suddenly, shockingly, silently on to splintered rock, and lie still. Around them on the scree were the scattered bones of Jasumatu, Priest-King elect of the Minoans, now reunited with the disks he tried so hard to save.

Chapter thirty

Sunday, 15th September: 0600 hrs

The night spent in the cave under Zeranokephala was cold and uncomfortable; neither Brian nor his three hunters had much food and none of them had any means of making a hot drink. Mateo made a small fire of thin dry wood from the hedgehog plant and added twisted lengths of cypress which crackled and spat sparks but gave off little heat. Leaves produced thick heavy smoke which was reluctant to leave the confines of the cave. An attempt to heat a small can of sardines resulted in burnt fingers and little else.

Conversation did not come easily and was confined to practicalities and platitudes. Night fell fast and they had no light other than from Brian's torch; all slept early then awoke with the dawn, cold and dispirited. Only Mateo, sleeping on the cold ground outside the cave wrapped tightly in his blanket and snoring loudly, seemed impervious to the cold and the hunger and the deaths of Robert and Nikos; the others suffered from uncomfortable memories of the previous day's events.

Was it a tragedy, or was it the end which they as hunters had sought? Had the pursuit only one possible result? How else could the stolen treasure have been recovered than by a physical confrontation? And for that confrontation to end in victory some injury had to be done to the quarry. And after that it was only a matter of degree: a bloody nose or a death, did it really matter? In undertaking the pursuit, the deaths of the Greek and the Scot had been the sought-after, inevitable, unavoidable outcome.

This conclusion was ignored by Mateo, rested lightly on Dimitris, but weighed heavily on Kenneth who spent the night dodging the stones under his blanket and wrestling with his conscience. Time and time again he felt that he should have done more to hold his companions back, could have grabbed Nikos as he fell, might have foreseen the awful outcome. And yet again, did his regret lie in the loss of

238

the greater part of the treasure and the disks, rather than in the deaths of the two men? In the more honest moments of the night, Kenneth realised unhappily that this might be so.

And what of Brian whose vacillation and indecision and amorality had brought the whole thing about? How did he pass his night, ostracised by the others and fearful of his future? Was there here a parallel with the young Priest-King Jasumatu whose own lack of leadership and indecision had brought about the loss of the disks and the treasures of the palace of Phaistos thirty-five centuries ago? Two weak men brought to a sad end by the stronger aims and ambitions of others and by events over which neither had control? Throughout the long night Brian longed for the courage to throw himself into the gorge to join Nikos and Robert on the rocks below. He pictured himself getting quietly to his feet, moving secretly past the sleeping bodies of his captors, standing on the edge of the gorge, waiting for the moon to rise before stepping forward to fall into the depths. Such a tempting prospect. If Brian had had a Sirute or an Asumunde to stand beside him and take his hands he might have done it. But the twentieth-century man had no ghosts, no beliefs, no certainties, no simple loves. He could not take the step. Instead he spent a lonely night shivering in the cold and in fear of what retribution awaited him below in the hands of the law. Or in the hands of Theseus, an altogether more frightening prospect.

At six in the morning the light of the rising sun struck the face of Volakias across the gorge and it was time to go. Four tired men started the rough trail back down to civilisation; Mateo led the way, Dimitris brought up the rear; the two Englishmen stumbled between them. By ten-thirty they were with Eleni, telephoning Yorgos the Merc, eating bread and honey and grapes, drinking hot black coffee. They caught the twelve o'clock boat from Hora Sfakion to Lossos and by half past were back in the comfort of the late twentieth century, drinking wine and eating before sleeping through the afternoon. The events of the last twenty-four hours in the high mountains seemed already remote, the memories fading in the banalities of the coast.

Sunday, 15th September: 1700 hrs

Theseus allowed Brian three hours sleep in the room which he had left in such high hopes less than two days ago. At five o'clock in the hot still afternoon as the sky darkened with the humid prospect of the first storm of autumn, a small boy roused him from his restless sleep. The imperative knocking brought him, tousled and disoriented, to his door to receive a short hand-written note: 'I expect you on my launch at six. Theseus.'

Brian showered and found a clean check shirt and jeans. He sat on his balcony smoking a thin cigarette as the clouds gathered and the colour left the village below him. Many have gone to their execution with lighter mind than Brian as he descended the concrete staircase with jelly legs in the ominous dusk. The walk seemed to last forever yet was over quickly; the last few steps along the wooden jetty seemed like the steps to the scaffold. All around him the village life went on. Children swam and shouted. Tourists gossiped and worried about the weather. Villagers sat under trees and watched and argued. Yet to Brian the walk seemed like his last, each step was significant, each crunch of pebbles beneath his feet loud and final, each breath a gasp.

Theseus' launch barely moved on the slight sea; a voice from within the cabin invited Brian to step down into the craft. Theseus sat at the chart table with his back to the bright western sky. A bottle of Glenfiddich and two glasses stood before him on the table. A diving set with twin air bottles and a weighted diving belt made an untidy pile on one of the cushioned benches, partly resting on a small hessian sack. "*Kathiste, parakalo.*"

Theseus sat with the sunset behind him, his face in darkness, a flash of white in his black beard. He poured measures of whisky into the two glasses and pushed one across the table to Brian.

"*Yiamas.*"

"Yeah, cheers."

"*Lipon.* So you chose to cheat me. That was foolish. And your friends are dead. That is unfortunate." Theseus filled the glasses again. "You have made a mistake, Englishman; a bad mistake. I asked you to come here to Lossos as my friend, my trusted friend, and you have failed me. You came to do a job for me for which I would have paid you well, and the job remains unfinished. Not only did you not complete the work, but you spent my time and my money in stealing from me. This was foolish. It was an insult to me, and no one insults me and steals from me without punishment. That is the way of things here, you understand?"

Theseus spoke quietly, as if with regret. "So, in some recompense, I want you to do a last little work for me. After that we will part and you will not return." Theseus poured two more glasses of whisky. "But first, we will drink together and you will explain to me why you cheated me."

Brian gulped the whisky; a light clammy sweat on his forehead, giving a furtive glance at the door to the cabin. He tried to speak calmly but his voice came oddly to his ears. "Well, yes, but I didn't, really, intend to cheat, it just, sort of, got out of hand ..."

His strangled speech ended on its usual note of apology as he watched the mooring ropes being untied by the same young boy who had brought the summons to his interrupted sleep, only half an hour ago. The ropes were thrown on board and the boat drifted away from the jetty, turning slowly so that the panorama of the village passed the cabin windows. Theseus drank the last of his whisky and filled Brian's glass again, to the brim, so that the golden liquid poured down its side, catching a sunbeam. "So you did not mean to cheat me? Does that excuse it? It just happened? It just happened that you spent days taking things from the wreck, and hid them, and arranged for them to be sold. That just happened? I am sorry; I do not think that these things just happen. You and your dead companions chose to cheat me. Deliberately. That was unfortunate, for you."

Theseus pushed the brimming glass across the table and leaned back to smile without humour at the Englishman. "No-one cheats me, remember that." He gestured at the glass, "Drink it, please."

Theseus went out through the forward door of the cabin and shut it firmly behind him; the roar of the twin engines filled the air as he spun the wheel to starboard. The craft heeled as it raced out of the bay, past the light beacon on the island, and turned along the headland. Whisky slopped from the glass and streamed across the table to make a small pool against its raised edge. Brian drank a little from the glass and went to try to open the door. It was locked, as was the forward door. The engines roared and the Lossos headland swept past, quickly followed by the two chapels, then the divers' camp, and the open expanse of Lavris bay.

Brian drained the glass and beat at the windows with his fists without purpose or result. The boat roared on, striking hard at the short sharp waves brought up by the freshening wind, into a western sky showing errant sunbeams escaping from dark grey clouds. Eventually the sound of the engines ceased abruptly and the launch slowed and drifted and rocked uneasily on the waves. Theseus came back into the cabin; the door opened readily from outside. He poured two more glasses from the depleted bottle.

"Drink, please. No, both glasses."

Brian jumped to his feet and pulled at the door "Oh, come on, you can't do this, you've got to let me go, this isn't right, you can't do this to me ..."

Theseus watched him for a moment, dispassionately, holding his eyes. A thin- bladed knife appeared in his right hand. He gestured with it. "Sit down. Drink."

Brian sat despairingly.

"This is Sfakia. Here I do what I wish, what is necessary." Implacable, unbending, Theseus pushed the full glass across the table toward Brian with the sharp point of the blade. "Drink." The launch rocked uneasily under the growing wind as the clouds grew in the west. The sun had gone; the black cloud had a thin golden edge; far beyond Rodhia, the sea was still bright, but in Maranes bay it was a dull, unfriendly grey.

Brian drank the whisky in one gulp and coughed, banging the glass down on the table. "What do you want me to do? I'm sorry. I didn't mean to steal anything, it was Robert – who had the idea – I mean, and then Nikos who made the plans. I didn't want to do it, not really ..."

"For you, it is always someone else, *ne*? Yes? Never Brian. Always someone else who gets you into trouble. Always someone else's fault. But now your two friends are dead and you cannot blame them any more. This time you will take responsibility, you will go down to the reef to complete the job which you came here to do. Drink it now, please."

Brian watched the horizon turn and sink. The motion of the boat and the effects of the whisky made him feel sick and he swayed and retched. The point of the stiletto in the back of his hand brought him back to the reality of his position and he sobbed and wiped his face with a bloody hand. He grasped the full glass and drank its contents quickly in a last desperate search for courage, not daring to look into Theseus' relentless eyes. He felt hot and sickly and the voice came indistinctly to him. "Now put the diving gear on, and the belt. You will finish your work on the reef."

The idea came to Brian through the haze of alcohol. He needed a swim, it would clear his head. Once in the water, his element, he could escape. He stumbled to his feet and swung the twin bottles around onto his back and fastened the clasp of the weighted belt. The click of its fastening sounded final. Theseus opened the cabin door and the cold evening air swept in dispelling the fumes of spilled whisky and the smell of blood and fear. "Come, let us finish the job."

Theseus' grip on Brian's shoulder was iron hard, dragging him to the side of the boat. Any idea of resistance was overcome by Theseus' strength and the sudden glimmer of hope that he might escape when under water. With the ample supply of air in the twin tanks, he just might reach shore before Theseus knew what was happening. A straw for the drowning man to grasp, taking any thought of fight from him.

Theseus' iron grip forced him down to sit on the gunwale of the boat. Brian fixed his mask, taking great gulps of air to clear his mind. Theseus looked at his watch. "OK. Time to go. Goodbye, my friend. *Kalo taxithi.*"

Brian fell backwards into the cold sea and dropped steeply under the tug of the heavy belt. The initial shock of the cold sobered him and he reached for the clasp on the heavy belt with frantic hands. His feet touched the reef and he staggered and fell onto the sharp spines of the urchin-covered limestone desperately fumbling with the catch which appeared to be jammed by a thin fishing line. He gulped air frantically and thrashed upward against the overpowering load of the weighted belt.

On the boat above Theseus picked up the sack from where it lay on the bench seat and took out two sticks of dynamite and a fuse. He set the fuse and pushed the explosive back into the sack and tugged at the fishing line which was fastened to it to make sure that it was secure, then dropped the sack and its contents into the water. He started the engines and slowly turned out to sea. The sun disappeared behind black clouds and the day was over.

Down on the reef Brian was struggling with the alcohol in his brain and his cold, clumsy fingers, fighting with the clasp of the belt which was holding him down, pulling in the fishing line which was tied around it. The line came easily to his hand but he did not see what was attached to its other end until it was far too late. The fuse had been timed perfectly.

Hearing an explosion, Theseus turned to watch the plume of water which burst from the surface. Dramatically he swung the launch around and raced back in to where the sea raged in a disk of white and green mixed with dead fish and small coloured bits which might have been clothing. He waited awhile, circling the spot, and then set off at high speed back towards Lossos.

He called Gillian on the radio. "There has been an accident. I was with the Englishman, Brian, working on that reef at Maranes. He went down to fix some charges and there was an explosion. I think that he is dead, but we need to search. Will you call the coastguard at Sfakia?"

Brian's body was found early next day. No one remarked that he appeared to have been diving while wearing jeans and a checked shirt.

Chapter thirty one

In the late morning Theseus made a rare visit to Andreas and was received with much deference and shaking of hands by the perspiring proprietor and Katerina, his wife. He was shown to a table in the corner where a tired red-check cloth was quickly replaced by a crisp white one. Surrounding tables were moved back to give privacy and Andreas stood anxiously by as Theseus sat.

"*Kathise, kyrie Theseus. Kathise. Ti tha piete, cafe, koniak.*"

"*Ne. Ena sketo, parakalo.*"

The coffee came quickly, Andreas placing the small white cup carefully, stilling his shaking hand with effort. A small carafe of crystal water and a polished glass followed. Andreas stood awaiting dismissal until Theseus turned from his contemplation of the sea and, as if recalling his purpose, smiled suddenly at him. "*Signomi, Andreas.* Please sit with me. I have a favour to ask." Andrea sat carefully, upright, unconsciously wiping his huge hands on his apron; Katerina brought a second coffee and retreated to the kitchen from where she watched anxiously.

"My old friend, I have a favour to ask of you. I want you to close your taverna to the tourists tonight. I want you to allow me to hold a private party here, for about ten or twelve people. I know that you will provide me with your best food and your own beautiful wine and I would like you to make sure that we are not disturbed. We will eat at eight." Andreas visibly relaxed; concern about what might have been demanded withdrew, to be replaced only moments later by more practical worries about the meal. Andreas was both flattered and relieved; if there was one thing he could do, it was provide food and service. In his mind he was scouring the village for the best fish, the freshest bread, the best hung goat, the crispest vegetables; he would provide a meal to remember.

The two men were of the same age and had lived in the same

village all their lives. They were both big men and strong but one exuded power, the other deference. As boys they had fought and climbed on the hills and fished in the bay. As youths one had gone to sea and the other stayed ashore, one led men, the other followed men; their paths turned widely apart. And now in late middle-age Theseus controlled Sfakia and Andreas ran his restaurant; one commanded, the other complied. "*Poli orea, efharisto poli.* There is no problem. My wife and I will be honoured to serve you as our guests; of course," he continued expansively, "there will be no charge."

"Thank you, my friend, I knew that you would help me. And we will not be your guests but your friends and I will make sure that you are fully recompensed for your efforts tonight. Thank you again, and for your hospitality. I must leave you now, for I have much to do. Please give my respects to Katerina." Theseus rose easily to his feet as Andreas struggled to his. There was a firm handshake and Theseus was gone, leaving Andreas standing by the table. Andreas sat down again and wiped his sweating forehead and hands on his apron and watched the tall figure walk purposefully back to the hotel, head bowed and stroking the white patch in his beard. He was relieved to hear that Theseus would pay; goodness knows what Katerina would have said if his offer had been accepted, but he had done it well, he thought, he had kept face. An image came to Andreas of two boys and a boat on a sunlit sea, long ago, but he could make no connection between the memory and the present. He shook his head as his wife came from the kitchen, anxious to hear what had transpired, and in an unusual show of affection he took her hand and patted it. "Don't worry, *yeneka mou*. We have only got to provide a meal, that's all. Sit with me a while and we will plan what we have to do."

With a formality unusual in Lossos handwritten notes were folded into white envelopes and despatched to Lavris, to the archaeologists' camp, to the hotel, to the sparse room with the rough concrete terrace above the village. 'You will be my guests tonight at eight o'clock at Andreass' taverna.' Only for Kenneth and Mary Ashworth, Jenny, and for Brad Slinger were the words 'if you please' added. For the rest this was a summons, not an invitation.

Some received the invitation with surprise but with anticipation of an interesting evening, others with dread. All knew what had happened on the wreck, most had heard a version of the events in the White Mountains, all knew of the deaths of Nikos, Robert and Brian. None knew what Theseus intended. The most unexpected invitations were those to Oscar, who had had a brief interview with Theseus that morning, and to Jackie who received the summons with some trepidation; she could not work out why she had been included. She felt that her role in the whole business had been blameless but could not resist a feeling that she might soon be on her way back to England. Oscar, on the other hand, had been involved from the start and had been compliant, if not participant, in the theft. He spent the afternoon chain-smoking and worrying about a clean shirt; he would have liked a drink but didn't want to risk it as he felt that he would need all his wits during the evening. He passed the time walking backwards and forwards across the concrete terrace of the rooms he had shared with Brian and Robert, missing their irritating companionship. He wished he had been more resolute and determined in his counsel, surely he could have made the others see sense. He cursed himself for letting his lust for Jackie distract him from what his friends were proposing. He wondered what the inside of a Greek gaol might be like and what the sentence for plundering an ancient wreck might be. He was almost glad when the time came to shower and dress in a white shirt which Jackie had freshly ironed, and leave. He did not descend the steep steps to the village in quite as desperate a mind as Brian had done only the night before, but near to it. He met Jackie by the hotel and neither spoke as they crossed the shingle to where Andreas' taverna lay strangely quiet.

Kenneth and Mary had a glass of wine with Gillian and Jenny on the hotel terrace in the early evening; Brad joined them later and his confidence served to relax them all but while they chattered about the day, no one mentioned those things which were uppermost in their minds. Fiona, subdued, in a dark dress, served drinks to hotel guests and suffered comments on her formal appearance brightly but without her normal wit. At quarter to eight Gillian announced to the guests that anyone wanting further supplies could help themselves for the rest of the evening. "We are going out, so look after yourselves for once. Don't worry about money, it's all free tonight, but I'll close the bar at ten, so drink quickly."

Such was the idiosyncratic way she ran the hotel that this was accepted as normal by her guests and none exploited her generosity, and at five to eight Gillian led her party down the stairs and across the beach. As they arrived at Andreas' a small outboard boat tied up at the wharf and Dimitris and Mateo came ashore. Mateo had found a nearly clean striped shirt which he had tucked into a pair of old trousers which he had unearthed from the depths of his room at Lavris. No one could remember seeing him in trousers before but his battered sandals and his callused bare feet detracted from his apparent formality. Dimitris wore a formal white shirt and dark trousers, and looked stern. He showed everyone to their allotted places at the large table which already carried carafes of water and golden wine and baskets of bread. Theseus was nowhere to be seen and the talk was quiet and uncomfortable. Andreas brought olives and mezes and poured wine and water and retired to the kitchen to watch. Even Gillian was uneasy; she was as unaware of the true purpose of the meeting as any, and she was glad when Dimitris spoke.

"Thank you all for coming to dine with Theseus and Gillian tonight. I am sorry that Theseus is not here to greet you, but he will arrive shortly. Please eat and drink and enjoy the food and company but, before we start, let us spend a moment in memory of those friends who died recently. Think specially of Jenny who has lost a husband, and of Oscar who has lost two old friends in such a tragic way. Please think also of Manolis in hospital in Hania." There was an uncomfortable silence around the table. Some thought the tributes overdone and unnecessary; after all, the Greek and the two British had done their best to cheat everyone and, particularly in Kenneth's eyes, had brought about the second and catastrophic loss of the disks. And, in Brad's mind, had irresponsibly damaged the wreck site. Others wondered about Brian's death and whether there was a connection with the others, or whether it was just an unhappy coincidence.

Jenny could not help thinking, happily, that she had 'lost a husband and found a lover', and found solemnity difficult.

Gillian was worried about what her unpredictable husband might be up to, and who would suffer in consequence.

Mateo had no regret about the deaths; he had done what had to be done in the interests of Crete and honour; remote from the others, he leant back in his chair to watch the rise of Saturn over the ridge.

Mary shivered in the cool evening and pulled her cardigan more tightly over her shoulders as she felt the alien hand of Sfakia in the air.

Unseen except by Mateo, high above the dark village, the vulture watched and waited.

The silence of the evening was broken by the arrival of a small outboard which tied up at the taverna wharf to allow Theseus, in black shirt and trousers, to jump onto the terrace carrying two small sacks which he lay carefully on an adjacent table. Turning, he approached the dining table smiling, with arms outstretched. "Welcome, my friends, welcome. I am sorry that I was not here to greet you. Come, let us eat. We will talk later." He sat at the head of the table with Dimitris and Fiona on his right hand and Brad on his left, next to Jenny. Gillian sat at the far end with Mateo and Kenneth and Mary; Oscar and Jackie fidgeted in between. Andreas was as good as his word, producing a beautiful meal of simple local food which tourists, accustomed only to moussaka and chips, would not believed possible of Cretan cooking. Mezes were followed by freshly cooked calamari, crisp in a light batter, then sardines, split and gently barbecued. Sea urchin in garlic dressing followed with onion and tomato salad, then sole in strips, browned in the grill. Next came tender lamb in a sauce redolent with local herbs, with green beans, then the goat, an enormous leg slowly cooked on a spit, juicy and tender. The golden wine for which Andreas was famous was the perfect foil to all the dishes, matching the stronger flavours, complementing the more subtle ones.

The earlier unease passed and the conversation became lively with even Oscar and Jackie joining in with tales of the village and the tourists and the fishing. The meal drew slowly to an end and Andreas brought tiny carafes of *tsikoudia*, and black, thick coffee. Gillian smoked; Oscar and Jackie were desperate but reluctant to indulge in this company until Gillian noticed their discomfort and chucked her packet down the table.

Theseus was quiet, drinking little, joining in with a social word only when the chatter died. He watched the ridge behind the village until a sliver of moon appeared over the crags and, as if this was the signal for which he had been waiting, he sat back in his chair and quietly tapped the table with a knife. Conversation ceased immediately and all eyes turned to his commanding figure. There was silence but for the slap of tiny waves on the hulls of the tethered boats. The moon, just beyond full, lifted itself clear of the ridge and caught the wide wings of a bird which drifted slowly over the bay.

"We have witnessed some strange events here in Lossos of recent times, events as catastrophic as an earthquake; the aftershocks will be felt for many years." Theseus spoke clearly but quietly in English, sure of the attention he was getting. "Strange events, from which, I fear, the village will not recover. But Sfakia always changes and yet does not change. The sea does not change, the mountains do not change; people come and go and scratch the surface of our land but they do not change it. But although the land is not changed, the lives of the people who live in it, who visit it, can be changed. Those events which we have witnessed will affect the lives of all of us. We will none of us be the same again."

Theseus paused and looked out to sea and watched the vulture cross the face of the moon. "I, myself, will change. I cannot resist and survive. Although the rocks and the waves will not be altered, the world gets smaller and the influences of its ambitions and hopes will have effect even here. I cannot resist this influence as much as I might wish to, and I must accept it." He smiled to himself. "This will not be easy for a Sfakian like me, but these days we cannot retreat into the mountains to wait for our enemies to tire and go away. Today we must meet the challenges, and adapt, or others will impose those changes upon us." He looked around the table. "You who are my guests tonight come from the wide world. Some come from England, one from Australia, one from America, you all bring ideas and hopes to which Sfakia must respond. Sfakia itself will not be changed, but the lives of its people must change. Even Sfakians must bow to the world. I am proud to be Sfakian and I have done my best to meet my responsibilities to Sfakia; I have been harsh, sometimes ruthless, always determined to ensure the best for my people, but now I must lead them in a new direction."

Theseus got up from the table and went to stand at the edge of the terrace, looking out across the bay. The moonlight chiselled his features from seamless stone. He spoke without turning, as if to himself. "I will not be the first who has had to make hard decisions for the future of their tribe which they lead; I will surely not be the last. Many men in the past, in Crete, have had to take hard choices on behalf of their people; some met success and some, failure. But I cannot now sacrifice a lamb and hope to appease the gods. Life today is a little more complicated." Theseus stroked his beard and sighed; a moonbeam struck his shoulder and moved slowly away. He turned from his contemplation of the bay and returned to the table. He looked around at his guests and spoke directly to each one.

"I will retire soon to my fishing and I will leave the future to younger men. I will retire, but do not fear, I and my chosen successor, Dimitris, will watch over you."

Did Theseus know that his words had been used by Asumunde, in Phaistos, thirty-five centuries ago? No matter, the intention was the same; the hopes for, and the duty to his people, the same. No one questioned the assumption of power and responsibility, here in Theseus' own land. The words were ponderous and anachronistic, but were appropriate and understood.

In the silence Andreas came to the table, apologetic and hand-wringing. "Kyrie Kosta, I do not wish to disturb you, but may we

249

clear the table? You will be more comfortable."

"Certainly, my friend, and bring more coffee and *tsikoudia* for us. We will stay some while longer, I think, if you do not mind."

The table was cleared quickly and a new cloth spread; more cups and carafes were brought and the moon moved slowly overhead to hide behind the awning; overhead, the vulture continued to watch and listen.

"And now to practical matters." Theseus cleared his throat to regain attention.

"The unfortunate deaths in the mountains of the young Scotsman and the Athenian, Nikos, have been reported to the authorities. I have sympathy for those of you who knew them, and in particular for Jenny who has lost her husband." Theseus looked for the first time into Jenny's eyes, and held them for a long moment. Jenny met his gaze and felt that he could read her thoughts. She stayed outwardly cool but her contradictory feelings made her pulse quicken. She recognised that this man knew how she felt about the death of her husband, might even know of her interest in Brad, but understood; she felt comforted and at ease.

"The deaths in the mountains will be treated as climbing accidents and Kyrie Ashworth and Mateo will have to make a statement to the police. Dimitris will not be involved."

Mateo did not care. He would tell the story with an easy heart. Kenneth had expected something like this and would worry through the night. Theseus or no Theseus, to an Englishman, death was serious. Although he and the others had not been actually involved in the accident, he nevertheless felt responsible. The fact that the two who died had broken the law and had stolen his disks did not, in his mind, make his involvement any less reprehensible. He met Theseus' eyes. The Cretan nodded, he understood the reservations of some Englishmen to the realism of the East. "Please do not worry, my friend, it will be a simple, straightforward matter and there will be no problem for you."

Surprisingly, Kenneth found himself believing him and felt a little easier. With a start he realised that he had begun to accept the power of this man.

"Now to the tragic loss of the Englishman, Brian, whom I had invited to Sfakia to carry out a simple job for me. You know that in attempting to finish the task he had started, to help me complete the plans which I have now discarded, he was killed while placing an underwater charge. A most unfortunate incident for which I will feel endlessly responsible. But the fuses which had been supplied to me have been found to be faulty and action will be taken against those who supplied them."

There was a stir around the table. Theseus' eyes met those of each of his guests in turn, implacably. There was no comment; none seemed appropriate; no one asked why Brian had dived wearing jeans and a shirt, possibly no one knew. The soaring vulture nodded in agreement as a small cloud crossed the moon. Theseus continued, "The authorities in Hania will be investigating this matter, of course, and the fuses have been taken away for inspection."

Brad permitted himself a small smile in the darkness. That the fuses would be found faulty, he had no doubt; no doubt at all. Oscar nervously lit another cigarette. It might have been he who had been fixing those charges. Theseus spoke directly to him.

"You, Oscar, have lost two good friends, and I am sorry for that. I understand that you were aware of what they planned, but took no part in it. Possibly you might have attempted to dissuade them from the course they had chosen but I doubt that you could have changed their minds. In other ways you have shown yourself to be a good man and have contributed to the village, and you are well liked." In a brief flash of humour, he added, "Too well liked by some." Jackie squirmed.

"I do not intend to involve you any further in my plans. The deposit in the bank in Athens is yours to do what you wish with, in its entirety. But I think your time in Lossos is at an end. As is yours, my dear Jackie." His dark eyes bored into hers and she could not meet his gaze. "You have served me well …"

'Too bloody well,' thought Gillian.

"… and have done a good job in the hotel. But we will not want you here any longer. Maybe you will go to Athens. But, thank you, all the same. We will not meet again." He sat back in his chair. "You may go now, both of you."

Jackie and Oscar struggled to their feet and said quiet goodnights; they wandered away feeling lost and excluded but also relieved. Only Fiona moved. She jumped to her feet and caught them up before they left the terrace. She hugged Jackie, "Goodbye, love, look after yourself," and kissed Oscar on the cheek. As she returned to the table, flustered and sad, Theseus spoke to her. "You gain my respect, every day. You will make a good wife for Dimitris. The future is in your hands as much as it is in his. This is the way of the world now, we must acknowledge the involvement of the women. This may be an improvement, who knows?"

Fiona met his look levelly. "It will be, I know. It can't fail to be."

The lights of the tavernas across the bay were being extinguished one by one as the tourists drifted back to their beds. The moon shone on the buildings opposite whose images, distorted, reflected on the black sea. The vulture circled in the dying thermals of the crags, swooping low over the sea to climb high over the land in its endless patrol.

"Now," Theseus was suddenly brisk, "Let me deal with some other matters. The discovery of the wreck of the Minoan ship will change Lossos. How long the work will take, I leave to the experts, but I am told that Kyrie Slinger and his team will be with us for some time." Theseus turned in his chair, "I hope, Mr Slinger, that you will be happy here and I am sure that all that you do will improve our knowledge of our forefathers, and will be to the benefit of Sfakia. I urge you to consider the land and its people in your work and I am prepared to help with this."

Theseus smiled for the first time and put a huge right hand, palm uppermost on the table. "I have found that the European Commission are much more helpful when it comes to cultural matters than they were when I was asking for their help in building the *Ioannis*. Dimitris and I have secured their assistance in three important projects which will affect all of us."

He looked around the table again, then out to sea. "Firstly," he went on, "a road will be built from the Liridiana track which will link Lavris and Philikas to Anopoli. It will not come into Lossos. I know, my friend," as Mateo stirred to object, "I know that this will disturb your peace in Lavris, but some things are unavoidable and sometimes I have to take decisions which are not palatable to all. The road is unavoidable." Theseus smiled at the small man whose clear eyes met his unflinchingly. "However, you have always been faithful to the country in which you have chosen to live, and in which you are much respected, and I have something to say later which you may find interesting. Please bear with me a while."

Mateo subsided. He had great respect for this man, despite Manolis' misgivings, and would give him time.

Theseus took a drink of water. He had not touched the *tsikoudia* and had drunk only a little wine. "The second contribution from Brussels will assist with the operation of the archaeological site. I am sure that Mr. Slinger will concede that the site is an eyesore, a blemish on a beautiful headland. I know how he has plans for improving it, but possibly the EC assistance will speed matters. They are willing to fund an excavation site compatible with the headland, but, after some persuasion, have gone further. A museum and workshop will be built at Likkos, on my land, in which all the finds from the wreck can be displayed and in which all the work of restoration and recovery can be carried out. This will be a low building of local materials which will fit into the landscape. It will be a pleasant place in which to work and which may provide," he coughed quietly, "will provide, to satisfy the Commissioner, much employment for our people. I trust that this will be acceptable to you, Mr Slinger, and I can, if you so wish, arrange for your secondment from Dallas for as long as you want. I have spoken to your people today. I trust that you are not offended by this, and they are content. My family will make certain funds available to them to enable them to continue their excellent work around the world."

Theseus sat back and awaited Brad's response. "You sure do things quickly, Mr. Theseus. I am delighted to accept. But on one condition." Brad leaned forward and put his hands on the table. "The condition is that I have total freedom to do the work on the wreck without interference, and that I have a say in the design of the project. I also would wish to continue my other work around the world during the winter when we cannot continue here. If you can accept this, I'm with you all the way. I look forward to working with you."

Theseus smiled. "I had expected no less. This is your project, and I respect your commitments elsewhere. But I have another favour to ask of you. I want you to employ Mateo as a sort of guardian of the site and its surroundings. He has, as you know, great sympathy for the land and its plants and animals and for Sfakia. His input will be invaluable."

"No problem there with me – how about you, Mateo?"

Mateo scowled down at the tablecloth, fiddling with a piece of bread. "Won't be easy," he growled, "But, since you're going to destroy Lavris anyway, I suppose I might as well have it done my way. But it will be my way, no matter what it costs. And I will not wear a suit."

Theseus grinned at him. "I take that as a yes?"

Mateo nodded.

"Now the third thing," Theseus went on, "the Commissioner has offered to assist in the building of a new hotel to accommodate the increase in the number of tourists who will wish to visit the area. It will not be in Lossos, where no further development will take place, but on the ridge between Lavris and Philikas. It will be part of the landscape and will be the only one permitted. It will, of course, be built on my land, and I trust that Gillian and Fiona will run it in the effective and charming way with which they run Lossos."

This was the first time in twenty years that Theseus had made comment on the hotel and Gillian was astonished. She looked up the table at her husband. "I didn't think you'd noticed." She lit a cigarette and blew the smoke out with great enjoyment. "Well, well, here we go again. I thought that I was going to be able to retire at last, like you. I'm sick of being nice to tourists." She looked down the table at the strange man who was the father of her children and felt that she knew him less well now than when she had been his naive bride. "You continue to surprise me; I thought you hated hotels."

She laughed and spoke directly to Fiona. "What do you think, Fi? Shall we do it?"

Fiona smiled back at her. "You're too young to retire. I suppose we may as well give it a try; after all, it seems that I shall be around here for some time anyway, and I've got to have something to do." She shrugged, "Yeah, OK, why not?"

The moon had swung round into the west; there were no lights on the far side of the bay and the blocks of moonlit buildings were scattered randomly across the hillside, interspersed with wedges of deepest black. Above them the crags appeared steep and impenetrable, holding Lossos in a tight protective grasp. Theseus turned to the Ashworths. "Forgive me, Mary, Professor, for subjecting you to this tedious monologue. I am conscious of the fact that you have not been here in Lossos for long and I hesitated to include you tonight. But I felt that you had both become involved, and would not wish to be left out. I also know that you, Professor, will not find it easy to resist the challenge which I now am able to offer you. You both come with the admiration and respect of your colleagues. You, Mr Ashworth, for your knowledge of ancient scripts and your skill in deciphering them. And you, Mary, for the capable way in which you have run the British School in Athens. I am told that the place has never been in better hands. I wish to offer to you the position of administrator of the new museum. I hope that you will accept it, but please, take your time, as it will not be completed for a while." He grinned wryly.

"This is Greece, you know."

Mary smiled at the big man. "I am very flattered by your offer, Mr. Theseus. You have done your homework very well although I cannot believe that you have talked to many in Athens. Most would not agree with you; they find me too demanding by far." She paused and looked out over the black sea. "May I think about it? It would be lovely to work here in Crete, but a lot depends on where Kenneth works, and I don't want to lose touch with Jenny."

Theseus looked quizzically at Jenny. "I think Jenny might be here for some time."

Jenny's blush was not seen in the darkness.

Theseus glanced at his watch, the village around them was silent and Andreas and Katerina had gone to bed. "One last thing, if you will permit me, and then we can all go home to sleep." He sat back in his chair and stretched. "This morning Mateo led an expedition into the Eligias gorge to recover the bodies of Nikos and Robert. The bodies were found and taken by helicopter to Hania. But the helicopter did not take these, which were somehow overlooked."

He nodded to Dimitris who got up from the table and crossed to where Theseus had left the two rucksacks earlier. Dimitris carried them to the table and put them carefully on it. "These, Mr. Ashworth," Theseus continued," were found near the bodies of our unfortunate friends. I understand that they carry the remainder of the Phaistos treasure and that there are a number of damaged disks there. From what Oscar has told me, there were some fifty disks in total and I am told also that this could be a sufficient number from which a decipherment of the script may be possible, if they can be reassembled."

He looked across at Kenneth. "It may be, Professor, that this will be of interest to you. I am sure that Mr Slinger will have no objection to my passing these into your care."

Theseus got to his feet. "Thank you all for your company. It is time for bed. We all have much to consider. *Kalinikta.*"

The vulture circled in the moonlight once more and returned to the crags to continue its ancient watch.

Chapter thirty two

Tuesday, 17th September

The clear skies of the previous night had gone; an early morning
squall brought the first touch of autumn. The crags around Lossos
were replaced by swirling curtains of mist and the sea was choppy
and sullen. Umbrellas left open on terraces turned into parachutes
and crash-landed on the shingle, closed umbrellas stood redundant
like petal-less flowers; boats jerked uneasily on their moorings, turning first one way then another, seeking freedom. In Nikos' room
where the debris of his hurried departure awaited Jenny's reluctant
perusal, a vortex of dead leaves spun on the floor and might have
been his restless ghost.

For the first time for many weeks Fiona did not swim. She had
been awakened early by a tearful Jackie but the two had little to say
to each other and had sat together on Fiona's bed watching the grey
day struggle to be born. Oscar had gone fishing for the last time, "I
promised ..." but would be back to catch the early ferry to Hora
Sfakion to start the long journey to Athens. Jackie had decided that
she would not go with him to Athens; she was too sad and shocked
by her sudden dismissal to be capable of making any firm plans and
wanted time on her own. She thought that she would go to Hania
and work in a bar or as a waitress for the remainder of the season
before deciding what she wanted to do, but could think no further
than that. She only knew that she was going to miss Lossos and
asked Fiona why she thought she had been sent away. Fiona muttered something about Theseus thinking she would want to be with
Oscar, knowing all the while that it was to convince Gillian that he
was changing direction, and that he needed Gillian's co-operation in
his plans. She was his sacrifice, banishment on a cold morning, not
death in the sunshine on the hot stained stone of Phaistos.

Oscar was back in time and changed into last night's white shirt.
He left, as he had arrived, swinging his holdall from one callused

256

black hand. He, too, was on his own for the first time for many years and the arm that held Jackie was to reassure himself as much as her. They stood on the front of the ferry as it reversed from the beach and turned across the bay, then walked down the side together to watch the waving party on the beach disappear in the driving mist and rain.

There had been quite a gathering on the beach; news of Jackie's departure had passed quickly through the village and tourists and villagers formed a group behind Gillian and Fiona to say their farewells. Oscar would be missed by only a few of his fishing mates but the loss of Jackie's vivacity would leave Lossos a quieter place. There was some speculation about her sudden departure; villagers tutted about her having a baby; tourists knew that she had fallen out with Gillian; no one knew of Theseus' decision. But summer girls come and go in the village and everyone assumed that Oscar would have wanted to go with her. In a few days scarcely any other than Fiona would remember her.

Fiona had not seen Dimitris since last night's dinner party. She had left him talking to Theseus and had half-expected him to come to her room later, but he had left a note for her at the hotel to say that he had gone to Athens with Theseus and would ring in the evening. She learnt later from Gillian that Kenneth and Mary had gone with them to enable Kenneth to make his statement to the police in Hania. Gillian had remarked that Kenneth did not appear to be looking forward to this and had gloomily insisted that Mary go with him 'to feed me buns through the bars'.

It was a much happier couple who arrived back on the last boat; Theseus' lawyer had prepared a statement for Kenneth in English and in Greek to the effect that two members of a party, attempting to climb Pachnes, had missed the path in the dusk and had fallen into the Eligias Gorge. The others had searched, but, overtaken by nightfall, had been unable to recover the bodies of their friends. The party had spent the night in the mountains and returned early next day to report the loss. These things happen in the Lefka Ori. After a formal hearing some time later, the matter was closed and a small memorial cairn was built on Zeranokephala to record the tragedy. It was more than Jasumatu had.

Mateo walked back sadly to Likkos after the dinner and paused at the top of the ridge to look down on his beloved country bathed in moonlight. He tried to imagine what it would look like in a few years time with the road and the traffic and the new buildings but his mind could not conjure the change. He had a thought that he might leave Sfakia before it all started and find a new place to live, untouched and innocent, as Lavris had been. But he also realised that changes happened everywhere and that Theseus had made a brave choice in accepting them, but on his own terms. And, if he, Mateo, left, who would protect the land and its animals and plants? Who could do that as sympathetically as he? He could not let that responsibility out of his hands. Theseus knew that very well, damn him, and had played the card cleverly. But he would never wear a suit, or a tie.

With a shrug of acceptance Mateo followed the path down to Phlikas and over the hill to Lavris where Argus greeted him by impressing two large dusty footprints on the not-so-clean striped shirt. Back to earth; it was a pity that men were not more like dogs, faithful, content, mistrusting change; but who, then, would think of the stars?

Jenny spent a much happier night. She and Brad strolled a little way through the sleeping village until a few wisps of cloud obscured the moon. They did not say much, each busy with their own thoughts, content to be together. Without conscious decision, they found themselves back at Brad's room where they slept, not making love, like an old couple. But it was different in the morning; they rose late, and planned an early siesta.

The early morning squall had passed; a pale sun made brief appearances through grey cloud. The crags had lost the shroud of mist and now hung colourless and forbidding above the village. Some tourists had set off along the coastal walks, some lingered in tavernas, moodily drinking coffee, watching the sea churn. Someone in Andreas' taverna was heard to mutter that he'd seen Bognor look better. Holidaymakers don't like change, even changes of the weather; it spoils the summer snapshots of memory.

Gillian and Fiona drank coffee in Gillian's office having despatched the last reluctant breakfaster from the terrace. Gillian was restless and prowled uneasily, upsetting Raki who sat on a bench watching her; she glared at a group of tourists struggling past on the rain-polished shingle. "Some people expect that it will always be the same here, always sunny, always warm. 'Oh, what a shame, Gillian, they've built even more since I was here last year, I do hope it won't spoil things too much.' 'Oh, Gillian, I do hope the weather will not change too soon.'" Gillian, drawing heavily on a cigarette, mimicked southern-counties English.

"What the hell do they expect, that it should be kept like it was when they first came, three, five, years ago? What about what it was like twenty years ago, with the bay full of shit and there was no fresh water for months in the summer? Do they want it like that again? And what about sixty years ago when it was crammed with defeated Australians trying to escape to Cairo, of all bloody places?" She squashed her fag-end viciously into a full ashtray. "I'm getting too old for this. Bugger Theseus and his plans, I don't want to go through it all again, being nice to people when Theseus just sits and glowers and wishes he was back at sea. I've had enough, I'll go home to dear old Middlesex."

"And be bored stiff. I don't suppose that Middlesex is the same as it was, either."

"I s'ppose you're right," Gillian said moodily. "I always hated England anyway, that's why I left; all starched and formal, no passion. No drawn knives, only sheathed ones, but just as nasty." Gillian lit another cigarette and grinned across at Fiona.

"And you're a bloody Aussie, what the hell are you doing here? Are you going to escape to Cairo some day?"

"I doubt it, not now. I suppose I'm here for the same reason that you are. A man. And the hope that we can make some difference to the place. The bay would still be full of shit if you hadn't come."

"The only shits now are men," Gillian sniffed. "I can't get rid of them, as much as I try. They keep turning up, like turds in the bay used to do." Gillian finished the dregs of her cold coffee and grimaced, reaching for a cigarette to take the bitter taste away. "So, what are we going to do about this hotel thing? Do you want to give it a go? It'll have to be different, you know, I'm not going on being nice to tourists for ever."

Fiona laughed at Gillian's transparent grouch. "You don't mean that really – you love it. But you can do less. Only be nice to people you like."

"I'll be pretty quiet." Gillian stood up and Raki joined her, they both surveyed the village from her window. "Are you going to marry Dimitris, then? Have lots of black-haired babies, get fat?"

Fiona got up to stand beside her friend and fondled Raki's ears. They looked out onto the village where the growing warmth and dying wind had brought colour back to the sea and the cliffs. A burst of sunshine shone through a gap in the thinning clouds. "Yes, to the first. Yes, but not lots, to the second. Certainly not to the third. We'll be too busy."

Together, at the window, they watched a large grey bird drift along the cliffs seeking a thermal. It found one and turned and spiralled into a patch of blue sky, high above the white chapel of Agia Katerini.

Chapter thirty three

Dimitris and Fiona were married in the tiny chapel of Agia Theodoris in early September in a ceremony in which the whole village participated. She had insisted on being married in Lossos despite the wishes of her parents and at the price of having to agree to a second celebration back home in Perth at Christmas.

Greek marriage services are feats of endurance lasting at least four hours, preceded by gunfire, followed by gunfire, and executed under barrage of sugared almonds thrown as confetti. The service is accompanied by a lugubrious keening chant which would be more appropriate to a funeral, sung by an unaccompanied male choir of three or four otherwise unemployable hangers-on. The congregation stands around and chatters, criticising everything, and moves freely in and out of the church.

The principals have no such escape and are trapped in the gloom and the heat of the tiny chapel. It is agreed that if the bride and groom can survive the wedding, they have a good chance of surviving married life. For a foreign bride the whole affair is even more demanding as she must stand for four hours with not much to do other than walk round in circles when encouraged by the priest. She must remain glamorous throughout and appear attentive to a service which few understand as it is sung in ancient Greek. To Australians newly arrived in Greece and unfamiliar with the ritual the whole business is a perplexing ordeal.

But eventually Dimitris and Fiona emerged into the bright sunlight, scowling at the glare, to be photographed looking like frightened rabbits, and led a long line of friends, villagers and inquisitive tourists down the path back to the village. The red dust of the track stained the hem of Fiona's white gown with a scarlet thought entirely appropriate by some of the older village women. Shotgun fire echoed from the crags and sugared almonds inflicted severe wounds.

Andreas walked with Fiona's mother, perspiring copiously and with his little blue eyes ringed with tears, solicitous and apologetic, wearing a thick black suit as if in mourning. Katerina followed with Fiona's father, uneasy in her prominent role, but proud to be seen on the arm of the tall Australian. From time to time she thought of her kitchen and hoped that the feast which she had prepared for weeks would be ready and that there would be enough to feed the wedding party which seemed to have doubled in number since she planned it.

But, of course, there was enough food, and after a little while even Katerina relaxed and had a glass or two of champagne and revelled in the compliments which Theseus paid to her in his short speech. The launch *Phaistos* which was Theseus' present to Dimitris and Fiona bobbed at the taverna railing. Theseus remarked that he would have preferred to give them a yacht but thought that Dimitris would have his hands full coping with Fiona. This joke was significant not for its quality, but its rarity; Theseus had never been heard to joke in public before.

The evening was a riot of dance and drink, and of occasional bursts of gunfire. Fiona treasured ever after a photograph of her father, shirt open to the waist, handkerchief dangling from his hand and leading a line of high-stepping Cretan dancers. It was only when they began the knee bending and spinning routines that he gave up and collapsed into his chair surrounded by Amstel bottles.

Dimitris and Fiona spent their first night together in the new flat which they were to share on the top floor of the taverna and the biggest crowd which Lossos had ever seen gathered on the beach early next morning when they left to sail the *Phaistos* round the island to the Elounda Bay Hotel for their honeymoon. They found the north coast cool after the heat of the south and the hotel too formal: their fellow guests showed no interest in Crete and seemed only to be interested in food and drink and in telling competitive tales of other places which they had visited. The bill for the five days was a shock even to Dimitris, who was accustomed to high Athens prices; he grumbled over dinner that for the cost of their brief stay he could have bought the whole of Sfakia in 1950. Fiona put a slim hand over his big one and scratched the back of it gently. "But it's been worth it, love, hasn't it, to be here with me away from the damn village."

"I not so sure," he grinned at her. "But, you're right; you've got to get away from Lossos now and again, to see it in perspective. It's too easy to be caught up in its whirlpool, but it's only an eddy, really. That's what Theseus has realised; he's brought the world into Sfakia, just in time."

She looked at him, affectionately, mockingly. "Philosophy, from a Cretan. Whatever next?"

They walked back, hand in hand along the manicured paths, to their small bungalow on the edge of the wide sea, and looked for the stars which they would see from Lossos. But they could not see the stars from here; the glare of the hotel had destroyed them. They were back at work by the end of the week, Fiona to the hotel in Lossos where she was taking over from Gillian; Dimitris to Syntagma and endless meetings.

* * * * *

The road from Anopoli to Liridiana and down to Philikas was completed in spring and a continuous stream of lorries brought materials for the building of the new hotel. Although she was at first reluctant, Gillian became involved in the plans and spent hours arguing with architects who seemed intent on creating a new Hilton rather than her simple design of stone bungalows with Cretan arches, scattered in the gardens which Mateo had created. By the time of Dimitris' wedding to Fiona the foundations had been laid and Gillian was giving her attention to the fittings. Battles with fussy designers were fought and won; if Gillian was going to do this thing, she would do it her way, with Mateo's connivance.

Similar battles were being fought over the design and construction of the museum. There are few good museums, and Brad Slinger wanted this to set new standards. He had soon realised that the wreck held a selection of what had been thought worth saving from the damaged palace at Phaistos and therefore had a unique capacity to portray life at the end of the second palace period. Brad insisted that all that was found should be displayed and not left to lurk in unseen rooms for the benefit of experts only. Again designers descended and had to be listened to and sent away to rethink.

Progress on the wreck itself was slow but the reference grid was finished by the end of the first summer and the excavation would start in earnest in the spring, and Jenny and Brad travelled widely during the winter after the wreck site had been shut down at the end of November. Brad had responsibilities in Dallas and lectures to give to archaeological faculties around the world and Jenny's father's reputation helped her acceptance in a society where it seemed that everyone knew everyone else, whether they were based in Dallas, London or Paris. She enjoyed the freedom with which Brad crossed the world and she contributed a depth of knowledge and an intuitive mind. She was happy and in love and the memories of her claustrophobic past in Athens with Nikos were rarely recalled.

One day in late spring when they returned to Lossos to check on the progress of the site, she climbed Pachnes with Mateo and Brad and spent the night in the cave where Nikos and Robert had fallen, but there were no ghosts. A griffon vulture flew below the cave as the sun set; Jenny had seen the bird from Lossos, sailing the cliff thermals, but only distantly. Here, in the mountains above the gorge, his wings seemed to embrace the whole of Sfakia.

* * * * *

Jackie was with Oscar in Barbados, sunburnt and fit and with a diving boat and school. She and Oscar had parted on the bus at Vrysses in a disappointing and prosaic way after the eventful summer. He had watched sadly from a cafe as the green bus to Hania turned the corner and disappeared and felt his life stretch ahead of him like an empty road. It was then that Oscar started to consider going back to Barbados and using Theseus' money to start a diving school there. Fourteen thousand pounds, while not a lot in London, was a fortune in the Caribbean.

Life as a bar girl in Hania was a constant parade of drunken American and Greek sailors and endless propositions, and badly paid as well. Although sometimes she felt tempted to revisit Lossos, she did not make the journey over the mountains; Gillian and Fiona came to Hania occasionally and brought her news from the village. She was tempted by a sailor from time to time, particularly the black men from the US ships, but rarely. She settled to a life of sleeping days and long working nights, snatched meals and infrequent afternoons on the beach trying to regain her failing tan. The season drew to a cool close and she dreaded the thought of the return to England and the prospect of more drunken men in more bars, but louder and nastier, and in everlasting drizzle.

The bar near the harbour was unusually busy for the time of the year and Jackie had an exhausting night, working without a break from ten in the evening until four in the morning, fending off lecherous US sailors and serving drinks as if alcohol was going out of season. There was a group of US men at the far end of the bar, some black, some white, all boisterous, and she did not notice a solitary man until a noisy gang had staggered out into the night. There was always one drunk who outstayed the rest, smoking and spraying ash, hoping that he would be the one who got lucky with her. Tonight was no exception. Here he was in the gloom at the end of the bar; she took his glass, "Come on, time to go, they'll sail without you."

"I hope they do." Oscar said quietly. "Come to Barbados with me."

Kenneth and Mary Ashworth were the only ones to decline Theseus' invitation to stay in Lossos. Mary found the village too claustrophobic and the prospect of being under the Sfakian's wing too restricting. She and Kenneth had talked over the proposition and had decided to return to the British School in Athens and the freedom and friends they had left behind. Kenneth had never been happy with his role in the recovery of the treasure and could not be free of the burden of guilt while he was in Crete. Now, back in Athens, with Mary content in her work and with his own skills in demand, he was far happier. His only regret was that the disks which had been recovered from Brian's sack were too few to make it possible to attempt a reasonable decipherment of the pictographs, and as far as he knew, those found in the gorge were too badly shattered to be recoverable. Still, there was plenty of work that could be done, and their visits to Jenny and Brad kept them in touch with the progress of the excavation. They were content to have been part of the recovery of the stolen treasure of Phaistos; what more could an archaeologist want?

In November a note from Brad was delivered to the British School. 'Ken, you may not trust computers, but there is quite a clever one, back in Dallas. It has been working on a number of badly broken clay disks which were recently recovered on the south coast of Crete. It somehow matches the bits by scanning them and then puts them back together again, God knows how. It takes a long time, even for a clever computer. You, of course, will not trust it, being cynical about these things. However a package is on its way to you with its conclusions. If you have a moment, check them over for me. Best regards; Jenny sends her love to you and Mary.'

The next day Kenneth received a package from the American Embassy in Athens, brought by a pedantic US courier who wanted seventeen signatures of receipt, both in English and Greek. He dismissed the offended man without a tip and called Mary on the internal phone. "Come and look at these," he said, pulling from the package crystal clear photographs of ancient clay disks which bore pictographs impressed in a decreasing spiral on both sides. "How about that," he said with an English understatement. "They look genuine, don't they?"

It was going to be an interesting winter.

* * * * *

A big man sat alone on his launch on a mirror-still sea in an early dawn, watching a sleeping village cradled in the protection of encircling rock. In the east a flush of pink threw Psiloriti and Kendros into black, jagged relief, and over Agios Ioannis a fading moon dominated a still dark sky. A vulture drifted down from the crags and turned wide easy circles, sometimes dark against the eastern sky, sometimes pale grey against the gloom of the west.

On the sea, and in the air, man and bird watched over Sfakia.